THE C CROSSROADER

The True Story of an English Casino Dealer

BY
CHRISTOPHER JAMES SHILLING

BOOK ONE: THE TRUE STORY OF AN ENGLISH CASINO DEALER

ISBN-13: 978-1512383386

First published in Great Britain in 2015.

more lucrative actually playing!).

You are about to learn how the casino industry works and how to beat a casino, and it is far easier than most people think; there are legal, licenced casinos over 100 countries around the world and it is nothing like what you see in films because casinos not only want people to win, they need people to win! Many professional gamblers take their holidays in resort areas where there are casinos and pay for their holidays with their casino winnings.

With most casino games the odds are only 1-2% in favour of the house and players who know how to play properly win every night of the week – and if every player walked out as soon as they were ahead by £300/$500 casinos would go out of business.

Of course casinos love mug punters but always remember that casinos need lots of people playing and winning a lot of the time, they don't even mind a regular punter who wins regularly but what they don't like is a player who beats them consistently and doesn't do the money back, long-term.

Anyone can get lucky for a night, a week or a month, but if you keep hitting a casino for thousands and thousands, rarely losing and never doing it back you are (a) going to be suspected of cheating, (b) get yourself noticed by the casino radar – and be tracked – and (c) almost certainly going to get barred eventually; these books will show you how to win consistently, not do it back and not get barred.

And so now, out of the kindness of my heart, I will pass on to you all the casinos' esoteric secrets that I learned during my international casino career as croupier, inspector, pit-boss, casino manager and infamous crossroader, in the entirely altruistic hope that it might benefit you, and, armed with this insider information, you too will be able to Beat The Dealer!

These books are not really aimed at people who want to merely punt and make their money last a bit longer, or for multi-millionaires who do not really care if they win or lose; these books are for people who genuinely want to win, long-term, and are prepared to quit when they are ahead – and spend their winnings elsewhere.

They contain a number of Golden Rules and plenty of insider information for players and professional gamblers, advanced betting strategies and hundreds of tips and fact-based stories that the casinos really do not want you to be aware of, the sort of insider info and techniques that will stop your losses immediately, keep you below the casino radar and get you winning long-term.

At present, on average, if a regular punter visits a casino ten times, he will usually win twice, break-even twice and lose six times; my aim is to stop those losses and turn most of the break-evens into wins.

The goal of these books is to stop your losses immediately, and that in itself will be a massive saving, but if I can turn your losses and break-evens into wins it will represent a massive difference on a yearly basis; I will also show you how to legally launder your cash and avoid the tax authorities.

You may be a casino gambler who's down on your luck and is beginning to suspect that the casino or a croupier is cheating you (and you might be right).

You could be a professional poker player looking for an inside edge to pass the time between poker tournaments or qualifying stages (in which case, you will might start making more money from the table games than you make from the poker matches!).

You might be a croupier who feels that they are being underpaid and overused by the casino (almost certainly true, especially when the greedy casinos keep up to 90% of the tips).

You could be someone who fancies going to a casino but doesn't want to look out of place as you aren't quite sure of the games, odds, strategies, etiquette, don't want to lose any money and are looking for some tips on how best to play and win (in which case, please read on!).

Hopefully, you are looking to supplement your annual income with tax-free casino winnings, like the idea of quitting winners, are willing to listen to how the professionals do it and follow the advice: play a little, take full advantage of the casino's free food and drink, win a modest amount, walk away and spend the winnings elsewhere (so you cannot lose it back).

Or maybe you are considering becoming a casino croupier (someone like me, not so long ago).

One last thing; I have a very real fear that what I am about to reveal will unleash a multitude of wised up players across the world who start turning the tables on the casinos; nothing wrong with that.

No; what I am afraid of is that some readers will learn how to beat the casino, go out and batter them – winning tens of thousands of pounds or dollars – and then become so hooked on the buzz of winning that they won't want to do anything else but gamble in casinos (and I have seen this happen thousands of times); the trouble is that winning money in a casino is extremely exciting, and what happens inside a casino is so much more interesting and entertaining than anything outside that many people start wanting to want to spend all their time in a casino, gambling endlessly and this is almost always fatal; so please be aware that if you choose to go down this road, you will be ignoring most of my advice.

But be that as it may, here, in brief, are a few of my Golden Rules:

Only gamble when you have a job or a regular income;

Hertfordshire town.

And as for the likes of Monte Carlo or Las Vegas, well, they were certainly not the kind of places anyone I knew had been to, so what the hell was a casino doing in my neck of the woods?

As far as I could imagine, the sort of people who frequented casinos were billionaire tax exiles and international arms dealers, the kind of people who owned yachts and private jets and whose only decisions in life were which 5-star restaurant to go to and whether to take the Rolls or the helicopter!

And as for the local population, even if some of them appeared fairly affluent, surely they could never have afforded it; after all, wasn't that why we had bingo, bookmakers and the national lottery: so that the working classes could indulge the basic human urge to gamble? Christ, I never even played on the one-armed bandit down the pub!

I perused the advert for a fourth time: "Don't be a Cinderella all your life!" the advert screamed at me; "Join our casino and enter the glamorous world of the professional casino croupier, conducting exciting games of roulette and blackjack! Evening work, good rates of pay, free meals from our world-class restaurant, free uniform, free taxi home plus other benefits; please call..." et cetera, et cetera, and then it went on to give the local telephone number, which was really beginning to bug me; surely there couldn't be casino in Hertfordshire – I just couldn't get my head around it!

Indeed, were casinos even legal in Britain? On just about every set of adverts on the telly there seemed to be an ad for an online casino, but these were all offshore and, to my mind, not regulated or policed and so obviously not to be trusted.

Maybe they were holding interviews around here for jobs in London or – much more likely – abroad; yes, that must be it: a local agent recruiting people to work in Vegas, on board luxury cruise ships or working in foreign casinos; being surrounded by so many multi-millionaires and with all that money washing back and forth across the tables, well, some of that money was bound to end up in my pocket (one way or another), right? After a couple of years of that I'd be rich!

So I marshalled my thoughts, grabbed my mobile phone, took a deep breath and dialled the number. When someone answered, I asked to be put through to the 'duty manager' (as instructed in the advert), who promptly asked for my name, age – "Seventeen, but I'll be eighteen in two weeks' time" – he certainly didn't sound like an East End hood, more like the graduate of an expensive private school – and then he asked:

"Have you got a criminal record?"

"You what?" I asked, somewhat taken aback.

"A criminal record; have you ever been in trouble with the police?" he asked me again.

"A criminal record? Of course not!" I spluttered, and this was the god's honest truth – because the police had never caught me!

"No criminal record, you're sure about that?" he quizzed.

"What? Yeah, of course I'm sure!" I went. I was most put out; all I was doing was applying for some lousy job and here he was giving me the third degree; I nearly told him to shove it, but then I remembered the money for the sports car I wanted to try to con my parents out of so took a deep breath and tried to remain calm, which was just as well since he immediately invited me along for an interview, straight away, that very evening.

"Where exactly are you?" I enquired, and he gave me directions to an industrial estate in Watford, which was only fifteen miles away, on the other side of Hemel Hempstead, which was only a few miles down the road and threatening to encroach upon my home town of Berkhamsted; apparently I was to look for a large nightclub and bingo hall, since the casino was situated behind them; I vaguely knew the area but had no idea there was a casino there. "Right, let me get my suit on and I'll see you in an hour!" I told him. A casino, in Hertfordshire? Surely not!

I then dressed in my best – and only – suit, borrowed

one of my Dad's silk ties — I'd have to remember to replace it before he came home or he'd kill me — crept downstairs and slipped into Mum's old Mini; it didn't even have a CD player, but I'd had my own secret set of keys cut ages ago and it was a lot more reliable than my leaky, 1962 convertible Austin Healey Sprite and looked somewhat better than my bright orange 1974 VW Beetle.

After a half-hour drive, I found the place without a problem; it was a huge, windowless building on the edge of an industrial estate with a massive car park in front of it, close to a large nightclub and next to a bingo hall, and to get to the casino one had to drive down a narrow passage at the side of the bingo hall and under a metal security bar upon which sat a large arch with the words: 'The Metropolitan Car Park.'

One entered a smaller car park, from where I could see some double-doors of bronze-tinted glass, and on the cream-coloured wall next to the doors was a large golden sign which read: 'The Metropolitan Casino.'

A casino in Watford; wonders would never cease!

I pulled in and parked as close as I could to the entrance, and as I was checking my hair and tie in the rear-view mirror noticed a tall, elderly fellow in a red overcoat came out from behind the mirrored doors who took three long steps over to me and opened my door.

"Good evening, sir," he said.

"What do you want?" I yelled, ever suspicious.

"Er, permit me to park your car for you, sir," he said, looking a trifle embarrassed.

"What are you on about, I've just parked it!" I said, staring at him like he was a moron.

"Er, pardon me, sir, but I'm the parking attendant; I'm here to park your car for you, sir." And then the penny dropped – he was the parking valet! And he was calling me 'sir', me, a fresh faced kid! A parking valet, in Watford! Honestly, you couldn't make it up! How very American, I thought, finally taking the keys out and handing them to him (yet another faux pas; apparently one leaves them in the ignition).

"Do I get a receipt?" I snapped.

"Oh, that's all right, sir; I'll remember you," he said, lowering himself into the forty year old Mini. "One doesn't often see these any more."

"No, more's the pity," I muttered under my breath as I turned, took a deep breath and walked in through the mirrored glass doors.

I didn't really know what to expect; actually, I was quite excited and mildly intimidated – which was exactly how the casino wanted one to feel – and once inside it wasn't too dark or smoky but actually quite nice: deep red carpets, cream wallpaper, faint piped music, muted lighting overall but bright enough near the reception desk, which was manned by two tall, immaculately dressed Arabs in dinner suits who were both staring at me curiously.

So in my poshest of posh voices I announced who I was and what I was there for; one of them reached for a phone and made a call while I wandered about, looking at a large glass display case opposite the reception desk which contained a pair of mannequins kitted out in the kind of clothes and jewellery that I could never even dream of being able to afford.

I sniffed, loudly, and stepped over to peer through an inner set of heavy double-doors, constructed of dark wood and smoked, toughened glass, but through which I could see, barely, into the casino proper.

It was even darker in there, but I could just about make out a few tables (they had low bright lights positioned directly above them) and some vague, shadowy forms moving around; I also thought I could make out a tall, bow-tied croupier conducting a game of cards – so that answered one question: they were open in the early evening, then. I turned back to the Arabs at the reception desk.

"Say, what time do you open?" I politely enquired.

"We are open from two in the afternoon until four in the morning," the taller one informed me.

"What, you're joking! Gamblers come in at two pm.?" I asked, aghast.

He nodded, smoothly. "Yes indeed; quite often, they wait outside for us to open."

"What, and they stay till four in the morning?" I asked, appalled.

He nodded again. "Indeed; our busiest times are after midnight."

"Jesus Christ," I muttered, shaking my head; it was a different world.

My thoughts were running wild (and I had an overly-developed imagination anyway) but I didn't have to wait long for a moment later a door next to the reception desk opened and a tall, blonde, very attractive girl appeared, immediately followed by another even more immaculately-dressed fellow (though a white one this time); he gallantly escorted the girl to the front double doors and showed her out then turned back towards me, looked me up and down, rubbed his hands together (as if he were about to serve me up for dinner), and in a clear, plummy accent, went: "Right then, who do we have here?"

I walked up to him, smiled, looked him dead in the eye, shook him firmly by the hand and introduced myself. He told me his name was Mr. Hunter, that he was the casino duty manager and after giving me another careful once-over he ushered me into his office.

He wasn't particularly tall, maybe a shade under average height, but he looked incredibly smart and dapper, what with his immaculate dinner jacket and silky white dress shirt, hand-tied bow tie, expensive haircut and red silk pocket handkerchief; he even wore good shoes: black and sparklingly clean. He reminded me of Sean Connery in the role of James Bond and I kept looking for the tell-tale bulge of a pistol in shoulder holster under his tuxedo, but I couldn't tell for sure.

The office was spartan and obviously functional; Mr Hunter went behind the large metal desk and sat down in a somewhat tatty but comfortable-looking leather reclining swivel chair; he lit up a cigarette and indicated that I take the only other chair in there, a cheap, hard plastic one: typical, I thought, just like being back at school.

He was muttering to himself, lighting a cigarette, dragging deeply from it and reading through the notes he'd made from our brief telephone chat, so I glanced around the room: there was a large year-planner on the wall, a TV monitor with various live images, a shelf full of bulging files, a couple of filing cabinets, some metal trays containing what looked like thousands of small plastic discs and hundreds of video cassettes, plus a doorway leading to a shower area.

"Right then," he said aloud, clapping his hands and

making me jump; then he grabbed his pack of cigarettes, took a new one out and lit from the end of the old one, stubbed out his fag butt and held out the fag packet towards me. "Smoke?" he went, almost throwing them at me.

"No thank-you, it's a disgusting habit," I replied, but then, remembering where I was (and my new sports car), I carried on in a quieter tone: "Er, actually, I'm trying to quit, but thanks," I lied, whilst adjusting the crease in my trousers and imitating his public school refrain, which wasn't difficult.

"You'll be in the minority there," he told me with a black look, inhaling deeply from the cancer stick, and then we recapped some of the stuff we'd been over on the phone. "Got a C.V.?"

"Sure," I said, pulling from an inside pocket a single sheet of A4; "It contains my entire educational history." I'd prudently omitted all the things that I was most proud of, such as my extra-curricular activities like selling air guns, knuckle dusters and flick knives to all the kids in school and reprobates around town.

"Hmm, so you were editor of your college magazine and you like reading, music, cars and motorbikes? Hmm," he went, paused, and then, looking me directly in the eye, went: "So, have you ever been in trouble with the police?"

I frowned and glared back: "The police – no, never!"

"What about family or friends – do any of them have criminal records?"

"No, of course not!" I snorted, looking him straight between the eyes.

"Well, it doesn't matter," he shrugged, "since we give everyone a full police background check anyway." I just sat there, staring back at him. So then he said, "I expect you're wondering why I'm asking you all these questions."

"Yes, I was – *rather*," I said boldly and he grinned, finished his cigarette, lit yet another and pulled out a great big folder, and from that he produced a large, impressive-looking document, almost like parchment, which was covered with lots of official-looking seals and stamps and signatures, and then he started reading it aloud and rambling on about how all casinos in Britain were state licensed and government regulated and totally legal and above board and that all casino owners had to be licensed and free from criminal convictions – or even criminal associations – and furthermore that the same rules, rigorously enforced (with the assistance of the local police) applied to all gaming staff, and so on and so on; frankly, most of it went completely over my head though I did manage to say, with a smile on my face:

"What, you mean that I won't be working for the Mafia then? Thank goodness, my mother will be relieved."

He laughed out loud.

"The Mafia, that's a good one! No, no; indeed: quite the opposite!" he said, laughing again – but I was secretly thinking: damn, what a shame!

"Would you mind taking a quick look at this?" he asked, and showed me a funny little book that had black pages covered in coloured dots, the dots making up different numbers. As I reeled them off, he told me it was a colour blindness test, which I passed with flying colours. Then he got up from behind the desk and came round to my side. "Hold out your hands," he told me, and when I complied he took them in his hands and carefully studied my fingers and fingernails (like some silly scene from "Jaws", I thought).

"Okay," he said, letting them fall and returning to his chair he asked how I was at mathematics.

"Maths? Er, I'm all right," I lied, shrugging; needless to say, maths was my worst subject. "Er, why is that?"

"Well," he drawled, "because mathematics is a major part of this job." When I just kept on looking at him – like a complete idiot – he continued: "You see, as a croupier, you will have to rapidly calculate a large number of bets, and so it's very important that you get the payouts correct."

"Er, pay... outs?" I queried. "I thought that it was only the casino that ever won." Well, that started him laughing again, then he started choking, and then he laughed again and didn't stop for ages.

"If only that were true," he said, laughing and coughing at the same time, struggling to get the words out (he had a terrible cough for such a youngish guy). Then he handed me what he called 'a simple maths test': "You've got two minutes; go!"

The test consisted of twenty questions, along the lines of 35 plus 34, 1½ times 10, 3 times 17, that sort of stuff; I went as fast as I could, struggling the whole way, and just managed to finish in time. After he'd marked it – 17 out of 20, which I was well chuffed with – he didn't seem happy at all. "Hmm, seventeen out of twenty," he muttered, looking at me as if I were a complete dunce; "That's not very good," he said.

"What are you talking about? That's eighty five per cent," I squawked, one of the best maths scores I'd ever had in my life.

"What's three times seventeen?" he snapped.

"Er, fifty one!" I said.

"That's right – so why have you written fifty three?"

"I don't know; I was on the clock!" I said.

"Hmm, well you'll have to do a *lot* better than that if you want to work here; the payouts have got to be *one hundred per cent* accurate, not just ninety five or ninety nine percent: one hundred per cent!"

"One hundred per cent? All the time? Impossible!" I said.

"No it isn't," he said.

"Yes it is," I replied.

"No it isn't," he shot back; "after all, it might be a lot of money that we're talking about."

"Yeah; how much?" I asked, but he just flashed an evil grin.

"All in good time," he told me. "How do you feel about working in the evening?"

"Oh, fine," I said; "I've always been a bit of a night owl (which was actually true). "So what are the hours?"

"You'll normally work from nine pm. till four am., though occasionally you'll be asked to do an afternoon shift: one thirty till nine pm.; when you are trained up, you may be asked to do a double shift, which is half one in the afternoon till four in the morning with an hour's break from nine till ten, the bonus being – once you're out of your probationary three months – that the second shift is paid at time and a half; how does that sound?"

"Yeah, that sounds great, no problem," I told him as he lit up another fag and enquired about my cars and motorbike. Then I asked: "Say, how long have you been here? Cos I've lived in Berkhamsted all my life and I never knew there was a casino around here."

"There's been a casino here for over forty years, but you've probably never heard of us because we're not allowed to advertise; it's a rule set by the Gaming Board."

"Not allowed to advertise?" I said out loud, wondering to the sense of that; "But how do you attract new members – cos I suppose it is members only?"

"Yes, of course; we're a private club, and people come here to play from all over the Home Counties but predominantly from North London; it's not really an English cultural thing, casino gambling, which is something of a shame because the odds we offer are far better than punters will get anywhere else."

"Really? How's that then?" I asked.

"All in good time!" he laughed.

"So how busy do you get?"

"Well," he told me, "we have over thirty thousand registered members and get five to six hundred players every night on average, so we don't do too badly."

"Thirty thousand?" I went, astounded. "Jeez Louise, they must be loaded!" He just laughed again, but I was seeing pound signs dance in front of my eyes.

"Well, that depends what you mean," he said; "Most of our regulars are very well-off, many of them own successful businesses, lots of cash-rich businesses, or have lots of property that they rent out or they have inherited wealth, and they come to us so they can have a safe, relaxed evening, a superb dinner, some drinks and maybe a flutter on the tables; if they win, great, and if they lose? Well, they can afford it." Oh yes, I was hearing everything that I wanted to hear, and was beginning to realise that I really wanted to get this job; within just a few months I'd be loaded – *loaded*!!!

"So, seriously; does the casino ever lose?" I asked, honestly wondering. He smiled.

"Well, yes, we do occasionally... but overall? Not very often," he said with a cheeky grin. "The odds are only very slightly in favour of the house, so what we like is lots of players, on lots of tables, placing lots of different bets, so that even with a house edge of only one or two per cent, that one or two per cent is chipping away at thousands of different bets over the course of an evening."

"Hang on a mo," I said; "One or two per cent, is that all it is? I thought it'd be, like, thirty or forty per cent in the house's favour."

"Oh good lord, no, " he said, shaking his head. "In my dreams!" he laughed. "No, of course we need the players to win, and win often, otherwise they would stop coming; in fact, on some casino games the odds actually favour the players, albeit only briefly, and those games we really have to keep our eye on."

"Holy mackerel, I'm beginning to realise that there's a lot more to this business than I thought," I said out loud, which was unlike me; normally, I'd think a lot but say very little.

"Don't worry about it," he said; "we'll teach you everything you need to know before you start, and after that it'll be down to you to gain as much experience as you can."

So then we talked money, although it didn't sound like much: £200 a week ('cash in hand') whilst training (which meant five mornings a week for two months); then £300 a week for the next three months (whilst we were 'on probation'), after which, he told me, it went up 'quite considerably.'

So not a lot to start with, but I wasn't really bothered by that as he had yet to tell me about all the most important thing – all the tips we going to get – and there he was rambling on about free staff meals, a free uniform, a free taxi home, good chances of promotion et cetera, and I couldn't be bothered waiting, so I blurted: "And what about the other stuff?"

"What other stuff?" he asked, looking at me strangely.

"You know," I went; "you've forgotten to tell me all

about the other stuff; the tips!"

"The tips?" he went, like a cretin.

"Yeah, the tips," I said again. "How much do we make in the way of *tips*?" I asked, mentally rubbing my hands together; holy sheet, with five or six hundred millionaires playing every night, I'd be rich within months!

"Oh, you're not entitled to tips," he said. "Tipping is illegal...."

"No it isn't!" I said.

"Oh yes it is!" he said, quite forcefully.

"Oh no it isn't!" I went; "I've seen it in the movies!" I was almost shouting.

He was looking at me with narrowed eyes, but after a moment lit up yet another fag, rolled his eyes and said:

"Look, I understand that that you may have seen some things in films and on TV but that's all rubbish, couldn't be further from the truth, in fact. I can't comment upon what goes on in other parts of the world, but tipping is illegal in British casinos and has been since the Gaming Act of 1968."

I expect I looked suitably shattered, since he went on (in a calmer tone, inhaling on one cigarette whilst fiddling with another): "No, like a lot of things people

33

associate with casinos it's a common misconception; tipping has been illegal in Britain for many years."

"Yeah, okay, but *why*?" I asked; obviously I'd have to re-think my wild plans of becoming rich just because I worked as a casino croupier for a few months.

"Well, you think about it," he said; "If you were a dealer, and you knew that every time a particular player won some money you'd get a big juicy tip, wouldn't you be slightly more inclined to try and help him win – even if it meant trying to unduly influence the game in some way?"

"Er, I don't know," I muttered, diplomatically.

"Yes, exactly," he smiled, "and that's why it's better we don't allow it, which means all the games are dealt honestly, do you see?"

"Er, well, yes, I guess so," I conceded, feeling both completely gutted and nonplussed, because if what he was saying was correct then surely every barman or waitress in the world would give extra drinks and other freebies to their clientèle (if they were big tippers) in the knowledge that a big tip would materialise.

After that I didn't have any other questions I could think of so I just kept quiet, and eventually he invited me back for a second interview and 'some more simple tests' on the following Saturday morning, which I agreed to attend. Then he shook my hand, showed me out of the office and came out into the car-park with me.

"My name's Carl, by the way," he said, and when I nodded he asked; "So, do you drive?"

"Yeah, of course," I replied. It was a warm, sunny August evening, and here I was, standing outside with this impossibly suave bloke in his immaculate dinner suit and I suddenly felt inordinately uncomfortable about being dressed in a cheap, grey M&S suit whilst waiting for the parking valet to bring over my mother's old Mini; damn, I needed a decent car, and I'd try like anything to get this job on Saturday – even if it didn't seem like I was going to make a fortune in tips – if only so I could squeeze some cash out of my parents to get one. "Er, thanks, I mumbled, holding open the door as the elderly gent in the red coat scissored his way up and out of the Mini.

"So is this your car, then?" Carl asked with a smirk. "Well, it's in pretty good nick."

"Nah, have a word, it's me Old Dear's! My father loves tinkering with cars, so he keeps it roadworthy," I told him; "He's got a classic Citroen DS 23, and I've got a couple of cars, a convertible Austin Healey Sprite and a Volkswagen Beetle, and a motorbike, but my parents have promised to front me the money to get a decent sports car if I get the job," I said.

"Yeah; what sort of car do you want?" he asked me,

grinning.

"A Lotus; or a Jaguar," I replied, "any Jaguar!" and he laughed yet again; the bloody bloke never stopped laughing! "Er, so what have you got?" I asked.

"Well," he drawled, taking another drag and blowing a plume of smoke into the air, "until I got married I had an E-type Jag." I nearly punched him in the face.

"An E-type Jag, holy shit," I said an awed voice.

"But now I've got a house and a kid," he said, with sort-of grimace.

"Oh, Jesus; I'm so sorry," I said, in an understanding sort of way and he laughed yet again, so I went: "So what're you driving now?"

"I've just taken delivery of a new Audi Quattro," he purred, grin plastered over his face; a new Audi Quattro – the bastard!

And then, as Carl stood there, smoking and grinning, I had the cringing embarrassment of clambering into my mum's crummy old Mini and crawling out of there while he stood there and watched the entire time, the bastard!

And yet I always liked Carl; he was one of the most professional people that I ever worked with in the casino business, and although it was plainly obvious that he wanted to be the the casino's general manager one day he always had time for you, no matter what level you were — trainee, dealer, inspector — and he worked *with* the dealers rather than against them, and that was something that I never saw any other manager do, not ever.

And so now, looking back, when can I honestly say that I don't regret anything, I do regret one thing: letting Carl down. It was Carl who interviewed, hired, trained and mentored me. Who can say why I did what I did? A combination of morally ambiguous entrepreneurship skills mixed with natural dexterity combined with the opportunities offered at the time (Q: why does anyone do anything? A: because they want to), but I just wanted to tell you now, if you're reading this, that you were the one thing that I did regret, Carl — and I hope you understand.

I spent the rest of the week trying to find out as much as I could about casinos, which wasn't much, and talked to all my friends about it (who all thought I was 'ideally suited', although none of them knew much about casinos either), and nervously waited until the Saturday, where I had another interview, with Carl and two senior inspectors, and then a large group of us had a battery of tests (and interminable instructions in the art of picking up small plastic discs as quickly and neatly as possible).

After what seemed like ages but was only three hours,

I was formally hired for the training school, along with about fifteen others (out of around sixty people who showed up that morning), and we were told to be there for training at nine am. sharp, Monday week.

I was relieved to have been offered the job but was now having serious doubts as to whether I would be able to cope with all the mathematics involved (we'd already been furnished with a pack of homework, largely consisting of, for whatever reason, combinations of multiplication and addition of the numbers 5, 8, 11, 17 and 35).

I spent the Saturday afternoon telling all my friends my happy news (and embellishing it as much as possible) and every one of them, to a man, thought it would suit me down to the ground, as did their parents, one of whom had a girlfriend who had worked as a croupier many years ago in a country called Oman and had earned a fortune; when I heard this story I was inordinately happy, and, once it had been confirmed that if I got a decent job I would be loaned enough money to get a decent car, I broke the news to my parents that very evening: that I had got myself a job, was going to be working nights, in a casino, as a croupier, and that I needed *at least* three grand so I could get a decent car.

Well, at least Dad took it OK.

Over dinner — dessert, actually; I waited till all the

knives and heavy crockery had been removed – I gently mentioned my news.

"What? A casino? So you're going to work for the Mafia!" Mum shrieked. "That's typical of you! Well, I'm not having it!"

"Oh, Ma," I placated, "it's really not like that; it's not even illegal," and quickly told them about all the licensing, the Gaming Board and even the police background checks.

"What, the *police*? I ask you!" she snorted. "Why can't you get a job in a supermarket? At least with food you'll have a job for life!"

"What, stacking shelves on minimum wage? No thank-you!" I hollered.

"Well, actually, having the police involved would probably indicate that it is a fairly reputable company," Dad said, trying to help out; he'd probably been in a casino himself (not that he'd have told Mum), and then he cut to the chase: "So how much are they paying you?"

Well, what could I do but lie? If I told the truth, I'd be fitted-up with a huge 'housekeeping' bill, plus repayments on the impending car loan, so I thought it better to tell them that I wouldn't be paid anything until I'd successfully completed the two-month training course (although I'd be allowed to sign on the dole as usual).

"And after that?" he persisted, and when I made up a piffling figure of around £150pw, he started banging on about it not being much at all, seeing as I'd be working nights ('unsociable hours,' he called it), dealing with a lot of cash money, having to be honest, reliable and trustworthy, etc.; Jeez Louise, he knew more about casinos than I did! I'd have to be careful there.

"Yeah, well, give me a couple of years, and I'll be making more than you are!" I yelled at him. "The geezer who offered me the job said he used to have an E-Type Jag, and now he's got a new Audi Quattro!" I went. "He's the casino manager, he's only in his twenties and he looks exactly like James Bond!"

"Yes, well, we'll see," Dad said, turning away and concentrating on The Times cryptic crossword.

"Yeah, we will!" I said belligerently. "Carl said you can work anywhere if you work hard: London, on board cruise ships, Las Vegas, Sun City – all over!"

"Yes, I'll bet," Mum said, looking over her glasses and down her nose. "Oh, really; 'Carl' now, is it? It still sounds to me like they're a bunch of gangsters; casinos – honestly!" And with that, she gave a loud sniff and began clearing the table.

"Look, I don't care who they are, as long as they pay me!" I threw back at her. Then (remembering my new

40

car) I continued in a much calmer tone: "Look, Mum, you wanted me to get out of the house, do something with my life and get a job, and now I've got one, okay? And if they really *are* criminals, I'll leave and get a different job, all right? Blimey, I'd have thought you'd have been pleased! I don't wanna go to uni and rack up a massive student debt!"

"No, no, that's not what we're saying," Dad interjected. "We *are* pleased; in fact, I'm fairly surprised that you've managed to find a job that could suit you and that you might actually enjoy."

"Oh, well, that's all right then," I said, deflated. "Say, er, when can I get the money for the car?"

Later, locked upstairs in my room as usual, I lounged on my bed, alternatively watching TV, shuffling a pack of cards and wondering what working in a casino would really be like, and after a while I realised that I was actually looking forward to the training school and, more to the point, with the odds as low as one percent in favour of the house, learning all the secrets on how to beat the casino; at that moment, I had little idea of both how easy and how difficult it would be.

Chapter 2

Apart from having to get up at the ungodly hour of seven to be at the casino for nine in the morning, the training school didn't start out as particularly difficult for me: five hours each morning, Monday to Friday.

For the first couple of weeks, all we did were endless maths tests and continual practising in learning how to handle, speedily pick up and neatly stack the small gaming tokens, which were like large plastic coins and referred to as 'chips'; all I really wanted to do was learn about the games and how to beat them, but that was to come later.

Twelve of us started the course, six of us completed it and two of them left within the next few months; some couldn't handle following all the strict instructions (the 'procedures'), a couple more were simply useless and quite a few got booted out when their police background checks came back with interesting comments; it was amazing how many young people had been arrested and either cautioned or prosecuted by the police (then again, I'd been dodging the authorities for years and was always very careful to avoid getting nabbed).

Carl Hunter mentioned that they'd interviewed sixty people to end up with the twelve that started the training school, and that ratio was pretty much the same every year; the only thing that I didn't really like, apart from the early mornings and the other trainees, was the masses of homework that we were supposed to take home and learn; well, I can honestly say that I always took it home.

After a couple of weeks of maths tests and 'chipping', we began learning how to spin the ball and the roulette wheel (always in the opposite direction, and changing the direction each time we spun) and how to mark the winning number, clear away the losing chips and make the pay-outs (in the correct order, so that no-one got confused and so you didn't pay someone twice).

If ever I asked why things were done in a certain way, the only answer I ever got was 'procedures,' which, I soon worked out, was a polite way of saying 'for security reasons' (or, 'because we don't trust you'), and so I quickly stopped asking those sorts of questions; even the silliest little rules had been invented and put in place for one sole purpose of trying to prevent theft, either by the players, or, more commonly, by the gaming staff; words like cheat, steal, thieve and 'have it away with' were never spoken out loud: it was always 'procedures.'

Occasionally I began to think that I was picking up the job quite well, but then Carl or one of his assistants would pretend to be a normal player, and then we trainees realised how little we really knew; whenever I watched Carl demonstrate how a fast game should be dealt, he completely blew me away.

Whenever anyone, and it was usually me, got less than 95% in a test, we were given a real dressing-down in front of everyone else, which annoyed me no end seeing as these scores, always above 90%, were the highest test scores that I'd received in my entire life.

One day, after a particularly ferocious verbal battering, I must have looked somewhat mutinous, for Carl did go to the trouble to explain that just a few silly little mistakes made on the tables could end up costing the casino a couple of thousand pounds each hour; multiply that by fourteen hours a day (and fifteen gaming tables, and ten casinos in the group) I began to see what he meant (in theory, the group could be losing tens of millions of pounds a year due to incessant dealer errors), so much so that for the first time in my life I started doing the odd bit of homework.

After a month on the training school, and now that I was showing an interest in the job and keeping at it, whilst on a daily basis hassling my parents for lifts in to work and home again, or to borrow their cars, or whingeing at dad to fix up my old 1964 British Racing Green convertible Austin Healey Sprite (which was a complete *bag of shit*, leaked like a sieve, was forever breaking down, cost as much in oil as petrol, was beyond even Dad's skills to fix up and had been an utter waste of money), they finally agreed to cough up enough money for me to be able to afford a decent car,

44

and we agreed on a loan price of up to three thousand pounds.

Of course, I'd hoped they would just give me the cash, but Dad insisted on coming with me when we went car hunting (needless to say, I'd hoped to scam them by making out the car had cost three grand whilst only paying around two grand for it, but no such luck; I was gutted)

I'd originally fancied a Triumph TR7, but my experience of old British convertibles had put me off for life, so I ended up searching for a 1992 Mazda MX5, and we found a 5th-hand, fully-serviced 1.8 Mazda MX5 convertible in black (it also came with an interchangeable hard top, which just as well since it rained just about every week of the year). The vendor had wanted £3,250 and I was gob-smacked when Dad offered the bloke £2,000 cash for it, and even more surprised when the bloke accepted £2,500. Overnight I was happier, and even more so when I offloaded the crappy old Sprite for nearly £500 (which almost what I'd paid for it); I began spending most of my free time winging around in the MX5.

I'd wanted one for ages, and was delighted; now I didn't feel so bad about parking in the staff car park, amongst the second-hand Alfa Romeos, Audis, BMWs, Porsches, etc.; most of the trainees couldn't even drive, so I had one up on most of them; the fact that I was now £2,500 in debt bothered me not at all.

Within the first couple of weeks of the casino training course, which we'd been told would be about eight weeks in length, we had to go, independently, in person and with all manner of identifying documents, to our local police stations, so the police could carry out a full background check on us, but they had nothing in their Big Brother files on me; I'd never been arrested or even questioned by the police.

They took our mug-shots at the casino and then proceeded with the applications for our gaming licences; it all seemed like a right lot of hassle to me ('procedures', no doubt), and in the those last weeks of the training they dropped a couple more from the course who hadn't been performing, which led me to study extra hard. I was now getting to the point that I was itching to start work and see what it was really like 'on the tables.'

I'd developed a huge amount of respect for Carl: he was always immaculately turned out − so much so that I'd even begun to try to emulate him, to the degree that I'd been risking slaughter by borrowing me old man's expensive silk ties to wear to work − and Carl never got tired of answering my continual questions, or correcting our silly mistakes; he always had time to go over something if you were unsure, and he worked hard to get your dealing as perfect as possible; he was always patient with everyone and there wasn't a single thing about the gaming industry that he didn't know.

In those last weeks, we dealt mock-games more or less continually, half-an-hour at a time, and Carl, and the various assistants he used – usually casino supervisors who were called 'inspectors' – really pushed us to get up to speed. And then there were a few curious things happened, none of which I ever forgot….

One morning, one of the other trainees was dealing and the remaining few of us pretended to be punters, placing chips on the table, to be cleared away or paid out. In doing this every day, I soon came to realise that by far the best odds were the 'outside chance' bets, that is, red, or black, or odd, or even, or the numbers 19 to 36 or 1 to 18. Why? Because the odds were only 1.35% in the house's favour, which was *half* what they were if you played the layout, i.e. on the numbers themselves.

And what I liked to do was place a chip – on 'red', say – and, if it won, I'd 'let it ride' for three or four times, till I had a decent amount… then I'd drop back to one chip, and start again. The reason I particularly liked this bet was that it was so easy on the pocket, as it was basically the 'casino's money' that you were playing with; if you lost, you only lost your one original chip; one could play for a long time in a casino like that, and with an excellent chance of doubling your money!

So as I sat there, staring at the roulette table and my homework sheets, day after day, night after night, I realised that maybe a slightly better way to play was to cover both 'red' and 'even'. Why? Because now, you would only lose if a black, odd number came up, and there are only eight black, odd numbers rather than say, eighteen black numbers (as you would if you just played a bet on 'red').

And if you 'doubled-up' when you won (a) you were playing largely with the casino's money, and (b) you only had to be moderately lucky to suddenly have a large pile of chips in front of you within just five or six minutes!

Similarly, you could play on 'black' combined with 'odd' (and only lose if a red, even number came in, of which there are only eight in total. Of course, sometimes you might break-even, but that was better than losing!

Indeed, a similar bet would be red and odd, or black and even; it just so happened that out of the eighteen red numbers, you might have reasonably expected nine to be even and nine to be odd, but in fact there were eight red even numbers and ten red odd numbers, and eight black odd numbers and ten black even numbers, and I preferred limiting one's potential losses by as much as possible.

Another variation was to play three chips on red and two on the centre column; you would only lose if a black number in the first and third column came in (again, a grand total of eight numbers!). Of course, one always had to be careful of the 'zero', because if zero came in, all even-chance bets lost half.

I played these bets on these training games for two or three hours every day, and hardly ever lost, and if I did lose, it was only a small amount of my original stake, as I would be winning and then doubling-up 'with the casino's money', so much so that I wanted to nip out to another casino and try it for real, but Carl had told me that it was absolutely forbidden for gaming staff to enter another casino, and so, tempted as I was, I had to rein myself in even though I was chomping at the bit.

And if I really wanted to get Carl into a frenzy (and thereby get a cheeky break from the constant training and practising), I'd ask him about internet gambling and online casinos (or playing anything on electronic equipment anywhere); he'd all but spit feathers, froth at the mouth and rage that because they were all off-shore, unlicensed, unregulated and unpoliced they were all, therefore, a total rip-off and a con, and to be avoided like the plague.

"Only in a British, land-based casino will the player get an honest game!" he'd rant.

"What about online poker?" someone would ask.

"Better to play in a real casino," he'd reply, "it's always going to be better when you are face-to-face and in a real casino."

"Are casino rules the same everywhere around the

world?" I asked.

"No they are not," Carl told me, "not by any means."

"Why is that?" I asked.

"I'm not entirely sure," he said, "although it may be that different countries cater to different types of clientele."

"How do you mean?"

"Well, Las Vegas, for example, only expects punters to be there for two or three nights, in other words, they are not worried so much about a regular trade of local members, so they do their best to take their punters money as quickly as possible," Carl said.

"But how is that possible? Do you mean that they cheat the players?" I asked.

"Not exactly," he said. "No, it's more to do with the odds. I'll give you an example; what are the odds, and I mean the house edge, if you play on our version of American Roulette?" he asked us.

"Two point seven percent if you play on the numbers, or one point three-five percent if you play on the even-chances," I said.

"Correct; but do you know what the odds are on American Roulette in the USA?" he asked.

"Haven't got the foggiest," I said, and everyone laughed.

"Well, they vary from five point two-six percent up to seven point eight-nine percent in the house's favour," Carl told us.

"What? But that's twice as bad as our odds!" I said. "How is that even possible?"

"Well, they have a slightly different wheel; you see, our wheel, the European wheel, has thirty seven slots, numbers one to thirty six plus zero, right?"

"Right," we all parroted.

"Well, the American wheel has thirty eight slots, numbers one to thirty six, plus zero and a double-zero, and, believe it or not, that one extra slot accounts for a further percentage in favour of the house, but to make things even worse, if you are betting on the even-chance bets, if either zero or the double-zero come up you lose your entire bet! So the house has a standard 5.26% edge against the player, compared with 1.35% in Britain and France, or 5.26% in Vegas compared with 2.7% if you are playing on the numbers rather than the even-chances in the UK.

"Now, that might not sound a lot, but that is an enormous difference when you factor in how many spins take place every hour at the roulette table!" Carl said. "And there is another bet, similar to our 'first four', which covers five numbers but has a house edge of 7.89%!"

"But that's crazy!" I said.

"I agree," Carl said, "but then, like I said, most people are only in Vegas for a couple of nights, so the casinos don't really care about long-term business. On the Continent, every casino and every country will have its own rules regarding zero, but in Europe everyone tends to use the single-zero wheel; the punters wouldn't stand for it if we suddenly switched to the double-zero wheel. I hear that in the States they prefer blackjack and dice − that they call 'craps', which we don't really play over here − because the odds are so much better for the players on blackjack and craps."

"But aren't there casinos all over the States, these days? In Nevada, Atlantic City and on Indian Reservations in lots of different States?" I said; the internet was a wonderful thing.

"Yes, something like thirty-eight States across America have legalised casinos now," Carl said, "but must of them still use the double-zero wheel. Stupidly, in my opinion, but there you are."

"So in other words, don't punt in the States!" I said.

"Well, I wouldn't say that; you can get some excellent games of blackjack, and the States is the only country in the world where I would play the slot machines," said

Carl.

"Oh, why is that?" I asked.

"All in good time, Mr Shilling, all in good time! First, we've got to get you up to speed on roulette, haven't we?" And there was me assuming that what we were being taught held good for every casino around the world; not so!

And so we continued with our chipping, our cutting, our stacking, our placing of chips on the numbers and positioning the payouts properly, our maths tests, our training games and a hundred other things. But Carl was obviously a casino expert, and I made a note to myself to pick his brain again when the opportunity presented itself.

One particular surprise to me was how relatively affordable it was to play; I has seriously thought – due to the fictional rubbish I'd seen on TV or in films – that the minimum bets would be something in the hundreds or even thousands of pounds: wrong!

The roulette chips themselves had a minimum cost of £1 apiece – although Carl had told me that lots of punters played with chips valued at £2, £5 and £10, some played at £25 per chip and a select handful of members played with chips valued at £100, but apparently these were only issued on rare occasions.

I was quickly discovering that with as little as £100,

one could have quite a good night out, including free snacks and drinks as long as one is playing, and with the massive bonus of being able to walk away a winner – in other words, a free night out!

In fact, I was thinking along the lines of going to the casino (with, say, £200) in the early evening, playing carefully for an hour or so, doubling my money, then going out somewhere else and using my £200 in winnings to fund my evening out – a free night out indeed!

And so I began paying even more attention to the intricacies of the training because a suspicion was growing in me that, due to the tiny house edge, there was a lot more to this casino business than I originally thought, and that a switched-on player, that is, someone who wasn't too greedy, didn't get addicted to the thrill of winning and could train themselves to walk away after winning a relatively low amount – hundreds, rather than thousands of pounds – might very well be able to beat the casino, long-term.

One day, Carl was sitting at the table, as I was, pretending to be a punter and placing chips on the layout while one of the other trainees dealt. I just sat and played red & even, until I spotted Carl doing something funny; in fact, at first I thought that my eyes had deceived me till I clocked Carl do it a second and then a third time.

And it seemed so simple, too – and fast; very, very fast! For as the 'dealer' neatly stacked out the winning bet, as we'd been instructed, and then turned, momentarily, into her 'float' area (to pick out the chips for the payout) – and her back was turned for only a second – Carl would smoothly reach out and slip a couple of his chips onto the winning number! And since the odds were paid out at 35-1, if he slipped two chips onto the winning number, he'd suddenly made himself £70! But that was assuming he was playing with £1 chips; if he was playing with £5 chips, he'd make himself £350! And she kept paying him out, almost every other spin; he was making money hand-over-fist!

I noticed Carl was doing it whenever a number came in that he could easily reach came in, which was around half of all the numbers, the cheating little weasel! And judging from the reactions of everyone else, no-one seemed to have spotted a thing! I had to stifle back a giggle every time he did it, which was just about about every other spin!

And he was quick! It might have looked as though he was just checking the bet, but he was definitely adding his chips to it, and I even spotted that he often slipped his chips underneath someone else's, thus make his cheating look far less obvious. It was brilliant!

Playing coloured chips valued at five pounds, and adding to the winning bet – 'top-hatting,' I found out later it was called – on every other spin or so, i.e. thirty spins an hour, meant, roughly, that he'd be creaming in over five thousand pounds an hour! And that was only if he stuck on one extra chip on; he'd rake in over ten grand if he popped two £5 chips on! Ten grand an hour, it was a *huge* amount of money! And then I watched him do it throughout the next trainee's stint as well, the cheating bastard – he was stealing an absolute bucket-load of cash!

And then it was my turn to deal – but I was ready for the scamster! So, I did a couple of spins, and then I hit a number that was within easy reach for him. *So*, I marked ('dollied') the number, called it out – "Twenty-two, black" – and turned to the float... and then whipped smartly round, catching him red-handed! Gotcha!

"Please don't touch the bet, sir," I said, sweet as pie, and then, completely straight-faced, I deftly removed his sneaky late bet, paid out the winning chips quickly and neatly, and then spun again. "Place your bets, please," I intoned, as was proper, avoiding eye-contact with Carl the entire time: got him!

After that, I was very careful not to make any silly cock-ups, and even more careful to watch Carl like a hawk, especially out of the corner of my eye (when the sneaky swine didn't think I could be watching).

And yes, he did try it on again, and yes, I caught him. And the best bit was that I remembered to play it really cool; at the end of my stint, I left the table without any fanfare, as if it was merely 'all in a day's work.' I then sat back down, and proceeded to play as if nothing had happened. After that, I noticed, Carl seemed to have slightly more time for me.

And so I was back to playing the outsides, red combined with even, as usual, and doubling-up and playing mostly with the 'casino's money', and I always seemed to do well; and I liked this bet for another reason: that a dealer, no matter how good he was, could never try to 'spin to miss'; oh, he could try to 'aim' for the zero – in which case you lost half of your even-money bet – but as I understood it, no dealer could do that; and if he could, he'd be the richest bloody bloke in Hertfordshire – if not the country!

Towards the end of the week, even the worst of the remaining six of us were finally showing some improvement due to the constant practising and cajoling into trying even harder. The six of us who were left were playing three to a table, taking it in turns to deal, with Carl and his two assistants, Joe Wallace and Gabriel Smithers, either inspecting, playing or both.

When it was my turn to deal, both Carl and Joe jumped on 'my' table, and started piling mounds of chips all over the layout. It was ridiculous; I had to get one of the other trainees to come and 'chip' while I tried to get all the pay-outs correct, while Carl kept on at me the entire time to 'speed the game up.'

Well, after ten minutes of this I'd had enough, so spat out a 'place your bets' instruction and flicked the ball round the wheel for about three revolutions, in other words, giving the idiots no time at all to get their chips down.

Luckily, perhaps, the ball fell into an empty number — well, it was easier for that to happen since only a few numbers actually had chips on them — and I yelled "No more!" and cleared the layout before any of them had a chance.

I then did exactly the same thing again, and again hit an empty number. In just two spins, I'd absolutely cleaned everyone out! I then immediately spun again, without giving them any more chips, just to rub it in — and sod 'em! And as soon as the ball had gone round three times and fallen, I reached into the wheel to spin again.

"Hey, hang on!" said one.

"That's not fair!" cried another.

"Carl, he's cheating!" accused a third.

I just shrugged, and looked my innocent best. "Place your bets, please," I intoned.

"Hey, gimme some chips!"

"More chips!"

"Hold up!"

"Carl, tell him!"

But funnily enough, Carl didn't tell me to do anything; he just sat there watching the proceedings. I slowly passed them all a couple of stacks each, and then did the same thing a fourth time: spun the ball, *then* announced for them to place their bets, and, three revolutions later, announced 'no more bets' then dollied the number and hauled in all their losing bets.

"Now wait a minute!"

"Gimme a break!"

"What's the rush?"

"'Have a word!" and:

"Carl!" But he just laughed.

"Hell, I'm just trying to miss 'em!" I said. Carl just laughed again, and then I slowly started giving out the 'colour' again.

"In general," Carl said, "we prefer the dealers to do long spins, because most of the time most of the players will not want to place a bet until after the dealer has spun the ball."

"Why is that?" someone asked.

"Well, a lot of our members are Chinese, and they are

all quite experienced casino gamblers, and what a lot of them like to do is watch the wheel for a few seconds before deciding where to place their chips; they like the feeling that they might be able to predict where the ball finishes up, and so, once you are fully trained, you should be able to make the ball go round for fifteen or twenty revolutions before calling 'no more bets'."

"But I thought you had to place your bets before the ball was spun," said somebody.

"No, no, no," Carl told us. "That's only with these fraudulent online casinos, or those fixed-odds-betting-terminals in betting shops, and like I said, they are to be avoided at all costs. No, in a proper casino, one is allowed to place one's bets right up until the dealer announces 'no more bets', and unless one can do that, one should not be playing at all. Any electronic device that makes you place your bets before the ball is spun is obviously a computer algorithm which will react to where the bets are, and obviously deliberately miss them, most of the time."

So then we started seeing how long we could make our spins last, and we all got shown up by Carl, Joe and Gabriel, who seemed to be able to do just over twenty revolutions (I could barely manage half that).

And then somebody (it could've been anybody) asked: "Say, Carl, *is* it possible for a dealer to, er, deliberately spin a number?"

The question brought a pause, and a sudden silence; obviously, it was a question that everyone, particularly myself, had been wondering for a long time (whilst practising, I'd made numerous attempts to hit a certain number, or area, on the wheel; I usually aimed for zero – since it was a green colour, and thus so much more noticeable than a red or black number – but my results were inconclusive. In fact, it seemed the harder I tried, the greater my failure rate).

"That's a very interesting question," he said; "Well, I don't know; do *you* think it's possible?" he asked us all. Some said 'maybe'; some said 'no'; but mostly, it seemed, no-one really knew. "Well, let's put it to the test then, shall we?" Carl asked, and had me chip and stack all the chips, and then got everyone around my roulette wheel; then he explained the rules: we were each allowed two spins, one practise spin, and then the 'real' one; the wheel shouldn't be too fast (or too slow); and the ball had to go round a minimum of seven full revolutions; that the number that we were aiming for was zero; and that he would go last. And then we all had a go.

Well, no-one had a clue about how to 'aim;' I did my best, and the ball ended up in number seven, six numbers away from zero. I was one of the closest but if I'm honest, it was just dumb luck, and even if it *had* ended up in the zero, that, too, would have been pure luck. Even when Joe and Gabriel, Carl's assistants again for the day, had a go, they got no-where near. Finally, it was Carl's turn. So he took off his jacket, pushed up his sleeves and grandly announced that he didn't need a practise go. We all clustered even more closely around the wheel and there was dead silence.

He set the wheel revolving nice and slow, and picked up the little white ball, then he held it in the wheel's rim, timing its release... and then he let it go. It went round about seven times – I counted meticulously – and fell away from the rim, bounced feebly a couple of times, and finished up – plop – smack in zero!

Well, I couldn't believe my eyes, and there was a moment of stunned silence. It was Carl himself who broke it. He let out an enormous 'whoop!' and jumped about five feet – it seemed – in the air, then danced madly up the pit, laughing uproariously the entire time. It was the first time that I'd seen Carl shed his suave urbanity, but, because of what I'd just witnessed, it didn't really register.

After he'd calmed down, and put his jacket back on, and straightened his (already immaculate) hair, he avoided answering all our demands for him to tell us how it was done, and then he somewhat spoilt it by refusing to even try to repeat what he'd done.

"I want to quit winners!" he cried.

"So it was luck!" we brayed back, and eventually he admitted it had been mainly down to luck, and reminded us that in real-game conditions, the wheel had to be fairly fast, and that the ball had to go round at least fifteen times, sometimes as many as twenty revolutions if it was a big game, so as to allow suspicious players, who would never place their chips till after the dealer had spun, to get their chips down, and there were many such players, he informed us, particular the Chinese, in the foolish belief that the dealer could influence the result.

"The dealer *can* influence the result," he said, "but only in the sense that he controls the *pace* of the game, and the amount of colour given out, and the 'atmosphere,' and the speed of the wheel – some players like it to go quite slowly, feeling that they'd have a better chance of predicting where the ball would finish up – or the number of revolutions the ball makes, or even things like whether the dealer is friendly, and says 'hello,' compared with one who keeps it strictly 'professional,' with no personal touches."

And so in other words, the dealers could control aspects of the game to quite a large degree but then, I also thought, if a dealer *couldn't* truly influence the result of the game, i.e. which number the ball was going to end up in, then *why weren't we allowed to receive tips?* Either he *could*, or he *couldn't* (in which case the non-tipping rule, for 'security' reasons, was completely ridiculous).

Of course, even if an experienced dealer *could*, somehow, work out how to get the ball to fall away from the rim above a certain part of the wheel each time, there were yet other factors to take into account: the metal diamonds that were embedded into the side of the wheel (they were called 'hazards', and the ball would usually strike a hazard one spin out of three); these would make the ball bounce all over the place.

Also, you had the metal struts between each of the numbers, and if the ball hit directly on to the top of one of these metal partitions, it could bounce off anywhere; and if the inner wheel was too fast, and the ball hit one of these metal parts, it quite often actually bounced out of the wheel!

Even the hard black plastic floor in each number's slot created difficulties: no matter what number the ball first fell into, it would not usually stay there; it would almost always bounce two, three or four times, and usually end up half the wheel away from where it originally fell.

Furthermore, the ball was flicked one way, whilst the wheel was set spinning in the opposite direction (creating even more of a scattering effect), and one had to reverse the spin each time; moreover, the dealer was always instructed to spin from where the ball had previously landed, so, in effect, the ball was probably going to be spun from a different part of the wheel each and every time.

In other words, if you factored in all the possible

permutations, it was going to be almost impossible to aim for a certain number and get it to come in – unless you were very lucky.

"And so, to answer the question," Carl concluded, "the answer is 'no'; 'section-spinning' cannot be done." But in that case, I asked myself, why on earth was there an actual casino term for it? 'Section-spinning' was a description of something which didn't actually exist! Funny, that; what was it, a UFO?!

Then again (I thought, as I resumed placing my chips on red and even), even if Carl had managed to hit zero twice, or even three times, or had got the ball in the 'neighbours' (the two numbers either side of zero), it still would not have been conclusive proof; only after I had witnessed him achieve it seventy or eighty times over the course of one hundred spins, under real game conditions, would I have been convinced. And I just didn't think that that was really possible – although I definitely liked the 'Chinese' model: never place your bets until after the spin; why give the game away and show the dealer where you are betting? Why take the chance?

In the seventh week of the training school some of our gaming licences began filtering through – not mine, of course, but some of the others' – and that meant they would shortly be starting work proper. Carl told us to check The Rota – which we were to follow as if our lives depended on it – which was on the wall in the staff room; as soon as our licences were issued, our names would be put up on the rota. I couldn't wait to get cracking and checked the rota three or four times every day, but my name never materialised; I even started to wonder whether the police had a file on me after all (I could always have been grassed-up by some envious ingrate).

And at the end of that week we got a visit from The Gaming Board; Carl had already mentioned that it was going to happen and that it was something that we should all be excited about: apparently he had put in a good word for us because they didn't do this for everyone, and so we were officially to give the gentleman from the 'Board the respect he deserved and to hang on to his every word (I took all of this with a pinch of salt).

Anyway, he didn't show up till mid-afternoon on the Friday and I was furious; Friday was the only day of the week that I itched to get away early; not only did we get paid our £200 in cash (usually four lovely £50 notes in a little brown envelope), but I wanted to get home, read my notes, take the dog for a walk, the MX5 for a spin and then spruce myself up to go out for drinks with my friends.

So I stood on my own in the staff-room and moodily leafed through the training manual (we'd long-since completed our roulette spinning and bet-calculations); it was nearly half-past one, and everyone else was sitting around in there: smoking cigarettes, drinking coffee, watching day-time T.V., the girls were applying make-up, chatting, shooting the breeze, checking the rota, or – in my case – minding my own business and not saying very much to anyone.

Although it was late in the day for us (especially me!) it came as a nice surprise when one of the 'real' dealers came in, in preparation for his afternoon shift – though he was nothing like I was expecting and I couldn't take my eyes off the bloke. I watched him slouch in (without even a casual jacket); just the usual dealer attire – black shoes and socks, black trousers, white 'dress' shirt, black bow-tie – though this geezer was also wearing a black tuxedo, which meant that he wasn't a dealer but an inspector.

He certainly didn't look like an inspector, at least he didn't look anything like Carl, Joe and Gabriel; those chaps were not only always immaculately turned out but tall, slim and handsome with it, whereas this guy looked completely different: short, plump, with longish light-brown hair, a longish drooping moustache, lazy posture, he had two or three rings on his fingers, a bracelet and a big, gold wristwatch – all of which we'd been told were strictly 'forbidden' – and he was looking round the room with a sort of retarded, dozy look on his face; not unattractive, exactly, just very, very different.

Up until then, almost everyone I'd seen had been tall, immaculate, slim, good-looking, well-groomed, smart and generally seemed to fit within a casino environment; this chubby little fellow looked well out of place. The funny thing was, as I leant against one of the dividing walls in the staff-room, staring at the telly and pretending to ignore him, he grabbed himself a coffee, lit up a fag and then zeroed-in on me like I was a drunken tart in a nightclub.

"You all right?" he asked me.

"I guess," I shrugged, looking him over again.

"New training school?" he enquired.

"New?" I went. "*New*? No, we've been here seven frigging weeks!" I said.

He laughed, and held out his hand, and I shook it. "Christopher Shilling," I said politely.

"Malcolm Philby," he replied, then took a long drag on his fag, though politely blew the smoke upwards, where the extractors could suck it up and away.

"Been here long?" I enquired.

"Nah," he went; "couple of years; used to work in Brighton."

"Yeah? You an inspector?"

"Yeah," he nodded; "Just been made-up; how are you enjoying the training school then?"

I pursed my lips, shrugged and laughed. "Can I be honest?"

"Yeah, 'course you can — as long as you whisper!" he said to me, so I laughed again and told him:

"I just want to get started, you know? It's beginning to bore me to tears."

"Yeah; two months training does tend to do your head in," he agreed.

"You're not wrong, though we've got a visit from the Gaming Board this afternoon," I told him; "Should be interesting."

"Eh? You're joking! It'll be the longest hour of your life!"

"Really; how do you mean? We were told it was really important to pay attention!"

"Well," he went, "they'll tell you how they think it works, and then, when you start on the floor, you'll find out how it really works — you know?" I didn't, but nodded anyway.

"What do you mean?" I quizzed; "Is it all crooked?"

"Nah!" he laughed, "at least, not mostly," and then he laughed again. Jesus Christ, was that all these blokes did: *laugh*? He then glanced at the huge clock, which was positioned immediately above the door: it read exactly half past one. "Gotta go," he said; "see you later." And then he was off, chucking his coffee cup in the bin, finishing off his fag, and then heading out of the door, and yelling down the corridor to some of the others to get a move on. I went and sat in one of the red velvet chairs, and fell into a half-slumber.

At just after three o'clock we were all woken up by Carl, who was suddenly ushering us into the restaurant, muttering: "Be nice! Ask him questions! Call him sir!" Sleepy as I was, it was as much as I could do not to blow a loud raspberry; three o'clock!

We sat ourselves down in the very plush, albeit dimly-lit, restaurant and the waiters brought us coffee (with a mineral water for me), and after yet more long minutes Carl materialised with a very nondescript geezer: tallish, overweight, in his fifties or sixties, with greased-back greying hair, dressed in a cheap, ugly, brown suit, and, worst of all for me, wearing a self-important, smug look on his face; I'd had enough before he'd even begun.

But I kept calm, if only for Carl's sake (or at least till I could control myself no longer), but when the old lump started talking in a drab, brash, uncultured Northern monotone, well, I just wasn't impressed *at all*. I mean, I tried to look interested, for a few minutes, as he banged on about how highly British gaming staff were viewed by the rest of the world, and how crucial the British Gaming Board had been in the development of world casino gaming (er...) and that the UK casino industry was regarded as the standard to aspire to the world over, etc., etc.....

In fact, the only thing of any interest that he mentioned was the fact that properly trained UK personnel could easily negotiate for themselves some extremely lucrative foreign contracts, at least it was interesting enough until he got on to the subject of 'fiddling' – for that was what he called it – and it was hard enough to listen to him at all, droning lugubriously on, but at least now he was muttering on about issues that I'd wanted more information on for ages, and so I finally began paying attention as he patronizingly banged-on:

"And don't think that any of you can try any funny business and get away with it – because you won't – you haven't got a chance: you'll be caught the first time you try it. Now, I know that no-one here has got a criminal record, so I'm just telling you: don't even bother. You might be tempted to try to on, but, believe me; you'll never get away with it. Think about it: you're all new here... but some of us have been in the business for over thirty years, and you'll be working alongside people who are a lot more experienced than you are – and they'll be able to spot anything remotely suspicious a mile off. So do yourselves a favour: just forget about it."

At last – something slightly interesting! This was the

first time, really, that the subject of thieving from the casino had been properly addressed; I mean, it had been briefly touched upon occasionally, but whenever anyone asked 'why,' the answer was always the same: procedures. In other words: security.

It was for this reason that dealers were strictly forbidden to touch the players, i.e. by taking cash, or giving out chips, directly to (or from) a player's hand, and why dealers always had to 'show clean palms,' i.e. wipe their hands and display them upwards, to show that they hadn't palmed any cash chips (which they could sneak out to the staff-room, hide in their coat and later give to a friend outside of work, who could then come in the casino another day and cash them in). The old fool was still rambling on:

"So my advice to you all is this: keep your noses clean, work hard, listen to what you're told, and above all – enjoy the business! Because this is a superb business to be in, and it can be a lot of fun." He paused, and looked at us dozing off in front of him (well, everyone seemed to be nodding off except me). "Hmph!" he snorted, and I spotted Carl off to the side, cringing; "Has anyone got any questions?"

Only one, mate, I thought: how can you be so damn sure that everyone who'd ever pulled a fast one in a U.K. casino actually had been caught? Wasn't it possible that someone could have pulled off a quick, lucrative fiddle, and then left before anyone was any the wiser? Or maybe a fast, experienced dealer was doing some real small-time − and thus unnoticed − fiddling, which had gone undetected for ages? I'd long-since worked out that a good dealer, pinching just two piddly little £25 chips a night, could make himself a sweet little 'bonus' of a grand a month; stupid northern twat.

Well, these were the questions that sprung to my mind but I knew I couldn't ask them out loud, and it was plain to see that none of the other trainees were going to ask anything, so, just to help Carl out really, I stuck my hand up (just like being back at school, it was).

"Yes, lad?" said Old Grease-bag. 'Lad'? − have a word!

"Yes, sir," I went, "well, I was just wondering why British croupiers are not allowed to receive tips, when croupiers are in other countries." I knew the answer already to this one ('security'); Carl had told me all about it when I'd had my interview. I just wanted to ask him *something*. Also, it bought me time to think of another question.

The old boy gave me the same story that Carl had, adding that the British 'model' was still the best, and that all British casinos were 'crime-free,' which was a lot more than most other countries could claim.

(I later discovered that this tipping story, which had become gospel in our club, was complete rubbish: a myth propagated by the casinos to try to feather their own stinking nests. The truth was that the greedy casino operators couldn't agree to the proportion of tips that the gaming staff would keep and wanted to keep the lion's share themselves – around 80% of the tips, in fact – so eventually the Gaming Board banned tipping altogether; it had never rung true from the start and anyway, what with all these procedures, how could a dealer help a player to win? And how on earth did all these foreign casinos manage to remain in business? I'd read-up a lot on the subject, and almost all Western countries and plenty of other nations around the world had some sort of casino industry and they all allowed tipping, although what percentage of the tips kept by the casino varied wildly).

"Any other questions?" he asked.

"How does one get on the Gaming Board?" I enquired, not honestly interested at all, but I was still trying to think of something interesting to ask. He self-importantly explained that one didn't 'apply' but had to be invited to join, and its members were predominantly retired army officers, judges, barristers, M.P.'s, policemen, titled gentry and the like; yeah, I thought: 'jobs for the boys'! And a bigger bunch of crooks you couldn't wish to meet.

Finally I thought of something. "Say," I went, "did you ever come across a 'system' that could beat a casino? I mean a legitimate one?"

"No, lad; I never did." Well stone me, it was all I could do not to jump up, point at him, and yell: 'Liar!'

"Er, but what about 'card-counting'?" I politely asked.

"Well," he drawled, pursing his lips, "a 'system' is supposed to be a sure-fire certainty, which is definitely *not* the case with card-counting; all a dealer has to do is cut the deck in half and any so-called advantage is immediately nullified."

By this time I felt I'd done enough and just wanted to get home, so slumped down in my chair. No-one else asked anything, and we were eventually allowed to go home at half-past four, directly into the Friday evening 'rush hour'; I didn't even feel like taking the MX5 for a spin which just went to prove how drained I was, it took me over an hour and a half to drive twenty miles and when I got home and slumped down in front of the TV, exactly like my old man after he'd had a long day, but I didn't remain there long.

I'd seen my younger brother, Simon, hanging around in the back garden with a couple of his stupid mates, and they had been wanting to give me a thumping for months, so I went to my bedroom, got my sheath knife and CO_2-powered air pistol, changed into some casual clothes and then put the dog on the lead. The last time they had tried to bushwhack me I had been expecting it and had taken similar precautions, and they had all taken a pounding, and for months I'd been itching for them to have another go.

(On average, brother and I would 'have at it' about twice a week, and there would be a serious set-to every couple of months or so.)

Checking that the repeater air pistol was primed and loaded (and I had spare magazines), I sauntered out into our long back garden pretending I was just going to play with the dog.

From long experience, I knew idiot brother would be down the far end of the garden, smoking and talking shit with his idiot cronies, hidden from view behind various fences and trees, and I gradually moved further down the garden, calling to the dog and throwing things for her to retrieve, and hoping brother would hear me and attack.

I played with the dog for over ten minutes until I finally sensed movement approaching, which I ignored, but let my right hand fall to within centimetres of my pistol, which was in the waistband of my jeans and concealed by a loose shirt, and then I knelt and stroked the dog (she was called Cinnamon, was a rough collie of excellent pedigree who looked just like Lassie on the telly); I was still facing towards the house, but Cinnamon was looking over my shoulder and I felt her tense and she let out a soft whine.

"NOW!" I heard someone whisper, and immediately dived to my right, rolling and then coming up into a crouch position while drawing the pistol and firing.

All three of them had got weapons, but none had the brains to get something decent as I saw they had a baseball bat, a cricket bat and a pickaxe handle. Fortunately for them, they all had jackets on and I wasn't aiming for their faces; I shot all three of them twice amidships and Cinnamon leapt up and bit my brother on the thigh, which started me laughing hysterically, as I set about them, punching and kicking, as they tried to flail their rude weapons as I grabbed them and threw away.

My brother lashed out at Cinny, so I kicked his knee hard at the side, and he went down, screaming. His idiot mate Robbie was out for the count, leant against a tree and rubbing his jacket where I'd shot him in the stomach, whilst the other genius, Danny, had lost his weapon and looked about to run for it. I raised the air pistol and aimed it at his groin, at which he squealed and took off up the garden.

"Cinny, down!" I told her, and she stopped attacking my baby brother (who was two years younger than me, much bigger but five times slower); "Had enough, you dumb fucks, or shall I shoot you again?"

"You've done my fucking knee in!" my brother screamed, going red in the face.

"Yeah? Well, I'm sorry about that," I said, as I stepped over and stamped on the injured knee, and he screamed in pain and yelled bloody murder whilst I laughed even more. "How are your guts, Robbie – you dumb schmuck!"

"Fuck you, we're gonna get you!" he whined, and I stepped over and slapped him with my free hand.

"Try it again, and I'll take your fucking eye out, you stupid prat," I told him, and kicked my brother in the knee again for good measure. "Come on, Cinny, heel! See you later, morons!" I then went back to the house – keeping a wary eye out for Danny, but it seemed he'd run off home – and fed the dog, spruced myself up, made a few calls and then took the MX5 out for a spin; the little melee had completely reinvigorated me.

The following week, our licences began filtering through, and people's names began appearing on the rota. And then Carl dropped a bombshell on us: we were to be allowed to visit the casino the following evening, to get a feel for what it was like 'on the floor' on a typical evening.

"Has anyone ever been in a casino before?" he asked, but of course none of us had; how could we, as kids in our teens and early twenties, have possibly afforded it? "Well, I hope you haven't got any plans for tomorrow night, because that's when I'm going to show you what it's really like." Our excitement levels shot up, and we were all asking him questions at the same time:

"What time?"

"Where do we meet?"

"What do we wear?"

"Can we play?" ("No!")

Carl told us: "Meet in the pub down the road and come over here together; I want you in reception at 10pm, sharp; dressed up to the nines, yes, but nothing too flashy. Is that understood, ladies? I'll get you all signed in, and then I will escort you, slowly, around the casino. I don't want you to talk to anyone, touch anything or get in anyone's way; remember, you'll be in the casino under live game conditions, so I don't want you distracting anyone, is that clear? Don't have anything to drink beforehand; anyone who turns up worse for wear *will* be sent home.

"Now this will probably be the only time you ever have a chance to witness a casino in operation from the punters' side of the pit, so make the most of it, all right? I've had to pull in a few favours to get this approved, so don't let me down. Has anyone got any questions?" No-one did, but it was obvious that we were all excited and we remained that way for the rest of the morning, throughout our practice games.

At the end of that day's training we were given another talk, by another old geezer – but this one was completely different to that pompous idiot from the

Gaming Board. Carl sat us all down and introduced us to a genial-looking old boy named Jacob Ambrose who looked a bit like Richard Attenborough in Jurassic Park, with a short white beard that was very well groomed, and he was dressed in a full-blown, spotless tuxedo, with a frilly white dress shirt, velvet bow tie, cummerbund, glittering cuff-links, razor-creased trousers, and shiny black shoes: just like Carl, in fact, though without the red silk pocket handkerchief and permanent suntan.

After saying hello and shaking everyone's hand, he explained that he was one of the gaming managers, and then he gathered us all around one of the blackjack tables, and showed us the actual gaming chips (and high-value plaques) that we'd be using on the live games (up till then we'd just been using 'practise' chips, which were old, chipped and valueless); then, in a rich, deep and cultured voice, he invited us to sit down, which we did (with me off to the side, as usual), and then he looked at us carefully in turn, and kept on doing so as he spoke to us.

And he wasn't at all like that old fart from last week; he spoke to us as equals, and without any hint of condescension; he told us what an incredible business the casino industry was, and how different it was from any other walk of life: it was a different world.

The casino would look after us, and teach us everything; not only how to deal the games properly, but how to walk, talk, stand, dress, and conduct ourselves: they would mould us into the perfect model of what a croupier should be.

He mentioned that British gaming personnel were highly thought of, but he didn't ram it down our throats. He said that the club was the company's flagship casino, and that both the drop and the hold were much higher here than anywhere else; the action was intense and constant, and it took total professionalism to ensure everything was conducted properly.

Yes, we had a lot to live up to, he told us, but we would be helped at every step of the way. And we were never to feel alone; his door, and that of all the other managers, was always open. If we needed any help or advice, be it about work or anything else, we weren't to hesitate.

"And if," he said, "it sometimes feels like show business... well, in a way, that's exactly what it is: a well-run casino is a place for wealthy people to meet and feel protected, and able to gamble in safety, and put on a bit of a show, and enjoy the spectacle of high-stakes gaming with all the style and showmanship that we have to offer.

"It is often like being on stage, ladies and gentlemen, so remember that every night you will be up in front of our members, wealthy people, and they will be expecting a good night out, and so we try to give them a bit of a show, and we don't want you to ever forget it.

"And yes, sometimes it might seem that you are under pressure, because you will be dealing with large amounts of chips, which can add up to a lot of money; but this all adds to the excitement and suspense of the game, and it's just part of the job; you'll get used to it, and, when you do, you'll begin to enjoy it.

"But like I say, if you ever feel that it's too much for you, remember that we are here to help you; come and speak to one of us, and we will set you right. All we want is for you to enjoy the business."

Then he gave each one of us a long, genuine smile... and then he actually stood up, came over to us each in turn, shook everyone's hand again and wished us well. I couldn't quite believe it: he was a lovely old chap, obviously sincere and completely up-standing.

Cynical and suspicious as I may indeed be, even I couldn't help but feel moved, and when I shook his hand I thanked him and said how grateful I was that he'd taken the trouble to speak to us. Then he took all the chips and plaques back to the cash-desk (in a soft, black velvet bag) and Carl let us go, reminding us yet again about the following night.

It was early in the week, and the weather was cloudy, chilly and blustery, so instead of going for a customary spin with the hood down in the MX5, I got home around 2pm., earlier than usual, and found Mum jabbering away on the phone.

"What was all that about?" I went.

"Nothing," she told me.

"What do you mean, 'nothing'? And what was that eighteen hundred quid you mentioned?" I quizzed her.

"Nothing; it's got nothing to do with you," she told me, but that was like a red rag to a bull.

"If it's eighteen hundred quid, than I want to know about it!" I told her, and eventually she threw her hands in the air.

"It's about that big pine tree we've got growing down the garden; Dad thinks it's getting a bit tall, so he told me to organise a tree surgeon to come and chop it down."

"What, for eighteen hundred quid? Not on your Nelly!" I told her.

"Well, Dad doesn't want to do it, and we need someone who's insured; after all, we don't want an accident to happen and be liable for damages, do we?" she said, with a supercilious look on her face.

"No, I suppose not," I admitted, but I was hatching a plan. "Well, you know best," I said, heading upstairs to lock myself in my bedroom as usual.

Eighteen hundred quid? To lop a tree down? Are you joking me or what? I knew that it was a matter of just a couple of hours work, if that.

So I changed into some old jeans, t-shirt and sweat shirt, and sneaked downstairs and into the back garden. I soon found everything I needed in our shed; Dad could have easily done the job. Eighteen hundred quid, what a joke! The so-called 'tree surgeon' was probably laughing himself sick; well, I'd show him: I'd have the bloody thing down in no time!

It was quite a windy day, but I wasn't stupid; I rummaged through the shed until I came up with some cord; not rope, exactly, but more like electric cabling, and good enough for my purposes.

I went down the garden to the offending pine tree, which wasn't particularly wide (I could put my arms around the trunk and touch hands) but was about fifty or sixty feet tall, and then, with the cabling over my shoulder, and using the fence to assist me, proceeded to clamber up into the lower branches and thereby gain a foot-hold and start climbing up the tree.

It had lots of branches, not particularly thick but strong enough to support me. When I was about forty feet high, and the tree began tapering towards the top, I tied the cabling to the trunk using lots of knots and them shimmied back down to the floor. By the time I got back down to the ground I was covered in grime, pine needles and bark, but no matter; eighteen hundred quid saved!

I then crossed to the opposite side of the garden, which was about twenty yards wide, a little bit wider than the house, and tied the other end of the cable to the base of an apple tree; the wind was blowing from east to west, and I didn't want the wind to blow the tree into next-door's garden, especially as their two young kids had been playing on their climbing frame (until I'd clambered up into the tree, screamed like a banshee and scared them off).

Tree securely anchored, I got out my trusty axe and started thwacking away; (I knew the drill, I was forever watching the Discovery Channel: make a concave 'V' with your axe on one side, saw through from the other side and then pull it down; easy as pie).

Unfortunately, my thwacking brought the unwelcome attention of my mother, who came hareing down the garden yelling fit to burst (I'd hoped to have the job basically done before she cottoned on), but I screamed at her to leave me alone so I could save us all eighteen hundred quid, plus I had my axe in my hand and was sweating and covered in filth, so she did a quick retreat but then stood in the dining room, looking out through the patio doors, arms folded and shaking her head.

I ignored her and continued chopping away; I kept all my weapons razor sharp and my axe was making inroads into the pine. If my idiot baby brother had been around, I would have let him take a turn; breaking inanimate objects was something he would have enjoyed, but he must have been out with his mates, the useless spastic.

After about an hour I was about half-way through the tree and I could hear the trunk beginning to crack a little, and the wind was gusting and the cable was nice and taught, so I got my saw and start sawing into the uncut part of the trunk; my plan was to then cross to the apple tree and pull her down towards me (whilst scooting out of the way yelling "Timber!"); the one thing I hadn't counted on was the strength of the wind.

Sawing rigorously, I knew it wouldn't be long before the trunk would start to give way, and so when the cracking and splintering noises started coming thick and fast, I knew the time had come; I glanced up the garden towards the house saw Mum still in the dining room, arms folded and shaking her head, lips pursed in contempt.

I ignored her, and starting tugging on the cable, attempting to induce the big fir tree to fall across our garden towards me.

"Come on, come on!" I called, giving it a really strong yank and then – *CRACK!* – I found myself sprawled on my back: the blasted cable had snapped! I looked upwards, fully expecting so see the tree falling down to crush me. No such luck. Another gust of wind blew, towards our neighbour's garden, and then there was another loud crack, then another, and as I watched in horror the sixty-foot tree teetered on it's stump... and then toppled, extremely slowly at first but gathering inexorable momentum, to crash across next-door's fence, garden and climbing frame.

"Oh dear," I might have said, as I looked up the garden and saw Mum, still standing in the dining room, arms still crossed but this time nodding her head, smiling and gloating. "Fuck it!" I muttered, racing up the garden, down the passageway, across our front garden, over the hedge and into the neighbour's front door; they were called Trish and Peter; at my insistent hammering, Trish answered.

"Trish, something terrible's happened! I've cut a tree down and some of it's fallen into your garden, are the boys inside?" I blabbered, like a lunatic, and indeed Trish was looking at me like I'd flipped (which I had).

"The boys are inside, everything's all right, calm down! They said you were up a tree doing something...."

"Well, okay, good, I'll just nip out back and tidy everything up," I said, dashing back into our rear garden, grabbing up axe and saw and then scooting back round to next door's back garden.

The pine tree had pivoted on the fence and partly come to rest on their climbing frame, buckling it somewhat, but I'd deal with that later.

It took me over three hours to cut the tree into manageable-sized logs that I could heave back over the fence, and then I thought it best to pick up every shred of debris, leaves, sticks, branches, pine cones and even the endless pine needles that I'd left, as I didn't want Peter from next door coming home and then, understandably, wanting to box my ears, or, worse, complain to my old man (the climbing frame was only slightly buckled; hopefully they wouldn't notice).

By the time I'd finished I was absolutely knackered and aching all over, but at least their garden looked very tidy, so tidy in fact that no-one would have believed the destruction I'd caused just a few hours previously (and I'd make sure I had an early night and hopefully by the time Dad returned home it would be dark anyway).

Of course, then I had to chop up the pine tree into manageable logs for the wood shed and fireplace, which took me another two sweaty hours.

Possibly my steadfast dedication – and abject terror – caused my mother to relent somewhat, though no mention was ever made of the fact I'd saved us £1,800; I might have been given dinner, but £200 for my troubles, maybe? £180? £100, even? Forget it!

The following day we had another fairly late finish, as

Carl and Gabriel worked and worked the trainees whose licences had been issued – which just happened to be everyone besides myself, in fact – and so, just after half-past one, as we were about to depart from the gaming floor, the afternoon shift came on the gaming floor to open up; the guys started removing the security tags and heavy covers from the roulette wheels, while the girls started brushing down the green baize table-tops.

I spotted one girl in particular, and you couldn't help but notice her: tall and slim and with beautiful, shimmering long golden-blonde hair, stunning blue eyes and a high cheek-boned, heart-stopping face. She glanced up at me and smiled, and I had to hurriedly lean against the nearest table in case my knees gave way. She was, without question, one of the most gorgeous creatures that I'd ever seen, and I failed miserably to return her smile. I sort of stumbled over to her table, and blurted:

"You all right?!"

"I'm fine, how are you?" she asked, giving me an even bigger smile.

"Er…" I went, my brain shutting down completely. "Yeah, anyway, what are you doing; don't we have cleaners who do all that?"

"No way!" she replied, in a wonderfully sweet-sounding voice. "The cleaners do the floors, the restaurant and bar, but they don't touch the gaming equipment."

"No?" I went, shaking my head like a complete half-wit.

"No way," she said emphatically, shaking her head and her long golden hair swept from side to side. (I couldn't be sure, but I think I did emit a small whimper.) "No-one touches the gaming equipment except us: this is *our* casino; we look after it, and the casino looks after *us*."

"Oh, right," I managed.

"So you're on the training school, are you?" it asked – because such a gorgeous creature shouldn't have a name.

"Aye," I replied, like a complete muppet.

"Are you enjoying it?"

"Aye," I went, wide-eyed, nodding and swallowing.

"Well, I hope you make it," she said.

"Oh, aye," I groaned, still nodding, and she gave me a strange lopsided smile, shook her head again and moved to brush down another table. I took a deep breath, tested my legs – they seemed OK – and then staggered off; damn!

This turned out to be my last proper day of training; all

the others had had their licences come through, Carl was working back on the day shift as of the next day, so it was only Gabriel, Joe and I until my licence finally arrived (which it did that Friday). I shot off for the afternoon but was itching to get back that evening for a look at the real live casino action.

The casino really did seem to be a different place, offering a highly unusual life. It was interesting, and, I guessed, could be quite exciting; throughout my life, I'd always been called a night-owl, black sheep, dark horse – by parents, teachers, relatives, friends, friends' parents; all my life, I knew I could never do a nine-to-five sort of job, and the casino seemed to be turning into exactly what I was looking for. And not only that, but it seemed to take an active interest in its personnel. I was beginning to suspect that I'd actually fallen on my feet and couldn't wait to get stuck in. A company that actually valued its people – amazing!

And such a shame it didn't last; such a great shame.

Harry Jarvis was a sixty-nine year-old, semi-retired quantity surveyor. He was twice divorced, lived alone, dated the occasional well-kept lady and generally lived a quiet life. He went to the cinema and the theatre, took his dogs for long walks, played golf with friends and business associates, took long winter holidays, went down the local village pub, hardly ever ate lunch at home, and, every once in a while, popped over to Jersey to collect some secret tax-free money which he'd stashed there over many years.

He still did the occasional well-paying job, and didn't have a mortgage any more – he'd struggled for 25 years to pay that off – but wasn't wealthy. Since he'd been self-employed his entire life, he hadn't been able to afford a decent private pension: too much money had been spent on paying mortgages, raising children (and giving them a start in life) and simply making ends meet to have the luxury of that.

So now he had just the state pension to live on (£110 per week), plus his tiny private pension (£75 per week), or to put it another way, he was expected to make ends meet for the price of a decent meal for two: terrific!

Harry drove a turbo-charged Subaru and liked it; he regularly attended aikido classes, a discipline he'd first learnt years' ago; he never courted trouble, and wisely avoided unsafe areas, though sometimes odd jobs took him into run-down parts of inner–city London and one never could be too careful, especially if one was a little old bald guy.

Something that not many people knew about Harry was that one of the other things he did was to attend various local casinos six or seven nights a week; not for hours and hours on end but just till he was up to the tune of fifty or a hundred quid.

It was something that he kept strictly to himself; not because he was ashamed of it – on the contrary, he couldn't give a monkey's what anyone thought about him; in fact, he was *proud* of it, had anyone deigned to ask – but simply because he'd learned to be circumspect over the years; a lot of people, he knew, would think he was wealthy if they knew he was out at the casino every night, and word would inevitably get around, possibly even to the ears of potential thieves. Life was far too short for all that nonsense, so Harry very rarely mentioned his casino hobby anyone.

Going to the casino, and playing the roulette tables for a couple of hours was one of the highlights of Harry's day. It wasn't that he was addicted, in the usual sense, but he'd certainly miss it should he somehow be prevented from going. And he certainly didn't think that going six nights every week was excessive. After all, what else was he going to do? Stay in and watch the soaps?

He usually played in Watford, and usually at The Metropolitan Casino; there was another casino in Watford, The Palace, which might have been easier to get to but the parking was non-existent, it was busier but it was smaller and much more down-market (and it far harder to get to the tables). He was also a member of casinos in Luton, Northampton and London, but overall The Metropolitan was by far the best and most convenient casino for Harry: he lived in Harpenden, just ten miles away as the crow flies.

Harry had first played in casinos years ago, back in the Sixties, when one of his big clients had invited him along. He hadn't become a regular player, but that was probably because when he did go he always seemed to lose. But he'd remembered what he'd seen, and, after he divorced (the first time), and had more disposable income, he'd gone back more regularly and had gradually learned how best to play: it was a hard lesson to learn, especially when it was your own money at stake, but the last thing that Harry was, was dumb.

He soon realised what *not* to do, and then, later, how to carefully take advantage of the best situations. After a while, he started winning regularly, and so began to go more often, never playing for much – he would take a maximum of £200 with him, and never his cheque book or bank cards – and he carefully developed a kind of system. Well, not a system, exactly; more a method of play that suited him.

Harry was a bright bloke, and although everyone makes mistakes – his first marriage being one – over the years his winnings slowly began to cover his losses. Eventually, Harry realised that for him the best way of playing was *carefully*, and as soon as he was £100 ahead, he'd leave – happily! £100 wasn't that difficult to achieve, though you might have to wait around for a couple of hours till the time was right.

The way Harry looked at it was, if the state were only willing to pay him a measly £110 a week, then why shouldn't he try to top-up his income by going to the casino six nights a week? He had time on his hands, and what more pleasant way to spend it than in lovely casinos, where there were no riff-raff to bother him, where he could get an excellent – and heavily subsidised – dinner, and then, maybe, walk out of there actually winning money?

Now that he was mostly retired – he'd only do a job now if someone actually contacted him by name, which was once or twice a month – he couldn't really afford to lose much, and nowadays he only ever took £100 with him, and as soon as he was ahead £50 or more, he got out of there.

Harry had realised that if he only ever won *small* amounts of money, then the casino would hardly even notice him, and his name probably wouldn't go down on those sheets that the supervisors were always writing on; and the £350 he made every week was a welcome addition to his income, and nicely subsidised his pleasures in life.

He'd worked out that there were some golden rules to abide by when playing at the tables: never, *ever*, play against a dealer who was 'on a roll,' and raking in all the chips; it was much better to play against a dealer who was generally paying out, and, not particularly lucky at that moment.

Sure, one might have to wait around a couple of hours,

but then you could easily make £50 – or more – in just a few minutes. So he'd always watch the dealer before buying in to play.

Also, it was very important to stop playing when a new dealer came to the table; he might be a lot luckier than the previous one, and Harry had spotted an insidious little trick that all casinos seemed to utilise: as soon as a dealer started paying out, they would get one of their hottest croupiers to take over, and he'd jump on the table, do four or five quick spins, and before you knew it, you'd just lost four or five bets on the trot!

So whenever there was a change of dealer Harry had learned to stop betting and just stand at the back and watch for a while, and if it didn't look good then he wouldn't hesitate: he'd move straight off to another table and see how the other dealers were doing. If he couldn't find a dealer who was paying out, or, at the very least, find a game that was chopping back and forth, then he wouldn't play at all! He'd go and have a free drink at the bar!

Sometimes, if he spotted a player who was a on a lucky streak, Harry would scoot over and back the same numbers; the other player might be playing £5 chips or even £25's, whereas Harry only ever played £1 chips, but it didn't matter: after two or three winning spins, Harry would have won his quota for the night and be off into the sunset.

Sometimes, if a player was hammering a certain section of the wheel and there was a hot dealer who was crucifying him – and seemed only to be spinning the opposite side of the wheel to where the other player was betting – then Harry would jump in and play the opposite section of the wheel; this method of playing had netted Harry some good wins over the years.

And as soon as he'd achieved the magical figure of £50, he'd cache his chips (he'd put them in a pocket reserved for "winnings only"); if he still had some odd 'table' chips, and was in a good situation, he would play on, and a couple of times a month he'd have a lucky night and often end up winning over £200!

(On one memorable occasion, Harry had had a wonderful night where he just couldn't seem to lose, and hadn't been wiped out of his table chips for *two hours*! He'd won over £1,900 that night – but that had been a long time ago!)

Always, always, the most important thing remained: as soon as you had achieved your set amount, *get out*. If it was proving difficult, then £50 was enough; if you were on a roll, and you'd achieved the £50 quite easily, then play out the remainder of your chips and see how much more you could make.

And when they were gone: *get out*! Even if you hadn't had a sniff and had lost your entire £50 bankroll: *get out*! Because Harry knew that the two surest ways of losing everything were to keep playing for hours on end, and to keep playing when on a losing streak.

Nowadays, Harry kept records of how much he won, and where; overall, each week he seemed to have two easy nights, one really difficult one, and three moderate ones, where it went back and forth till he finally achieved his goal.

It was rare for him to lose the entire amount he took with him, but it happened once or twice a month, which was why he never took a lot with him in the first place – and at least he'd had a 'free' night out, with dinner and a few drinks. Harry had worked out that if you have three or four losing bets on the trot, it was better to walk away and find another dealer who might not be so lucky; Harry had learned an expensive lesson by trying to ride out a losing streak, it was far easier and cheaper to just walk away.

By checking his records, Harry had averaged a win of just over £350 a week for the last three years. The way Harry looked at it was that £350 a week, tax-free, on top of one's regular income, and at next to no risk, was a result in anyone's book.

Later that evening I sauntered downstairs and found my old man sitting as always in his armchair watching the news and puffing on his stupid pipe; he had started smoking a pipe in a concerted effort to quit cigarettes, though I regularly caught him outside with a crafty fag. I sat myself down on the settee opposite, coughed violently until I had part of his attention and then I explained what I needed.

"Now that I've successfully completed the training course," I began grandly, "I've been invited to an evening in the casino proper – tonight! So as a favour, I thought you'd lend me a bit of loose cash so that I can afford to buy all the managers a drink and make a good impression, know what I mean? Oh, and let me borrow your car for the evening; again, so I can make a good impression. And as soon as I get paid, I can start paying you and Mum back, can't I? What do you say?"

"No," he went, not even looking at me.

"Eh? What do you mean, 'no'?"

"Like I said," he said; "No."

"You miserable old slag!" I yelled. Then (much more calmly): "But I'd have thought that you'd have wanted me to get off on the right foot! Eh? And make friends with all the managers and the big punters; you do, don't you?"

"You're not borrowing the car," he went. "You'll only crash it."

"What? No I won't," I told him. "I've never crashed a car in my life; in fact I'm a probably a better driver than

99

you are!" Then I cracked up, giggling wildly, since I knew it would wind him up.

"Take your new car! God knows, you made enough of a fuss till you got it!"

"Nah, can't take that; everyone knows I drive that! Gotta take something more up-market; something special," I went, trying to flatter him to death. "I want to make a statement, and yours is the only car in Berkhamsted that can do that."

This time, he didn't say anything.

"Oh, go on Dad, *please*! When do I ever ask for anything?" (Apart from all the time!) "All the managers and big-wigs will be there and see me!" I wailed.

"Well, you're lucky that I'm not out on business tonight," he began.

"Oh Dad, you're an absolute diamond!" I hollered. "Oh, and can I borrow one of your silk ties? You know I'll look after it."

He immediately whipped his stinking pipe out of his mouth, and waggled it at me: "You touch any of my ties and you'll never get to use the car again!" he said, slapping his the pipe down on his little table next to his malt whisky and almost getting out of his chair.

"Oh flipping hell!" I cried, scooting out the door. I went upstairs, got into my suit, put one of my ties on, stuffed one of Dad's in my pocket and then rushed back and presented myself downstairs, where I managed to wheedle £20 out of him, which I had to (again) promise to repay. Then I was grudgingly handed the keys to his car – which I hadn't yet been able to get copied – and went outside, fired her up (not that you could really hear the engine running) and got on my way: whoopee! Because an immaculate, black 1975 Citroen DS 23 Pallas was still, even after all these years, one of the most beautiful cars in the world.

I left the house at half-past seven and took the DS for a long, leisurely drive, popping in to a couple of my favourite pubs for a couple of drinks en route to the casino.

The other trainees had arranged to meet at a pub-restaurant near the casino at nine o'clock and I got there at nine forty-five: still far too early, and thus I was forced to have a drink with them and listen to their mindless chatter; but at five to ten I made my way to the casino by getting in the car and driving the 500 metres in the DS; I didn't offer anyone a lift, and met up them in the reception.

The casino, even though it was a Tuesday night, seemed extremely busy; the car-park was jammed, there was of course the valet parking (something I'd seen only in American movies) but now there was also a couple of big, thickset – but nevertheless immaculate – geezers standing outside and in reception (obviously part of our 'security'), along with the usual crowd of Arab receptionists, most of whom knew me by now.

We chatted, waiting till the others got there (and even as I waited, two well-dressed couples came in, the ladies depositing their fur coats, the gentlemen signing in, and then they were ushered inside).

I sidled up and peered in through the inner double-doors, and the place was heaving; no wonder they needed more croupiers! From what I could see – which wasn't much; the interior was always kept pretty dark – all the tables were open, and all the spaces around the tables occupied; it looked really busy!

Eventually the other trainees turned up, and I thought that the girls looked particularly tacky, in all their fake jewellery and cheap, revealing dresses; so I peered into the glass display cases, looking at clothing that I couldn't afford even if I *could* afford it, my dreams were suddenly interrupted by a flurry to my left, as the inner glass doors burst open and I looked over to see something that I definitely didn't like the look of:

"Right then, you're all here, then?" a harsh Scottish voice spat out. The voice belonged to a very thin, very pale, middle-aged white-haired witch-like woman, with bright blue eyes, bright red lips, and bright red claws for fingernails; she was dressed in an expensive, form-fitting black dress, with a short black jacket over it and black high heels. She gave us all the once-over and she had an awfully evil glare. I tried bravely to stand up straight and smile but as those searchlight blue eyes lit upon me my immediate thought was: Oh, Christ!

She looked very alert and no-nonsense, and after signing something in the book she turned back to us and said: "Right, listen you lot! Carl's gone home, so you're with me tonight and we're very busy, so I can't spend a lot of time showing you around, so listen carefully: follow me around the casino, *anti-clockwise* – have you all got that? Try to take in as much as possible, stay close together, don't dawdle, and DO NOT crowd anyone or distract them from the tables, is that clear?

"Then I want you to follow me into the staff-room, where I'll introduce you to the staff; remember to check the rota to see if your names are up there and then I'll show you out the back exit, which you'll be using in the future; any questions? Good; right then, follow me!" And then she was off, with the others following her like sheep.

Me? Sod 'em! I thought; I'm going to take my time and check out as much as possible, so I got to the rear of the group and dawdled along, trying to take it all in.

As soon as I walked through the set of inner doors what struck me immediately was how completely different it was from my experience of the gaming floor; there was an amazing atmosphere which I couldn't

103

quite define but could simply *feel*: excitement, expectancy, hope; the place was packed and every table was heaving; I was looking at the dealers – or trying to, when I could spot them through the press of bodies – and they were calling out the bets, spinning the wheels, taking bets as the roulette wheel spun round, adding up and paying out with lightning speed – you could hardly see their fingers move – and they looked so poised, refined and professional, even though it was all so fast, that I was thinking that there was no way in the world that I would ever be able to do it.

And as for the punters, they seemed like quite a mixed crowd, to say the least, mostly foreign, mostly smoking, and they were dressed pretty much alike: the men in jackets, but mostly without ties, and almost everyone, male and female, appeared to be middle-aged (or older), most were overweight, not English, and there wasn't a single person wearing a dinner jacket or bow tie. Some of the older women were dressed up a bit, and most of these were overdressed. Mostly, they seemed to be Jewish, Arab, Greek, Italian, Indian or Chinese and though few of them were black they were almost all most definitely not from Berkhamsted.

And all of them seemed to know exactly what they were doing; the place was extremely noisy, what with the punters calling out the bets, the dealers repeating those same bets and then the inspectors doing likewise, and what with dealers calling out 'no more bets!', the punters yelling to each-other about what they were doing and how it was going, many apparently invoking some god or other to help them win and above all of this was the constant sounds of the balls whizzing round and then bouncing around the wheel, and the dealers calling out – loudly – the winning number, and over and above all this was the constant clicking and clacking of the playing chips, as they were slapped down by the punters, or cleared off the layout by the dealer, or 'chipped up' by another dealer (or clattering around in some of the expensive, electronic chipping machines); it was a racket, but it all went to add to, rather than detract from, the overall atmosphere.

Almost all the men (and most of the women) were smoking and there was a lot of heavy cigar smoke around, but I noticed that after it floated around a bit it soon got caught under one of our powerful extractors (which were located in the low, 'hidden,' black ceiling) it was instantly sucked up and away.

The roulette table layouts were plastered in chips, with each player – five or six (or more) per table – placing fifty to one hundred chips each spin, and I thought there was no way on earth that I could handle that lot!

Soon enough – far too soon for my liking – we had traversed the bottom end of the casino and were now passing the roulette then blackjack tables on the other side of the pit, with the restaurant on our right. All the blackjack games were open, with what seemed to be a lot of tall stacks of chips on each 'box', but then suddenly we were through the staff-only door with the witch-like woman ushering us into the staff-room, telling us to wait in there and that she'd be back soon.

I wandered in, trying to assess all I'd seen, but found that I couldn't concentrate for the staff-room itself was in chaos: dealers (and inspectors) were all over the place, all attired in their evening-wear and looking very smart, sitting around in the soft red armchairs, watching the TV, drinking coffee, smoking cigarettes, chatting, coming in and out of the room, calling through the hatch (into the kitchen) for dinner and then slagging off the TV.

In fact, everyone seemed to be moaning, cursing and slagging everything off: the TV, the dinners, the punters, the managers, the (lack of) breaks and even each-other. It was a right old racket, and the overhead extractor fan, which was rattling noisily away in the ceiling didn't really help; it also didn't really extract the cigarette smoke, which was a pain because as far as I could tell I was the only person in the entire room who wasn't puffing away like an addict.

So I stood by myself, leaning on a dividing wall, looked over into the canteen area and saw a handsome dealer tucking into what looked like a good beef stew with roast potatoes and other assorted vegetables on the side; he glanced up, smiling and chewing at the same time.

I smiled and nodded back to him, and called out: "Any good?" He nodded back, still chewing and smiling. I just grinned, and stared over at the TV. A moment later, I noticed the dealer at the dinner table put down his knife and fork and light up a cigarette whilst still swallowing his dinner, and I couldn't help but grin even more.

I hardly recognised any of the staff, which seemed to suggest that only a few of them ever did a day-shift (or double-shift); most of the dealers seemed to be in their mid-twenties, with the inspectors – you could tell them apart because they wore a black dinner jacket – either late twenties or early thirties; and all of them, both male and female alike – although there were a lot more men than women – were good-looking, above average height, slim and immaculately turned out.

Some of the women were wearing flowing, deep-blue, diamanté encrusted evening gowns: these were the dealers; others were wearing short, smart black dresses worn under a short black jacket: the inspectors. Others were in long, flowing black dresses: the cashiers. And the girls in the low-cut, shortest, most revealing black dresses were the waitresses, and all of these, without exception, were stunning. Needless to say, all of these uniforms were bespoke-made, and all were without pockets! I just stood back and watched the show.

There was a huge clock above the door, and at exactly twenty-past ten, the whole lot of them, like clockwork, stood up en masse and made for the door, stubbing out cigarettes and downing the last of their coffee en route. Within seconds, a strange silence enveloped the room, broken only by the buzzing but useless extractor fan. The other trainees then realised the place was empty and made a dash for the armchairs, but I just remained leaning on the partition wall, still trying to take it all in.

Moments later the next wave of 'breakers' started coming in and performing the same rituals that the others' had: lighting up cigarettes, grabbing coffees, turning the TV station over, plonking themselves down in the armchairs, and then slagging-off everything and everybody.

The only person out of this new crowd that I recognised was the chubby guy from the other week: Malcolm Philby. None of the other staff showed the slightest inclination to talk to him (or me!) but I thought he seemed friendly enough and when he spotted me he came trotting over.

"All right?" he went.

"Oh, aye; you?" I asked. He shrugged. "Looks like a busy night," I said.

"What, you're joking! This is nothing; just you wait till Friday; 'Wankers Night', we call it."

"Oh?"

"Yeah: Wankers Night, when all the young idiots bring their new girlfriends along and try to impress 'em, acting like big shots with just a couple of hundred quid and faffing around all night; it's a waste of our time, but we slaughter 'em anyway!" he laughed. Then he took a deep drag of his fag. "When you starting on the floor?"

"Dunno, still waiting for my licence; end of the week, hopefully. So, what; tonight's not that busy then?" I asked, definitely worried that I might not be able to handle all the action.

"Oh, it's about normal; lots of bodies, but not a huge amount of action. It'll die off around eleven-thirty, twelve, and then pick up again around one, when all the Tids come in."

"Tids?" I enquired.

"Chinese," he explained.

"Er yeah, but 'Tids'?" I asked nonplussed.

"Tiddly wink," he went, spelling it out: "*Chink*."

"Oh," I muttered; "Say, who's this woman who's been showing us around tonight; the Scottish one?"

"Oh, her," he said, looking around guiltily and lowering his voice to a whisper; "That's Mary MacCreith." He looked around and lowered his voice even more, so that he was whispering directly into my ear. "She's one of the managers." He glanced quickly round again, to make sure no-one was eavesdropping. "She's good, very good at the job, but if she's in a bad mood or we're losing... phew-ee! Just keep well away! And if you're on the receiving end...." He whistled, with his eyebrows raised. "Well, just make sure you never are." He stared thoughtfully into space for a moment, pursed his lips and shrugged. "Or any of the managers, come to that."

"Oh, right," I managed, thinking about (and committing to memory) what he'd just said, and then Mary herself came bursting in, glaring around the room and searching us out.

"All right, you trainees, you can go now," she yelled, stepping back into the hallway but continuing to hold the door open and waving for us to get out there. "Come on, chop chop!"

"Jesus," I muttered.

"Yeah, but you don't want to keep her waiting," Malcolm muttered in return, so I whispered a 'laters' and dived last through the door and nearly banged straight into her: whoops! I just managed to avoid her, and gave her a silly grin.

"Who the hell are you?" she yelled.

"My name is Shilling," I replied, in my poshest of voices.

"Oh, yes," she all but sneered; "*Christopher* Shilling

isn't it?" she glared, as the others filtered in.

"Yeah, that's it," I croaked, and as soon as we were all stood out in the corridor she pressed an intercom buzzer. After about two seconds, when the big security door didn't buzz to let us out, she banged on the buzzer again, and screamed:

"*Vernon, open this fucking door!*" and as it buzzed she pushed it open for us, and waved us out, muttering, "Goodnight, goodnight."

I boldly replied: "Goodnight!" and then we were all outside, with the heavy metal door slamming behind us. "Blimey," I muttered, walking off and looking for the Citroen DS (and no-one wasted their time asking me for a ride.)

After taking the DS for one final naughty spin, I arrived back home just before midnight and found my father slumped in his armchair, asleep, pipe in ashtray, a half-empty bottle of malt whisky on his side-table and a book open across his chest; I knew from old that he was either celebrating a successful day or drowning his sorrows.

Dad used to be an accountant, but three years ago had been convinced by one of his golfing buddies to become a life insurance salesman, and for the last three years he'd been banging on about 'residuals', and I later found out that he got 5% whenever someone paid a premium, and this was usually monthly, and that went on forever, so he was making good money without even leaving the house nowadays, although he was, according to him, one of the best salesmen in his company (if not Europe).

I'd recently overheard him telling Mum that he was earning more than twice what he used to make as an accountant and hardly paying anything in tax (he always used to say to me: "Don't steal - the government hates competition!"), so not wanting to pay much tax was in my DNA.

I sat on the settee and started flicking through the TV channels, but when I turned up the volume slightly it woke him up and he roused himself, peering blearily over at me. He tried to struggle up, saying, "Oh you're back! Is the car all right? How did it... here! That's my bloody tie!"

"Eh?" I went, staring down at it; "Oh, shit!" I'd completely forgotten about borrowing it!

"Hey, come 'ere!" he bawled, floundering in his armchair and struggling to heave himself up as I ripped off his stupid tie, flung it at him and darted out of the room, up the stairs and into my bedroom, slamming and locking the door behind me. As I stood quaking behind the door, I listened for signs of pursuit and was quite ready to slip out of the window and onto the garage roof, but thankfully I couldn't hear any, so I guessed he'd had a successful week, praise the lord!

By the end of the week, I was the only one still on the

112

'school' not to have a licence, and had spent many a boring morning with only Joe or Gabriel for company; but come lunchtime on Friday we finally got word from the Gaming Board that my licence was being issued that afternoon, and when Carl came in to work the afternoon shift he stuck my name up on the rota; he'd given me the Saturday and Sunday as my days off, and I was to begin work proper the following Monday night.

"Come in at eight," Gabriel told me, "so we can get you a uniform sorted out; and make sure you comb your hair!" Bloody bloke!

So I finally had a start-date, at last; I could hardly believe it, after all this time. I left the building, both elated and worried at the same time, and took the MX5 for a long spin in the country; it was cooler but not raining, so I had the top down (and heater on) and grinned the entire time. I liked the MX5 but I wouldn't be keeping it forever, no sir; I'd start on the tables at the casino, make them lots of money, get promoted, get huge pay-rises (plus bonuses for winning big) and then I'd get a Lotus Esprit... *and* a flipping E-Type Jag!

Chapter 3

I'd been itching to start work for weeks; now I fretted about it. I'd been panicked by how busy the place was and how much action there'd been on the tables, no matter what the inspector Malcolm Philby had told me.

I'd gone out for a drink over the weekend with some of my mates from college (Maurice and David) and talked to them about it – as I had throughout the entire training school – but they just told me not to worry about it and just to enjoy the first few weeks – and take in as much as I could, obviously – because in the early days the new starters would be almost expected to make lots of mistakes. David, who knew me very well, said that he thought working in a casino would be 'just about perfect' for me – whatever that meant.

So I went in on Monday evening, at a quarter to eight, was let in through the back door and then sought out somebody to get me a uniform, and eventually one of the pit-bosses showed up, a guy with black receding hair and a big black moustache (whom I'd never seen before) called Keith Blackwood; he seemed like a nice enough chap, and took me down to the office and sorted me out some shirts, dress trousers, clip-on bow ties and showed me to the gents changing room, which was roomy enough, with a shower area, sinks, loo, benches, open coat rack and lots of lockers (of which I got a small one).

As soon as I'd got my uniform on (and combed my unruly blond hair) I went and sat in the staff room and watched as it gradually filled up with night-shift personnel; no-one deigned to speak to me so I just eavesdropped on all the gossip, but found it to be much the same as the other day: moans and groans about just about everything and everybody. As it got closer and closer to nine, the room gradually filled up with plenty of faces that I hadn't seen before and I just sat quietly, smiling and nodding to anyone who looked over enquiringly.

At exactly ten to nine everyone stood up en masse, stubbed out their cigarettes, drank down the dregs of their coffees and marched out on to the gaming floor, so I followed them.

Again, the casino seemed very busy, and as soon as we had entered the roped-off 'pit,' which no punter was allowed to set foot inside, the senior pit-boss, Percy Collins, began directing the inspectors to 'take off' other inspectors, and then direct the dealers to replace other dealers (the afternoon shift) and telling the extra bodies to open up more tables.

When he finally got to me he must have deduced who I was (seeing as he'd already dealt with all the other names on his list) for he introduced himself and we shook hands, and then he directed me to go and 'chip,' which allowed me to move around the pit helping to empty the chipping machines and physically chip-up chips on all the roulette tables without a chipping machine (which was four out of the ten roulette tables that we had).

It actually wasn't *that* busy (once I'd calmed down and taken proper notice of my surroundings) and I moved around quite happily, helping out here and there, watching what was going on, not saying anything to anybody – as we'd been endlessly instructed – until just over an hour had gone by and one of the other trainees came and tapped me on the shoulder, indicating that it was my turn for a break. So, I remembered to 'show clean hands' and made my way to the staff room, where I sat for twenty minutes without anybody speaking to me.

For the entire rest of the night all I did was chipping-up; I didn't know whether to be angry or grateful. But I did get a couple of short stints dealing roulette the following night, and though I might have been slower than expected, I didn't make any cock-ups, and over the next couple of weeks I got to deal somewhat more frequently, increasing slowly from two or three quick stints (when we were quiet) to hour-long stints (with not-too-bad action on my tables); I was only allowed on '£1' (per chip) tables, mind you, and never if we had a 'big' punter hanging around, but after a month I felt myself getting up to speed.

Hardly anyone spoke to me, which might have bothered some people but didn't bother me whatsoever since I reckoned most the staff were so far up their own ass-holes – and for no obvious reason that I could see – that I wouldn't have wanted to talk to them anyway.

I discovered from all the gossip in the staff room that some weeks previously the casino had lost a large group of experienced dealers, who had all resigned and left on the same night because they'd been offered good positions in some of the top London clubs, thereby almost doubling their pay overnight.

Even with us six trainees now on the gaming floor we were still relatively short-staffed and there was plenty of overtime available to anyone who wanted it, so I started doing quite a few double shifts.

Staffing was a problem that had begun affecting the casino lately more and more, I learned, and in fact not more than three months since I started on the floor the casino was obliged put another advert in the local paper advertising for experienced casino personnel, and soon managed to poach four dealers from our competition in town, 'The Palace Casino,' and after they'd been with us for a month, four more of their mates also came up. And it was out of this latter group that I made my first friend in the casino: Sinclair Peterson.

One evening, while I was chipping and he was dealing,

117

he'd had a game build up so I went over to help out, and as he dealt he kept muttering asides to me, completely taking the mickey out of his punters – who were now starting to lose – but, more particularly, the other gaming staff, especially the ones who strutted around like jumped-up little Hitlers, making out they were God's gift to the casino world.

Now this was highly unusual (a dealer dealing yet talking to the chipper at the same time) but I was enjoying it since the attitude of most of the older gaming staff had really begun to annoy me; they tried to act so superior, yet all they did was spin a little ball around a wooden wheel, or pull cards out of a plastic box; honestly, you could train a monkey to do that!

And it wasn't even as if any of them could actually control – or influence – a game, was it?; I'd been watching like a hawk to try and determine whether any of them could do it and I couldn't be sure; I'd seen lots of dealers win lots of money, just as I'd seen lots of players win lots of money as well.

Of course, I was just a mere trainee, what did I know? I wasn't really even supposed to speak (apart from to announce the betting on the tables; what were we, back in Victorian Britain? I honestly heard the phrase being sneered: " A good dealer should be seen but not heard"); and so the important thing, at this stage of my career was not to make any stupid mistakes, so all I was doing was making sure the payouts were correct whilst trying to get up to speed as quickly as possible; I hadn't got the leisure to practice any of that 'section-spinning' malarkey, but it was something I thought about all the time.

I had thought it through and it was simply going to be too difficult – impossible, actually – as there were far too many things going on to be able to concentrate on aiming for a certain section each time, and all this without taking into account all the problems of bounce, scatter, speed – of ball and wheel – and remembering where you'd previously spun from, and then get all the stacking of the bet, the payouts correct, the acknowledgement from the inspector etc., all done in under a minute, etc.; no, it was all too much for me to focus on at the moment.

Anyway, Sinclair had me giggling away as he slagged-off the other croupiers and managers whilst dealing a fast, competent game, and he gradually wore the punters down till they eventually lost back their chips, bought in for some more, lost those as well and then gradually sloped off to try their luck on another table.

"So how come you come up here from the Palace?" I whispered to Sinclair.

"Dunno, must've been mad!" he replied, causing me to crack up even more.

"Do they pay more here?" I enquired; I'd been wondering how we compared with other clubs.

"Well, the standard pay is exactly the same, but here you get time-and-a-half for a double, and I need the blasted money!" he told me. "You got your own place?"

"What, on this money? You must be joking! Nah, I live with me parents," I told him; "How about you?"

"Yeah, same here, living with me parents, but me and the girlfriend are saving up to get a mortgage on a flat," he said.

"Jeez," I muttered, because the idea of me getting my own place, even though I dreamed about that sort of thing, was about as likely as me being able to hit a number on demand; with my basic net pay being about a grand a month, and rent or a mortgage being a minimum of £500 a month, I had no chance! "Is the work here about the same as at the Palace?" I asked.

"What? Low pay, few breaks and constant hassle from the idiot management? Yeah, I'd say it was pretty much the same," he said; "The bloody twats!" I giggled but unfortunately I then I had to go and help out on another table, but at least he had broken the ice and after that 'Sincs' and I started chatting all the time.

Those first months shot by in a blur: I was always in on time, I chipped a lot of the time, I dealt a few decent games and generally tried to learn as much as I could; if they had left me dealing all of the time no doubt I would have improved a lot more quickly, but the bosses obviously preferred to use more experienced dealers on the bigger games.

I just kept my mouth shut and my head down, smiled at everyone, did what I was told and tried not to mess-up. I noticed that the girls from my training school seemed to deal far more often than me, and that wound me up a bit, especially as I thought they were rubbish, but there you are; sometimes it's better to just keep your head down and say nothing. And eventually I had to stay behind after work and do The Count.

The count was when a few poor souls had to stay behind after the night shift and count all the money that had been 'dropped' down the table boxes by the dealers; everybody hated doing it and I'd been warned about it, yet I was looking forward to it; apparently it was a real pain in the ass and took anything up to three hours, meaning that I wouldn't get home till seven-thirty in the morning, but in many respects I was looking forward to it, particularly because I was dying to see for myself how much money the casino actually made.

There were two dealers and one trainee (that would be me) on the count, plus one inspector, one manager, and, sitting on a separate table, two cashiers. Once we'd closed all the gaming tables, locked away all the chips, the other staff had been released from duty and we'd locked all the doors behind them (including wrapping a massive locking chain through the door handles of the inner set of double doors), the dealers went around the casino, unlocking all the drop-boxes from under each table and piling them up next to American Roulette 10, down at the far reaches of the casino (and about as far away from the front doors as one could get), which was where we would be doing the count; then, once the manager and inspector had got their paperwork ready, we began, and the most senior dealer unlocked the first box, from 'AR1', and emptied all the money out on to the table.

I just stood there, goggle-eyed: it was an absolute pile of cash, a bloody mountain of the stuff! I just stood there, mouth hanging open, at least until Mrs Mary MacCreith, the assistant manager and, unfortunately, the manager for that count, from two feet away screamed at me at the top of her voice: " Shilling, what are you, *DEAD* ? Pick up the money *YOU CUNT!*"

Startled into animation, I quickly began sorting through the immense pile of banknotes, of which it was mostly fifty pound notes – there must have been at least fifty grand, I reckoned – and as fast as possible putting the correct denominations together, with all the notes facing the right way up (with the Queen's head on top) and stacking them at the side of the table. Try as I might and going as fast as possible it seemed that I was really slow whilst the two other dealers were racing through the cash, their hands moving faster than I could see.

"Don't worry about it, Chris," said the inspector, Kara Allsop, one of the few half-decent people in the entire place and who had actually spoken to me a couple of times. "You'll get used to it."

"It's more money than I've ever seen!" I wailed.

"Oh just get on with it; we don't want to be here all fucking night," snapped Mary MacCreith – who else?

Then the most senior dealer laboriously counted all the bills out, in rows of twenty, and the next-most experienced dealer scooped them up and put them to the side. It took absolutely ages, but I was so entranced by all the cold, hard cash that I'd forgotten about the lateness of the hour.

Once we'd done one box, and Mary and Kara's totals both tallied, the dealer next to me placed all the money in a plastic sack, zipped it up, and then passed it over to the cashiers on the next table, who proceeded to unzip it, and count it all out again to double check it; what a palaver! And then we cracked on with AR2.

Kara was right: after three or four boxes, the fifty pound notes were just so many pieces of paper, which I had to pick up, sort and count, the faster the better. By the end of it, my head was spinning and my hands, fingers and arms ached like the devil. Once all the cash was counted, handed over to the cashier and we'd rammed and locked all the boxes back under their individual tables, we were allowed to go and sit down on a settee and have a coke and some crisps from the kitchen (very generous!); then we waited for the cashiers to complete their double-checking of it all. I just sat there like a lump, too tired to try to make conversation – not that I'd have wanted to anyway, as the other two dealers were both miserable sods, neither of whom had made the slightest effort to even be civil to me – so screw 'em!

After what seemed like another hour, we were called over to sign the paperwork and I made a mental note of reading the results (and wrote them down when I got home); and my estimates had been way out! AR1 had a drop of only nine grand! The total cash 'drop' was £108,884 and the 'result' £19,922. So slightly less than the 20% 'hold' that the casino expected every night, but still, twenty grand!

Now correct me if I'm wrong, but isn't that about seven million pounds a year? Taken from just one provincial casino (and supposedly there were ten casinos in our group)? Jesus Christ, I thought, as I tooled home at half-seven in the early morning traffic in the MX5: someone, somewhere, is absolutely creaming it! And then I had another thought: what they were paying me – diddly squat – was an absolute insult.

As the weeks went by, and I started dealing roulette on a much more regular basis – sure, my games weren't quite as fast as some of the others', but I never made any silly mistakes − I noticed that some of the older hands began to nod the occasional 'hello,' and chat to me a little in the staff room.

I was always pleasant, and of course always listened politely when the more experienced personnel were telling 'war stories' about how they'd nailed some punter or other, in the hope that I'd pick up some hints on how to win more money − and keep the management sweet − but the truth was, at the end of the day, all one could do was 'keep the game going,' and it seemed to me that being a successful dealer was as much down to confidence rather than anything else; after all, the dealers themselves had nothing to lose; even if they were 'unlucky' and dished some money out, it wasn't their money, whereas for the punters it might be money that they couldn't really afford to lose, and feel under a lot of pressure, and have less confidence (seeing as they were gambling against the odds).

And as I dealt more, with my games getting gradually faster, my confidence began to grow; and when I was chipping, I'd regularly witness the likes of Susanna Filton − for that was the name of that gorgeous blonde creature that I'd 'spoken' to just before I came off the training school, when she'd been brushing down the blackjack tables − dealing huge games of roulette, with stacks of chips on almost all of the numbers, and literally thousands and thousands of pounds being wagered on each and every spin, and she'd just spin, pay, spin, pay, and nothing would faze her at all, and before you knew it she'd simply wiped everyone out! I would just stand there flabbergasted... so god knows how the punters must have felt!

Strangely, I'd noticed during my brief stints at dealing that the more I tried to miss the players – which was little more than wishful thinking, in truth – the more I seemed to get flustered and end up paying them out: typical!

Yet I'd noticed that the dealers who truly didn't care one way or the other about the result, and just got on with the job at hand, usually walked away winning; and, similarly, the punters who seemed particularly at ease, those who genuinely didn't seem to care what happened – no matter how illogical their bets – often got good wins, whilst the players who really tried, playing all the best odds and doing what seemed to be the most sensible bets... well, they were the ones who usually lost; I just couldn't figure it out at all!

But maybe that was the point: playing against the odds simply wasn't sensible from the outset; after all, no matter what you did before the spin, there was only ever going to be *one* number that finally came in – and no-one knew which one it would be.

And there was another other thing that I'd noticed which irked me a little, so much so that I'd finally asked to Sinclair about it in the staff-room one night.

"Say," I whispered to Sincs, "how come when you clean-up on the tables none of the managers ever tell you 'well done,' but if you do your brains, they treat you like a piece of shit?" Which they did; I'd witnessed the management's attitude towards certain dealers every night since I started, and thought it was appalling. (Fortunately, I was too new to have been risked on the bigger games, so my faffing around on the smaller roulette games had been largely unnoticed.) Sincs just laughed.

"Ha, why do you think; it's cos they're a bunch of plonkers!"

"Whaddyamean?" I hissed in a whisper.

"Oh, they're so short-sighted they make me sick!" he replied. "If they're gonna bollock you when you do your crust, then they should compliment you when you do well, right?" he said. (I nodded.) "Exactly! But no, instead, they completely ignore you! Of course, if you do your bollocks they spit at you like you're scum, or kick you under the table, or threaten you with poxy Tuesday/Wednesday as your days off, ah, they're all flipping morons!"

"Yeah, but if they gave out some decent rewards, like more regular pay rises, or a cash bonus, or an afternoon shift with a nine o'clock finish, well, blow me, our profits would through the roof!" I said.

"Yeah, tell me about it," Sincs agreed; "Tell me about it!"

Later on, when I was on a break in the staff room, I found myself sitting next to Kara Allsop, one of the few people in the whole place who would talk to you normally, and I asked her:

"Er, say, Kara, remember when we did the count a couple of weeks ago? And we won about twenty grand?"

She shrugged. "If you say so, Chris; I honestly can't remember."

"Yeah, well," I continued, "what I was wondering was, is that pretty much about average – do we normally win that much?" She nodded. "And how much does it cost for the casino to stay open every day?"

"Well, I don't know for sure, but I think it costs around and ten thousand pounds per day; it's not cheap to run a casino any more!"

"So, what, in other words, we make about ten grand in profit per day?"

"Yeah, about that," Kara nodded with a shrug.

"What; and we never lose?" I went.

"Oh, no," she said, "we tend to lose a couple of times a month, and we tend to break even a couple of times a week; but then on other nights we'll win twenty or thirty thousand, so it all tends to even out eventually."

I dropped my voice to a whisper. "So how come the managers get so stressed when we're losing?"

She laughed, shaking her head. "I wish I knew!" she said.

"It doesn't make sense!" I said.

"No, it doesn't," Kara agreed, smiling. "And because the punters don't seem to be able to walk away when they are ahead, however you look at it, owning a casino in this country is simply a licence to print money."

"Phew!" I whistled. "But it seems strange that with the odds being only slightly in favour of the house, why is it that we win so much? Surely we have lots of players that win something, and then go home, no?"

"Well, it might seem like that, so if I could sum it up in just one word, I'd say it was down to greed. You're right, the odds are only a few per cent in favour of the house, and because they are that low almost everyone is up at some stage of the night, but it's like I've always said, if everyone left as soon as they were a hundred quid ahead, we'd be out of business.

"But people don't stop when they are ahead; they are enjoying themselves too much, and when they win five hundred pounds in just a few minutes, they tell themselves that they can now win ten, or twenty or fifty grand."

"Sheet," I went, working it all out.

"Oh yes, the brain is a funny thing," Kara said; "And I've seen it a thousand times: if you start winning, your brain tells you to keep playing because tonight is going to be your lucky night and you're going to win twenty grand, or whatever; but if you start by losing, your brain tells you to keep playing, because in a minute you are going to get on a winning streak which is going to be much luckier than your losing streak!"

"So, psychologically speaking, if you are the average punter, whatever happens, unless you've got really strong will power, you're buggered," I said.

"That's right," Kara agreed; "Owning a casino is simply a licence to print money."

"Jeez Louise," I whispered, but I was actually thinking hard: could it be possible to train your brain in such a way so that you could leave the casino as soon as you were, say, £500 ahead, and do it two or three times every week?

One evening, I was left standing at an almost-empty £1 roulette table; it was our quiet time, just after midnight, which was the slow half-hour between when the

Europeans started making a move for home and the Tids and other foreigners began pouring in from their takeaways and restaurants.

So there I was, just stood there like a spanner, dealing to a couple of old Jewish ladies who were each playing about ten chips per spin, until a young Chinese guy that I didn't recognise wandered over and stuck a few cash chips down on the first and third dozens.

I spun and missed him, hitting number 18. Then I spun again, and the Tid quickly rooted around in his pockets and pulled out a couple of £25 chips, one of which he stuck down on the first and third dozens again. But I missed him again, raked in the losing chips and spun again. Now he was plonking £50 down on the 1st and 3rd dozens, but this time I hit number 19, and so again pulled in the losing chips. Another spin: and £200 went down, as he 'doubled-up.'

But I missed him yet again: number 16 came in. Now my inspector was taking an active interest – it was Grenville Aston, Kara Allsop's boyfriend – and he'd stopped watching the other two (quiet) tables that he was supposed to be inspecting and was concentrating on mine.

Another spin and the Tid now had £300 on each dozen: it was the table's maximum allowed bet, but stone me if I didn't repeat number 16, again wiping him out. As soon as I reached into the wheel for the next spin, he was suddenly reaching for his wallet, so I paused to see if he wanted to buy-in, but he just indicated that I should spin, so I spun, and he threw a load of banknotes notes down on his two favoured dozens.

"Cash plays!" I called.

"Cash plays to the table maximum!" Grenville announced loudly (and somewhat more professionally), and we all watched as the ball fell away from the wheel's inner rim, hit a diamond, bounced all over the place, fell towards the numbers, bounced again as it hit a metal stanchion, and eventually settled in number 24; I quickly reached out, grabbed up all the notes, flung them into the 'salad' (my float area), and then cleared away the losing chips belonging to the old Jewish ladies.

Grenville then had me sort out and count the notes – it amounted to £500 – which I shoved down the drop box, and then I spun again. The young Tid quickly searched through his pockets and shoved down a couple of crumpled notes, a few fives and tens, onto the third dozen – it was obviously his last money – Grenville announced (in a quieter voice):

"Cash plays to the maximum," and I hit number 22, missing him again, and so again whipped in the notes, cleared the layout of losing chips, counted out the banknotes – it was a grand total of £40 – and pushed them down the drop-box. The young Tid looked baffled, searched through his pockets again – this time coming up empty – and after a moment wandered off, so I shrugged and spun the ball for the old ladies.

I glanced to my left and saw that Grenville was doing a table check, which was supposed to be done every hour on paper, and every half-hour only visually, and now he was adding up the drop box (we had a little clicker by the salad area, which we'd click once for every ten pounds we dropped); by comparing the figure on the clicker from how much was missing from the float he could gauge a fairly accurate table result, and I could see that my table was up a fair amount, of which I was responsible for over a grand at least, I reckoned; I'd certainly earned my wages tonight!

Then another dealer came and took me off – it was Tracey Houghton, who was a totally useless but fairly attractive blonde; she'd probably dish the whole lot back out again! – and so I went on a break, along with Grenville (who'd been taken off by William 'Bill' McCoy, who seemed like another half-decent inspector), and when we got to the staff room Grenville actually started a conversation with me, asking me all about the MX5 and he suddenly seemed much more open. Not that he was one of the miserable ones, mind you; he was good enough at his job and mature enough not to have an 'attitude', but I realised what it was: he'd seen me win money!

You see, that was the important bit; just being able to deal competently wasn't enough: you had to actually *win money*, as that took the pressure off the inspectors, which in turn took the pressure off the pit-boss, because then the managers were happy because the casino was winning money... which was all a bit ridiculous really, seeing as, long term, we were almost always going to win money anyway... but that was how it was.

And yes, as a dealer, you did want to try and win money, almost trying to will the ball into an empty number, but, as best as I could figure, it was still largely a matter of luck (with a bit of confidence thrown in). So I chatted cars with Grenville for the remainder of the break (he drove an old – but decent enough – 2.5litre Vauxhall Calibra) and although I hated to admit it, part of me was pleased that some of the more experienced staff could see a respected senior inspector giving me the time of day.

And the following evening, at just after nine pm., I was stood at another quiet table when a very young-looking, fresh-faced guy came over to play. He threw £100 over and muttered 'colour by a pound', so I passed him over 100 £1 chips, and shoved the money down the drop-box. Then I leaned over slightly towards the inspector, and whispered:

"Er, excuse me, but have we seen this guy before?"

Then inspector stared at me as though I'd just slapped him with a wet fish.

"What?" he spat.

"Er, well I was just wondering if we've seen him before; I mean, he looks awfully young," I said.

"Well, so do you, Shilling! They would have checked all that at reception; get on with it!" he whispered poisonously. Jesus Christ, I thought, I'm only trying to ensure we don't lose our licence for letting in under-age kids, sorry for breathing!

So I started dealing, and he started playing, and within a few moments I could tell he was casino-familiar from the way he handled and stacked the chips; he might even be a croupier, I thought, at least until he started buying in for £100 every spin and I took £700 off him in a matter of minutes, but then felt a light tap on my shoulder, so showed clean palms and announced, "Thank you, you have a new dealer," and made my way to the staff-room for a break. Obviously, I wasn't up to the job, I thought sourly.

Later on, I saw the fresh-faced guy on another table, and later still, on yet another table. And at the end of the night, I had the temerity to ask the pit boss, Percy Collins, if I could ask him a question.

"If you must," he said, barely looking up from his paperwork.

"Er, I just wanted to enquire after that young-looking kid who was playing in here earlier, first on AR8, and later on AR3 and 4; how did he do, in the end, if you don't mind me asking, sir."

"No, that's all right," he said, still not looking up; "he won forty-four grand."

"How much?" I went. "Forty-four? Well, we'll never see him again, will we? Forty-four grand, by god! More than four years' wages," I said. "Oh no, we'll never see him again."

Percy slowly removed his spectacles and looked up at me. And then he went: "*What*?"

"Well, I mean, forty-four grand; that's real nice money, that; we'll never see him again, will we? He'll probably pay off a chunk of his mortgage with that, or buy a nice new Lotus, or put down a thirty percent deposit on a flat; oh no, we'll never see him again." In my infinite wisdom.

"Shilling," Percy drawled, still without deigning to look at me, "he will be back in here tomorrow night."

"But how can you say that?" I spluttered. "We've never seen him before, have we?"

"No, we haven't ever seen him before; but you mark my words: he will be back *tomorrow night*."

"Oh yeah, sure," I said. "Anyway, thanks anyway, and see you tomorrow," and with that I breezed off. What an idiot, I thought; if I'd won forty-four thousand pounds, you wouldn't see me for dust, I'd go and live like a king in the Bahamas (or Vegas) for a year, or just rent a flat, buy a nice 2nd hand Jag and take two years off work.

So after I turned up for work the following night, who should be the first person I saw hammering away at the tables? Yes, you guessed it: the fresh-faced kid, banging down hundreds of pounds on every spin. I couldn't believe it, and couldn't bear to look Percy Collins in the face all god-rotting night.

At the end of the shift, I'd heard that the young-looking kid had won money again, so I timed my moment as best I could (at the end of the night, after the chips had been put away and after ascertaining that the casino had won nearly eighteen grand overall, so hopefully he would tolerate my presence for a few minutes), over I went, 'cap in hand'.

"Excuse me, sir," I said without preamble, "but I would just like to apologise for my stupidity of yesterday; it's about that fresh-faced kid that we'd never seen before, sir."

"Well, what about him?" Percy went, without looking up from his paperwork.

"Well, sir, you were right, and I was wrong, sir, so I'd like to apologise."

"Hmm, well you're new to the business, so maybe I can

forgive you. When you've been in the industry as long as I have, certain things become almost predictable. And it is all psychological. It's Shilling, isn't it?" he said, glancing at me, however briefly.

"Yes sir, that's correct, Christopher Shilling."

"Well, Shilling, do you know what?"

"No, sir; what's that?"

"Well, young Shilling; if I could have any wish in the world, if I was allowed just one wish, do you know what I would wish?"

"No, sir, sorry, I don't know; maybe to win the lottery or something, sir?"

"Don't be so bloody ridiculous, Shilling; if I got hold of that kind of money, I'd be dead within a year. No, if I could have any wish in the world, I would wish that the first time that any punter came to our casino, they would win big: forty, fifty or even one hundred thousand pounds; yes, at least a hundred thousand. Yes, indeed; that would be my wish."

"But surely, sir, if that happened, then we'd be out of business within a couple of months," I said, but he just looked at me witheringly.

"No, young Shilling, we would not be out of business at all; we would be the busiest and most successful casino in the entire history of the world."

138

"But, er, excuse me sir, I don't understand," I said, pitifully.

"Shilling, it is important you learn this lesson early-on in your career – if indeed you go on to have one," he scoffed, "so let me try and explain; if, on the first time any player came to our club, they won a sizeable amount, let us say, over twenty grand in just a few hours of play, and anything up to one hundred thousand on their first ever visit, then let me assure you of something: they would not want to be anywhere else – in the entire world! The only place they would want to be is here, in our casino, gambling away – and nowhere else – because we are lucky for them! Wild horses would not be able to drag them away from our tables!"

"But, but..." I spluttered.

"No; no 'buts', Shilling; because do you know what then happens?"

"Er, no sir," I said.

"Because then what happens, after they win, and win, and win, and win... well, then they lose, and lose, and lose, and lose... and then we get everything back that they've won, and then we get the house, the car, the business, the inheritance – even the kids, if we want them. We get it all! And so it goes on, year after year, decade upon decade: we get it all!"

"Really, sir?" I said, dumbfounded.

"Yes; really, sir! Goodnight, Shilling," and he waved me away, yet I was still thinking: nah; I would have partied for two years solid!

How wrong could I have been? I had been completely and utterly wrong, because over the next three weeks I saw that fresh-faced kid come in our casino on just about every night of the week, and on just about every night he won anything from two to twenty grand (although never quite achieving the big win he secured on his first night in our club).

And then one night he lost *eighty* grand, roughly half of everything that he'd won from us up until that point, and the following night he did back the other half, plus another ten grand of his own money on top.

And then he simply did his bollocks, night after night; he just couldn't seem to get a single bet to come in, and on the rare occasion it did, he'd chase his money and lose it all immediately. Again, and again and again, and chasing his money with ever increasing stakes.

In less than two months, I witnessed that young-looking kid win over one hundred and sixty grand from us, lose it back and then spunk a further £600,000 of his own money (which, indeed, probably was his house, his car, his business, and finally his inheritance).

And then we never saw him again.

It was a painful lesson learned, but never to be forgotten: don't get sucked in! If you win, walk away; if you lose, only lose a little, and walk away! (I do hope he didn't do anything even more foolish, but like I said, I never saw him again.)

It still annoyed me when I would watch experienced dealers confidently win money on the tables, because most of these blokes were the most obnoxious people you could ever (not) wish to meet; they were loud-mouthed, swaggering braggarts – and, for the most part, completely stupid to boot – but as I say: if you ran a fast, efficient game and you won money regularly, all sins could be forgiven – so no different to being in a premiership football team really (apart from the appallingly low wages), and we were constantly reminded that we were only as good as our last result.

However, as much as I saw these characters winning money, I often wondered how their results evened out because as my experience grew I started noticing various things and I saw that even the most experienced hands made plenty of pay-outs as well, and as soon as they started losing heavily the pit-boss would try to replace them.

Also, and most suggestive to me, was that none of them seemed capable of turning a sudden losing session into a winning one; some of them tried to speed their games up but that seemed to be about as much as they could do; I made a mental note of this, and many other seemingly minor things.

It peeved me no end when my three months probationary period came and went and there wasn't a sniff of my promised pay-rise, or even a pat on the back and some friendly acknowledgement for all my effort, the miserable, tight-fisted bastards; I won them tens of thousands of pounds and I was only clearing a measly grand a month after tax. I told Sinclair about it and he invited me out for a drink on the Saturday after pay day and I accepted immediately.

For some reason both Sincs and I – though hardly anyone else – had been given Saturday and Sunday as our days off, which was somewhat strange, us not having families (i.e., married with kids), and the week-end being extremely busy in the casino, and the only thing I could guess was that it was because Carl did the casino rota, he also had the Saturday and Sunday off, Sincs and I were so easy to work with, never complained about being missed out for a break and left out on tables, and more to the point, we both seemed to have lots of winning sessions.

So when Sincs invited me out on the piss I accepted happily, and looked forward to getting together with him, having a major drink and giving the casino a right proper slagging-off.

Sincs wanted to meet up quite early on Saturday night so – he said – we could have a quiet chat and get some drinking done before the night really kicked off, and who was I to argue?

Sincs lived in Watford, so I drove over in the MX5 to collect him, whizzed back home and parked up and then we trooped into Berkhamsted and got started just after seven in The Nag's Head, a busy pub in the town centre of Berko; he got the drinks in (him: a pint of Stella; me: a large Bacardi with diet coke) and we started drinking and chatting.

It wasn't long before we were half-tipsy and cursing the casino, and the arrogant, more experienced croupiers, and the inspectors, and the pit-bosses, and – particularly – the casino managers, and then we cursed the low pay, long hours, impossible targets, greedy owners, the general uselessness of some of the girls who worked there, the stupid, moaning punters, the non-existent tips, the incredibly miserable atmosphere… and then we slagged-off the crummy managers and our piffling salaries some more.

Sinclair was the only bloke there (other than myself) who tried to have a good laugh and not let the bleeders grind him down; actually we were similar in many ways: above average height, slim, fair-haired, and we liked music, cars, drinking and girls in that order (at least for me; Sincs seemed to like girls far more than cars, which I thought was ridiculous); we were both completely broke (and so had to live with our parents) and were pretty good dealers and hated most of the casino management.

After a few more drinks we adjourned to The Saracen's Head, where we paid for overpriced drinks, found a couple of seats, got deafened by the awful music, looked at the mostly under-age girls who were drinking in there, played on the fruit machine (he lost) and then cursed the casino some more. I asked Sincs about his future plans, and he gave me a funny look.

"What you mean?" he hollered.

"How long you gonna be staying at The Metropolitan?" I bawled in his ear.

"Well it ain't gonna be for the rest of my life; sod that!" he replied, laughing.

"So what you gonna do, then?"

"You know, the usual: work there another year or so for the experience, get me inspector's licence, maybe go to London for a year, and then go and work on the cruise ships or something; why?"

"Just wondered," I replied with a shrug.

"Yeah," he went, guzzling his lager.

"I've heard that the money's good abroad," I yelled. He nodded.

"Good? Good? It's fuckin' excellent, especially compared with here!" he laughed. "You get a good salary, tips and bonuses, free lodging, and on the cruise ships, it's all found, know what I mean? Christ, a few years of that and you'd be able to come back here and buy a place outright, you know?" He laughed again.

"Nah, surely it ain't that good!" I said. "Is it?"

"Bloody is," he nodded. "A couple of the managers they've got down at the Palace went abroad in their early days, and they saved up enough to be able to buy a couple of houses each! Now they're quids in: decent paying job, renting one of their houses out, money in the bank and no mortgage to pay."

"Phew!" I went.

"Yeah, that's what I wanna do: get some experience under me belt and then push off abroad for about ten years; it don't matter where. The cruise ships, Sun City, Las Vegas, Monte Carlo, Australia; I don't care. As long as the money's good – and if you move around often enough it's usually tax-free – you should be able to save at least thirty or forty grand a year and every three or four years you come back here and buy a cheap flat, do it up and then rent it out.

"Then, in ten or fifteen years, you come back here for good, get a flat in north London and go to work in one of the top London clubs: it's easy money, plus you'll have the rental income from your two or three flats:

sorted!"

"Blimey! And that's what you want to do, is it?"

"What? You'd be crazy not to! Who wants to work here, in *Watford*, on the rubbish money that we're on? And putting up with all the crap from all the managers all the time? Jeez, it's only worth it if you do plenty of overtime!"

"Yeah," I said, "though at least there's plenty of that at the moment; I'm hoping to be offered some soon."

"Yeah, it's cos we're so short-staffed, but even that gets you down after a couple of months; how do you like doing two or three hours on the tables without a break?"

I shrugged. "You know me," I said.

"Yeah, I do," he replied, laughing yet again.

After a few more drinks we meandered up the road to The Greyhound; it was now after nine o'clock and the pubs were beginning to fill up so we stood at the bar and screamed at each-other.

"You know, the money used to be a lot better years ago," Sincs hollered.

"Eh?" I screamed back.

"The money!" he bawled in my lug-hole.

146

"I got the last one!" I shrieked. He rolled his eyes and pushed some money at me to go and buy another drink for us. Within half an hour the place was jammed, so we got another drink each and headed for the door; once outside, we sat on a nearby wall, drank our drinks, watched the young women walk by and tried to talk, even though my ears were ringing.

"You know, croupiers used to make much more back in the Sixties and Seventies," Sincs commented.

"Yeah?" I went.

"Yeah," he affirmed, nodding vigorously.

"Yeah; how much more?" I enquired, money always being a subject close to my heart.

"Well, I know that croupiers in Watford back in the Sixties used to be on over a hundred quid a week," he told me, "and that was a lot of money back then; back then, you could get a brand new E-Type Jag for a couple of grand, know what I mean?" he asked, looking at me. I nodded and took a swig of my Bacardi. "Yeah, my uncle was a plumber back then and he was only earning ten pounds a week – I asked him!" Sincs bent over to place his drink on the floor and nearly toppled over but I grabbed him, pulled him back upright and he continued without pause. "Yeah, croupiers, man, even in the late Seventies, even in Watford, were on twenty grand a year, and in London it was more like twenty-five grand a year."

"But that's, like, fifty grand a year in today's money!" I said, trying to work it out.

"More like seventy," he said.

"Jeez!" I whistled. "Yeah; Carl Hunter told me that he used to have an E-Type," I said, remembering.

"But he's a rim merchant!" blurted Sincs, and I laughed.

"So basically, what you're saying is, us croupiers haven't had a decent pay rise in donkey's years," I said to him, "and even though we still have to deal the same poxy games, to the same stupid punters, and stick to the same silly procedures, and put up with all the same old shit from the dozy managers, right? And we're not even getting the same as dealers used to get back in the Sixties – right?"

"That's right," he agreed.

"Jeez Louise; a dealer back in the Sixties must have been creaming it! You could've probably bought a house in London back then for about five grand; damn!"

"You said it," he said.

"So what the hell happened?" I asked him.

"What happened?" He shrugged. "Who knows?" He paused to leer blearily at a trio of under-dressed, under-age girls who were leaving the pub and heading into town. He struggled up to try to follow them, but I dragged him back down.

"Eh?" I hollered, to remind him.

"Eh? Oh, who knows, but I think the casino accountants began to think they were paying too much in salaries and so stopped giving out regular pay-rises, and then they started taking people on for less and less each year, and everyone just rolled over and took it," he said.

"Yeah, except we're now doing the same thing," I said, laughing.

"Ah, but I got plans," he said, looking well hammered, peering at me and wagging a finger under my nose.

"Yeah; what plans?" I asked.

"Ah!" he went, grinning drunkenly; "You'll shee!"

I managed to get him to his feet and we swayed back into town, winding up back in The Nag's Head, where Sincs was apparently known to the bar staff; after getting our drinks we went and propped up a fruit machine, where Sincs started mindlessly popping pound coins into the slot, pressing buttons and cursing.

"Screw!" he said. "Aw, screw it!" He swallowed half of his vodka and coke and then smacked the top of the fruit machine.

"Aw, why do you even bother, mate? You know all electronic games are fixed, mate!" I went. "That's why they call 'em one armed bandits, mate," I yelled. "Save your money! Let's have another drink!"

"Hang on, I think I'm on a... oh, fuck it," he said, losing his money and finishing off his drink.

"You deal blackjack, don't you?" I asked him.

"Eh, what?" he went, still staring at the thieving machine.

"You deal blackjack, don't you?" I asked him, and he nodded. "So what do you think about card-counting? Reckon you could do it yourself?"

"Eh? How could I? We're banned from playing in any other casinos, you twat!"

"I know, I know! All I'm asking is do you think you could make a living out of it?"

He mulled it over while I swigged my drink waiting for him to reply. He shrugged.

"I dunno," he said; "Yeah, maybe; maybe I could make it pay – though it would mean a lot of travelling around, you know? To avoid becoming too well-known and barred, you know?" I nodded. "So that would probably cost you quite a lot in expenses; and you'd probably lose every now and then as well, even if you were doing everything right. So nah, I dunno; yeah, maybe I'll try it

150

one day; why do you ask?"

"Just wondering," I told him; "Have you ever thought about sneaking into another casino to try your luck, cos I know I have."

"Yeah, but I'm known at the Palace, and I can't be bothered trekking up to Northampton or down to London, and you've gotta show photo I.D. which might be monitored by the Gaming Board, you know? Or someone might recognise you and grass you up; I can't be bothered, to tell you the truth."

"You could always get a mate to join, sneak you in as his guest, sign you in under a false name, wear a false beard, that sort of thing," I pointed out.

"Yeah, I guess; so, what, you wanna try it?"

"I'd like to try out some even-chance betting, yeah; you know, red plus even, you can only lose on eight numbers and you double-up when you win; I never see any of the punters trying it at our place and I played those bets all the time during the training school and only ever lost once or twice." Sincs stared glassily into space. "I'm sure it's one of the best ways to win, Sincs; what do you think?"

"Yeah, that or counting; or cheating," he said, and laughed.

We had another couple of drinks and then I found him

a cab; if I stuck him on a bus he'd fall asleep and end up who knows where. I walked home, merry but not drunk, yet the ten minute walk somehow took me half-an-hour.

I seemed to have settled into the routine of casino life without any major upheavals; I'd always preferred staying up late and not having to get up to an alarm, so the hours seemed to naturally suit me. I'd usually finish work around four thirty am., be home and in bed by five and then sleep till noon. Sometimes I'd stay home and read, sometimes I'd go to a village pub for lunch and sometimes I'd just take the MX5 out for a spin; damn, I loved that car!

Mum would usually have dinner ready around seven pm. and after that I'd get washed and changed and drive in to work; from what I'd overheard in the staff-room, compared with many of the other dealers I lived a very quiet social life. I still looked forward to battles with my brother and his idiot mates, but they had tailed off lately, as I'd been doing lots of overtime and was hardly ever at home unless I was asleep, and my parents had been strict for once with Simon about not waking me unnecessarily (well, it was either that or he knew I'd scrag him). Come to think of it, I hadn't seen the mong in weeks.

From listening to the gossip in the staff room, most of

our gaming staff (at least those who weren't married), seemed to sleep all day, get up around six pm. (or later), take a shower get to work not much earlier than 8.30pm. After work, it'd be back to someone's flat for drinking or − more commonly − a heavy session of smoking dope, playing poker and chatting about work or what they had planned for their nights off. These usually consisted of a trip to a London nightclub where various drugs would be imbibed, helping them to dance the night away; just before dawn, they would repair back to someone's flat to smoke themselves into oblivion.

Seeing as I didn't smoke, alcohol was the only drug that I liked and the fact that I hated most of the other croupiers, I didn't think it likely that I'd be invited to any of their little soirées any time soon; I only talked to about five out of the complement of fifty or so gaming personnel we had working there. One of the main reasons I hated them was their attitude towards the newer members of staff (to wit: myself); anyone who was simply less experienced was treated like a mere peasant and fit only to be sneered at.

One of the casino's most important rules was that we were to blindly obey the instruction from any senior member of staff, no matter how ludicrous the demand might appear to be, and this rule was forever being employed by the petty, pathetic, power-crazed jumped-up little Hitlers who worked there to prove to the new dealers how low down we were on the pecking order.

But I didn't lose sleep over it and always tried to show willing whenever a manager instructed me to speed my game up.

Now that I understood the most important unwritten rule – that one had to win money – I just got on with learning the job; I had witnessed the most loud-mouthed, cocky, obnoxious, boorish dealers – who I surely would not have spoken to in the street – being given all sorts of little comments of flattery by the managers and pit-bosses; sickening to witness, it was.

It seemed that as long as you ran a good game and regularly won good money for the casino, you could get away with all sorts of minor transgressions, even to the point of being borderline-rude to our very bread and butter: the punters. But like I've said – I was simply looking for an easy life (and regular pay rises).

After my three-month probation period had passed without a sniff of the promised pay increase, and another couple of months also went by, and still with no raise or recognition in sight, I decided that I'd think about getting another job; I'd always fancied being self-employed any way, becoming some sort of entrepreneur (and buying and selling black market goods, in all likelihood); obviously it didn't matter that I was always on time, always well turned-out, always happily followed all instructions and was always polite and friendly: all that mattered were results. So it irked me all the more when I found myself doing well on the tables.

Now this was curious — to say the least — because whilst we had been on the training school we had been specifically told — by Carl — never to worry (or even think) about the results because they would come simply as a matter of course; all we were ever told was: get it right. But now, actually working 'on the floor,' it was plain to see that getting it right came a distant second to the reality of getting a result.

Certainly everyone makes minor mistakes (particularly in their early days), and everybody has to go through the learning curve, but in time one becomes a very proficient, effective dealer, regularly securing a healthy 18-22% gross profit for the club; however, no matter how efficient or capable you might be, it all counted for nothing unless you could actually be relied to win money for the club.

It was a slow, careful, insidious method of management that had existed in most casinos since the dawn of time because nothing specific was ever really said (and certainly never to new personnel), but I came to recognise the signs: the manager's looks of disgust when a dealer had failed to secure a result; dealers who had been in the good books the previous week suddenly being given the cold shoulder; the management ignoring (or sneering) at the dealers who tended to lose money (and who were then left for hours on the smaller 'Mickey-Mouse' games because they couldn't be trusted on the bigger games); the 'accidental' missing you off the break list by the pit-boss if you had lost money on the tables earlier in the evening; the holding back of promotions and pay rises; the frequency of being given the detested 'count'; and who on earth would want Tuesdays and Wednesdays as their permanent days off?

Of course, if you were in their good books (because you usually won large sums of money), you might be given the odd day-shift (even before your days off!), you'd get regular pay increases, you'd be looked on favourably when promotions were due, you'd get the occasional week-end off, you might – though rare, this – get congratulated by the managers in front of the other gaming personnel after achieving a solid result, you wouldn't be looked at like your were a piece of dog dirt on their shoe, you might even be spoken to – civilly – by a manager occasionally and you got to tell some good 'war stories' (and thus gain peer-group respect) in the staff room.

Once I woke up to what the job really entailed, I wasn't entirely convinced that I wanted to remain in the casino industry, but the truth was that I did enjoy the basics of it, and anyway, what else was I going to do?

So I decided that I'd try to stay with the casino for the time being (unless of course a better opportunity presented itself), and the one thing I did (indeed, had always done) was begin paying much closer attention to what the experienced hands seemed to do whilst dealing, hopefully pick up some pointers and do my best not to lose money, if only to keep the blasted management off my back (and not get left out on the tables for three hours without a god-damned break); at least I was smart enough to realise that if I voiced my concerns to any of the managers, I'd be given pretty short shrift, and − in all likelihood − be shown the door at their earliest possible convenience.

By my careful watching of how the most experienced (and cocky) dealers worked, I noticed (usually when I was chipping for them) that as soon as a heavy punter came to their table (or any money started getting paid out) they would increase the pace of their game, and then start altering the speeds of ball and wheel, and even begin cutting down on the number of chips they handed out; in fact, as I paid more attention, I noticed that this was how almost all the 'hot' dealers operated: once they had the punter under the knife and felt in control of the game, they would then tend to hit a lucky streak and fleece the punter savagely, regardless of how they were spinning.

Unfortunately, I noticed that a great many punters would continue playing even when it was patently obvious that not only were they on a losing streak but that the dealer was out to get them as well.

One thing all of the club's best dealers had in common was that they rarely, if ever (unless they were already in a strop about something), got flustered by a game, but what this said to me was that if you were a player and you were winning and they changed the dealer on you, it was time to stop and move tables; or, if you lost three or four bets on the trot, it was time to stop and move tables; and, very importantly, never to 'chase your money' and continue to play against a dealer who was taking your money.

The casino odds were so small in favour of the house that I was slowly coming to believe that a switched-on player might just be able to beat the house, long-term, and so was beginning to formulate some plans – and 'golden rules' – of my own. I'd recently read in The Times – so it had to be true – about an online survey that had found that what a person needed, for financial happiness, was £43,000 (on average) per annum.

Now this was interesting, because I knew a lot of people who were earning around £43k per annum, but they were almost always miserable and flat broke (due to all their bills, taxes, expenses, outgoings and direct debits); what I was beginning to wonder was whether these 'average' people could benefit from the knowledge I'd gleaned from working in the casino for half a year, so that they could, maybe, double their income with tax-free casino winnings.

In an effort to keep Saturday and Sunday as my nights off (and get my bloody pay rise), I endeavoured to ingratiate myself with the management by copying all the hot-shot dealers and began constantly trying to angle for a result.

One of the things that I most liked most about the job was the cut-and-thrust aspect, i.e. the fact that it was real, actual, cold, hard cash that was sloshing back and forth across the tables every night, and the fact that a player on a big losing streak would try everything he could to win his money back, and that I, as the dealer, had to watch out for – and actively prevent – a big loser getting back to 's-p,' and thus I could have a major impact upon his finances (I just hoped that it was money he could afford to lose).

However, once I'd begun to really understand the intricacies of the job, get some decent wins under my belt and knew that I could win good money on a regular basis, do you know what I really enjoyed?

What I really relished was when the casino suffered a very bad night, and lost to the tune of thirty grand or more, thus affecting the nightly, weekly and monthly result – and, of course, all the managers' bonuses.

Sometimes I could see (out of the corner of my eye) the managers snarling and circling around the pit like sharks looking for weak prey to pounce on, getting on everyone's backs by issuing stupid instructions, 'sweating' the result and cursing the gaming staff... which caused most of the dealers to become even more intolerant and highly-stressed (and dealing could often be an extremely stressful job).

Quite often, the managers' behaviour would create panic and cause otherwise quite capable dealers to lose control (or become truculent and actually want to give the money away, because most of the dealers hated the managers), and then they'd start to pay out even more money!

Oh, I used to *love* this, but was always very careful to keep my head well down and still try to angle for a result on my own table; it would have been fatal if any of the managers saw me standing there grinning like an idiot just as they were witnessing their monthly bonuses go down the pan!

And so, all gripes about money aside, one of the biggest surprises of my young life came when I had completed fully six months of work at the casino and actually began finding myself looking forward to going in to work!

In the normal course of events, I'd have dinner at home, go up to my room to wash, change and do my hair, return back down the stairs wearing my casino evening wear and then get the MX5 fired up and head off to the casino.

Occasionally, my younger brother and his awful mates would be hanging around, and he'd normally call me some name or make a sarcastic comment and I'd be more or less obliged to lump him one, the idiot, but fortunately for him I couldn't really get involved in a proper scrap for fear of rumpling my immaculate white 'dress' shirt, or, indeed – and I'd only just realised it, in fact – if we got into a major scrap, and I did some serious damage to one or more of them, and the police became involved, and a criminal conviction, then I might lose my Gaming Licence, and I really didn't want that! So baby brother, unbeknownst to himself, was free to abuse me at will, and only get the mildest of slaps.

Indeed, it came as quite a shock to me that one could actually 'enjoy' one's work; I had sort-of suspected that most people put on a brave face while inwardly hating what they did for a living. I certainly believed that most jobs really sucked and that given the opportunity, 99.9% of people would choose not to work for a living.

Of course, I didn't have much experience in the workplace, and apart from the casino staff my only close contact with working adults were my father, parents of friends and school teachers, and from what I'd seen most of them hated having to work; of course, whilst at school and college I was continually being told that one's school days are the best days of your life, and it was better to try to stay in education for as long as possible, but that's meaningless to a school-kid (particularly to one who was bored rigid at school); I used to wonder all the time that if school was this bad, what the hell is work gonna be like?

As for my old man, well, when he was having a good week and selling plenty of life insurance, head-office were staying off his back and he was earning good commissions and bonuses, then great, he was fine (and I had an easy life) but if he'd had a bad day?

My Dad's bad moods were something to behold (or preferably not behold); years ago I'd learned to sniff the air in case he'd had a bad day and if that was the case go and hide quietly in my room or take my dog for a long walk – and yet he was constantly winning prizes and competitions and was one of their best salesmen in the entire country! (And what on earth must it be like for the merely average performers in his company?) I figured to myself that Dad, along with just about everybody else, would much rather not have to work; although I now spent a lot of time wondering whether £43,000 (tax-free), on top of Father's usual annual income, would make him exponentially happier.

And then there were the casino managers, most of whom you could tell were sick of their jobs: a couple of the older male managers just came in and spent most of the night sat around in the bar, talking to the big punters and getting half-sloshed on the free booze; I reckoned that most of them only stayed in their role job because (a) they had been there so long that they would be useless and totally unemployable in any other job, (b) most of them liked the 'status', however false, that being a 'casino manager' afforded them, and (c) it gave them access to plenty of fresh, attractive females.

Needless to say, I hated almost all of the casino managers because the only manager who seemed to enjoy the business (and his jobs) was Carl Hunter, who, at twenty-eight, was the most junior casino floor manager; the kindly old fellow Jacob Ambrose I hardly ever saw, since he mostly did day shifts and Sunday night.

Carl was friendly, funny, likeable, knowledgeable and intelligent, and a guy who absolutely revelled in what he did (and loved everything about casinos); and then there was Mary MacCreith, the Evil Scottish Witch, who was just as capable and knowledgeable as Carl but unnecessarily nasty with it, so I avoided her like the plague.

The vast majority of the rest of the staff seemed to moan about everyone and everything and yet they kept on coming in and doing exactly the same job as Sincs and I, and we never complained − at work − about anything; in fact, I enjoyed most aspects of the job, even the things that everyone else seemed to hate.

And thus I found myself, getting on for nineteen years old working as a roulette dealer in the casino business, with an inkling beginning to form in my mind that I could just about see a future for myself in the industry, an industry which I had often found to be annoying yet equally often quite good fun, very interesting, and quite definitely different, and I did like to be different! Now, if I could just manage to squeeze some regular pay rises out of the cheapskates then so much the better!

So I decided, all things being equal, to give it another six months and had little idea what I was letting myself in for; funnily enough, neither did they.

Chapter 4

Most things spouted about casinos are lies, generally because those in the know don't want anyone on the outside to know the truth!

A regular casino punter will never tell his friends, family or business acquaintances that he plays in casinos, and if the punter's friends discover he's a casino gambler he will never tell them the truth about how much he loses as he won't want them to think he's a loser or addicted and possibly on the way to becoming a degenerate gambler; and when he does get to that stage, he'll probably start stealing from his company, his spouse, his family, the tax-man, or even his friends to finance his play, all of which probably goes some way to explaining why people are absolutely forbidden to take a camera or any electronic equipment into a casino.

A casino owner (or manager) will never choose to reveal the truth about how they operate, how they pander to people's greed, try to get the suckers in and encourage them to play on and on and not want them to leave until their last penny is finally sucked up into the well-oiled casino machine, secure in the knowledge that not only are the odds forever stacked in the house's favour but that even the legal, licensed clubs will have no compunction about having their staff use arguably dishonest methods for swindling any lucky or competent player. Of course, if one of their employees were rash enough to start spilling the beans on their operation he would either be immediately fired or – more likely – accused of stealing from the casino and then fired.

Casino personnel are forever fibbing about the business: pretending that they earn far more than they would in any other semi-skilled job (even though they only receive little more than a low-to-average wage), continually implying that they work for the Mafia (or some shadowy crime syndicate), that they win millions of pounds every night and that the job (and themselves) are far more interesting and glamorous than they really are.

Casinos in Britain have never been allowed to advertise and you can understand why, because if they were brutally honest about it, what would they say? "Come in and play against us, with the odds – and a large number of incredibly surly staff – always stacked against you!" It's hardly a good way of drumming up business. Of course, these days the casino doesn't have any hidden electronic magnets under the roulette wheel for the simple reason that they don't need them! The pit-boss, with a stable of experienced, cocky, lucky dealers has no need for such devices; and the best bit is that a primed, hot, lucky, 'killer' dealer leaves behind no evidence.

Casinos, whilst forever making out that some player

has nailed them at the tables, very rarely court publicity (because they know it's usually bad for them), to the degree that most are unwilling to even prosecute known cheats due to the unfavourable press coverage such a court case brings; it is only ever a former employee who has nothing to lose and who has been both sides of the table that can genuinely be relied upon to openly reveal the true inner workings of a casino and the facts about life in the green felt jungle.

In an effort to try to increase the success of my table results, I would sit at home and study all of the notes and instructions we had been given during the training school, but these soon proved useless; they were just to help you learn the basics of the game of roulette.

So then I would use every opportunity at work to study the style of those whom I considered to be the best dealers in the casino; putting their methods into practice on the gaming floor was more effective than studying all my training notes at home. One day, I went down to the local library to get everything they had on casinos (they had nothing) and so I proceeded to a good local book store, accosted the owner and hollered:

"I want everything you've got about casinos!"

He was a helpful chap, and we had a good look round, but the shop itself had nothing on casinos. He offered me a book about card games (which I took) and then a book of crossword puzzles (I just looked at him). After looking in the back of the shop, he unearthed a guidebook for Las Vegas which we perused and found had a decent bibliography in the back, so I took that as well, and he took details of some of the books mentioned in the Vegas guidebook and said he'd do his best.

But I wasn't expecting much; casino gambling never had been much of a cultural British pastime, even if the true odds available in a casino – as long as you knew all the little tricks and traps to be aware of – were far better for the player than the odds available elsewhere (bingo, the lottery, the horses, sports betting etc.).

I continued ploughing away at work, and when I was certain my nightly and weekly results were noticeably improving I began carrying a little notebook around with me, and every time I went on a break I'd write down how well I had managed on the tables and then I'd tot it up at the end of each week; as the weeks went by I found that most of the older hands were now starting to tolerate my presence and even beginning to talk to me, but by this time I wasn't interested in talking to them and would generally just smile and nod and try to look my most retarded best (it wasn't difficult); Sincs, Malcolm, Kara, Grenville, Bill and Carl were the only ones I had any time for in the entire place.

Just before pay-day, Sincs would usually mention about getting together for a drink on the coming Saturday night, and I would always agree. I loved pay-day, but not for the usual reasons; for me, the best thing about pay day was that for all the newer employees like myself (we had such a high staff turnover that the casino didn't automate our payments till we'd been there at least a year), the casino paid one's wages in cash, and one's pay-packet (a little brown envelope) was always made-up using (predominantly) fifty-pound notes!

On pay-day I always felt like a million dollars, walking out of the casino at dawn to get in my convertible with around £1,250 in fifty pound notes shoved carelessly down the front of my shirt; no matter that I was always completely borassic two weeks after being paid (and that my car was a twenty year-old heap that I still hadn't paid for), it was always great to be able to go into a pub and buy a drink with a fifty, they were so rare! And this was exactly what Sincs and I ended up doing the following Saturday night.

As soon as we had got the drinks in at The Nag's Head, Sincs went:

"So what do you reckon to your pay rise, then? Though an extra fifty quid a month ain't much, is it?"

"What're you blabbing on about? 'Pay rise'! I ain't had a bleeding pay rise!"

169

"Yeah, you have," he told me. "Everyone has."

"Well I flipping haven't!" I roared. "The motherfu...!"

"Calm down, calm down!" he told me. "You can go in and get it sorted out on Monday; you're easily as good as anyone else in the place... well, except me, of course."

"Yeah, yeah, of course; I'll never be that good; being able to bend over forwards whilst dealing roulette and taking it up the ass and kissing Mary's ring at the same time, that's pretty good going mate, I'll never be as good as you mate," I said, seething. He laughed, as usual. "And assuming I do get a pay rise next week – and I'd better, I tell you that, otherwise I'm doing the offski – have you ever stopped to work out how much money we actually make for the casino? In relation to how much they pay us, I mean," I asked him.

"Course I have. We make them thousands, and they pay us jack-shit."

"No, seriously, I mean," I went on. "How much do you reckon we make for them pieces of shit every month, on average?"

"Well, I dunno," he replied, frowning, and taking a long pull at his pint of lager; just to keep him company, I swigged at my Bacardi 'n' diet. Eventually, he plonked his glass back down, still frowning. "I dunno," he said again; "it's hard to say, actually; I mean, some nights it's pretty quiet and they stick you on crappy little games where even if you're making twenty percent you're probably only making a couple of hundred quid an hour."

"Yeah, but then there are other nights when it's heaving and you can cream in a couple of grand an hour," I reminded him.

"Yeah, yeah, I know all that, Chris the Piss," he said. "And then of course we all have nights where they stick you on a big game and you do your crust, losing five grand in ten minutes and there's nothing you can do about it and then they make you chip-up the entire rest of the night; hmm, it's hard to say, actually."

"Yeah, well, just saying, if you had to," I badgered.

"All right, all right," he laughed. "Honestly?" I nodded. "I reckon about twenty-five, maybe thirty grand a month," he said.

"Thirty grand a month, is that all? I'd have thought a lot more than that – maybe even as much as fifty," I told him.

"Yeah, maybe; if you have a very good month."

"Yeah, well, anyway, let's call it thirty, OK?" I continued. "And how much do we get paid? Not even two grand! Not even five per cent of what we make 'em! Is that fair?" I wailed. "I tell you Sincs; it makes me wanna bloody scream!"

"Yeah, well, don't give yourself a heart attack, mate! That's just the way it is, you knob-end! What do you want to do about it, ask Mary to put you on a percentage?"

"Yeah!" I went.

"Nah!" he replied; "If she did, you'd only end up doing your brains!"

"Yeah, I'd end up owing *them* money!" I said, and he laughed.

"Ha! Here, let me get another drink," and off he went, leaving me to stew; but he was right: what could I do about it?

After a few more drinks we commenced our walkabout, and I was already feeling the effects of my five quick doubles. We walked around, going from pub to pub, nodding hello to people we knew – Sincs knew an awful lot more people than me – and looking at the girls. We talked about work, the games we'd dealt that week, the punters whom we either liked or disliked and all the casino personnel that we hated.

"But seriously," I said to him later, "couldn't they put us on some sort of bonus system, like a percentage of everything over, say, twenty per cent that we made them every month? That wouldn't be illegal, would it?"

"Bloody hell!" he cried. "Is that all you think about, money?"

"Er... yes!" I yelled back.

"Thought so!" he said, laughing.

"It wouldn't be illegal, and it might make us more profitable," I said

"Oh, just forget about it mate, it's never going to happen. Really!"

"All right, all right, you knobber!" I hollered, and he cracked up; "Anyway," I said, "how the hell did you get into this flipping business anyway? How come you're not a road sweeper or something? What did you want to be when you were growing up – apart from a bell-end?" I asked him.

We were now sitting, drinks in hand, on a low wall outside The White Swan, which sat between The Saracen's Head and The Greyhound and the inside of which was packed.

"Actually," he answered, "when I was at school I wanted to be a motor mechanic; there's pretty good money in that, you know?" I grunted. "Well, anyway, I was doing all the engineering courses and what-not at school, and quite enjoying it – you could muck around, at least – when me parents took me on holiday to Spain, and that was when it all changed."

"What you mean?"

"Well, that was when I got my first proper look at a casino," Sincs told me.

"Oh, yeah?" I said.

"Yeah," he went on, "and after that, well, all I wanted to do was get involved in the casinos business, one way or another. You see," he said, taking a quick swig, "we were booked into this hotel on the seafront, and it was nice enough, but it was about a mile from the centre of town where all the restaurants, bars and nightclubs were located, you know?" I nodded. "So every evening me and the old parents would have dinner at the hotel and then walk along the promenade into town; it was actually a really nice place.

"Anyway," he continued, "on the second or third evening that we'd done this, there we were, strolling along, enjoying the warm breeze and looking out to sea, just me and me Mum and Dad. Well, this promenade thing was sort of set back quite a bit from the beach, and it kind of rose up this gentle slope, away from the beach and through this nice park, all covered in tended lawns, colourful flowers and palm trees; nothing like the crappy parks covered in dog shit like we get over here, know what I mean?"

"Yeah," I laughed.

"So as we walked through this park, gradually getting

closer to town, we got to the crest of this hill and looked back, and there was this spectacular view over the park and then with the yellow sandy beach and deep blue sea beyond that, and then the setting sun off in the distance; oh mate, it was absolutely glorious, I can still see it today, clear as a bell.

"And then we'd walk down the path which was now curving into the town, and then we came back to the promenade thing again, although at a much higher elevation, and as we walked along, I stopped and looked over the wall, to have a look at the beach again — and guess what I saw?"

"What?"

"The casino, of course; their local casino — and Jesus, what a casino it was, and nothing like our crappy old place; it was set down by the beach but on its own private road and bit of promenade, and there was all this activity going on so I leaned over the wall to have a look. It wasn't a massive building, or even particularly grand, but it just oozed class, you know? It weren't anything like I'd ever seen before, know what I mean? Certainly nothing like anything in Watford, and nothing like our poxy place! Nah, mate, it was a large, single-storey building, all made out of white marble, but with golden brass lampshades and glittering lights dotted all over the place, and it was set back from the road with a couple of long marble steps leading up to some tall glass doors with brass railings and door handles, with two doormen standing there, dressed in red coats and looking the business."

He looked at me, probably to check that I was still listening, which I was; he was never normally so expansive, but he had me picturing the scene, the glass of Bacardi 'n' diet coke in my hand largely untouched. He continued:

"But it wasn't just that, the building, the palm trees, the gardens and beach, in the evening's, er, twilight, that had grabbed my attention; nah, mate, it was this: this huge line of limos and sports cars slowly pulling up to the casino's front steps, and the valet's opening the doors, and these fucking old men in dinner suits an' all getting out, and then the other door being opened, and these fucking women getting out, these *women*, man, these gorgeous women, tall, slim, suntanned, all beautiful, with long summer designer dresses, and covered in gold and diamonds and everything, and then they were walking arm-in-arm into the casino together, and the valets were scurrying around to go and park the car, and then the next one pulling up, and the same thing happening. And the men were all short and fat, and all the women were young and tall and slim and beautiful; and the cars mate; oh Shills, you should have seen the cars!"

"What about 'em?" I said, thoroughly entranced (Sincs being fully aware that I liked nice cars above all things, including most people).

176

"Oh, those cars, man! It was the cars more than all them other things that had caught and held my attention, and they had everything there, man: limos, Lamborghinis, you name it; long black Cadillacs, Mercedes convertibles, red Ferraris, dark-blue Rolls Royces – both saloons and convertibles – E-Type Jags, Porsches, Aston Martins... oh man, I tell you, they had the cream there that night mate, phew-ee!"

"Jeez Louise!" I said back as we both downed the remainder of out drinks and paused for a moment deep with our thoughts. Then I jumped up to get us a refill.

When I came back from "The War Zone that was The White Swan on a Saturday Night", Sincs went on: "And this was just the south of Spain, remember, not Vegas or Monte Carlo. And yet there was everything there, the best of all the Italian, English, German, the world's super-cars! Well, it had me awe-struck, I can tell you.

"Eventually, my parents had to drag me away but I never forgot that scene. And then, of course, every night for the rest of the holiday that we walked in to the town I'd peer over that wall and see the casino, and all those rich slags in their bloody cars, with their, god, impossible women, and I'd think: bastards! I want some of that!"

"And so, what?; you think you're going to get it by working in some miserable casino in *Watford*? Ha!" I laughed.

"Bollocks!" he said, and I laughed even more.

"But no, seriously," I said, when I'd calmed down; "What did you do; come back from holiday and start enquiring about casinos?"

"Er, well, yeah, more or less! Found out that you had to be over eighteen, and with no criminal record, and that they were legal over here, cos I'd wondered about that" – I nodded – "and discovered that most of 'em were in London, but that there were two crappy ones in Watford, so I just carried on at college till I was old enough to apply and get on a training school, which was down at the Palace as it turned out, but what the hell; cheers!"

"And then… what? You found out the difference between being a filthy rich punter and an overworked, underpaid dealer?"

He made a face. "Yeah, yeah, you could say that."

"Yeah; sucks, don't it? I said, laughing.

"Bloody does!" he replied. "Yeah, but I've got a few plans up me sleeve," he said.

"Yeah, what's that then? Get lashed and try to forget all about it?"

He laughed, and gave me a funny look. "Nah, you retard; you'll see, soon enough!"

178

"What? Get stoned for the rest of your life?"

"You'll see, mate, you'll see!" he went, waggling his finger at me and giggling. "Anyway, knob-end, how did *you* get into this business?"

"Me? You know why! Cos I wanted a sports car!"

"But it's rubbish!" he yelled.

"It's better than your poxy Ford Escort!" I hollered back.

"Yeah, but it's still just rust on wheels!"

"Yeah, I know," I muttered – cos at the end of the day, he was mostly right. "Well, you know I wanna get something else, don't you; something better?"

"What?"

"I dunno; something better!"

"Yeah, but what?"

"I haven't got a clue," I mumbled, drunk; "About anything."

Back at work on the Monday night I went straight in and got the question of my salary increase sorted out with Carl; I was fully expecting a full-on row (which might have resulted in my storming out), but instead I

179

was taken into the managers' office for a half-hour while Carl shuffled through paperwork and then grandly announced (without talking to anyone else) that I was to be awarded a generous raise (his words) of £250 per month, backdated by three months, no less, so I would now be earning the tidy sum (his words again) of a very respectable seventeen thousand, four hundred pounds per year (before tax).

Furthermore, the casino was 'moderately pleased' with my performance and that I was now eligible for overtime payable at time-and-a-half on a double shift.

Moreover, he told me seriously, that if I continued in a like manner I would soon be considered for a promotion from Trainee (Level Two) up to T1 (with all the commensurate pay-rises that came with it) and after that I would be classed as a full-time Dealer (Level 4) and might even be taught blackjack!

Yes indeed, it was so very generous – especially considering the fact that I estimated I was making them at least £30k per month – and it might have upset me but hell, anything was better than nothing, right? So for the time being I decided it was better for me to keep ploughing away at work regardless and hoping that things would continue to improve; and anyway, what the hell else was I going to do?

Just doing little things, like speeding my game up when a player started winning seemed to get the money start coming back in, and if it merely chopped back and forth I'd alter the entire style of the game, slowing it right down, then speeding it back up, and changing my spins each time and generally trying to keep the punters second-guessing.

During my off-duty hours I'd spend hours figuring out ways of gaining and maintaining a result: for example, if a player hit his stride and wanted plenty of fast and furious action, what would I do? I'd stop dealing altogether, fiddle around in my float area and make them wait till I'd got my breath and felt 'in control' again. Sometimes I'd give the ball an almighty spin, of 20-plus revolutions; other times, I'd rattle the ball around for only seven or eight orbits of the wheel, always keeping an eye on the speed of the inner wheel; anything to put the winning player off, in fact.

Without doubt, these sly tactics seemed to pay off overall and even if my luck was out completely I would try to fight a holding action till I could get the word out for another dealer to be sent to replace me. As the weeks went by, I saw from the figures I made in my little notebook that my results were steadily improving, and I noticed that more and more of the older, more experienced dealers were beginning to talk to me.

Once my basic game was in order and flowing smoothly, I'd try to remember each individual player and make a mental note of how they played, so I'd be ready for them next time; often, I'd try to lull them in to a false sense of security and then hammer them with everything I'd got... but I always remained smiling and friendly; I figured that if they felt really at home (and thought that I was trying to look after them) they'd continue playing with me even though they were getting badly beaten, and from me they would always get a welcoming smile and a 'hello,' which was a damn sight more than they got from ninety percent of the other dealers.

It used to surprise me that the regular punters kept coming in so frequently until I realised that (a) they were loaded, and had plenty of ready cash that was better off spent in a casino than declared to the tax man, (b) they liked to show to the world that they could afford to lose, and (c) there were very few places in the immediate vicinity where they could feel secure whilst throwing such large sums of money about.

Fortunately for us, there wasn't another casino anywhere in the area that treated its players with anything other than the same contempt with which we did; in fact, compared with the crummy Palace Casino down the road we were viewed as quite an up-market club!

And thanks to the stupid Gaming Board, a wealthy businessman couldn't just open up a casino willy-nilly but had to go through all sorts of red tape, background checks and licensing procedures, particularly relating to whether there was enough of a potential local, 'unstimulated' casino trade – not to mention having the huge cash deposits (apparently in the region of £10,000,000) needed to buy a licence and bank-roll (another £10m) the operation in the first place.

Most of our punters were older men, and most of the time they came in on their own though often playing in the same groups; only on a Friday or Saturday night would younger men come in, often with friends or some dolly-bird they were trying to impress, and it takes far more than a couple of grand to impress a casino dealer, and these budding young Romeos were mercilessly slaughtered (whilst the male dealers tried to impress the girls); our only regular younger players were the grown-up children of our more successful Chinese or Greek members (who were mostly restaurateurs).

The truth is that before starting work at the casino I'd always thought of myself as coming from a fairly typical, fairly well-off, middle-class family; well, now that I'd seen the other side of the coin, I realised that wasn't the case at all! Having witnessed the sort of stakes normally gambled by the casino's regular players, 2-3 hours per night, 2-3 times per week, I realised that we weren't particularly 'well off' at all, and the sort of money often lost in one night by one of our regulars would be enough to make my poor old Dad weep!

My family's financial state (i.e. having a nice detached house, both parents having their own car, a small mortgage, money in the bank, a couple of foreign holidays per year, etc.) didn't even come close to the sort of wealth carelessly gambled away by our members every week of the year; and the worst of it was that when a regular player hit a winning streak and walked out with twenty or thirty grand (or whatever), he couldn't wait to rush back to the casino the following night (or afternoon!) and do it all back, because the money didn't mean anything to him; what a joke!

And yet most of the players seemed to somehow enjoy themselves; certainly if they'd been winning money and you jumped on and gave them a beating you might get the odd glare, but this was surprisingly rare; if they muttered anything at all, it was to curse their luck (rather than the dealer, who'd might well have been doing his utmost to miss them!).

I supposed that because we were in England, where it was supposed to be all legitimate and honest, most players were aware that they were playing against the odds but were completely unaware that they had the greedy 'house' managers and under-pressure dealers to contend with; if only they knew one of the most important Golden Rules: if you are winning money, and they change the dealer, stop! Find another table to play on, and only start playing if you see that the dealer is paying out as often as he is taking!

When I had first started as a dealer, and had seen all these old people throwing money away across the tables, I had thought of them as all quite sad; surely there was something else they could find to blow their money on! Didn't they realise what an amazing night someone like me could have had with just five hundred quid – let alone five grand?!

But after six months of witnessing all the goings-on in the casino, I slowly came to realise that I had completely missed the point: the point was that they were already loaded, with many of them possessing more money than they could ever spend, so obviously losing (or winning) a few thousand pounds in an evening was not really going to bother them much – if at all; and if achieved a nice little win, they probably felt it was well worth it (even if they could never quite got back to the point where they'd originally started); the important thing was that they had *won*, and Fortune was smiling down upon them.

Indeed, how better for a semi-retired multi-millionaire to spend a relaxing evening out on the town, starting with a few decent cocktails (on the house), followed by a little punt at the tables, then a superb meal with champagne – again on the house – in the sumptuous surroundings of a private members-only club, rounded off with another punt at the tables, secure in the knowledge that you can afford to lose and everybody else in the building is also rich and one isn't going to be bothered by any riff-raff; the (fiction-inspired) concept that a casino is full of pick-pockets, prostitutes and with a management of gangsters out to steal from its clientèle was obviously complete and utter balderdash

185

– otherwise they'd soon have run out of players! I suspected that if I'd been loaded I'd probably have spent many an evening in a casino (though not necessarily in Watford!).

And thus I'd experienced a complete change of heart towards our regulars: they weren't a bunch of sad, boring old codgers but were actually to be admired; so much better to get out of the house, away from the mindless television soaps and to pit your wits against everything the casino had to throw at you!

Yes indeed, it was much, much better to get a thrill from your gambling and try for a win than have the highlight of your evening come when your children ring you up to ask to borrow some money!

Even going out playing *bingo* was better than sitting around vegetating in some old folks' home and none of our members seemed to be giving up on life and going senile (like my Mum's parents had done); they were getting themselves dressed up, going out for dinner and hitting the roulette and blackjack tables two or three times each week!

Gambling, in truth, seemed to be keeping these older people alive, and not only did they seem happier than most people I knew but seemed even more alive and vital than most teenagers; indeed, I began to like them a lot more than people my own age... though I still tried to nail 'em!

The staffing situation at work had reached chronic levels yet again and even an advert in the local paper had failed to inspire any interest from local talent; and the situation was made all the worse when a couple of the more experienced personnel resigned (and went off abroad to work).

It was the same old story: low pay, which led to staff resignations, causing staff shortages, leading to advertisements promising greater pay and yet more training schools, causing less staff to be available on the gaming floor, leading to longer stints on the tables without a break, creating more bad feeling amongst the remaining dealers... followed by yet more resignations.

If only head office had paid a little bit more to begin with all this hassle would have been avoided from the outset! But what did they care, stuck away in their ivory towers? I often wondered if much of the scamming that was said to go on in casinos was as much to do with the head office policy towards its staff as it was to do with the financial temptations that went with all the fiddling; probably it was a bit of both.

One night soon after my pay-rise Carl collared me on the gaming floor. "Hey, Chris!" he called out. Oh blimey, I immediately thought, what have I done now?

"Hi Carl, what can I do for you?" I replied, keeping a pleasant smile on my face while being frantic to get to the staff-room for my fifteen-minute break (always fifteens nowadays, never twenties) and hoping that he hadn't caught me breaking procedures.

"How would you like to learn blackjack?" he asked me, without preamble.

"Blackjack!" I blurted, my brain going in to immediate overdrive; I'd always been led to understand that one was never even considered for bj training until one had been there for at least two years (for the last thing the casino wanted was you learning all the games immediately and then 'doing the offski' to London – or abroad – as soon as you'd passed the training course); so this could be a right result for me! "Yeah, sure!" I said.

"OK, good," Carl said; "It's got to be next week, seeing as we're starting a new training school the week after; you'll have to come in every morning at 10am, we'll train till 2pm and then you can do the day shift, okay? And you might even catch the occasional double; can you cope with that?"

"No problem!" I told him. The 'occasional double'; he'd slipped that one in smart enough (though the extra money would come in damn handy). I was forever asking for more overtime, but only rarely got put on the rota for a double shift (although this might improve for me now, as we were so short-staffed).

"Good," he said, turning to go.

"Say, er, Carl, er, once I've learned bj I'll be what they call a 'two-handed' dealer, is that right? So I'll be entitled to a better pay scale, isn't that right? Er, just asking," I said.

He didn't say anything, but he looked me in the eye, nodded ever so slightly, then shook his head, and pursed his lips; how well he knew me! "Yes, that's right," he said, walking off, still shaking his head. I immediately rushed to the staff-room to give Sincs the good news, though unfortunately he wasn't on a break (but when I told him later he was ecstatic; for some reason, he was even more excited than I was).

When I got home later, my brain still spinning, I rooted from my shelves all the books that I'd been able to find on the subject of blackjack (and there were a rake-load), and began re-reading various passages.

Blackjack (or 21), was, of course, a casino game that could theoretically be beaten, and thus had spawned absolutely hundreds – if not thousands – of libraries of 'how to' books (I'd even been foolish enough to buy some of them; hell, I'd have bought anything related to casinos, and almost all of it was complete and utter bollocks).

Now I knew that punters could win money playing bj, just as they could by playing roulette, but even I, not yet a bj dealer, was wised up to the fact that all a dealer had to do to render all card-counting skills nullified was simple: cut the deck in half. And all the books in the world were not going to alter that basic fact.

But I still wanted to know more about the game and was already looking forward to my bj training, if only to learn how to beat the casino (and not have them cut the deck in half).

As usual, Sincs and I went out on the Saturday night after pay-day. And as usual, we had a good time, going from pub to pub, getting drunk, slagging off the casino and talking about our plans. We'd both noticed that even doing sixty-hour weeks had not made any real difference to our pathetic financial situation.

"I mean," I wailed, "I still have to pay 'housekeeping' and a hundred quid a month to me old man for me MX5, for god's sake, and I'm trying to save a couple of hundred a month towards getting a place of my own – though I never do – and I wanna get a better car and I just can't bloody well afford it! I mean, Christ, is this any way to live, working just to pay bills? Jesus, we're no better off than slaves! We're just wage-slaves!" Needless to say, I was getting just a little bit miffed with everything.

Like many another 'profession,' being a croupier could often be a highly stressful job, and so like many other professionals many of the dealing and supervisory personnel would use various methods to help them unwind; just like famous TV personalities, movie legends, pop and rock stars, sportsmen, those involved in producing TV shows and films, or lawyers, city traders, high-pressure salesmen – you name it – we croupiers needed an outlet for our stress.

For some, like Sincs and I, it was alcohol, and we enjoyed getting slaughtered together (we went out one or two nights every month; not a lot, I grant you, but it was all we could afford and boy, did we get slaughtered!); and I liked to have a drink with my other, non-casino mates (I had always seemed to be able to put away a lot more booze than they did); and I'd occasionally have a drink at home, locked safely away in my bedroom; and, when I couldn't get out of it, I'd go down the pub with my old man (using the opportunity, and his money, to get plastered).

But overall, I didn't think I drank that much and indeed was vastly different from the other gaming staff, most of who appeared to spend not only their two days off but also most of the nights after work getting completely wasted; in fact, they seemed to spend their entire lives off their faces – yet the strange thing was that the people who got 'out of it' the most were usually very proficient at work; their focus was total. It had to be, and after spending seven hours a night in full-on concentration and not making one single mistake they surely needed to relax.

Most of the dealers seemed to use drugs; drugs were what they spent most of their disposable in on: pot after work, speed or coke in the afternoon when they got up, and ecstasy or coke at the weekend.

And it was all quite normal and accepted – as anyone with a high-pressure job will tell you – so as Sincs and I chatted, and got drunk, and cursed the rotten casino, we gradually purged ourselves of the week's accumulated stresses. If we'd had no form of release, we'd have definitely cracked up and probably ended up decking the first person who talked shit at us.

"So what do you think you'll be doing in five years' time?" he asked me.

"Dunno," I replied, "though I like your idea of working abroad, saving hard and buying some flats over here to rent out. You know; save up the cash, buy in a slump and sell in a peak." He nodded. "And keep shooting off to work abroad, on top money, till you've got enough to retire on – or, at least, get some cushy job in a London club."

"So what would you wanna do if you weren't in the casino business, then?" he asked me. "What did you want to do when you grew up?" And then he laughed.

"I dunno. I think I told you once before: I wanted to have a car dealership that just bought and sold convertibles."

"Yeah, yeah, I get it," he said, and he laughed again.

"What?" He laughed yet again. "What?"

"Only a dimwit like you could want to run a business flogging convertibles… in a country where it pisses it down 350 days a year!"

"Oh, do one!" I spat, but that only made him laugh even more. "An' I'll tell you something else, as well; I ain't impressed with working fourteen hours a day and trying your best on the tables only to be given a slagging if and when you do your crust! Too much flipping stress for me, mate."

He shrugged. "You might get stressed, but they can say what they like to me: I don't give a monkey's!" He laughed again; he always laughed.

"Yeah, I know," I said; "I had noticed. But no, seriously, for that sort of unrelenting pressure, pressure to get a result I mean, we should be on top money, man, and I mean top money – you know? After all, there's no difference between us and, say, any other entertainer, is there? We're still up there, performing as it were, with pressure to do well from the bosses, not only to entertain but also to get a damn good result as well for gawd's sake!

"So you tell me, what's the difference between us, say, and a top premiership football player, eh? And they're all on, like, fifty or one hundred grand a week and what do we get? A poxy two hundred and fifty quid and a load of abuse – know what I mean?" I nearly spat in disgust, but thought better of it and merely finished my drink and snatched Sincs' empty glass out of his hand.

When I came back with the fresh drinks and said again: "Know what I mean?" he went:

"Yeah, but you're forgetting one thing: when a premiership player belts one into the back of the net, that's due to his skill, not just down to luck. Cos at the end of the day, all we do is spin the ball, or pull cards out of a shoe; there's no real skill involved, is there?"

"Oh do me a favour!" I yelled; "You mean to tell me that you and I get roughly the same results as all the other mongers there? Gimme a break! We work at it, not like some of that lot, and what do we get in return? Sweet fuck all!"

"Yeah, but what can you do?" he asked, rhetorically.

"I dunno; what can you do?" I asked to myself. "Cheap, poxy rim-merchants, that's what they are; there's no justice!"

"So what're you going to do, then? Come abroad with me?" he inquired.

"Yeah, sure; I guess." I shrugged. "Give me a year or so to learn bj properly, and to perfect my roulette – cos I'm slowly getting there, I reckon – and yeah, I'm up for that. Jeez, there's no way I'll ever be able to get my own place – or a decent car – working for this lot!"

"You said it," he said.

"Yeah, I know I did," I said; "Just then!"

"So where shall we go? Abroad?"

"Oh, I dunno; why don't we give the agencies a call in six months and see what they've got?" I said.

"I fancy somewhere hot," Sincs told me. "Somewhere like the Bahamas or the cruise ships or Sun City."

"What about Oman? I've heard the money is phenomenal over there."

"Oman? Where the hell's that? Nah, let's go to the Caribbean! They sell rum over there!" he said enthusiastically. "You'll love it!"

"Yeah, whatever; but I'll tell you what."

"What?"

"Before I go, I wanna put down a deposit on a flat, and then rent it out. Like a nest-egg, know what I mean?"

"Oh blimey," he went, "you can't even pay off your car, let alone buy a decent one, and now you're talking about a deposit for a flat?! How long do you think that's gonna take you?"

"Well I don't know," I hollered, "but I wanna start as I mean to go on, don't I?"

"Nah, mate," Sincs said, "I ain't waiting round here for another five years till you've saved a couple of grand; I want to be out of here within the next six months."

Later on, when we were somewhat drunker, Sincs said:

"So, let's say we do go abroad, in six months, a year, whatever, and we get on really good money, and you get your ass in gear and start managing to save fifty grand a year..."

"Or a hundred," I interjected.

"Or a hundred, whatever, is that what you really want to do? Set up some stupid garage, selling stupid convertibles? Or buying and selling cheap, crappy flats? Bor-*ring*! Seriously, if you were fairly well off, what would you do with your money?" He stared at me, drunk.

"Casinos," I told him.

"Casinos?" he repeated. "What the hell are you talking about?"

"I just told you: casinos."

"But you're already in the casino business, you bell-end! I was talking about after you leave the business! Don't tell me you still want to be an inspector in fifty years time!"

"No, mate," I went, slowly, "I wanna see if I can beat

the casino, as a *player*."

"What are you on about?" he went. "They'll never let you in!"

"Nah, not our place, mate; other casinos, around the country, or around the world. I'd love it, punting carefully and stopping as soon as I'd made five hundred quid, or whatever, and then moving on to the next one; it can't be all that difficult, the odds being what they are, and now that I know what to watch out for I would move on as soon as I spotted that they were changing the dealer on me."

"I always thought it'd be a laugh to own a casino, and it would," he went, ignoring what I'd said. "But what's was our place up for, nine or ten million, ain't it? And that wasn't the bond or the premises, that was just for the licence!"

"Ah, but you're talking about legal clubs, ain't ya? Well, that's not the way I'd do it."

"Eh?"

"No mate; how about setting up an illegal place somewhere, like in an old mansion out in the country, or an underground club in Chinatown; I've heard that the Chinese have their own private casinos there anyway."

"What?" he went, the knob-end.

"Listen," I explained, "this is how I picture it. We save up...."

"Nah, it'd never work," he said, stopping me in my tracks. "I've already thought about it; as soon as you got set up, you'd have the Old Bill and Gaming Board come down on you like a ton of bricks and you'd end up losing everything, cos as soon as word got out all the legal casinos would grass you up to the Old Bill to get rid of the competition, and the Inland Revenue would want to shut us down cos we wouldn't be paying any taxes! And as soon as a player lost a load of cash, he could threaten to dob us in to the authorities if we didn't give him his money back."

"Oh, shit, I hadn't thought of that," I said. "I thought we could rent some dilapidated old mansion out in the country, set right back off the road up its own long drive; it shouldn't cost too much seeing as no-one wants to live in those draughty old places anyway, and then we do it up – just a bit of paint and nice curtains – and maybe even make our own gaming tables...."

"A great idea," he said, "but completely open to blackmail and all sorts. Just forget about it mate."

"Oh, man," I said, thinking about it briefly and then admitting to myself that Sincs was right. "But what about my idea of playing professionally? I mean, there are plenty of professional gamblers out there, so they must be ways of beating the house, long-term. Do you think we could do it? We probably know as much already as any so-called professional gambler, and the knowledge hasn't cost us years of time and tens of thousands of pounds to obtain."

"Well, we could probably do it, but you couldn't hammer the same place too often or they would bar you, so you'd end up spending a fortune on travel and hotels, so much so that it would probably eat up all your profits," he said, fairly intelligently and coherently.

I took a long pull at my drink, whilst Sinclair sat there looking at me, but I didn't know if he was just wasted or, in actual fact, seriously considering whether my plan to play and win in other casinos was workable. I thought it was achievable, I just didn't know if it could be realistically achieved someone like by me.

Eventually, he lifted his glass and took another swig, and then looked back at me.

"So – what; you think the idea sucks, then?"

"What, playing in other casinos?" I nodded. "Well, I'm not saying that," he said. "But you just learn blackjack next week, and then I might have a better idea for you."

"What, like go abroad and rake it in, in tax-free money and tips?" I said.

"Just you wait and see," he said, cryptically. "Come on, let's get bladdered."

Because I already knew how to handle the chips properly, it was just the correct payouts and the professional handling of the cards that I was taught on the blackjack training school, and after a couple of days – when I was allowed to deal bj on a 'live' game – I very quickly mastered the cards and immediately found it to be very boring; the problem with bj for me, as the dealer, was that it was the *player* who controlled the pace of the game, rather than the dealer: you always had to wait for him to make a decision about his hand; in roulette, it was the *dealer* who was the one who dictated how fast (or slow) the game went, and indeed how it was dealt.

Right from the word go I knew that blackjack was not going to be a game to interest me as the *dealer,* but from the *player's* point of view, this was definitely the best game to play. For a start, it was the only gambling game that I knew of where the percentages actually favoured the player (incredible, but true), so if one wanted to 'gamble sensibly' (if one could say such a thing) it was surely blackjack where one would begin – and why not wait until the odds swung in your favour before placing a bet?

Of course, I looked at everything from the dealer's perspective, and tried to do everything I could to beat the player (unless a manager had upset me, which was common enough), but I could also approach things from the player's side. So, it was the player that made the decision – that was the first good thing for the player. The player didn't have to draw a card if he didn't want to, although the dealer did: the dealer dealt to a very strict framework of rules, and the individual dealer made no independent decision. This made the game extremely attractive for the player, who could adapt his play to suit the odds at the time.

This came as a complete revelation to me, and when I asked Carl what the true odds were for blackjack, for once he couldn't actually give me a definitive answer.

"Well, Mr Shilling," he said, "that's hard to say, exactly, because they fluctuate with each individual shoe and it slightly depends on how the players play."

"Really," I went, a bit nonplussed. "How is that possible?"

"Well – and most people don't know this – the casino makes a lot of its money without even working for it," he told us.

"How's that then?" I asked, thinking that I'd learn this fucking game and then go and batter another casino, even if I had to go abroad to do it.

"Right then, let's pretend we've got a full table, that means seven boxes are being played, usually by five or more players, because a player can play as many boxes as he likes, and other players can play behind them, as well; we can have twenty-one individual players on any one table, in theory, up to the table maximums, of course."

And then he got us to place training chips on all seven of the boxes, and indeed, some of the boxes had up to three separate bets. Carl then proceeded to shuffle the four decks, cut them and place them in the dealing box (or 'shoe').

"Right then, I'll be the dealer and you be the players, and remember the perceived wisdom, you play your hand according to the dealer's up-card, all right? And remember, this isn't the parlour game 'pontoon', this is blackjack, and if the dealer gets the same as the player, it's a stand-off, or 'push', in other words, nothing happens, the player doesn't win or lose, all right?"

And so Carl proceeded to deal, myself and the other trainees played and I noticed something that Carl had been talking about, at least that was what I hoped, before I opened my trap and made a fool of myself.

What I noticed was that if Carl had a high card, like a nine or ten (and all 'court' cards counted as ten), we players would tend to draw extra cards to make our hands stronger, to try and get as close to 20 or 21 as possible – but if we went over 21, we were lost, 'bust'. And that seemed to happen quite a lot, before Carl had even drawn a card, so when Carl asked, half way through the shoe, if we had spotted how the casino makes a lot of money without even working for it, I took a chance.

"Is it when the player goes bust before you take a card?" I said.

"Well done, Mr Shilling, that is exactly correct. The perceived wisdom is that the player should play his hand depending upon whatever card the dealer has, so if I have a strong card, like a ten, most people will keep drawing cards until they get a good hand, eighteen or more, say; but, in the process, most people will get anything from a twelve to a sixteen, and then keep drawing, trying to improve their hand, but in doing so they will go bust."

"So they lose before you've even taken a second card!" I said. "And we've won without having to do anything! Talk about a licence to print money!" Carl laughed.

"Well, like I said, it's the player's own decision whether to draw or stand, but if it were me, even if I had a twelve or thirteen against an ace or ten, I would still stand; I always say: let the dealer earn his money, but it is amazing how many players will draw and go bust, only for the dealer with a ten or another high card to then pull a four or five or six, followed by another high card and go bust anyway. One sees that happening hundreds if not thousands of times every night."

"Have you ever played yourself, in a foreign casino?" I asked, and there was a long silence as he looked at us and smiled. "And if you did, was it blackjack you played?" Another pause, another smile. "And did you win?" Another broad smile. "Aw, come on, Carl , tell us," I begged.

"Well, due to the way the odds fluctuate on blackjack, and it is said that they sometimes favour the player, well, when that happens is the best, and indeed only, sensible time to play. Of course, nothing can one hundred per cent guarantee a win, but if you were to play that way, carefully, for around a week, you will definitely win overall. Which is why we in the casino watch our blackjack players very carefully. We have to."

"So have you ever played abroad," I asked again.

"Well, I'd be lying if I said 'no'," he said, "and occasionally the missus will book us a foreign holiday and there might happen to be a casino nearby; you will usually find a casino or two in every major town or tourist area, and usually if you're playing you get free food and drink, so it can work out a really cheap night out, especially if you know what you are doing on the tables, which most people don't!

"For example, in Las Vegas, you can get free drinks for as long as you are playing, and of course once you're drunk you'll make stupid decisions and the casinos fleece the punters something terrible, it's not even sporting," he said. "Many years ago, the Gaming Board of Great Britain made it illegal to serve alcohol at the gaming tables, and that was the right call, if only to save people from themselves."

"So how much did you win?" I asked. Another broad grin.

"Well, that would be telling – but let's just say that I've never lost," he said.

"Seriously? That's amazing," I said.

"Well, not really," Carl said. "I've played about sixteen times in ten years, in other words, we've been on around sixteen foreign holidays where there has been a casino or two, and I have played in lots of casinos on lots of nights, and yes, I've had a losing session, but never a losing night; I only usually play blackjack, and I only play when the odds are favouring the players, and never draw a card if I can go bust.

"Following these simple rules, I have managed to pay for most of the costs of our holidays, but I have another rule, and this is probably the most important rule: as soon as I have won the equivalent of a weeks' wages, I walk out. Even if I've only been in there half an hour, I walk out. Oh, sure, I can go back the following night, but the rules are the rules. Remember, chaps, I've been in this business for over ten years."

"You don't look old enough!" I interjected, and Carl smiled and I got called a 'wanker' and a 'creep' by the others, but what did I care? I just wanted to keep him talking; a person could make a lot of money from this information.

"Thank you, Mr Shilling, you're not the first woman to have told me that today," Carl said, and everyone laughed.

"But no, I have been in the industry over ten years, and you wouldn't believe some of the things I've seen; people wandering in here with fifty quid and turning it into five, ten, fifteen grand — and then walking out with nothing — *nothing!* It's insane, absolutely insane, some of the things one sees. Well, you've all been here long enough to have seen some things yourselves, I imagine," and I thought immediately about that young-looking, fresh-faced kid who had won over one hundred and sixty grand, lost it back and then lost another half a mil — and then stopped coming in; I'd always suspected he killed himself. And for what, some money? I'd never understand it, and I *loved* having plenty of money.

"No," Carl continued, "all we can do is make sure the games are run correctly and the gambling is controlled, because if people want to gamble, and they do, it is surely more preferable to licence, regulate and police it, than let it be run by crooks."

"So would you say that the hardest part is walking away when you are winning?" I asked, because I remembered the pit boss, Percy Collins, had said something along those lines to me, about the psychology of it.

"Yes, definitely," Carl said. "The most important thing is to set a maximum amount of time you are going to play, and a maximum amount of money you want to win, and as soon as you hit that limit, you walk out. Also important is not to take too much with you; I've always thought that your gambling 'pot' should be a maximum of about half a week's wages, so even if you do everything properly and still lose, you don't get too badly hurt.

"The reason I'm telling you this is that you've probably been here long enough to know whether you like the job enough to stay, and long enough for us to see that you are capable enough to do the job.

"But now we're talking about blackjack, and yes, you'll all get a pay rise, but with this game comes more responsibility, and you have to be more alert to the players around you. The last thing we need is hundreds of players waiting till the odds are in their favour and then jumping in and giving us a hammering," Carl told us.

"But I've been reading that not many people have the ability to count cards," I said. "That's what you are talking about isn't it? Card counting?"

"Well, essentially, yes, that and all the other rules for playing well that I've been talking about," Carl said.

"I've been reading about card counting," I said, "and I think I could do it; that would save us from a counter, wouldn't it? If I could count, and then saw a punter raising his stakes when the deck was in his favour?" Carl looked at me oddly.

"You've been practising how to count card?" he asked, and I smiled and nodded. "Well, how is that going to help us? Do you think we ought to have people positioned round the casino counting all the decks, and when one becomes favourable to the player, what are we going to do? Suddenly announce that we are not going to deal it? No, no, no, that's never going to work, and you are never going to be able to count the cards whilst dealing the game without making lots of mistakes. No, no, no," he went.

"Er, I was just trying to protect us," I muttered.

"Well, it was a good thought, but no. Does anyone else know anything about card counting?" There was a deafening silence from around the table. "Does anyone know how to spot a counter?" I thought I knew the answer to that one.

"Is it when someone plays the table minimum until the odds favour the player and then he increases his bets," I offered.

"Yes, correct, that is essentially it, and because all of our players are members, and most of them have been coming here for many years, we know everything there

208

is to know about them, particularly how they play.

"With most punters, I know how and what they are going to play the moment they walk in. Most people in our club play roulette, it's around a seventy-thirty split between roulette and blackjack, and less than ten per cent of players play both games. Which is sort of funny, because when I'm abroad I usually play blackjack to start with, get ahead by a couple of hundred quid, and then play some long shots on roulette; it's good fun, and if you're lucky you can walk out with anything from five hundred quid to a grand. But no-one seems to do that in Britain.

"But what I'm saying is, it is at this point in your careers that you should start remembering and mentally tracking the players. If you see someone approaching your table, you should be able to remember what he plays, where he plays, how he plays: everything! And you should know this instantly, before he even buys in, and you know what you are going to before you deal you first hand or spin or whatever; you should be prepared."

"Forewarned is forearmed," I intoned.

"Correct, Mr Shilling," Carl congratulated. "Forewarned is forearmed; so if you see someone coming in who you suspect is a counter, make sure you are cutting your shoes deep before he even gets to your table, and it never hurts to throw in a double shuffle at frequent intervals. Of course, you are all new to blackjack, and the inspectors will warn you if a suspected counter is about."

"If a card counter is really good, why do we even let them in?" I asked.

"Good question; can anyone answer it?" Carl enquired. Dead silence all round. "Well, if a counter is really good, we probably don't know for sure if he is actually counting, and they are the really dangerous ones; we would bar those in a heartbeat. But if we don't know they are counting, they are not giving themselves away by massively raising their stakes when the odds favour them, so even if they win, they are not hurting us too badly.

"Of course, we will bar anyone who wins too much in the long run whether or not they are counting, and as you know, we keep careful records of all the winners and losers, which are regularly checked for any odd results. If someone is winning too much, long term, they are either very lucky or possibly cheating, and as such, will be monitored extremely closely.

"And remember, we have all their personal details, so we can check with any other clubs that they are members of, to compare betting patterns, results or just about anything else."

"So how are we expected to remember everyone who comes in," one of the other trainees asked. "There must be thousands upon thousands of people coming in every week."

"And how can we remember all the Chinese, who all look the same anyway?" asked another.

"You aren't going to be expected to remember everyone," Carl said, "just the players who come in regularly and play a lot, and especially if you see them picking up."

"So just the winners, then," I said, and Carl agreed with that. "Because I've noticed that some players are just fools to themselves and no matter what they do they lose when they play on my table."

"Yes, some people are just born unlucky, and never seem to realise it," said Carl.

"But we've got our share of lucky players as well, haven't we," I said. "There are smart players, and lucky players, and a small number of smart, lucky players – and they are the hardest to beat," I said. "We should bar all the smart lucky ones."

"Well," Carl responded, "in the short term, anyone can get lucky, but we like to take the long term view, and if no-one ever won the casino would be empty. We need lots of players, and we need lots of winners, if we are going to be a place that people want to come to, because if they don't want to come we are finished, and so is every other casino.

"If ever I'm abroad, and I walk into a casino that is completely empty, I walk straight out. There is probably a good reason it is empty, and that reason is probably because it is not giving the players an honest game; 'honest' as compared to 'fair', if you see what I mean; never play in a quiet casino, and never be the only player at the table, or indeed the 'big' player at the table.

"And if you do find yourself in a holiday resort, such as Las Vegas, Monte Carlo or even the Canary Islands, bear in mind that the casinos there know that most players are only in town for two or three nights, or a week at most, so they will aim to take as much money from you as they can, as quickly as possible; here, it is different, and we rely on lots of regulars playing as frequently as possible, and for as long as possible.

"So, we are happy for people to win, and people are always going to win, but like we were saying earlier, overall, most of them are going to lose, but that's a fair trade-off for most of our wealthy players; most of them enjoy coming here, even if most of them lose most of the time, but they were all, almost all of them, up at one point!"

"And how about playing blackjack online? Is there any chance of counting cards and winning online?" I asked.

"No, there isn't," Carl told us. "Like I have told you many times before, there is no point in playing online because you are playing a computer that reads your bet and adapts its payout, so no-one can win long-term, and it's all 'off-shore' and unregulated in any case; yes, here in our casino the player has to place his bet before he sees his cards, but we are still using a shoe with four decks.

"When you play online – or if the casino is using an automatic shuffling machine, for that matter – the player is not getting a fair nor an honest game, because every hand is like it is the first hand of the shoe, and there is no way for a player to get a 'feeling' for the shoe, let alone a 'count'."

"What's a shuffling machine?" someone asked.

"A shuffling machine is exactly what it sounds like; it's a little black box that sits on the table, and after each hand the dealer pops the discards into the box, which continually re-shuffles the cards," Carl informed us.

"Casinos think they are being smart by using them, because the dealers don't have any 'down time' because they are not shuffling any more, but all it has done is swing the odds massively in favour of the house, so that most of the wised up blackjack players have simply stopped playing in clubs that use automatic shuffling machines.

"It's a really stupid, short-term answer to a minor problem; a good shuffle should only take a couple of minutes, and it all adds something to the game itself, players can take a break, order a coffee, chat to each-other, chat to the dealer even, and re-group and get ready for the next shoe, because remember that blackjack is a game of skill, and playing online or when a shuffling machine is being used nullifies any element of skill.

"So now, the casinos that are still insisting on using shuffling machines are getting a big percentage of very little – and anyone who keeps playing is a mug who deserves to lose when they are using a shuffling machine – yet clubs like ours are still taking a small but respectable percentage of a much greater volume."

"So what are the percentages, roughly?" I asked.

"Would anyone like to hazard a guess?" Carl asked us. "Come on, you've been here long enough now! Hands up who thinks the house edge is greater on blackjack than roulette?" A couple of people put their hands up. "Who thinks it is about the same as roulette?" A couple of people put their hands up. "And who thinks that it's less than roulette?" I put my hand up. "Hmm," Carl went, obviously not very impressed with us.

"All right, let me put it another way: out of every one hundred hands dealt, how many would the casino expect to win?" He grabbed a pen and piece of paper, and asked each one of us in turn; some said 70 out of 100, some said 60, one idiot said 80 and I, knowing what I did about card counting, guessed 55.

"Wrong!" he went. "The true percentage, if one can say that about a game where the percentages fluctuate after every hand, varies from around 0.8 to 1.5 percent in favour of the house; in other words, for every hundred hands dealt, the casino would expect to win around 52 and lose 48."

"But that's incredibly low," I said.

"Yes, it is," Carl agreed, "and if we were only dealing one hand per night, we couldn't afford to remain in business; but we are dealing hundreds if not thousands of hands per night, and that one-to-two percent is chipping away at every hand we deal, which is why we get an overall 'hold' of around sixteen percent from our blackjack action."

"And what would it be if we were using shuffling machines?" I asked.

"Well, estimates vary, but they seem to suggest that the casino's percentage goes up from roughly one percent to around four or five percent, and that is on every single hand, which is why most decent blackjack players have learned to give the casinos that use shuffling machines a very wide berth."

So there we left it for a while, taking a break from the psychology behind it, and going for tea and a sandwich, but I was making a list in my mind of Golden Rules on how to beat the casino, in the long term, and I had certainly added to that list this morning.

I very much liked Carl's philosophy about only taking half a week's wages with you when you played, and fixing both a time and money (win) limit, again of around a week's wages. If one could do that two or three times a week, playing little and often, only winning hundred of pounds rather than thousands, one could stay under the casinos' radar long-term.

Now I really was itching to go to another casino and try out some of my strategy, and I didn't think I could wait until I went on a foreign holiday. But would I lose my Gaming Licence if I got caught playing in another casino in Britain? I would have to carefully look into all this.

The blackjack training wasn't anything like as intense as the roulette training, and it was actually both interesting and instructive, and picking Carl's brain for little tricks was great fun; the only unfortunate thing about it was having to get up at eight in the morning to get to casino for a ten am. start, but at least we got a nine pm. finish, so I could go out for a drink with my mates David and Maurice (my other best friend from school, Andrew, was away at uni).

I soon managed to get the cards to come out of the shoe correctly and place the cards neatly next to each box, and the payouts were easy enough as everything was paid even-money, except on a 'blackjack', which was an ace and a ten, in which case the payout was 1½, i.e., the payout on £10 was £15.

Once I'd mastered the basic procedures, it was just a question of speed and neatness – maximum speed with maximum neatness – and, of course, no mistakes. The standard shuffle was more difficult to master, but shuffling four decks soon began to take less than three minutes, and by the end of the week, I could do it in almost two minutes flat.

They 'rewarded' us on the Friday with overtime, so we all worked from ten in the morning till four the following morning, and because we were so busy no-one ever got an early finish on a Friday night.

After I'd been dealing blackjack for a week, I really began to loathe dealing the damn game and dreaded being sent to deal it, so much so that within a couple of weeks I started to make deliberate mistakes: I'd fumble the cards, make a complete hash of the shuffle, deal far too slowly (from the casino's point of view) and would basically deal like a complete amateur; I'd even mishandle the chips, anything to look like the klutz of the blackjack pit!

I didn't say anything to anyone about preferring roulette (I knew better; a petty-minded pit-boss or floor manager could easily leave me on bj all night just to spite me), but I soon noticed that I was being sent to deal roulette far more than I was blackjack, where nothing had changed: I still angled for, and achieved, very good results (or, at worst, a stand-off). Looking at my weekly results in my little notebook, I saw that I was securing a 30% hold rather than a mediocre 20%.

And so my life jogged along for a couple more months as I tried (and failed) to save any money; Sincs talked less and less about swanning off abroad and I had no inkling whatsoever that anything was going to change this state of affairs, not even when Sincs summoned me for a 'private drink to talk about my future' on the coming Sunday evening; it sounded exciting, and I knew just the place to take him.

All summer long (weather permitting), I had been driving around the countryside in the MX5 to go fishing, and after spending a lazy afternoon down by the Grand Union Canal I'd often treat myself to a drink on the way home, and had been acquainting myself with a fair number a nice little country pubs around West Hertfordshire and South West Bedfordshire, usually within a few miles of the Grand Union, so I well knew which ones would be the quietest on an early Sunday evening.

As soon as I heard Sincs pulling up outside in his clapped-out silver Ford Escort, I was quickly down the stairs, getting the hood of the MX5 down and making ready to go; we jumped in and I motored out of Berko, carefully obeying the speed limits, and headed for a little village out towards Dunstable called Totternhoe.

"Hurry up, for God's sake," he yelled; "this is

important!"

Once in Totternhoe, we went into the back bar of The Old Farm public house (they called it 'the lounge bar'), and I was pleased that I had chosen well as there was no-one else in there. So we got the drinks in, took a couple of hasty gulps and then I followed Sincs to sit at a little table in the furthest corner from the bar.

"Cool," I grunted, sitting myself down and looking round the place.

"Good," said Sincs, looking around himself. "There's no-one else here."

"Well, you said you wanted to go for a quiet drink," I replied.

"Yeah, well that's cos I wanted to talk to you about something," he said.

"Yeah, well, what is it?" I asked.

But all he did was look at me, holding my gaze.

"What?" I said, but there was something in his steady, unblinking stare that filled me with vague dread, and I felt a curious sinking feeling in the bottom of my stomach. "What is it?" I whispered.

After what seemed like an age, he put down his drink, looked me in the eye again and said: "Right, I'm going to tell you something now, Chris, but you've got to promise me that you won't tell any one else, and I mean no one, not your mother, not your father, not your girlfriend, your dog: *no one*. All right?"

"Yeah, yeah, yeah, okay; no one," I agreed. "What the fuck?"

"No mate, cos this is serious; you promise?" Sincs was just about as serious as I've ever seen him.

"Okay, mate; I promise," I said, staring back at him, and then he stuck his right hand out, which I looked at for a few seconds and then shook. Holy shit!

"You promise?" he said again.

"Yes, I promise," I confirmed, getting a horrible tingling sensation spread over me; I felt sure he was about to tell me something that would change my life – and not necessarily for the better. "So what is this about?"

Sincs just sat there for a moment, looking at me, and then he nodded to himself, as if coming to a decision, and then he reached slowly into his tatty brown vinyl jacket and pulled out his old brown wallet – I'd seen it a million times – only this time, as he inclined it towards me, I'd never seen it so full and bulging.

He opened it up, I leaned forward and looked inside, shackles rising; it wasn't fear, exactly, but more like a sort-of superstitious premonition of the unknown: something highly unusual was about to occur, because

220

Sincs' wallet was full of what looked suspiciously like fifty pound notes – hundreds of 'em! And after riffling his thumb across the edges of the notes, like a magician he withdrew from the great wedge a crisp fifty and held it up.

"Do you know what this is, Chris?" he said… and that was all he had to say.

You know, it's funny how the mind works (and how quickly it can move), because before he'd even finished asking his question I'd realised what the score was and had already mentally pictured the entire scenario, because his wallet must have contained a minimum of ten thousand pounds – and I knew my money!

And I also knew that one doesn't obtain that sort of cash legally. Indeed, no; my good friend Sincs was definitely up to something, up to something at work, some big scam, and now he was about to ask me to come in on it with him. Hell, I even had a good idea of what was taking place and who else was involved! All these thoughts flashed through my mind in less than a split second.

"Course I do!" I replied in answer to his question, with a silly sort of laugh; my mind was racing, for I realised that even though we were sitting here in the most ordinary of settings – a quiet English country pub on a sunny Sunday evening – I was about to be thrown head-first into a really delicate situation which would forever change my life and status at work (in my own mind, at least).

However, I also knew, without any shadow of a doubt, that no matter *what* Sincs was involved in – and even though he was about to implicate me – there was simply no way that I would ever turn my back on him or grass him up to the management (as, I supposed, I was legally obliged to do). Whatever had caused him to approach me had obviously been tempered with the belief that I wouldn't turn him in and that I was a stand-up guy.

I have no idea how fast these thoughts flew through my mind, but it was no longer than a couple of seconds; I found myself unable to meet his eyes and realised that I was sweating all over, and took a big swig from my drink; but then I realised I had to say something to reassure my friend, so slammed my glass back down and met his gaze head-on.

"So what's this all about, then?" I asked, giving him a broad grin. "It's some sort of scam at work, isn't it?"

"Could be," he nodded, grinning back.

"Well tell me all about it then, you bell-end!" I hissed.

"Oh, I'll tell you all right," he said. "But you've got use your brain on this one, mate. Cos if you're careful, and keep your trap shut, I might just let you in on it... if you're interested."

"Oh I'm interested," I lied, "depending on the risks involved." And the money, of course.

"The risks; well that's the beauty of it mate; there aren't any risks! If ever there was a fool-proof scam, then this is it!"

"How do you know that?" I quizzed.

"Ha!" he laughed. "Cos we've been doing it for nearly three months and they haven't spotted a damn thing!"

"You're joking!" I said.

He laughed again. "Nah," he continued, "it's so simple even a bell-end like you should be able to handle it!"

"You're the bell-end!" I hissed; "Oh, all right then; get the drinks in and tell me all about it!"

And so he did just that.

The story went that some months previously a player had started coming in our casino and he was playing big money: anything up to £500 a hand on the blackjack tables, and up to seven boxes in one go. which was pretty big money for our casino (when Sincs described him I knew immediately who he was, even though I'd never dealt to him).

After a while, this punter had approached one of the female inspectors, Wendy Wilson, and asked her out for a coffee; she'd refused, as it was absolutely forbidden for gaming staff to associate with a punter outside of work.

(We'd been instructed on the training school that even if you bumped into a member of the casino in the street or in a bar you were supposed to ignore them and walk away, and if they tried to approach you, you were expected to report it to the management.)

Anyway, this player asked her out a couple more times; she was not particularly attractive (and unhappily single); the sort of tall, slim, dark-haired girl who looked fairly good when expensively dressed and done up to the nines but not when otherwise; you know the sort. She was flattered by this guy's advances, and finally agreed to meet up one morning for a coffee, at a time and place where she could be reasonably sure no-one from work would be (and thus spot them together).

Well one thing led to another and eventually Wendy became romantically involved with this player (whose name Sincs told me was 'Albert;); Wendy had insisted on total secrecy, which basically meant only getting together at her place when she wanted a jump, but soon enough they were meeting more often, and slowly she got to like him.

After a while, Albert had mentioned that he was a great card-counter, and that he had made a lot of money from casinos over the years. And some time after that, he asked her whether she would be willing to let him show her a really great blackjack scam that he claimed to have invented. (She was.) After listening to three months of Wendy bitching and moaning about how poorly the casino treated her, Albert felt he was on fairly steady ground when he broached the tricky subject of, maybe, and only if she was 100% happy with everything, ripping off the casino for a couple of hundred grand in the space of a month or two. By this time she had become completely besotted with him (so Sincs said), and they had spent a few romantic trips, down in London and out in the country, and by this stage she would probably have done anything he asked her to do - although £100k for a couple of months work was also acceptable enough.

And so Albert showed her what to do (it involved a simple crooked shuffle whereby a batch of cards were left un-shuffled), and in between their bouts of torrid lovemaking (as Sincs put it) they practised with the cards until one day, on an afternoon shift – when the casino was always run with a skeleton crew and most of the inspectors took turns dealing – Wendy dealt to Albert, and they put their scheme into practice, and they cleaned up big-style, especially considering that in the afternoons Albert could only play £200 maximum per box, only got to play one or two boxes and Wendy only got to deal to him for about three, forty-minute stints per seven-hour shift. But he was a good player anyway, so could hold his own till she came back on, and when she did, they would usually make £2-3k per stint, so it wasn't too bad but Albert often had to wait around for many hours before he'd get another go with Wendy as the dealer.

So then Albert had asked Wendy whether she knew of any other dealers that might be interested in making an extra ten grand a month. Now, Wendy wasn't particularly friendly with any of the other gaming staff (they never invited her along for a night out), but she knew Sinclair well enough; indeed, she'd come up the road from The Palace Casino at about the same time as Sincs.

So she'd invited him round for some drinks after work, got him half-drunk, asked what he thought of the casino, the wages and the managers, and then plucked up the courage to ask whether he thought it was morally wrong to scam an employer who enjoyed taking the total mickey out of you. Sincs had just laughed, and told her he'd be happy to shaft them at every chance he got. And so Wendy had shown him the crooked shuffle, and Sincs had taken to it like a duck to water, needing hardly any 'training' whatsoever. Everything was just so easy, so simple... and just about foolproof. So when Wendy told Sincs that she had someone in mind to act as the punter he was all for it, and it was no more than a couple of days before Sincs was making more money across the tables with Albert than Wendy ever had. But now Albert needed more dealers.

So after racking his brains for a while, Sincs told me

that he would now do me the honour (his words) of inviting me to come in on the scam since I was the only other decent bloke in the entire place.

I was listening with half my brain, and letting the other half race at a hundred miles per hour trying to assess the risks involved in getting mixed-up with such a venture.

Well, I don't know about Wendy being flattered by Albert's interest (it seemed to me he was just using her as a means to an end), but I'll tell you what: I felt genuinely flattered by Sincs' considering me, because for the life of me I couldn't recall anyone ever really trusting me with anything like this before. After all, he knew I didn't have a criminal record or come from a criminally-inclined background (as none of us at the casino did); then again, from talking to me on our nights out he must have realised I wasn't with what I was doing and wanted a lot more out of life than to merely be a lowly-paid worker-ant.

And he must have carefully weighed the chances of me going all funny on him and grassing him (and Wendy and Albert) up to the management, but that wasn't going to happen; he knew that I thoroughly despised the casino management, and he must also have concluded that I'd never spill the beans on a friend, and in this he was absolutely right, no matter what sort of 'crime' was involved; he had judged me well. But then he'd had to, considering how much there was at stake; I wondered how long he'd mulled it over before deciding to let me in on it.

All of these things I thought as Sincs jabbered on, telling me how easy it was, how foolproof and what a bunch of cretins (and horrible pieces of work) the casino managers were; however, I knew another thing: even though Sincs had flashed a wallet with a *minimum* of ten grand in it at me, and mentioned a figure of a hundred grand for two months' scamming (which was, of course, extremely tempting, especially as I was always skint), I honestly did *not* want to get involved (even though now I already was!).

I genuinely felt, from the bottom of my heart, that no matter how 'foolproof' Sincs said the scam was, there was just no way that anyone could get away with it over a period of more than a couple of months or so, and that the longer it went on (and the more money it involved) then the greater casino 'heat' the crooks would attract, until, eventually, even the fools who ran our casino would finally latch on that something was amiss, and what good was £100k if you lost your gaming licence (and casino career) and were banged up for five years?

God damn it, I was happy with my casino job! It was just unusual enough to maintain my interest (and make me feel somewhat special and different); I really enjoyed the basics of dealing roulette, and relished the aspect of angling for a decent result and beating the mug punters!

Fair enough, I hated most of the casino managers and most of the more experienced staff, and didn't agree with the low pay (now that I had seen what the work entailed I thought it was an massive insult), I didn't have any friends there (apart from Sincs) and I despised all the creeping and back-stabbing that went on; but I just kept myself to myself, got the dealing done and was even beginning to earn a begrudging respect from the older hands.

I was slowly managing to pay off the loan on the MX5, at some distant point (after various promotions and pay rises) I might even be able to save enough for a deposit for a mortgage on a flat, and I was even starting to get on with my parents for once (possibly because I so rarely saw them); certainly, the dealing, cut-and-thrust of the 'action' and even the hours really seemed to suit me – what more could I ask for in a job? And so I really did not want to get involved! So the immediate question was: what the hell was I going to do now?

Well, I knew that whatever happened I was never going to grass up my friend, so I was already 'implicated' – so it made no difference now if Sincs told me how the scam went down.

I tuned in again to what Sincs was saying and once I begun to comprehend how the scam actually worked I slowly started to understand that Sincs was right: it *did* seem foolproof.

"So why do you need me to come in on it?" I interrupted.

"Cos like I was saying, if you'd listen, *twat*, Albert says he needs as many dealers in on it as possible, so as not to draw too much attention down on just a couple of people. Though, frankly, you were the only person who I could think of asking."

"But why me?" I persisted.

"Look – it don't matter *who* it is as long as they can do the shuffle properly, not give the game away and keep their gob shut! But if Albert's always winning with just two people the whole time, eventually it'll be too obvious!"

"Oh, so you just want me to draw the heat off you! Thanks a lot!" I cried.

"Oh, shut your noise, for God's sake! No, course not." Then he shrugged. "Well, OK, yeah, I guess you could say that. But like I've been telling ya, it's foolproof." I gave him a look of obvious disbelief, so he went on: "Look, listen; the dozy managers have been watching me and Wendy deal to him for the last couple of months and we've given away an absolute fortune, and we've been doing the special shuffle right under their noses, and no-one's spotted a thing! Hell, I had Mary, Jacob and Grenville all watching me shuffle and deal for a whole hour the other night as I paid Albert out on every hand and they never spotted a thing!"

"How much did you pay him?" I blurted.

"Oh I dunno; 'bout five grand," he replied.

"Yeah;" I couldn't help but ask; "And how much do you get?" Because the money, should I eventually decide to get in on the scam, *hypothetically*, would be purely incidental.

"Er, 'bout half," he said.

"What, really; he always gives you half what he makes?"

Sincs nodded, proud.

"Well, I think it's ludicrous," I told him.

"Oh, what, so you're not interested then?" Sincs bridled. "You're not interested in making yourself five grand a week, tax free?" he went, touching on a subject he knew was close to my heart.

"Oh, sure, I'm interested in that," I said to him. "I just think you're bound to get caught eventually – and I'm not interested in any of *that.*"

"Oh, blimey," he shouted, rolling his eyes in exasperation. "Look," he went on, lowering his voice conspiratorially, "I'll tell you what; come round to the house and we'll show you what to do. And if you can get your head around it, everything will be fine; you'll see for yourself how simple and undetectable the shuffle is. And if you're not happy, we'll all club together and give you something to keep your mouth shut and you can forget all about it, OK? Now I can't say any fairer than that, can I?"

"Well," I laughed, "I can hardly just 'forget all about it,' can I?" I laughed again, and sipped my drink. "So what do we do now? Are you gonna let me have some time to think about it or do you want a snap decision right now?"

"You wanna think about it; okay, what do you want to think about, you spastic?!"

"Look, I wanna think it over," I repeated.

"I wanna think it over," he mimicked, scathingly.

"Yeah!" I went; "Cheats always get caught eventually, and the more money we take, the more likely it is that we'll get caught; the more money we pinch, the more money we will want to pinch, and then we'll get too greedy – and it's always the greed that gets you in the end; come on, Sincs, you know the score, we've seen it a million times!"

"I knew you'd say this," he said with a knowing grin; "I told Wendy you wouldn't want to do it, no matter how much money was involved."

"Well, how long have you known me?" I said.

"Yeah, but I've been listening you bitch and moan about the casino six months now; all you do is whine about how much you make for the casino and how little they pay you!" he said.

"Yeah, I can't deny that," I agreed.

"And you really don't want to earn five grand a week for two or three months?" he asked.

"Oh no, I do; I just think it's too likely that we'll be caught," I replied. "It's just a question of whether or not we can get away with it, and I don't think we can."

"Even though Wendy and I have been doing it for over two months and no-one's spotted a thing."

"Even so," I said.

"Okay, I can appreciate that; no, honestly I can. You don't want to do it for the money, fair enough. But there's something else you ought to consider: you're one of the best dealers in club, but they pay you peanuts and treat you like shit; you've said this to me a million times, so I know it's true. So forget about the money and think about it this way: what a lovely way to shaft the managers out of their monthly and yearly bonuses, and make those wankers at head office start giving some grief to our managers, the pieces of shit!"

"Nah, mate, I know where you are coming from but if

the shit starts flowing down from head office, ultimately it'll be us, the dealers, who get most of the shit! Yeah, I'd like to scam Mary and the other managers out of their bonuses, it's a great idea, but it's just not worth it, especially if we could get busted and lose our licences; it just ain't worth it."

"But how long would it take you to save fifty grand? Seriously?"

"At this rate? I never will!" I admitted.

"And so you'll never have enough to get a place of your own – or a Lotus!" he said.

"No, you're probably right," I said.

"How long would it take you to save even ten grand; for a car, or a deposit on a flat, like?"

"At this rate? Never!" I told him.

"So why not try it just for a month? Make yourself ten or fifteen grand, and then, if you're not happy, knock it on the head; why not do that?" Sincs suggested.

"No, no, you are right; everything you are saying is right, it's just that I know the greed will get to us, it always does, and then we'll all get pinched! Honestly, Sincs, thanks mate, but no thanks; if you want to do it, fine – I hate blackjack anyway – but I'm not getting involved," I told him with finality. He just sat there looking at me, and then said:

"You know what?" he went; "You're the only twat I know who would say 'no', even though you know full well that you make the casino a fortune while they pay you squat; you know the managers are wankers who take the piss out of you and treat you like shit, even though you're one of their best dealers; you know you'll never have a realistic chance of getting your own place, and here I am giving you a golden opportunity to get your own place, and still you say 'no'. But that's okay; I get it. You're a funny bastard, I know that. But if you won't do it for any of those reasons, I can think of the one real reason that you should do it; not for the money, or for yourself, or to screw the managers or the casino; no, I can think of a much better reason to do it."

"Oh, yeah? What's that then?" I asked.

"Annie."

"Say what?" I said in a whisper.

"Do it for Annie," he said – and I knew he'd got me.

Annie Olney had been one of the casino's longest members, and my most favourite customer by far. She was a tiny little sparrow of a lady, under five feet tall and 84lbs soaking wet, at least 84 years old and one of our oldest regulars: she had been coming in the casino almost every night for over fifty years.

I'd only really got to know her over the last few months because she would come in the casino just after seven pm and leave just before nine, and since it was only after being taught blackjack that the casino had started giving me double shifts with any great frequency, I hadn't really got the chance to see much of her before that.

She would come in the door and make her way to AR5, the roulette table nearest the door.

"Hello, everybody!" she would say, and buy in for twenty pounds, for a stack of £1 chips, and then proceed to play one or two chips each spin on the six-lines or corners, where one chip would cover six or four numbers.

She would have a cup of tea, ask the dealers about their social life and she knew everyone by name, even the Chinese regulars. Everyone loved Annie, and I remember the first time she saw me getting ready to take off the out-going dealer, she was asking me my name and how long I had been with the club almost before I'd tapped the other dealer on the shoulder.

The casino indulged her; she was absolutely adorable, she was no threat, she was a typical example of a 'bread and butter' punter and everybody loved her. She was just about the only player than the managers allowed us to talk to socially at the table (to everyone else, we were supposed to deal like a robot, and not engage in small talk: 'procedures'); of course, Sincs and I had long worked out that as long as we were raking in the cash, we could say and do just about anything we wanted.

One evening, I think it was a Wednesday, I turned up for work at 8.30pm as usual and was mildly surprised to find the staff-room completely devoid of troops. I checked the clock above the door, but it read 8.31pm. That's funny, I thought; did I go home, have two hours' sleep, wake up and then come in to work again? I looked at the TV and it was definitely showing evening television.

As I stood there frowning, the internal phone on the wall buzzed; being by far the youngest and most 'inexperienced' trainee, I never answered the phone; I'd quickly worked out that I'd either get a mouthful from a more experienced twat, or it would be a pit boss needing a dealer to open up another table (or take off a dealer who had started doling the money out), so there was simply no mileage in my picking up the phone.

It kept on buzzing, so I wandered over, signed in, put my bow tie on and then finally picked up the receiver.

"Staff room," I said.

"*Who's that?*" yelled a voice.

"It's Christopher Shilling," I said, calmly. There was a brief pause, then:

"Get out here, *now!*" *Click.*

"Dear oh dear," I muttered, "what has happened? A

robbery? A fire? A fight? Or have the toilets backed up?" but then I hustled out of the staff-room and onto the casino's gaming floor and thereby into the pit, but as I looked around me, I could hardly see any one at all. Somewhat nonplussed, I walked over to the bureau, where four of five managers were clustered, and then a roar went up from the vicinity of AR5, which was being screened from my line of sight by the bodies round the bureau, and as I looked over I saw that all the punters in the building were clapping and cheering, all of them crowded around AR5, so now I knew: someone was on a roll (and good for them!).

I looked around the casino and saw lots of dealers stood at lots of empty tables, but all the players in the entire building were clustered around just one table, AR5. As I approached the bureau, one of the managers glanced up and snarled, "What do you want?"

"Er, nothing in particular, I was just told to come out here," I replied coolly.

"Shills, get on AR5 and see what you can do," said Percy Collins, the pit boss.

"Yes, sir," I said walking over to the cluster of staff around AR5, during which another cheer went up, with lots of clapping and hooting, causing the managers and senior staff to mutter curses. "Excuse me, please," I said politely to a manager who was stood by the float of AR5 and impeding my progress, and he grabbed me by the arm.

"Where the fuck do you think you're going?" he spat.

"Er, I've been told by Mr Collins to deal on here, sir," I replied. He stared at me for a moment, let go of my arm and snarled, "Well, what're you waiting for?" And so I stood behind the dealer, a useless female named Tracy Houghton, and tapped her on the right shoulder, as per procedures, seeing as I was being watched by about seventy people, including inspectors, pit bosses, managers and even the casino's general manager, along with around fifty-to-sixty punters, and it was at this point that I noticed that my favourite player, Annie Olney, had about twenty five thousand pounds in chips in front of her! It was as much as I could do not to punch the air in celebration! Twenty-five grand, holy sheet! But I kept a straight face as Tracy called 'new dealer after this payout, no more bets', and everyone watched as the ball dribbled away from the edge of the wheel's inner rim, bounced a couple of times and came to rest in number 20, upon which Annie just happened to have a £25 chip.

Again, I had to keep a poker face as another huge shout went up, with everyone clapping and cheering, well, everyone except the casino managers, that is. Tracy paid Annie thirty-five £25 chips (for a £875 payout) and showed clean hands upwards.

"Thank-you, you have a new dealer now," she

239

announced to the table, and all the punters started clamouring for Annie to have one more spin from Tracy, who had obviously done her brains; Annie wasn't asking, but all the other punters kicked up such a racket that Tracy looked at the inspector, and the inspector looked at the manager, and he nodded, and muttered, "Yes, one more spin," so Tracy said to Annie, "Place your bets, please," and since no-one else seemed to be betting, Annie placed a handful of £25 chips on the layout, on the straight-up numbers, and Tracy spun the ball and wheel, a nice long spin and a nice fast wheel, announced – as per procedure – 'finish betting' and 'no more bets' and the ball trickled away from the rim, bounced a couple of times and fell right back in to number 20, a 'repeat', and another deafening roar went up.

I had to turn my head away from the managers and stifle a smile: another £875 going out! Oh, Annie, well done girl!

But now Tracy showed her clean palms again and stepped off to her right and I stepped in from the left.

"Good evening, Annie," I whispered, "Place your bets please!"

"Spin!" one of the managers spat at me, so I said to Annie, "Annie, place your bets, I'm spinning now!" and I reached into the wheel.

"Oh, no, don't worry about that, Chris," she said to me,

"I'm late as it is, I've got to be going," and no sooner had she got the words out before Carl Hunter had materialised by her side, sat down next to her, put his arm through hers and said:

"Now then, Annie, you don't want to be doing anything silly like that, do you? NO, no, no; tonight's your lucky night, Annie! You should never leave the table when you're on a roll, never!"

"Oh, no, Carl, I really must be going, I'm late enough as it is," and before Carl could reply, quite a few a the customers, who were all still clustered around the table, chimed in.

"If she wants to go, you let her go!" etc., etc., and they called for some chip trays, which were eventually brought from the cash-desk 'cage', and a lot of the regular punters formed a sort-of protective cordon around little old Annie, helped stack all her stacks into the chip trays, helped her over to the far side of the casino – the 'cage' was just about as far from the exit as possible – and then, after she'd been given her cheque (it was for just over twenty-five grand), they escorted her over towards reception. Carl was stood, with his arms folded, in front of the doors, and as she came towards him, backed up by a group of about thirty regular punters, Carl said:

"Annie, I've known you for over ten years, and when did you ever have such a lucky night? So if you leave

241

now, it'll be the craziest thing you've ever done; no-one walks away from a lucky table, and if you ride your luck you could win fifty or even one hundred thousand pounds tonight!"

Which was a fair point, I could hear and see everything from my vantage point on AR5 (just near the doors), but still, if a winning player wanted to go, no-one should try to stop them. There were some mutterings of the crowd around her along these lines, but it appeared Annie didn't need anyone's help, and in a clear voice said:

"I quite understand all that, Carl, I really do, and if I could stay, I would... but I'm late for bingo as it is, and I don't want my friends to become worried about me, and the last thing I need is for someone to telephone my husband, because I've been coming here for over forty years and he has absolutely no idea – and I don't know how I'm going to explain this cheque to him!" Well, everyone was in hysterics, and I wanted to be but decided to celebrate later, on my own, and I was delighted that the casino were in a twenty-five grand hole before the night's gaming had begun.

So off Annie toddled, and my fervent wish was that she didn't come in the following day and do it all back. And I was actually on a double-shift the following day, and my heart sank when Annie tottered in at seven o'clock, but nearly jumped for joy when she said, "Good evening, Chris; how are you," and bought in for £20, and after that went, and she'd had her tea, and a sandwich, and she bought in for another £20, and when that was gone – so was she! Up the road for two hours' bingo, as usual. Hallelujah!

The looks on the managers' faces were like thunder, so I kept my head well down and focused on dealing a very tight game all night.

And when I rocked up for work the following Monday night, Sincs was stood in the corridor waiting for me.

"Heard the news?" he went.

"Nah, what?" I went.

"About Annie," he said.

"About Annie? Oh no, what; has she had another big win?" I asked, getting all excited.

"Nah; they've barred her, mate," he told me.

"They've *WHAT?!*" I hollered.

"Shhh, for fucks sake!" he whispered. "Yeah, mate, they fucking barred her, as of today."

"But why? What the fuck happened?" I whispered.

"Well, apparently she came in yesterday and got chatting to one of the valets, and she said that she'd given five grand apiece to each of her five grand-kids, and this valet went and told one of the managers, who's probably fucking her anyway, and they've then had a management meeting, and now they've just had another one, and apparently it's because (a) she wasn't doing any of the money back, and (b) now they've heard she's given it all away, so she can't do it back, and (c) someone said that if she has another big win, even if she doesn't give it away, due to her age we'll never get it back anyway. So yeah, they've barred her, told her on her way out tonight that a letter was in the post to her and not to bother coming back."

"The pieces of fucking shit!" I said. "This was part of her life! She was part of the furniture, and everyone liked her, for fucks sake! What a fucking travesty!"

"I know, mate," Sincs sympathised.

"Well," I said, "if I didn't hate them before, I definitely do now. I'm going to do my absolute bollocks tonight, mate; I'm going to shovel it out tonight, I don't give a fuck!" and Sincs laughed.

"Yeah, I will too," he said – and, as I recall, we did.

Well, that had happened about two months previously, and I'd bitched about it just about every single day, and particularly when Sincs and I went out on a Saturday, and it had obviously registered somewhere with Sincs, because now he was hitting me with a really strong reason to give his little scam a look: to pay back the casino managers for their appalling treatment of my friend Annie. I didn't know what else I could say, except to repeat: if you get too greedy, you'll get caught. Sincs was just sat there looking at me, as I processed everything.

"How about this," he said. "You at least let me show you how it's done, and if you can spot anything, then fine: forget about it. But if you *can't*, then let me show you how the shuffle is done so that you can practise at home till you've mastered it; it ain't difficult, it only took me a couple of hours; all right?"

I slowly shook my head, but finally nodded and said: "Yeah; yeah, all right."

He sat there, just looking at me and shaking his head.

"What?" I demanded. "*What*?"

"Oh, nothing," he went, grinning. "It's just that I was thinking."

"What?"

"That only a tool like you could be given the chance to make five grand a *week*, in cash, with absolutely no risk to yourself, and wanna 'think about it' – you bell-end!" We both laughed. Though at that moment, I must confess, I was slowly coming round to seriously considering having a closer look at the scam.

Finally, I reached for my glass, untouched except for that initial swig (which must be some kind of record, I thought); it must be because the conversation had kept me hooked. And I certainly wasn't interested in getting lashed now; I had too much to think about and even went so far as asking Sincs if we could call it a night.

We walked out to the MX5, my head spinning, and it struck me vividly that although *my* world had suddenly turned upside-down, everything else had remained exactly the same: my car, the pub, people coming and going, the birds singing in the trees, everything; and yet the inside of my own head (which, of course, determined my whole life) had altered irrevocably.

As I drove us back to my house to let Sincs collect his battered old car, we maintained a complete (and unnatural) silence throughout the entire trip. I was still thinking furiously, a million questions running through my mind: Do I want to get involved? Do I need the cash that badly? Is it worth the risk of losing my job and career? Or prison? I liked my job! Should I look into it a bit more? What if I *did* make a hundred grand in a couple of months? How would that affect me? Jeez, I could buy a Lotus Esprit *and* a Rolls Royce Silver Shadow with that sort of money! But if I looked into it and thought it was too risky, how would I let my friend down gently? Oh, man!

I also thought that my friend Sincs, who was sitting beside me in silence, was wondering whether he'd just made a terrible mistake in asking me.

Although the trip back to my house took less than

twenty minutes it seemed like much longer, and we barely said a word; I headed for home but at the last moment instead of turning into our close I continued up the road, round the corner and parked-up behind some local shops; switching off the engine, I turned to my friend. For all my rapid mental juggling (and doubts about the scam), I still really felt for my friend and the risk he'd taken in spilling the beans to me; it must have taken an awful lot of guts for him to ask me. And I felt that whatever my ultimate decision would be, I had to set his mind to rest (and, in a way, repay him) by doing a good deed.

I turned towards him and stuck out my hand.

"Sincs, put it there, buddy."

"What?" he went, looking at me like I'd lost the plot.

"Just put it there mate," I told him, so he reached out and we shook. "I just wanted to say thanks; thanks for asking me, and thanks for trusting me; and whatever happens, I won't grass you up to those miserable slags at work."

He shrugged, and said: "Yeah, well, there weren't all that many decent people to choose from!" But then he laughed, and I felt a lot of tension go out of him.

"So what we gonna do? When are you gonna show me this shuffle thing?"

He laughed again. "I'll talk to Wendy," he said, "and you'll have to come round to her place one night after work, meet Albert, and let him show you properly; talk to you tomorrow night, all right?" I nodded, fired up the car, dropped him back at his car, and off he rattled. I then parked the MX5 next to Dad's beautiful black Citroen DS, put the roof up on the MX5 and locked it up, let myself in the house and proceeded directly to my bedroom, where I immediately poured myself a large drink from my secret stash of Bacardi 'n' diet coke (which I'd hidden in a box under my bed) and downed it in one. I then returned back downstairs and into the lounge, where Mum and Dad were watching telly, grabbed my rough collie Cinnamon and she jumped all over me and gave my face a big lick.

"You're back early," Mum said, to which I replied: "Yeah, I'm pretty tired; I'm just gonna take Cinny out and then I'm gonna have an early night, cheers," and then off out I went; going for a long walk, followed by a good night's sleep, I knew from long experience would help calm my thoughts.

It was still fairly early and quite light out, so I headed along a few local roads and then up a lane and across a golf course and on up to a local beauty spot called Berkhamsted Downs, my brain still buzzing furiously.

Already I was wondering if I could somehow pull-off the blackjack scam for just a couple of months and then get out of it; after all, I wasn't exactly starving (my silly parents would always look after me anyway); it wasn't like I really *needed* the money (though an extra five or ten grand a month would come in damn handy).

But what if I could squeeze something like *fifty* grand out of the scam and then get out? Fifty grand would set me up nicely and I'd be well ahead of the game! Realistically, it'd take me *donkey's years* of working my guts out five nights a week in Britain, and probably five years – or more – abroad to save anything *even close* to that sort of money.

As I walked, I thought it through.

No; it wouldn't be anything like fifty grand in two months; as things stood, I'd be lucky to deal to Albert more than a couple of times a week (assuming that I lost big money to him), and even then he might not be able to control all of the table's boxes. And if I paid him out even two grand a time, and he really did pay me half, I'd only be getting paid something like two grand a week (at best); was it really worth me risking my job for a lousy two – or even ten – grand?

If the scam really was as good as Sincs reckoned, then it might be possible to steal one hundred thousand pounds over a period of six months or so – in theory – but I knew that the casino would never let it get that far: they'd bring so much heat to bear that eventually someone would be bound to spot something; I honestly didn't think that any scam was really foolproof, especially not in the 'long-term' (i.e. fiddling for anything more than a few months).

And even if we *didn't* get caught – which was entirely possible – then the casino would simply bar Albert, and if he was winning in the region of ten grand a week that wouldn't take long: possibly three to four months and certainly no longer than six. In other words, if one *was* going to commit a casino scam one was much better off hitting them hard over a very short period, or alternatively for much smaller sums (amounts they would not even miss) over a much longer period. In this case, it'd probably be better if I paid him out – assuming that I got involved – ten grand a week for a couple of months, to hopefully end up with forty grand in my pocket for two months' work, and then let the idiot get banned; *forty grand*!

But then I laughed, and thought: hang on, Chrissy, old boy; you're talking about forty grand and you haven't even seen how the scam is worked yet! Better to wait until you're seen it a couple of times and *then* make a decision as to whether it's worth getting involved (and get a couple of weeks' profits under your belt) before you start jumping to any wild conclusions, otherwise, you're living in cloud-cuckoo-land, Chrissy, old boy.

I was definitely warming to the idea of skanking the casino; the crummy money they paid us (and particularly *moi*) had certainly begun to rankle. I privately estimated that I made the casino, conservatively, around forty grand a month (assuming I worked about twenty days a month); oh, yes, I definitely made them at least two grand a night and that's aside from the 'atmosphere' that I always tried to generate when dealing, which would – hopefully – bring punters back to our club. I was only being paid just over a grand a month (and my doing lots of overtime meant that I was now being clobbered by the tax man for 25% of anything over a grand a month, for fucks sake!): in other words, I finished up with less than two percent of what I made them: *two*! What a joke!

I can honestly say that I wouldn't have shed a tear over ripping-off such a bunch of mean-hearted thieves, and it wasn't as if I hadn't done anything slightly illegal before (though I'd only been in my mid-teens at the time, and importing and selling loads of flick-knives, air guns and contraband cigarettes was hardly going to get me banged up).

However, this was my first real job, I was nearly nineteen and what else was I going to do – stack shelves? And for far less money? Hell, I couldn't exactly see that happening, I'd rather be on the bloody dole (and importing more knives, guns and fags!).

Damn, what was I going to do? It was a real knotty problem, made even worse since I could hardly go and talk the problem over with my friends or parents, now could I? Not that I really wanted to involve my friends anyway; hell, all my friends came from normal, middle-class backgrounds like mine; they'd all probably try to talk me out of it anyway (and some of them might even 'dob' me in it 'for my own good'!). Oh, why oh why did this have to happen at this point in my casino career? I was a nice boy from a good background, it shouldn't have happened at all!

I continued walking and considering all the possible outcomes – all of which looked bad! Even with this long stroll I knew I wouldn't get much sleep tonight; by the time I got back home it was completely dark and it was ages since I'd taken Cinny out for such a long walk; she seemed even more tired out than I was. But at least I think I'd come to a decision: that probably the best thing to be done, at this moment in time, was to have a look at Sincs' silly little scam; if I didn't like it (and hopefully I wouldn't), then I could always make my excuses and try to weasel out of it somehow; but if I was genuinely one hundred percent convinced that it was undetectable, and that I could get away with it? I didn't know for sure, but maybe I'd give it a go.

As I suspected, I got very little sleep that night, and woke up – after experiencing many vivid dreams – with the feeling that I needed to go for another long walk. So, after an early lunch (prepared and dished-up by Mum), I got the MX5's top down and took it for a spin out into the country, found a place to park along by the Grand Union Canal and went for another stroll.

I had awoken with the strong feeling that I really

shouldn't get involved in the scam and so was left wondering how I could somehow extricate myself from the situation whilst trying to preserve my friendship with Sincs.

As I wandered and pondered, my mind kept returning to the philosophical question of whether it would be 'wrong' (morally, rather than legally, of course; I didn't give a stuff about any archaic legal niceties) for me to take my rotten employers to the cleaners. I examined the argument from every conceivable angle but kept on coming back to my situation: I had been hard-working, efficient, honest, and was, potentially, very loyal; I had worked now for my casino company for nearly a year, which is a long time when you're not even nineteen!

I'd given them nothing to complain about — in fact, I reckoned I'd out-performed almost everyone else in the place — but I felt that I was treated very poorly by the casino management, but more than that I mean they *paid* me very poorly; less than two percent was a downright insult, yet even would five percent have been. Was ten percent too much to ask? Ten percent would have made *all* the difference: the difference between struggling, always being skint, being somewhat depressed, having a crappy old car and being unable to afford a place of my own, compared with being just... *OK*. That was all I wanted, nothing more than that: just to be *OK*; money that I worked really hard for; money that I deserved; money that they *wouldn't even miss*.

In my own mind, what had happened since I had started at the casino was that the work had got harder, the requirements of the job greater, the overall standards had fallen, the management had treated everyone like dirt, the rewards were negligible – and yet expectations had remained high.

I remembered what Sincs had told me about what croupiers used to earn back in the 1960's and '70's: in real terms, our money had plummeted and we were now being shafted. There was nothing morally 'right' about how dealers had been treated in general over the years, and I personally felt very ill-done by, yet the casinos' profits had kept going up and up. I wondered how I'd feel had I started as a dealer, say, five or ten years' previously, for the way I was figuring it, my employer was even less moral than I was.

So what to do: Leave? Stay and get shafted? Stay and do the shafting? What if I stayed and did a bit of entrepreneurial appropriation of funds? What if I stayed for a while, stole a bit (considerably less than I was making for them, mind you) and then left; would that be wrong? I was now very much in two minds as to whether it was.

We were busy in the casino that Monday night, but Sincs and I managed to have a brief whispered conversation in the corridor:

Him: "Had any thoughts?"

Me: "Nah."

He told me that we could go round to Wendy's house after work that very night unless either of us got the dreaded 'count' in which case we'd have to make it the following night. I told him 'OK,' and, lo and behold, both of us did get the count. The count was always a pain, and annoying as hell to see all those piles of cash being stacked up in front of your eyes; the feeling, for me, had never really faded. They never told anyone in advance about the count for 'security' reasons; they just stuck your name up on the board in the staff-room at around 2.30am. But their idea of security was complete codswallop cos when we were short-staffed you always knew when you'd get the count: on the first night back after your days off.

And so, after another restless night and very thought-filled shift, I followed Sincs back to Wendy's when we finished work on Wednesday morning; she lived in a small, two-bedroom terraced house down one of Watford's horrible back streets and Sincs managed to squeeze into a space right outside Wendy's place whereas I had to continue half-way up the street before I found a god-rotting parking place; but once we'd parked up (with me casting apprehensive glances all around and feeling distinctly unhappy about leaving my convertible in such a dump) and gone inside, I found she kept her house nice enough.

Wendy, never the most attractive of women even at

the best of times, looked a right mess at four-thirty in the morning after her day off, but she greeted me politely enough, even though I still held grave misgivings about the whole affair. She offered us a can of beer, which Sincs gladly accepted and I declined; then she said she'd go upstairs and get Albert.

It felt indescribably strange sitting there, on a cheap sofa in a run-down house in the crappiest part of a crappy town, waiting to meet a bloke who could supposedly steal a hundred grand a month from the casino, this 'Albert.'

Because this was where it *really* became serious; up to now all I'd done was have a chat with my mate Sincs, but now it was about to involve an actual punter in the flesh; this was when it became real. I felt a violent urge to take a leak, though I hadn't wanted to go a couple of minutes previously, and then I started panicking and the thought suddenly came to me that this Albert wasn't upstairs at all, that this whole thing had been an awful ruse, that I'd been lured along under false pretences and in a few seconds I wouldn't be meeting Albert at all but in fact was in a trap set up to test my 'honesty and loyalty,' and I almost began hallucinating and actually thought I could see Carl's evil little head appearing from behind the hall door and sniggering "Gotcha!"

On the verge of a panic attack I almost leapt up and scarpered, and it was only my fast-wilting belief that Sincs would never dob me in it that kept me there; I asked him to get me a crummy beer just to try and take my mind off everything but even as Sincs headed for the kitchen I could've sworn out of the corner of my eye I saw Carl's head peep round the door! I blinked hard and looked back and forth and jumped up with the intention to go and see if anyone was really there, but then I heard footsteps coming down the stairs. Oh well, I thought; this is it.

Wendy came in first, and said: "Chris, this is Albert," and then in came a geezer that I recognised immediately; he was a little bit shorter than me, a little bit skinnier and had a sort of foxy look; he had sandy hair, blue eyes and looked to be about forty-five, but had one of those unlined faces that was hard to date (and could have been anything from thirty to mid-fifties).

He smiled, held out his hand and said (in an American accent): "So this is the guy."

I shook his extended hand, managed some sort of smile-like grimace and said: "Yeah, that's me."

He nodded, and said: "I think I've seen you in the casino; you deal a lot of roulette, don't you?" and I muttered something in reply, but felt some tension go out of me; the casino management weren't there at all, thank God, and hopefully we could now cut to the chase – but we all just stood there like lemons with no-one seeming to know what to do next. So I piped up:

"Well come on then; I ain't got all night you know and I'm shagged! Show me how to do this shuffle thing!" Sincs laughed, and without any further ado Wendy opened up her ironing board and draped a thin towel over it, to somewhat duplicate the feel of one of our table layouts at work (shuffling cards on a hard table surface is nigh-on impossible, especially the way we croupiers shuffle cards); then we all clustered round as Albert instructed Sincs to do the special shuffle and talked me through what was happening. I listened and watched, entranced; and at the end of the shuffle, Sincs showed me the section of the deck that he had left un-shuffled. "Do it again!" I said, and they went through the whole sequence twice more for me, whilst Wendy went and found some novelty chips that we could use to show me precisely how the betting went.

In essence, the shuffle was basically exactly the same as our usual casino shuffle, using the standard four decks, only this time a portion of cards – around thirty – were left *un*-shuffled – and would remain un-shuffled for the entire duration the dealer was doing his stint at the table. The dealer would do the normal 'riffle' shuffle, and simply not shuffle the portion at the bottom of the deck in with the other cards; it would look as if he was, but in fact he would just riffle the few cards from one batch of cards in one of his hands into the few cards on top of the un-shuffled lot.

He then placed the sequence, which was always to be placed towards the start of the shoe towards the

258

bottom of the deck for the player (i.e. Albert) to cut, upon which he'd place the un-shuffled sequence of cards towards the front. With his trained memory, Albert would watch the un-shuffled sequence for a couple of shoes, and then, when he had remembered the order (and values) of the cards, he would start to bet heavily as soon as the un-shuffled sequence was due to come out; knowing the values of the forthcoming cards, all he had to do was draw out a number of cards until he had the correct sequence of cards to bust the dealer and he was guaranteed a win.

I watched Sincs shuffle from both the side and from above and couldn't see any sign that anything fraudulent was taking place, and then I finally twigged the ace up Albert's sleeve: the crooked shuffle was indeed almost 'foolproof' because the dealer's very own hands prevented the scam from being seen by anyone watching! I was rocked by the simplicity of it; rocked, stunned and extremely impressed.

Also, because the fixed sequence never came out directly at the start of each shoe (albeit within the first couple of hands), no inspector in the world was going to be able to remember any kind of sequence of the cards. It really was brilliant! Now that I knew what I was watching for, I tried again to see anything untoward when Sincs shuffled but again I couldn't see anything remotely suspicious; man, was I impressed!

Then it was my turn to have a go, and as I shuffled

Albert stood right in front of me, leaning over and peering directly at the cards. Of course, I made a complete hash of it and Albert ordered me to do it again, and then again, and again. Over and over he made me do it, till at last I had worked out the basics of what to do; the fine-tuning could come over the next couple of days.

I was still making a fair old mess of it, and Sincs started calling me names, but I threw a few back, and everyone laughed; slowly everyone began to relax as I shuffled on and on, fumbling the cards all over the place.

"Blimey, you're rubbish!" cried Sincs. "How did anyone like you get a job as a dealer?"

"Oh, look who's talking, Mr Do My Crust!" I replied.

Him: "Shilly-Shally Shilling, Shilly-Shally Shilling!"

Me: "Shut your noise, you muppet!"

Him: "Useless plank!" etc., etc.

Wendy and Albert were both laughing, but Albert, with his face down next to the towel and watching me with eagle eyes kept urging me to carry on practising the shuffle, muttering instructions and whispering to me to concentrate and get it right.

After another hour and a half – it seemed longer; Sincs had long-since retired to the couch to guzzle Wendy's beer – I felt that I was beginning to get it right, and finally told Albert it was time for me to make a move.

"Have you got any decks at your place?" he asked.

"Yeah, I've got loads of old packs lying around," I replied.

"Okay, well tomorrow you're gonna have to go and get four new, identical decks and practise at home; you've got to be able to do this shuffle with your eyes shut; you've got to be able to do it automatically and absolutely accurately," he told me. "And all you gotta do then," he said with a grin, "is keep your nerve." He looked me dead in the eye. "Think you can do it?"

I looked straight back at him. "I'll give it my best shot," I said, and he nodded.

"Fair enough; but you gotta get it perfect, you know? Practise at home tomorrow, and every day till you're perfect. And I'll see you across the tables later in the week, okay?"

"Okay, sure; but I ain't doing it if there's too much casino heat," I said.

"Oh Shilling, what the hell are you blabbering on about!?" Sincs cried; "Too much heat! What heat, you monger? I already told ya, there ain't any heat! I been doing it under their noses for two months now and none of 'em have spotted a god damn thing, an' some of them have been in the business over twenty years!

261

Heat – oh please! They're all useless!"

"Yeah, yeah, okay, but for the first couple of times I'm only gonna do it if there's no manager looking over me shoulder and I've got Wendy as my inspector," I told them.

"Oh, blimey," Sincs went, throwing his hands up in the in disgust, but Wendy nodded and Albert just shrugged, and muttered something like 'fair enough,' and then Wendy said that maybe I should ask for extra overtime at work which would give us a better chance of getting corresponding afternoon shifts, and I nodded.

"Actually I'm on a double tomorrow, as a matter of fact – so everything seems to have worked out nicely. Oh yeah, one other thing before I go," I said; "Assuming all this goes as planned, how am I going to be paid, cos obviously I don't wanna be popping round here after work three times a week, do you know what I mean? Better in fact for us not to meet up at all outside of work, you know?" Wendy nodded. "So how am I gonna get my money? And how much am I going to get? Cos obviously I'm only doing it if I'm going to get at least half," I told Albert bluntly.

"Yeah, half, more or less, minus expenses," Albert muttered.

"Well, why don't we give your share to Sinclair, and then he can give it to you at the weekend, OK?" said Wendy; "To save you coming round here," and I glanced at Sincs, who nodded, so I shrugged and nodded as well.

"Fair enough," I said, and then I stepped up in front of Albert and stuck out my hand, which he shook, then me and Sincs said our 'good-nights' and let ourselves out to go to our respective cars, so after a moment's chat I walked up the road where (surprisingly) I found the MX5 still there (and in one piece), and just as I was fumbling the keys into the door-lock a car came sidling along and it slowed down as it drew up alongside me and as I glanced up *I couldn't bloody believe it*: it was Malcolm *flipping* Philby, the chubby casino inspector, on his way home from work after the count; of all the stinking luck! And then I belatedly remembered: the fool only lived in the next street along from Wendy! Unbelievable!

He wound down his window and went, "All right?" Thinking fast, I replied: "Nah, mate, knackered," and he laughed, so then I went, "See you later," and hurriedly got in behind the wheel, slammed the door and fired her up. A second later, Malcolm pulled away in his tatty red Ford whilst I just sat there pouring with sweat, shaking my head, banging my fist on the steering wheel in rage, cursing my rotten luck and imagining all sorts of horrible scenarios: unbelievable!

Chapter 5

Because I'd been fretting about this card scam thing all night, I only managed to get a few hours sleep but still managed to crawl in to work by one thirty and help the rest of the afternoon-shift crew get all the table chips and cash chips out; I then rushed back to the staff-room and ordered up a huge breakfast (from our staff 'mum') and wolfed it down.

And it wasn't long after we'd opened our doors (with me spinning endlessly away at the roulette table as per usual) that I saw Albert come in and start playing blackjack, where he stayed for about three hours, during which time the pit boss sent all our best blackjack dealers over to have a go at him, including Sincs (who I saw pay him out a couple of grand before being sent to take me off).

Albert had been plugging away at the table on both of the occasions that I was sent to the blackjack table, but seeing as I hadn't had a chance to practice the crooked shuffle I had no intention whatsoever of trying to do the scam, and in any case the pit boss didn't leave me on the table for long either time. I'd had a look at the decks of cards I had at home but they'd all been old, tatty and mismatched and I only wanted to practice with four new decks (the casino insisted on using brand new decks every day; it must have cost them a fortune);

but the real reason I wasn't going to be attempting the crooked shuffle was that Wendy wasn't working this afternoon. Albert soon realised that I wasn't going to be doing anything naughty so didn't attempt to try anything on (and there were too many bodies around – both players and staff – for us to have even the most muted of conversations), and he left the joint a little before six pm.

The following lunchtime I was up bright and early and walked into town, where I was able to purchase four identical new decks, after which I returned home and spent the remainder of the afternoon and early part of the evening standing over our ironing board with a towel thrown over it in my poxy bedroom practising the interminable shuffle.

The idea of the scam was this: to leave the first thirty (or so) cards in each shoe un-shuffled, but I was aiming to try to leave about thirty-five cards out of the four decks un-shuffled, just to be on the safe side; you then had to arrange it so the un-shuffled portion was at the bottom of the stack, which you offered to Albert to cut, and who would then cut the 'slug' of un-shuffled cards up towards the front: perfect! This way, Albert would always get a minimum of two complete (seven box) hands at roughly the beginning of every shoe (and the more boxes he could play, the better; it was also essential that he controlled the last two or three boxes). I found it to be really quite difficult to leave thirty-five-odd cards un-shuffled (twenty would have been easier), but if done quickly enough I thought I could get away with it. Now all I had to do was keep my nerve.

I'd already decided that if I felt unhappy about pulling the scam, for whatever reason, then I simply wouldn't risk it; I wouldn't give Albert 'the nod.' I was sure I'd get an opportunity sooner than I'd have liked, but as it happened Albert didn't come in that evening, which was fine by me (and Thursdays were generally quiet anyway), but he was in bright and early for the Friday afternoon shift, which both Sincs and I were working (as part of yet another double).

I couldn't fail to spot the cheating dog come sauntering in, seeing as I was dealing on A.R.5, the closest roulette table to the entrance. Sincs himself was next to me on B.J.1, and Albert wasted no time in walking directly up to the table and buying in for a couple of grand of chips. The inspectors we had that afternoon were Malcolm Philby and Keith Blackwood, both of whom were a bit of a joke but Keith had worked for the casino for so long that eventually they had to promote the idiot to the position of assistant pit boss (though he'd never go any further); the other dealers that afternoon were Peter Connaught and Dave Gill, both mates of Sincs who had come up with him from the casino down the road called The Palace (which I'd heard was a dark and dingy dump of a place); we all got along fairly well, maybe because we were all capable of dealing a winning game of roulette, but the others were much more experienced on the blackjack table than me (indeed, I was still considered to be a mere blackjack trainee, so might not even be pitted against Albert unless all the others all did their crust). As I furtively peered over, it seemed that Sincs was already dishing out mounds of chips to Albert; Christ, he'd only been playing for twenty minutes!

We had plenty of roulette players in that afternoon but not many blackjack punters, so Keith was able to keep things sweet for us – with just three tables open – till around half past six, when more punters started coming in and he was more or less obliged to open a second bj table for Albert (who had been requesting a £500 limit for the last couple of hours). So now we were down to one fifteen-minute break every hour and a quarter – wonderful! Keith even had fat Malcolm taking turns dealing, particularly to Albert, who seemed to hold his own against everyone except Sincs, who'd been paying him out something like a couple of grand per shoe for three or four shoes on the trot; Keith was changing dealers on Albert every thirty minutes (unless they won) so inevitably I was going to get a crack at him sooner or later, and the sooner bit came just after seven pm., when Keith told me to go and take off Malcolm (who'd obviously just done a packet of money to Albert) on B.J.5.

I was nervous and not feeling *at all* confident, but as it happened events were conspiring in my favour; no sooner had I started dealing on B.J.5 when a veritable tribe of Jewish punters came flooding in and Keith was instructed by the casino manager – the old boy Jacob

Ambrose – to open another blackjack table, so now we had nobody on a break at all, which meant we'd all be slogging our guts out on the tables till ten to nine!

Another eureka moment was when I'd twigged that that no-one would actually inspect me when it came to the shuffle time, which made the scam even more of a great brainwave, so I completed dealing out the remainder of Malcolm's shoe and, mentally shrugging to myself, went straight into my first crooked shuffle, which would not be hammered by Albert; it was simply so he could remember the values of the first thirty cards that came out.

I then cut the deck (in half, as instructed by that bell-end Keith) and proceeded to deal, quite slowly for the first five hands and then racing through the rest of it. I say that events were going in my favour because now Keith was inspecting three roulette tables and two bj tables almost single-handedly, though old Jacob Ambrose was also wandering back and forth, helping to keep an eye on things, and so it was that I pretty-much had no inspector watching me whatsoever. Also, there were no other players at my table apart from Albert himself, who had commandeered the entire seven boxes for himself (he'd placed a pony on each); it didn't look like he was going to do anything by halves!

And thus we came to the point when the cutting card came out, time for me to do my next crooked shuffle and the first time I had ever knowingly scammed my employer (in any real sense). And as I went carefully through the crooked shuffle, Albert leaned forward, keeping his head close to the baize and watching my hands intently, and – since no-one else was hanging around – he even started muttering encouraging little comments as I proceeded through the bent shuffle (the twat); and once I had given him the deck to cut and positioned the un-shuffled bit towards the front (and placed the blank 'postillion' card considerably less than halfway from the front of the shoe) he whispered, "Good, good." Yeah, yeah, I thought, I'll give you 'good, good,' you miserable, thieving *slag*!

So once more I dealt out the cards, again to only one £25 chip per box, so that Albert could get the card values straight in his head (and to make sure that I had done it right); after the first five hands, with Albert nodded his head and muttered, "Right, right, let's go," so again I raced through the rest of the shoe and then repeated the crooked shuffle, Albert watching me like a hawk the entire time.

I had noticed that he'd played extremely loosely for the first two shoes, stupidly drawing cards when he had a 17, 18 or even a 19, in fact drawing out as many cards as possible, so he could lose a bit (so that I'd be left on) and we could get the shoe over with as quickly as we could. This was an excellent strategy for he'd lost on almost every hand and when Keith wandered over he could see that the table had won over £1,000 from the first two shoes that I'd dealt; hopefully he'd now leave me on the table for another half hour – or three more shoes – at least. Once I'd completed the crooked shuffle for the second time, I handed Albert the postillion with which he cut the deck and then I positioned the fixed cards towards the front, cut the deck just slightly deeper than in half and then I banged the cards in the shoe.

Yet again, he just placed one £25 on each box, as I slowly dealt out the first five hands; this time, he muttered, "Perfect, perfect," and then started drawing cards at every possible opportunity, so I raced through the rest of the shoe.

With crooked shuffle number three complete, the deck cut and placed in the shoe, Albert now proceeded to bet £500 on each of the seven boxes and then out came the cards; Albert only drew a couple of cards out before declaring, "Stick on all," so I pulled out a four to go with my nine, which was followed by another nine – bust! – so I paid out £3,500; then I dealt out the next hand, once again he 'stood' on all, my 'up' card was a three, on top of which I drew two tens (and so bust again): another £3,500 payout. Then he dropped back down to £25 per box, and I whizzed through the remainder of the shoe; now the table was losing at least seven grand.

I quickly shuffled again, let him cut the deck, and got ready to deal. Again he placed £500 on each of the seven boxes, very rapidly ensured that I went bust on both the first two hands and so I was obligated to pay him out £7,000, and then I once more raced through the remaining cards. Keith was now beginning to 'sweat,' (he was famous for it), the table had to have a 'fill' of ten grand (in the form of one hundred brown £100 chips which were brought over by Jacob), so I signed for that and then shuffled again, though this time Jacob and Keith were standing nearby, talking – but they were watching a roulette game rather than me shuffling. I was still nervous, but I was now eager to make another big payout before Keith sent someone to take me off (I'd realised that if I didn't keep working the bent shuffle already in place it was extremely unlikely that I'd get another chance to pay him out).

It amused me that most inspectors, pit bosses and managers all tended to wander off and watch other tables whilst the shuffle was taking place on; funny, that! Talk about playing into our hands! And anyway, the way I was looking at it was: Sod it – in for a penny, in for twenty grand! So I finished the shuffle, banged the cards back in the shoe, dealt out the cards, made another £7k payout in two hands and proceeded through another speedy deal to the end of the shoe (which was again interrupted by Jacob, bringing another £5000 in £100 chips).

Just as I was about to pull the cards out of the shoe, I felt a tap on my shoulder so gently brushed my hands together, showed my palms up (and thus empty of chips), and announced, "Thank-you, you have a new dealer," and heard Sincs – the dealer that cretinous

Keith had sent to replace me – mutter: "Well done, knob-end! Go and see Blackwood," so I walked over to A.R.7, where Keith was dealing since he'd replaced Sincs to get me off.

"Where to, boss?" I asked.

"Oh, just deal here for a while, mate," he told me, showing clean hands and looking at his clipboard with the pit control sheet.

"Place your bets, please," I called and spun the ball, whilst Keith pencilled in some changes to the sheet.

"What do you reckon to that American guy?" he asked me quietly; "Reckon he's counting?"

"Counting? Nah, I can't me head round it; he places all his heavy bets at the start of each shoe! I won three or four shoes, the table was winning a couple of grand, and then he gets two good shoes and suddenly the wanker's winning five grand – of all the luck! No more bets, thank-you!" I called out to the roulette punters.

"Oh, don't worry about it mate, I know you were cutting it in half," Keith said. "Everyone seems to be struggling against him; I might even have a go myself in a minute."

"Yeah, good idea; go and give the slag a hammering for me," I said but he was already walking off, so I just made my pay-outs and spun the ball again. Cutting it in half; of course I was cutting it in half! I might have been new to blackjack but I wasn't a complete idiot; everyone in the casino knew that when you were faced with a heavy player you cut the deck in half!

But this was yet another reason why the scam was working so well; the only hands in the entire shoe that Albert was interested in were the first three and so – by some miracle – Albert's scam actually played against the casino's very own procedures and still ended up winning: because the casino always preferred to give a shorter shoe to the players when it started losing, Albert would get in even more crooked shoes; it was little-short of brilliant!

How Albert managed to remember a sequence of thirty or forty cards still baffled the hell out of me, but I guessed he'd probably been practising mnemonic tricks for ages (as all good card counters had to do). I ended up staying out on A.R.7 till the night shift started, but at least I now got an hour to chill out in the staff room. Sincs and I managed a very brief, whispered discussion in the men's changing room, but to do this was a big risk and so we soon ended up going back to the staff room and dozing off till ten o'clock (I was exhilarated, worried and knackered all at the same time).

As usual I spent most of the night dealing roulette and hammered many of our regular Greek and Chinese players, probably recouping most of the twenty grand I'd earlier helped steal from the casino (like their millionaire stock holders were going to miss it; yeah, *right!*). And at twenty past two the senior pit boss, Percy Collins, sent me to deal on B.J.4, where Albert was still plugging away (the greedy swine).

However, as soon as I saw I'd be dealing to Albert I decided that there were plenty of very good reasons for me not to do any more messing around tonight: it was late and I was tired (and might make a mistake); there were too many other bodies around (so Albert and I wouldn't be able to have even the briefest of whispered murmurings), and on B.J.4 this was particularly the case as all the other players were Chinese, and I respected them more than any other punters (and they didn't miss a trick).

Also, I had Grenville as my inspector (the smartest, craftiest and most dangerous − to any scamster − inspector in the building), and he was assigned to only one other table − BJ5, right next door − so he could stand right at my elbow and watch both games (and I reckoned this was *far* too close for comfort).

Additionally − and most importantly of all − I'd realised that I couldn't afford to have my name on the pit sheets indicating that I was responsible for paying out too much money to just one punter. So I decided I wouldn't be paying Albert anything out on this stint (and thought that if Albert was really smart he'd have tried to lose some money back to me − though I don't think he would!).

You see, good as the scam was, I'd had a major epiphany whilst standing at a quiet roulette table earlier in the evening and decided – there and then – that in future I'd only pay Albert out if Wendy was around to 'doctor' the paperwork, otherwise (I'd belatedly realised) even our amazingly dozy casino management would eventually review the table control sheets, put two and two together and realise that not only was something crooked occurring (the more a player won, the more the management scrutinised everything) but that Mr Christopher James blue-eyed-boy Shilling just *had* to be in on it!

I knew that at the end of each night an assistant pit boss (or senior inspector) was designated to go through all the table control sheets and make a note in a log-book of all our big winners and losers. However, because it was such a tedious, time-consuming job, it was never going to be a pit boss who'd worked the afternoon shift because (a) they never usually did a double shift, and (b) if they did, they'd be allowed to go home as soon as the casino closed, and so they'd never get to see if any afternoon-shift paperwork had been doctored by Wendy. Now I know these might sound like trivial little things, but believe me, if you're trying to keep a big casino scam like ours from being discovered by the management, they're *absolutely crucial*.

Thus I'd concluded I would only do the scam if Wendy was inspecting and I'd try to limit my scamming to the afternoon shift only, so apart from the big payout I'd given him earlier (which was too late to do anything about, and hell, I might as well get *something* out of it!), I guessed it was better to hit them big when they were least suspecting it rather than build up to some humongous hit once they already suspected something; I should be getting at least ten grand out of it, which was a nice-enough amount (even if I did get sacked), and from now on I wouldn't be taking any more silly chances.

I don't think Albert did deliberately try to lose some money back to me but I was so shattered I really didn't care, and when I was 'chopped' at four am., I shot off home immediately, physically and mentally exhausted. But at least it was now Saturday morning and I could look forward to my two days off; as soon as I got in from work I went straight up to bed and as I dozed off I was already looking forward to ringing Sincs that afternoon and having him go and get my ten g's, whoopee!

Excited as I was, I slept through most of the Saturday and it was only when Mum banged on my bedroom door just after four pm. yelling that Sinclair was on the phone that I roused myself; he must have impressed upon my Old Dear that it was extremely urgent to wake me because I always turned my mobile phone off when I went to bed and had long since impressed upon everyone that I wasn't to be disturbed for *anything*. It must have been fairly important, because I don't think we'd ever phoned each-other before, so I told Mum to tell him I'd call him back and turned my mobile phone on; he answered on the first ring.

"Shills?" he went.

"Uh," I replied.

"We meeting for a drink?"

"Yeah, come over and pick me up."

"Okay," he replied, we hung up and I dashed back upstairs to have a shower, get dressed and wait for him. He arrived not long after I started peering out of the downstairs window and scanning the street, so I nipped out, jumped in his old silver Ford Escort and he pulled swiftly away and headed out of town.

"Where're we heading?" I asked.

"Somewhere we can't be overheard," he said.

"What's wrong with here?" I went.

"Just hang on a minute," he said impatiently, and he drove us to the top of the Berkhamsted Downs, parked his old wreck in the car park up there and then we walked across a field till we were well away from any other walkers and could see if anyone started to get too close. Then he turned to face me and said:

"Albert's not impressed with you at all!"

"You what?" I hollered; "Then he's a prick!"

"What do you mean?" But I'd now got the right hump.

"He's an ungrateful piece of scum; I paid him out over twenty grand yesterday and he's not impressed with *me*? Well he can go screw himself! It's me who's taking the risk, and if he don't like it he can sod off!"

"Hang on, hang on, calm down," Sincs told me, going into his 'it's undetectable' spiel until I told him to put a sock in it.

"What's he so unhappy about, the twat? When did you speak to him?"

"I went round there earlier," he explained.

"Did you get my money?"

"Yeah," he nodded, and, glancing around yet again to make sure the coast was clear, reached into his jacket, pulled out a thick brown envelope, stepped up close to me and shoved it towards me; I grabbed it and hurriedly shoved into my jacket pocket (it was a squeeze to get it in, which for some reason made me grin inanely).

"How much is it?" I asked, but he shook his head.

"Dunno, didn't ask."

"So what did flid-features have to say, then?"

"Not much, except that apparently you had a golden opportunity to pay him out again last night and you did absolutely naff-all about it, and he wanted you to understand that these chances don't come along very often so when they do you have to make the most of 'em."

"Oh blimey, I know that," I said, "but I already told you: I ain't going to be doing it at all unless I'm one hundred percent happy with everything! Look, Wendy weren't around, that fucking Grenville Aston was inspecting, I was tired and I'd already paid him out fourteen grand in the afternoon; jeez, what does he want, blood?" Sincs laughed.

"Oh blimey, you ain't still worrying about getting caught, are ya? I already told you, it's undetectable – especially by those spastics!" he railed at me.

"Well, I was more worried about my name going on the paperwork again, to be honest," I said.

"Oh, don't worry about it," he breezed, waving a hand. "We hit 'em hard for a few months and then we move on before they get suspicious! Do that for a few years and we'll all have enough money to retire – and then you can set up your own stupid casino!"

"Oh, have a word! I ain't moving clubs every couple of months!"

"No, think about it!" he enthused. "Every six months we can change casinos and even move countries; we'll never be caught!"

"Aw, flipping hell, I ain't upping sticks every six months! All I wanna do is to get a small place of my own and retire."

"Yeah, with a Rolls Royce and Aston Martin on the drive!" he said, the sarcastic slag.

"Yeah, so what?!" I went.

"Yeah, well, you can hardly get a small place in *Watford* then, can ya – not if you want your cars to still be there the following morning!" he laughed. "You'll need to get a big pad out in the country somewhere, with gates, a big drive, double garage, alarms and lights all over the place; hell, that won't be cheap!"

"Yeah, maybe," I said.

"Hell, yeah," he went; "For all that, you're gonna need a least a couple of a mil! Which means doing the scam for at least a couple of years, don't it? So we're gonna have to move around."

"Okay, yeah, I see what you mean," I said, shrugging. "We'll have to see." At that precise moment, all I really wanted to do was get home and count the money.

"So are you going to keep doing it?" he asked.

"Yeah, I guess so," I told him, "as long as Wendy's inspecting."

"What? Oh for god's sake, I don't know what you're

worried about!" (Only losing me god-rotting job and getting banged up for five years.) "Just do it like we showed you and make yourself five or ten grand every week." (Not if the heat is on, mate.) "It's so simple even a knob like you can do it; it's foolproof!" (Not if we get caught, it ain't.) Just to shut him up, I said:

"Okay, okay; Jesus!" But I had already decided that I'd only do it if Wendy was inspecting. "Though I'll tell you what," I said, "if ever there was a time to do it, it's got to be this coming Monday."

"Why do you say that?" Sincs asked quickly.

"Cos I've checked the rota, and you, me and Wendy are all on a double and the rest of the crew are no danger," I said. "We can really nail 'em!"

"Who else is on?"

"Georgie Shields is the other inspector, and then there's Tracy Houghton and Sharon Jacobs," I informed him. "I dunno who the manager is."

"Well they're no threat, and who cares who the manager is?"

"Yeah, well," I said, laughing; "We should all get at least two or three good cracks at it!"

"Yeah, seeing as Sharon and Tracy are both crap!" he laughed in return.

"Yeah," I agreed as we turned around and headed back towards the car; "Not a bad idea of mine, this: coming up here away from spying eyes," I told Sincs.

"Yeah, and no talking about anything on the phone, either," he told me with a look.

"Course not, I'm not daft; I've seen 'The Sopranos'! No, let's just keep it really low-key and meet in a different place every week, somewhere even more out of the way than this, okay? Somewhere that no-one from work would ever go, and early in the day if possible, before any of those cocks from the casino are up and about." He nodded.

"Yeah, though you never know!" he said, and we both laughed. "And don't put any of the money in a bank or anything, all right? Don't leave any records that might be traced; keep it hidden at home, somewhere your parents won't think of looking."

"Yeah, I know." Where, though? "What are you going to do with yours?" I enquired.

"Save up, buy a flat outright and rent it out; and then do it again and again, as often as I can," he said.

"Yeah; smart!" I went, almost unable to take it all in; looking around again, I said: "Come on, let's get going; hell where am I going to stash this lot?" He shrugged.

"Dunno; I've put mine in a plastic bag which I've

shoved in a hole in my mattress; hardly ideal, but better than in my underwear drawer!" Sincs laughed.

"Yeah, my Old Dear would find it in mine immediately; maybe I should bury it in the garden."

"Nah, you'd only forget where you'd buried it!"

"Oh, have a word!"

"Or your Old Man would dig it up when he was doing his potatoes!"

"Oh shut up, you penis!" I went, and he started laughing, as usual.

"Or your dog would dig it up while searching for a bone!"

"*Screw... you!*" I told him, causing him to crack up even more.

We arrived back at the car and clambered in. Glancing around, I ripped open the envelope and pulled out the big wad of notes but even as I started leafing through them I realised that it was *nowhere near* the ten grand I was expecting.

"Whoa, whoa, hang on a sec!" I cried; "What the hell's this?"

"What?" Sincs went.

"Here, look!" I said, and started counting out the

284

money into Sincs' hands. "There ain't nothing like ten grand here, look!" I told him, as I quickly counted out the few thousand quid that was there; it came to a grand total of three grand, all in twenties. "You've gotta be joking!" I said, "I ain't putting my career on the line for three poxy thousand pounds; stuff that for a game of soldiers!"

"How much did you pay him?" Sincs asked.

"At least twenty grand," I told him.

"Twenty? Are you sure?" I nodded. "Hmm, yeah, you should have got more than three grand."

"Damn right I should," I went; "Cos this is taking the total bloody piss!" I was furious, and try as he might Sincs couldn't calm me down. "Bollocks!" I shouted, "I ain't doing it on Monday and that's that – screw him!"

"Oh, shut up!" Sincs cried. "What – you don't want to make yourself another three grand in one day?"

"Eh? You don't get it, do you? He's taking the total Mickey out of me; out of *us*; he's as bad as the frigging casino! Well, mate, you go back, you go back now and tell him that if he expects me to do it again he owes me at least seven grand, and I ain't doing a thing until I get it! And he can lose out on another ten large on Monday if he wants to treat me like some kind of *twat*."

Sincs tried again to calm me down but just made me

285

worse, so much so that I eventually insisted we drive to a phone-box (all thoughts of being careful on the phone momentarily forgotten); he tried to talk me out of it, but I went on and on about what a piss-take it was till he finally caved in (and also, I think, he started coming round to my way of thinking).

We drove over to Aldbury, a village nearby, and found a call box just near the small duck pond they had there. We both squeezed into the box and I stood with my ear next to the receiver as Sincs rang Albert and told him the score. After some time, with me listening to all of Albert's bluster, and getting more and more annoyed, I finally grabbed the receiver out of Sincs' hand and bawled down the phone:

"Hey! I paid you twenty and I want ten; end of story! Otherwise you can forget the whole blooming thing!"

He started twittering on about the losses he had incur while playing whilst waiting for one of us to be sent to deal blackjack, but I interrupted him in mid-flow by yelling that any losses were to come out of *his* end, not ours. He tried to mollify me, but I went:

"Hey, listen mate, what are you risking, eh? Yeah, you're risking sod-all! For us, it's our careers on the line!" He tried to explain that he'd only 'won' thirty grand throughout the week and had paid us out fifteen, but I cut him off. "Hey, I hate to be blunt but it ain't like I'm being paid a salary, is it? I'm only gonna get paid on what I pay you, right? And I paid you twenty big ones, mate — so I'm expecting half of *that*, mate, not half of what everyone else paid you! And what's more, just to remind you, like, you *did* agree to half before I started with all this, didn't you?" (I'd give him 'more or less,' the chiselling piece of shit!) "Half," I went on, "and I ain't doing anything else till I've got what I'm due, okay? We've got a golden opportunity on Monday, we're all working the afternoon shift, but like I say, you can kiss good-bye to me helping you out any more unless I get my other seven grand; your choice, mate!"

And with that I handed the phone back to Sincs. "You talk to him," I told Sincs, pushing my way out of the booth. I went and sat in the Escort, from where I could see Sincs listening to Albert; when he didn't quickly hang up immediately I turned his crappy radio on. Sincs stayed on the phone for a good ten minutes (I know because I was staring at my watch throughout). I touched the envelope in my breast pocket, and I have to say: even with only three grand in it, it felt bloody good! After an eternity, Sincs hung up and returned to the car.

"He says he'll give you another three grand, but that's it; take it or leave it."

"Jesus Christ, I can't believe this guy: makes thirty grand in a *week* and refuses to cough up my fair share!"

"So what do you want to do?" Sincs asked me, and he

didn't look happy (but I didn't care as I was still fuming). But after taking a deep breath and thinking things through, I shrugged, let out a laugh, and in answer to his question, said:

"Well, I think we should go and get the other three grand, park up somewhere... and get on it!" He shrugged, muttered an 'OK' or something, and started the engine. I don't know what he was so peeved about; after all, I might have just done him a big favour. "You all right, mate?" I asked; after all, he was still my friend. He gave a sort-of laugh.

"Yeah," he went; "Honestly; you and your bloody money, for gawd's sake!"

"Do what?"

"You're *so* tight!"

"No I ain't!" I hollered.

"Yeah you are!" he yelled back, "And now you're making me drive all the way back to Watford to get you some more!"

"I just don't like being taken for a ride!" I said.

"Yeah, yeah," he went, sighing.

"And I hate flipping Watford," I said, "it's bad enough having to work here, let alone visit it on my day off," I whined.

"Oh, for heaven's sake!" Sincs wailed.

He negotiated the back streets into Wendy's road and managed to find a space not far from her house. "I'll wait here," I told him and he nodded and, leaving the engine running, nipped across the road, banged on her door and I soon saw him disappear inside but I didn't have to keep up a vigil for spying casino eyes for long; after a couple of minutes he was back and had stuck it in gear and we were on the move again. "You got it?" I went, and he nodded; we didn't say another word till we'd gone all the way back to my house and he was parking up outside. "Come in for a sec," I said, and we went inside and straight up to my room. Locking the door behind me – I'd have to do that all the time from now on, I reminded myself – I said: "Where is it?"

"Here," Sincs replied, pulling out another thick brown envelope and handing it to me; I tore it open and counted it out on my bed: another three grand (and this time in fifties, whoopee!). I nodded.

"Fair enough," I said.

"So now you've got six grand; you happy now?" Sincs whispered sarcastically, which jolted me into action and reminded me to turn on my stereo and I whacked the volume up. "What's this rubbish?" Sincs went, as the Cocteau Twins blasted out.

"Aw, shut up! So is he gonna give you half in future?" I asked him.

"Yeah, we talked about that and I think he is from now on."

"Well, we'll see what happens on Monday, won't we? I ain't gonna take any shit, you know? Not where me money's concerned," and he pursed his lips and nodded. "So," I asked, clapping my hands and laughing, "where're we going for a serious drink?!"

On Sunday I had a lie-in and then went for a long walk with Cinnamon; there was no sign of my brother Simon, so I could relax and think things through, concluding finally that it had been an OK start to the scam; six grand, whoopee!

Whilst getting ready for work on Monday lunchtime I was feeling both nervous and excited at the same time. I shaved, took a long hot shower, went downstairs to have a bite of lunch with Mum, passed through the kitchen into the dining-room and bumped straight into my Old Man; on a week day lunchtime he was normally either out at work or — more usually — skiving off somewhere playing golf, but here he was at home, sitting at the dining table and reading the paper! In the normal course of events I tried to avoid him mid-week, but today he seemed pleased enough to see me, the miserable old sod.

"You're up early," he said.

"Overtime," I grunted, plonking myself down at the table across from him.

"Oh well, you'll be rich soon," he said, in a pathetic attempt to be funny.

"Yeah," I muttered, waiting for Mum to bring the lunch in.

"So how's the job going?" he enquired, folding up The Times, placing it on the table and giving me the eye-ball.

"Er, yeah; okay, I guess; tiring," I told him.

"Have you met any nice girls there yet?" I just shook my head in disbelief and just stared at the moron; Jesus Christ, did he really want to have a 'conversation' with me about my taste in women? He was nearly *fifty*, for god's sake! Well I'd give him conversation, the idiot! I'd got six grand − *six grand*! − hidden in my room, which was more money than I'd had in my entire life, so I launched right in:

"Rich? *Rich*? I'll give you rich!" I went. "Let me tell you something: I'm trying to save up for a deposit on a flat; I'm trying to pay you back for the loan on the MX5; I'm trying to put a bit aside for when I upgrade the MX5; I wanna put aside some cash for a rainy day − an' I'm *still* trying to give Mum some housekeeping money every week!

"Of course, any decent parent – once they realised that their kid was working his nuts off trying to save up so he could get a place of his own – would let him off the housekeeping and postpone the car loan – after all, that's what parents are for, right? – but nah, not me, *I* have to pay for everything, even if that means me doing sixty-hour weeks almost every single week as that's the only way that I'll ever get ahead, isn't it, otherwise I'll never be able to get a place of my own, will I? Damn!"

Bloody bloke! But he just sat there, regarding me mildly. So I said:

"So yeah, after next pay day, I've decided to pay off the money I borrowed from you for the car and then I'll be moving out, how does *that* sound, *father*?"

He shrugged. "Very admirable," he sniffed. "So, have you been looking at anything in particular?"

"Eh?" I went.

"Are you looking at any flats or properties in particular?"

"Eh? Oh, no, not really." And then: "But it'll defo be a place out in the country, a big place with a double garage that I'll need for the Rolls that I'm gonna buy myself as a house-warming present," I said.

"Very nice too," he said, leaning forward to pick the newspaper up again and obviously not believing a word

I'd said. "Houses like that go for what, five or six hundred thousand?"

I shrugged.

"So they've given you a pay-rise or two, I take it? Then whatever you like, kiddo," he said with another sniff.

Bloody bloke! I was just gearing up for a proper old row but then Mum came in with one of my favourite lunches – home-made vegetable soup and fresh bread rolls with cheese and pickle – so I tucked in and completely ignored the Old Man for the five minutes that it took me to scoff down lunch, after which I dashed upstairs, grabbed my keys, bow-tie and jacket and then ran back down and out to the car.

Bloody bloke!

After about an hour at work (and a lot of pussy-footing around), I managed to get five minutes in the staff-room alone with Wendy and explained to her how crucial it was that she doctor any incriminating paperwork (related to me), and she said she could 'sort it, no problem', which put my mind at ease somewhat; all she had to do was change my name for that of another dealer on the pit sheet (or even just change the amounts on the win/loss table sheets) and it would look like other dealers had been making all the big payouts. It was tricky, but simple enough – as long as Wendy could get away with it.

In truth, I liked all of the crew who were working that afternoon: Georgie Shields (an inspector, like Wendy), Sharon Jacobs and Tracy Houghton (mere dealers, who might not have been as efficient at the table games as Sincs and I, but they were all likeable enough – and with far less of the attitude that so many of the more experienced dealers and inspectors developed); ordinarily I'd look forward to working with this crew, but today I had bigger fish to fry and a lot on my mind, so might have been a little stand-offish.

The only downside to the afternoon was that our manager was Anthony Nilsson, a complete and utter arsehole, but fortunately for us he usually spent most of the shift on the gaming floor acting the big-shot in front of the girls (to get in their pants) or in the bar acting the big-shot in front of the punters (and getting pissed); yes mate, I thought, you're going to need a stiff drink after today, you useless prick! He was probably in a fairly good mood (for him), seeing as there were two attractive girls working the shift, but that meant nothing to me since he was always a complete tosser to all the other blokes there; I hated him, I really did – and suddenly decided to pay Albert out *an absolute rake-load*.

I didn't have to wait long, seeing as Albert was one of the first players to come in that afternoon; he walked straight over to BJ1 and Wendy (as senior inspector and acting afternoon pit boss) instructed Sinclair to shuffle and then deal the cards. I was already standing at AR5, and spent an infuriating forty minutes watching Sincs pay Albert out about three grand per shoe whilst I dealt roulette to two elderly ladies and a miserable old Scottish bloke; after we'd all been on a 20-minute break (Sincs and Wendy wanted their greasy staff breakfasts) I spent another forty minutes doing exactly the same (dealing on AR5 to pot-less punters with Wendy inspecting); what a joke!

Then we went on to breaks of 15 minutes during which Georgie took a turn on the BJ game and won a few shoes, so he stayed there for over an hour. Then Wendy had a go, and out went over ten grand in half an hour. Nilsson had been bringing a five grand 'fill' to the table on almost every shoe, so then he ordered Wendy to open up BJ5 – our £500 box-limit table – and Wendy stuck me on there immediately, and so I finally had the chance to start paying Albert out around seven grand per shoe; I got through four shoes before Sharon got sent over to take me off, and I actually lost track of how much I paid him (and certainly wasn't going to carry around any pieces of incriminating paper with reminders on them), but I figured I was surely in for a ten grand payout next week, which was just as well seeing as I overheard Nilsson tell Wendy to change the dealer the moment any money started going out.

So then we were pretty-much buggered for the rest of the shift, and after a couple of hours of that – with us slowly beginning to pull back some piffling amounts back from other players and Albert – he slunk off home.

When we couldn't be overheard, I asked Wendy how we did.

"We're doing twenty five grand," she told me, "though that includes winning five on the two roulettes, so we've probably paid him out around thirty altogether; Nilsson's doing his nut."

"Good," I told her; "Screw him," walking off to the staff-room and giving Sincs an enormous grin when I saw him sitting in there. We sat in front of the TV grinning like idiots for the entire fifteen-minute break; no words were spoken but every couple of minutes Sincs would glance at me and start fizzing and then we'd just piss ourselves laughing. And I really enjoyed dealing roulette that afternoon, trying to keep the games going as fast as possible and recoup as much money as possible.

By the end of the shift we'd really hammered the poor punters on roulette, and what with the straight blackjack shuffle we'd made almost ten grand (which was excellent for a Monday afternoon, but it still meant we were losing twenty grand overall; BJ5 was losing almost that entire amount alone!).

And so when Albert sauntered back into the casino just after eleven, the word went round like wildfire and everyone wanted a crack at him.

Percy Collins (the casino's senior pit boss) was now in charge of the pit, and kicked-off the battle with our most experienced, efficient and (currently) luckiest dealers; after that onslaught, he used some of our better dealer/inspectors and finally he resorted to our most senior inspectors (most of whom had worked there for aeons and expressed an interest in battering him).

Late in the night (just after three) I was given another crack at him, but I didn't even bother with the crooked shuffle, and after a nod, whisper and wink from me, Albert did back about a grand and finally departed the casino just before we closed; I later learned that he'd done back six grand in the course of those five long hours, and the casino itself had clawed its way back to being almost in the black – but not quite – so I was very glad when I was 'chopped' at four am. (since I *really* didn't want to have to stay behind and close tables for an hour, not with all the managers acting like jumped-up little Hitlers and like looking like thunder, the frigging twats!).

I headed straight back home and went directly to bed; I was physically and mentally exhausted (yet again). I'd seriously underestimated the stresses of running a scam along with trying to deal efficiently (and win money) elsewhere, and it was really taking its toll on me; after all, I couldn't afford to make even the smallest of errors and had to be 100% alert at all times. I'd worked hard on all the other tables to try and get a result and I think it was simply the pure adrenalin (and the money, and the fear of getting caught) that was seeing me through.

Albert came in the casino and played for long sessions every day that week but I only got one longish stint with him, managing to shell him out about five grand, but that was it for the week; circumstances prevented me from paying him out anything more, and to tell you the truth I really didn't mind; working as a dealer was taxing enough at the best of times, let alone with all these extra pressures!

On Saturday afternoon at four o'clock, I was parked in a lay-by, on a rise, in a quiet lane opposite the London Gliding Club near Dunstable; it was a little-used road, and when parked on the brow of the hill one could easily see any approaching vehicle (or dog walker, or horse rider, or rambler). I knew Sincs would be late but I didn't care: it was a sunny day, I had the MX5's hood down, the CD player was up loud (I was moaning along to This Mortal Coil) – and I was about to be paid twelve thousand pounds in cash – so what did I care? The way I was feeling, the casino could have sacked me and I still wouldn't have given a monkey's.

I had woken early, around eleven, and had nearly driven out to a pub for a heavy celebratory luncheon, but in the end decided against it, as I didn't want to have – what I hoped was going to be – a great day spoilt with a boozy head, so I took a shower and then went for a long spin in the MX5 (hood down, wondering what to blow the twelve – no; eighteen grand! – on) and took a thoughtful stroll along the Grand Union Canal. Then I had a late lunch in a pub, went for another spin and finally made my way to the pre-arranged meet.

When Sincs clattered up in his old banger (at four-thirty) I was still sitting happily in my black convertible, grinning like the Cheshire Cat; but as he pulled in behind me in his old Ford I waved at him, fired up the MX5 and he followed me to a deserted car park near a local picnic spot in the nearby village of Totternhoe. We locked-up and left the cars and went for a walk, and (as I'd hoped) we didn't see a single person all afternoon.

"So, how much did you get?" I immediately asked, as Sincs grinned, glanced suspiciously around and then handed me a *really thick* brown envelope.

"He gave me fifteen grand," he replied, "And Albert says there's ten in there for you." So then there was a bit of a pregnant pause, while I decided whether there was any point in flying off the handle again. I was owed, I reckoned, at least twelve, maybe even fifteen grand. The question was: would I get the other two-to-five grand that I *thought* I was owed, even if I did kick off? And I knew the answer: probably not. So I smiled and said:

"Cheers mate, that's great; now I've only got to find another, oh, four hundred and eighty four grand towards a nice place!"

"What you on about? You can get a crappy flat in

Watford for around two hundred grand!" he went.

"I'd rather eat my own shit!" I cried, and he laughed. "I wanna move out this way and get a big house in a nice village, and that'll cost at least half a mil! So yeah, anyway, did he say anything else?"

"Only that he felt you had a couple of opportunities that you missed, but overall he's okay with you."

"Well, he can go screw himself," I said; "In fact, I think we should give it a break for a week or so."

"What; *why*?"

"Aw, just to the heat cool down a tad; the idiot managers have been running around cacking themselves even more than usual."

"Yeah, I noticed," he said, laughing.

"Yeah, I know, but still," I went; "No harm in lying low for a week or two, is there? And Albert could even do back a bit, every now and then; it makes it look a lot more realistic and generally straighter, know what I mean?" I thought it was an eminently sensible suggestion, but Sincs just laughed.

"He ain't going to want to be paying them back anything, is he?" Sincs cried. "No mate, forget about him doing that."

"Well, okay then, how about us just not doing it for a

week or so?"

"What? But that'd be the same as him just handing the money back, wouldn't it – you div!"

"Well, okay then; but in that case, just tell him that I'm going to be giving it a miss for a week or so." But Sincs just stood there, looking at me like I'd lost my marbles. "What?" I went.

"I ain't telling him that!" Sincs railed; "No way; you can tell him yourself! But I'll tell you what: he won't be happy; no way will he be."

"Oh blimey, it was just an idea; no need to mess your pants."

"Look, you can't just do this for a couple of weeks and then stop, you know," he told me shortly. "The way to do it is to hit them hard, and for as much as possible over the shortest period of time! After all, they could bar him or sack us at any time."

"Bar him for what?"

"For winning," he said.

"Eh? They ain't gonna bar him yet though, are they? Not while he's holding the casino's money!" I pointed out.

"They might do; you never know. They might do, if we go on for another month and he keeps winning." I hadn't even considered this possibility, but would definitely have to mull that one over. We had arrived at a large meadow and found a warm, sunny, windless corner where we could sit out of the way and talk, and where I could see immediately if any ramblers were approaching and – most importantly – count my money.

It was mostly in twenties, but there were some nice fifties in there, and yes, there was exactly ten grand. I pushed it back into the brown envelope and shoved it back in my jacket pocket, and try as I might I couldn't get a massive grin off my face. Even if they sacked me, I was sixteen grand up; it would've taken me *forever* to save that sort of money; Jeez Louise, I was almost levitating with delight!

"You bell-end!" Sincs said, laughing at me grinning inanely.

"What the hell am I gonna do with it all?" I laughed; "If my Old Dear finds any of this in my underwear drawer she'll shit!"

"I told you already: stick it under your mattress."

"Nah, that's too obvious, and anyway, my parents have never trusted me; they're forever looking for guns and what not! Maybe I'll come up here one day and bury it under a tree."

"You bell-end!" he said again, laughing and rolling around on the grass.

Seeing as Sincs was under orders to take his girlfriend out that evening, I ended up driving home and stashing all the money he'd given me in between the pages of some large hardback encyclopaedias I'd got under my bed (that I knew no-one would ever look at). I'd have to remember to keep the door to my bedroom locked at all times from now on; not that this would prevent a determined police search, but hopefully it would keep family pests at bay (to wit: my Ma and the cretin that was my brother Simon), till I could remove the cash to a safer place. I was now seriously obsessing as to where that place might be; hell, I'd always pictured myself as a pirate burying his loot, and all being well I'd soon be doing just that!

After I'd put all the cash in my books I sat on my bed, suddenly at a loss for what to do; hundreds of thoughts were whizzing around in my head, and I needed time to sort and file them. I almost picked up the phone and called my mates Maurice and David to see if they wanted to go out for a drink, but something made me pause; Maurice and David were my best friends (I'd known Mo since school and met David at college) but they were both totally straight blokes, and I knew I could never tell them what I'd been doing at work (they'd probably try to talk me out of it, though I doubted they'd dob me in it or waste their breath telling me to turn myself in – though you never knew!).

I still saw them fairly regularly, as I did with my other best friends from school and college – Andrew, Sarah and Vanessa – but again, they were all law-abiding people (just like most people in my social circle), and my partner in crime from school, Jerry, had joined the Army on his sixteenth birthday (and was currently in Thailand, shagging anything that moved and doing a roaring trade selling stolen army equipment to the black market; damn, I missed Jerry!).

Well, I say I saw them regularly but it wasn't nearly as often since I'd started at the casino since the truth was – as any gambler will tell you – nothing outside casino is remotely as interesting as what goes on inside, yet non-gamblers will never understand the attraction. I'd actually found it quite hard to talk to non-casino people about all the goings-on at work, and perhaps this was why they had so many parties after work, so that they could talk about the casino intricacies with people who understood.

So instead of phoning anybody, I decided to take my rough collie Cinnamon out for a walk; I didn't want to sit around the house on a Saturday night like a complete loser and particularly not tonight since my moronic brother Simon was hanging around with some of his horrible mates, and we'd only end up having a ruck which could easily escalate into serious violence, as it had numerous times in the past; the last time they'd ganged up on me they'd definitely got the worst of it (since I'd had my 8-shot CO_2-powered Beretta on me at the time).

My younger brother was a great big lump of a twat, two years younger, four inches bigger and five years slower than me; he was like a rather stupid bull in a china shop – yet people thought he was the nicer of the two of us, can you imagine?! Normally I'd look forward to a semi-harmless ruck with the mong but tonight I needed a quiet think, so (just in case) I slipped my loaded Beretta (plus a couple of extra mags) into the waistband of my jeans and took Cinny out.

Whenever I had a knotty problem to solve, I would spend days or even months scheming and plotting; this hadn't helped me pass many of my exams, but boy, had I acquired (relatively) large sums of money (and met a lot of interesting people) over the years! And deciding what to do with the equivalent of almost two years' pay (in cash) would likewise take many weeks of machinating.

The truth was, that for someone like me (white, middle-working class, with about average looks, about average intelligence and few family connections) there was no easy way of achieving an exceptionally good lifestyle (except by committing a big crime); in other words, not a lot had changed in society for five hundred years (if ever): to scam or not to scam, *that* was the question.

And not scamming meant a life of drudgery – if not

downright slavery – for the next forty years: forty years! Unless one went to uni for seven years, gained a good degree and then had a stepping-stone into a great job afterward you were buggered, doomed to be a wage-slave for eternity; there was simply no way for a chap like me to live anything close to the good life.

As I walked along with Cinnamon, I pondered; it seemed that I was now in the fortunate position of having been given a goose that laid little golden eggs – up to a point. But one thing was clear (even to a guy like me): the more Albert (or any punter) won, the more the dozy casino management would begin to suspect that trickery was involved, which added further weight to my belief that it was better to hit them hard for a sizeable amount cash and then stop the scam completely. In fact, after stopping the scam it might be a good idea for us to really try to clean up on the tables (in the house's favour) so that the casino managers could see that we were working hard to make them big profits.

I knew that having large amounts of loose cash lying around, especially at my age, could be dangerous, since it was just so easy to find enjoyable things to blow it on: cars, clothes, jewelry, girls, booze, drugs, bling, gadgets, you name it, hell, it was almost frightening – but if my Old Dear found sixteen grand in my bedroom she'd blow her stack!

In many ways, one of the best things I could do with all

the cash would be to plonk the entire amount down as a deposit on a house, but even that would leave a dreaded paper trail (that investigative prosecutors might uncover at some later date); and absolutely the worst thing that I could do would be to buy a big, flashy car, for that – more than any other thing – would show the whole world that I just had to be doing something naughty; Jeez Louise, there'd be eyebrows shooting up all over the place if I started tooling around in a bright red convertible E-Type (or new Jaguar F-Type)!

So probably one of smartest things I could do with all my loose cash was simply to hide it, not tell a living soul, try to forget about it and see what the next few months might bring.

I was very pleased that Sincs hadn't traded his tatty old Escort in for something more expensive; it proved to me that he was being smart about things and that I'd made the right choice to trust him; I was both pleased and proud of him.

I walked to our local park, smoked a cheap cigar and wandered round for an hour, mulling things over. I was asked by a couple of girls for a light (which I politely provided; I always carried an expensive lighter, though I rarely smoked anything other than a cheap cigar), and we ended up wandering around and chatting for another hour till we were asked to leave by the park keeper (who wanted to lock the gates).

I briefly considered asking the teenage girls for a number but didn't because (a) I didn't need any new romantic distractions at the moment, and (b) my bottle went, so I walked home, locked myself in my room, poured a stiff glass of Bacardi and made a few obscure notes about what to do with all the cash; then I had a couple more stiff drinks and eventually fell into bed, half-pissed.

Simon Shilling was loitering with two of his mates round to the side of his parents' house, where they were sharing a crafty joint and taking surreptitious swigs from the third can of lager he'd pinched from the fridge.

Simon had just seen his hateful older brother stalk out of the front door with his devoted (and ferocious) hound, and momentarily considered following him and giving him a smack; but he didn't want to take Chris on when he had his vicious mutt with him, and it was quite possible that the bastard was armed with his nasty black Beretta or a flick-knife; you never knew with him. He decided against mentioning the idea to his mates, Robbie and Danny (since they'd been with him the last time they'd tried to bushwhack Chris, and all three of them had received a hiding); better to wait until they had got Tom and Stan with them, and then really batter the bastard.

It made Simon's blood boil how that everything Chris touched seemed to turn into gold: the contraband cigarettes and flick-knives he'd smuggled back from their Spanish holidays (and sold to all the teenage tearaways at school); the booze and the air guns (plus sights and pellets) that he'd bought and sold (at massively inflated prices) to all the under-age town hooligans; the off-road motorcycle Chris had rented out to the local teenage motor-bike nuts (at extortionate prices to kids who knew no better) and he'd never once been caught – not once! It made Simon's blood boil.

Even when Simon had gone out for a 'friendly' afternoon's shooting with his brother and Chris had shot him in the back, wounding him painfully with his powerful air rifle, he'd *still* managed to avoid being nabbed (mainly because Simon had been carrying an illegal air pistol at the time and had narrowly missed shooting Chris in the face earlier).

And now the bastard was working as a dealer in a casino or something (and no doubt stealing them blind) and posing around in a convertible MX5, the wanker! Simon shook his head, swore and took another guzzle from the can of lager.

"'Sup, dude?" grunted Danny, already half-stoned; he was a tall, pale, seventeen-year old drop-out who wore dirty dungarees and sported a great mop of shaggy red hair.

"Aw, nothing; just my fuckin' brother," Simon muttered.

"That fucking wanker!" spat Robbie (who'd received a slap, a black eye and two pellets to the stomach – and come off by far the worst – during their last semi-violent encounter with Chris).

"What do you wanna do, go and bottle the dick head?" asked Danny.

"Nah, I just seen him fuck off for a walk with his fuckin' dog, and he's probably got his pistol on him again; nah, fuck him," Simon replied.

"Yeah; fuck him," said Robbie. "We'll get the cunt another day."

"Why don't we just key his car?" asked Danny.

"Yeah, cool!" went Simon, brightening considerably.

"Oh, no way man!" wailed Robbie.

"Why not?" yelled Simon belligerently.

"Cos he'll know it was us and do us for sure!" said Robbie, shaking his head and dragging on the roach.

"Oh; yeah," went Simon and Danny in unison.

"Remember what he did when we kicked in the door of that fucking old Beetle he's got? The fuckin' cunt," muttered Robbie.

"Yeah, Si, your fucking Mum caught us and grassed us up to him, the bastard. Maybe we could jump him when he comes back," suggested Danny, but the others shook their heads.

"Nah," said Simon; "He can be an evil fucker when he's in the mood; let's just grab a couple more cans and head over to yours before he comes back; we'll get him another day, the snide piece of shit."

"Yeah; do him good and proper with baseball bats," said Robbie.

"Yeah; get Stan and Tom over as well; they hate him too," said Danny.

"Yeah, that sounds cool; come on, let's shoot over to Tom's, he's always got some weed," said Simon, and they grabbed another couple of cans and loped off.

Late the following morning, after Mum, Dad and Baby Brother had driven off in the stately old DS (to my grandmother's for lunch) I slunk downstairs and crept out into the back garden. I had come up with a cunning plan, and although I knew it wasn't perfect it was a helluva lot better than leaving sixteen large in between the pages of my dusty dictionaries and encyclopaedias.

First I went into the garden shed and rooted out my Old Man's garden spade and a battered old trowel; then I went round to the back of the shed where Dad kept an old oil drum; heaven knows where he'd got it, it was rusty, pitted with ugly gouges and was currently half-full of dirt and crap; the last time I'd been near it was when I'd gotten my brother to try to walk on it (and then kicked it out from under the twat; happy days). I man-handled the drum to the side of the shed and proceeded with my plan, for although I wasn't wearing an eye patch or cutlass I was about to bury my loot.

I got the spade and started digging, piling load after load of dry earth next to the shed, taking frequent breaks to stop and listen and make sure no neighbours or spies had spotted me. The digging got harder and harder, and then I belatedly remembered that we lived in a 'hard water' area: in other words, we had high chalk content in our local geology (the Chiltern Hills). Cursing – cos the last thing I needed was a *fucking blister* – I banged the shovel into the hard chalk and continued digging. After another hour I would have given up except I didn't know what else to do.

You know, digging a deep hole in a hard-earth area is bloody hard work, even at the best of times – in a forest, say – and it's difficult going down further than three or four feet, but you try digging six feet down through solid chalk in your own back garden! I could see that I was going to have to slightly revise my cunning plan; I'd been digging for over two hours, at possibly the only time in the entire week that I knew everyone else in the house would be gone for three or four hours, and I'd only managed to delve about three feet down! No wonder they buried stiffs six feet under;

no-one would *ever* be bothered in digging 'em up!

Giving up with the back-breaking digging, I nipped back inside the house and rooted out all the banknotes, neatly double-wrapped them in cling-film, then placed the bundle of ten grand into a seal-able plastic container and then placed *that* inside a couple of plastic carrier bags which I thoroughly taped up; back outside I put the package into the hole, hurriedly covering the sealed package with chalk and then dry earth till the hole was level with the rest of the garden; finally I manhandled the old, black oil drum back into its previous position.

Obviously I was hoping that if there *was* a police search, with metal detectors and all that bollocks, they would detect sod-all. I was using this episode as something of a dummy run, of course, for I'd soon be buying a little metal detector of my own and I already had in mind some little-used spots where I could bury my treasure where the digging would be easier; in future, though (in some out-of-the-way spot) I would place an old tin can half-way between the package and the topsoil, thus making it easier for me to locate the stash.

I returned to my room, replaced the six grand back inside an encyclopaedia, took a shower – I'd been sweating like a dog – and then changed into some nicer clothes; then I fired up the MX5 and drove round to show my face briefly at my Grandma's. I'd always got along pretty well with my Grandmother and my step-Grandfather, more so than with my parents really, and in my early teenage years had often gone round to their flat for lunch and a few games of cards (Canasta, mostly); nowadays I only saw them four or five times a year, so it was the least I could do to pop round for a while now that I had a spare hour or so but I wasn't very good company that day (seeing as the entire time I was round there I spent wondering what to do with my ill-gotten gains), and as soon as it was polite I made a move.

I jumped back in the car and went for a drive up to Ashridge Forest, a local beauty spot only six miles away from home; seeing as it was a Sunday afternoon, and a nice one at that, I knew there would be plenty of day trippers out for a stroll, but that was the point: I wasn't going to be burying any more money today but I wanted to go for a walk in the woods, somewhere not too far from a car park but at the same time somewhere that wouldn't, for whatever reason, attract a large number of walkers.

The soil up here was far less hard and chalky than in Berkhamsted, and I figured that it would only take me an hour or so to dig (and then conceal) a four-foot-deep hole in the ground (assuming I wasn't being disturbed by ramblers). I drove up to the most popular area, around the Ashridge monument, but, much as I'd suspected, it was jammed with cars, people, kids, dogs and all their stuff, so I proceeded back to the main road, swung a left, drove a mile or so and took another left turn, driving along a narrow road and finally pulling over into one of the little car parks on the left hand side of the road, which looked much quieter than the main car parks. I got out but left the hood down – there was nothing in the car worth nicking once I'd removed the face-off stereo – and wandered off up the trail, making a mental note of the bigger trees which sat to the right and left of the path.

I took a couple of short detours and within the space of half an hour had picked out four or five good possibilities; I then returned to the car and drove over to the Totternhoe Knolls, the picnic area in a village about ten miles from home (where Sincs and I had gone for a walk the previous day). There were two other cars parked there but this didn't dissuade me from having a wander and taking a look, so I got out once more, mooched along up the slightly muddy path which lead to the large squarish meadow below the old 'castle mound', and here I wandered around for about an hour, again making a mental note of any good possibilities for a burial site.

The earth was chalkier up here and the digging would take me longer, but I had to weigh this with the fact that it was a much quieter area than Ashridge and seldom, if ever, busy. I reminded myself to pop back up here in the early evening, maybe before I went in to work, to see if anybody came up here at such times. I was very familiar with the area, which helped, and already knew which ramblers' paths and bridleways were the busier ones (and thus to be avoided). I found a number of likely places to bury my loot, then headed back to the car and went home for a doze; all that digging had worn me right out!

I was back in to work the next day, and wasn't looking forward to it whatsoever; I had another double shift and Wendy was one of the inspectors (though Sincs was only doing the night shift), so I knew Albert would come prowling around at some point. I'd had yet another restless night, trying to figure out what to do, and had finally decided to do the crooked shuffle only when Wendy was inspecting me, pay the bastard out five or ten grand, and then indicate that I wasn't going to give him any more; Wendy could easily doctor the paperwork if I didn't go too crazy with the payouts. I was dreading the day that some conscientious manager would check the 'pit control sheets' and see that golden boy Shilling had paid Albert over one hundred thousand pounds (or whatever)... if *that* happened, my career wouldn't be worth the paper it was written on. I didn't regret all the massive payouts of the previous week, but from now on I'd have to be much more careful. If in future Wendy could make the payouts disappear – or, even more preferably, indicate that some other dealer had made the payouts – the scam would be just about as close to perfect as possible, but even that was risky.

And that afternoon when I was alone in the staff-room with Wendy I said as much, and was surprised when she agreed, although even when she said she could fiddle the paperwork so that ten grand could be made to represent other dealers' payments (and apparently show that I had had some winning sessions) I told her point-blank that I'd be taking things easy today.

The manager of the shift was Mary MacCreith, the awful, witch-like casino assistant manager, and today she was worse than ever: she was like a dog with a bone, hanging around the tables all the time and trying to make small-talk with Albert, in a pathetic attempt, I guessed, to distract him from 'card-counting' (she was still instructing all us dealers to cut the deck in half, silly old slag), but whenever I was dealing blackjack (and Bloody Mary wasn't skulking around), I'd do the crooked shuffle and was slowly managing to pay Albert out around three grand each time I dealt to him; and on the roulette tables, to try and keep my results up, I went in to 'pay and spin' mode and really went for the jugular. It wasn't a method of dealing that I enjoyed but it usually got results for the dealer, and by the end of the afternoon shift I was knackered, and dozed straight off when I got in the staff-room, oblivious to all the noise; no doubt someone would wake me up just before ten.

The rest of the week was similar: me doing as little fiddling as I could get away with, but if the timing was right I'd pay Albert out as much as I could (with Wendy cooking the books). By the time I left work just after four on the Saturday morning I was mentally shattered and ended up sleeping soundly through most of my Saturday off.

When I finally met up with Sincs at six that evening in one of the crummy pubs in Watford that he favoured, and he looked like the cat that had got the cream; as soon as he saw me enter, he got up without a word and proceeded to the gents, with me following, where – after making sure nobody else was lurking in there – he pulled out my biggest envelope yet.

"How much is it?" I whispered.

"He said fifteen large," Sincs replied – about what I thought I was due, to be fair – and so I nodded and forced the fat, brown, beautiful envelope into my already tight jeans pocket, whereupon we headed back to the bar and got the drinks in, though I was only staying for a couple because I had arranged to meet my friends Maurice and David later. "Mary's shitting in her pants," Sincs said; "We ain't had such a big winner in ages; well, not someone who didn't do it back, anyway."

"Nah," I went; "I reckon we should call it a day."

"Oh, shut up!"

"Okay; you want another?"

"What do you think?" So off I went to the bar, finding

it hard to walk what with the enormous package I had in my pants; I couldn't help but giggle.

Soon enough we went our separate way and I was back in the MX5, racing back to Berkhamsted and my friend David's mum's house, where she was having a bit of a get-together involving pizza, red wine and a game of Scrabble (allegedly).

But just before I turned into David's street, I pulled over into a small car park and, after checking there wasn't anybody hanging around and pulling the soft top up, I pulled out the thick brown envelope and quickly counted out all the money: fifteen piles of £1,000 was soon stacked across the interior of the MX5; £15,000, whoopee! I then gathered it together (it was all in tens and twenties), stuck it back in the envelope and squeezed the whole lot into the pocket of my skin-tight, sky-blue jeans; £15,000!

By the time I arrived at David's mum's house there were already quite a few people there, mostly friends of David's mum and partner Mick, though there were a fair number of people I knew from college; the pizzas and garlic bread had already been delivered and were lying around in boxes all over the kitchen but I wasn't interested in all that, and as soon as I had located myself a pint glass, filled it full of ice and poured out a sensible quantity of Bacardi 'n' diet coke – from the bottles I'd bought on the way over – I found myself a perch and got stuck in. My pal Maurice arrived soon after and he came over as soon as he spotted me; we hadn't seen each-other in what seemed like ages.

"All right, Chrissy, mate?" he asked, grinning. "How's it going?"

"Any better it'd be a crime," I said, biting my tongue to prevent myself from going: 'Oh, I scammed fifteen large from the casino last week.' Instead, I asked: "And yourself?"

"Same old, same old," he said; Mo worked for a big telephone operator doing some sort of office job. "Where's David?" he asked.

"In the back garden, talking to his old dear," I told him. I'd seen David through the kitchen window and made a rude gesture to him. "The pizza's here already."

"Oh, I had dinner at my mum's," he said, and I knew he wouldn't be boozing; no young black guy that I'd ever known touched alcohol: they preferred dancing and shagging white girls to getting drunk (whatever were they thinking?!). "How's the casino?"

"Still winning money," I replied and though he laughed I really had to change the subject fast; as I necked the rum, the desire to tell somebody about what I had been doing was becoming stronger by the second, and heaven knows what I might say if someone got me started on the subject once I was pissed.

"You still dealing roulette?" he asked.

"And blackjack now," I told him, taking a massive swig, gulping it down and then saying: "Come on, let's go rescue David;" Mo nodded and followed me out into the small back garden behind the small terraced house that David's mum Lesley lived in; en route we bumped into most of the friends I'd made whilst at college: Fiona, Vanessa, Sarah and Nicola. Come to think of it, I hadn't seen any of my college friends in months, and we were soon chatting away and telling each-other what we'd been up to.

None of my friends had ever set foot in a casino, and compared to what they were doing – office work, factory work, pub work, uni – my job must have seemed quite glamorous, so naturally I did nothing to dispel the urban myth of Mafia involvement in the casino business; in fact, I'd usually make up a few stories about our big winners and losers, the sort of clientèle we catered to, along with the greedy managers and dodgy owners that had.

Almost on cue, Fiona asked whether I'd witnessed any big losers lately.

"Yeah, the whole of the club," I told her.

"Are you on any bonuses for what you make for the casino?" Nikki inquired.

"Not exactly," I said, taking another enormous gulp of

rum and getting ready to pour another glass. "Wish I was; even ten percent would be nice. But no, that's not how it works; we get slagged-off if we don't win and we never get congratulated if we do, end of; so how are things going with you?" Nikki had gone to uni (albeit to Leeds), and she was just back home for the summer holidays. She shrugged.

"All right, I suppose; so do you make good money?" she asked, and it was all I could do not to spout a whopping great gout of Bacardi 'n' diet out through my teeth all over her. But I managed to force it down, take a deep breath, and say:

"It's getting better all the time, and I'm saving up for a new car."

"Have you still got the Beetle?"

"Oh yes, and I've also got an MX5 – and I'm soon to be getting a Lotus!" I told her, "and after that I'll get something even faster; anyway, what have you got?"

"What? I'm just a poor student, Christopher; I can't afford a car!"

"No, I suppose not," I went. "Maybe next time you're down we can go for a spin in my new Lotus."

"You bastard," she said, eyes narrowed, but I just laughed and moved on towards the back garden. "I'm going to talk to David," I said; "See you later." And it was at that moment that Vanessa chose to point at my trousers and pipe up:

"Christopher, what on earth have you got in your pocket?" Oh, shit, I'd forgotten about my little package completely. For some reason Albert had unloaded all his used tens and twenties on me, which made for quite a thick wad.

"Oh, it's nothing," I said; "Just what I was born with," trying to make a pathetic joke. I quickly pushed myself through the crowd as fast as was politely possible and finally got outside where a small crowd were gathered, all of whom seemed to be drinking red wine: sod that!

"All right, David?" I bawled, waving my glass at him; Mo was just behind me, and he'd grabbed a big slice of greasy cheesy garlic bread which he now shared with me. "Hmm, not bad," I said, munching away. "Who're all these?" I asked him.

"David told me it was Mick's birthday," Mo said; Mick was Lesley's boyfriend. "They're all social workers, or something."

"Yeah, they look like it," I said. "Well, this should be fun," I said, and he laughed.

"So work's going all right, then?" Mo asked.

I shrugged, and took a swig. "Up and down, mate, to be honest," I lied. "They get the arsehole when you lose and you get sod-all in the way of congratulations when you win; the managers actually stand next to you and kick you under the table if you pay money out, believe that? Oh, they're a bunch of arseholes, really," I said, "but what you gonna do? I'm getting paid more than I'd get doing anything else; hell, I'm probably making more money than me Dad!" He laughed.

"I wish I was!" he said. Mo's old man was a car mechanic, welder and part-owned a garage in Watford and did all right for himself; however, unlike my dad, he was extremely generous to his kids and gave them all nice cars – which he then serviced for free! Mo was currently driving a gorgeous classic car that his dad had given him which was almost as nice as our Citroen DS23: it was a Mk 1 Ford Granada, the 3.0 litre, two-door coupe automatic in dark blue; Mo had been my first mate to pass his driving test and so he'd had it since college, and it had been so much nicer than all the poxy clapped-out Nissans, Vauxhalls and old VWs the other students drove (if they drove at all); I loved that old Granada, and it made me realise that it was definitely time for me to trade-in my crappy MX5 (although I was already formulating a plan, the basis of it being that I'd keep the old Mazda as I wouldn't want to be showing off my new Lotus to the twats at work!).

"Yeah," I went; "When I get my next pay rise I think I might get another car, a fast coupé or something; a Lotus Esprit, maybe." I took another drink as David walked over to us.

"Hi," he went; "Oh, you've got yourself a drink, I see; what's that, your wallet?" he asked, pointing at the enormous package in my light-blue jeans.

"Yeah, with my weekly salary, and they only pay me in fifties," I replied dead-pan, then we both laughed.

"So how's the job going?" he asked.

"Well, it's full of surprises in one respect – how small the odds are in our favour, for example – but it's like I was just saying to Mo; the job's all right, it's just the people who have been there for a while; it's all a bit like being back at school really."

"School?" asked David.

"Yeah, school, or being in the army or something; you know, we're still just a bunch of kids really, all dressed-up in silly uniforms, being ordered around and told to behave ourselves and follow all the rules and regulations; the procedures, they call them; we used to hate the teachers and now we all hate our managers; everyone's got silly nick-names…."

"What's yours?" Mo interrupted.

"Oh, it's 'Shills' – Shills! I ain't been called that since I was twelve, for fuck's sake!" I laughed; "And then you've got the great-god-almighty rota; do you remember having nightmares about losing your timetable when you we at school?" They both grinned and nodded. "Yeah, well it's the same for us at the casino; you get a massive bollocking if you're a few minutes late or not at your table in time, not that I'm ever late; it's not worth the grief." I took another swig and then poured myself another half a pint.

"And there's like the school reports book – we call it the 'incidents' book – where any minor transgressions are noted down, and the jobs-worth managers are always justifying their stupid jobs by grassing you up and writing every tiny little event down. And do you remember our school dinners, and how crap they were? Well, it's like deja-vu, it really is; the casino dinners: what a joke! I was told when I started that we'd get a choice of an a la carte dinner from the restaurant every night; well, it turns out that the chef has got a separate budget for us gaming staff, and we don't get a choice at all; last night it was a choice between a rancid pork chop or squat!" Mo cracked up.

"It's a joke! And when you get in to the casino, normally at around half-eight, you ain't allowed outside again till you're chopped – and that's not normally till half-four – so all you can do is sit in the staff-room watching the shite on telly and breathing in everyone else's cigarette smoke! You ain't even allowed out to buy a sandwich or go for a breath of fresh air or anything! So yeah, it's *just* like being in school – or prison."

"Why won't they let you out?" David asked.

"Oh, security procedures or some such bullshit," I said. "But really it's just cos they can't be bothered and cos they're assholes, if you really want to know. No, what really riles me is that the casino are so damn *cheap* that they get the restaurant to order in separate, cheaper, crappier food for us than give us the stuff they dish up for the punters! And what are we talking about; how much more would it have cost them - fifty pence difference per dish? Compared to all the goodwill they'd have got back from us? Jeez Louise, it does my flipping swede in!"

"It's probably because the head-office accountants have never set foot in the casino," David said.

"Yeah, you're spot on, mate," I said. "The bean counters probably think that if they can shave fifty quid off one casino's food bill for the week then they're saving the group over five hundred pounds a week across the ten clubs, which means a saving of, what, twenty six grand a year? Sounds a lot, don't it?

"But think about this: say I go in to work and sit down to dinner and they serve me up a grey lump of inedible meat. Well, what am I gonna do with it? Stick it straight in the bin, like I did last night, right? And then I go out on the tables pissed off, because I feel I'm being treated like shit, you know?" They both nodded. "And so then I won't be bothered about trying to angle for a result on the tables! And this is the bit that I love: the bean counters, sitting in their ivory towers, thinking that they're being so smart by apparently saving the company twenty six grand have actually *cost* the company hundreds of thousands, maybe *millions*, in lost profits!" I laughed. "Laugh – I nearly shat!"

"Have you made any new friends at the casino?" Nikki asked, having wandered over during the tail-end of my litany of woe.

"No, not really," I lied again; "I'm still very much the new boy in town at the moment, and none of the older people give the new dealers the time of day; they're a bunch of arrogant pricks, really. Like I said, it's just like being back at school: you've got your groups, your 'cliques'; we've got the creeps, the rebels, the swots, the arse-kissers, the loners, the poseurs, the nerds, the druggies, the gays, you name it; and I'm the only completely normal one there."

"That must be a nice change for you, Christopher," said Nikki.

"Oh, do go back to Leeds and do some more studying at the tax-payer's expense, dear Nicola," I wheedled, and we all laughed.

"How busy does the casino get?" Nikki asked. "I wouldn't have thought there was enough money around here to support a casino."

"'Au contraire, Blackadder', we're certainly busy enough; apparently we've got over thirty thousand members, but we seem to get the same punters in two or three times every week; I guess we get about five or six hundred people in most nights, though it might just seem busy because we're so short-staffed, which is just crazy. You know what I said about them being cheap? Well, if they paid just slightly more in salary – an extra 25%, say – they wouldn't get so many of their dealers doing the offski down to London all the time; you can almost double your salary overnight if you do that.

"See, when we're short-staffed you get left out on the tables longer, and I'm talking for two, three or even four hours without a break, so all that happens is that even the best dealers eventually get tired and start dishing the money back out that they'd won earlier, so by apparently saving money on the wage bill it actually ends up costing them millions more in reduced profits, the mongs!

"I mean, there's no sense of team spirit at all, the management's attitude just seems to turn everyone against them and it's a wonder we win any money at all; I suppose it's just that the players get greedy and continue playing on when really they should quit and go home when they're a couple of grand ahead. I just try to keep my head down, smile, say bugger-all to the managers and do my best to win money on the tables; you get less grief if you win money on the tables, and of course I always get offered loads of overtime, and that keeps my wages healthy."

"So when are you going to be getting a place of your own?" quizzed Vanessa, who had drifted over with Fiona; "If you're earning so much, you could get a big house and we could all come and live there rent-free," she suggested.

"'Ness, have you ever heard the expression…." And I leaned over and blew her a huge raspberry and everyone laughed.

I loved all this, being the centre of attention, drink in one hand, fifteen grand in the other, wearing an expensive watch and designer clothes; mind you, it would have been ten times better if I'd pulled up in a flashy *Lotus* rather than the poxy old MX5 – but it was still all right! Even David, who was three years older than the rest of us, and who had gone to some technical college for his degree and now worked as a draughtsman for a steel manufacturing company, only drove a crappy old Renault!

(He'd had to buy it after he wrote off his convertible Spitfire when he'd overturned it into a ditch, and the only reason he wasn't crushed to death was because he fell out of the car as it flipped over and he nearly drowned instead. And it had amused me considerably that instead of calling for an ambulance – which might have brought the police sniffing around – he had hobbled home for three miles, bleeding from various wounds; he'd gone *right up* in my estimation after that.)

I extricated myself from my friends and went and poured myself another drink, and then wandered around Lesley's little house, nodding to various people that I didn't know and browsing at the books on the shelves that covered every spare inch of space; hers was the only house I'd ever been in that had plenty of books around the place (though my bedroom would have run a close second, inch for inch).

I'd always been a big reader (whenever I wasn't out and about getting up to all sorts of mischief, I'd have my nose buried in a book), and it always made me feel relaxed being surrounded by books (and people who read them), though after looking at the shelves I didn't think I would be doing much book-borrowing; stuff like 'Mores in Local Government' and 'Social Work for the 21st Century' was not exactly my cup of tea. There weren't even any young women to talk to – apart from the ones I already knew – so within a matter of minutes I was sitting inside on my own, drinking my Bacardi and trying to decide where to dig another hole.

Actually, it was more likely to be three holes, as I'd already decided to remove the ten grand from the hole behind our garden shed; it was far too close to home for comfort, and I'd concluded that a diligent police search, should there be one – and there was *bound* to be one if we carried on giving Albert seventy grand a week – was likely to find my little stash without too much trouble, and there was no reasonable explanation that I could invent as to where the money had come from.

In which case the holes would have to be somewhere far away from home, such as up in Ashridge Forest or at the Totternhoe Knolls; I might even do some burying tomorrow along with continuing to look for other potential hidey holes; I was becoming more and more paranoid by the day, but had utterly failed to convince Sincs or Wendy to cool it for a while. Having said that, considering the way we were treated by the managers the only justifiable reason for me staying on at the casino was to try to skank them for every damn penny that we could.

Now that I'd seen my friends, had a drink and sussed out that there were no interesting girls to talk to I was beginning to get bored at this party, and I was just about to finish my pint of rum and slink out of there – my friends were used to my idiosyncrasies – when I saw Vanessa coming over. Ness and I had been close at college, and although I didn't see her very often it was the sort of relationship – for me, anyway – that if she ever needed anything I'd be there for her; so I poured another glass and she came and propped herself on the edge of my armchair.

"So you're all right, then?" she asked.

"I guess so; I've got a lot on my mind, and the job isn't nearly as easy as people might think," I replied, looking up at her. "And all the money I get I have to put aside to go on a house down-payment, so basically my life sucks at the moment," I lied smoothly. "How are things with you; the pub still OK?" Ness worked as a cook in The Hope and Anchor, a country pub a few miles down the road in a village called Eaton Bray that I occasionally popped into.

She shrugged. "Oh, it's all right; I can't think of anything else I want to do. So are you going to be staying at the casino for a while?"

I grinned; "Well, it's always a trade-off, isn't it: the minimum amount of work for the maximum amount of pay, except the way it works is that you've gotta do loads of overtime just to get slightly ahead of the game."

"So how come you're not working tonight, isn't Saturday their busiest night?"

"No, that's Sunday night, but I don't work Sundays either cos I'm their blue eyed boy, and I make enough for them during the week to be given Saturday and Sunday as my days off."

"You've got green eyes," she said, smiling and running a finger through my hair.

"You know what I mean," I said, rolling my eyes and grinning.

"I haven't seen you much lately."

"Er, I've been meaning to pass by, maybe drop in for lunch, but I've been doing fifteen-hour overtime shifts three days a week and sleeping the rest of the time. I'm not getting out of bed till six o'clock on a Saturday evening!"

"So you've still got the Beetle?"

"Yeah, and a black MX5; you still driving your Dad's old Mini?"

"Yeah; so have you been looking for a flat or anything?"

"Hmm," I nodded; "I've been out to see some little houses, cottages mostly, in the villages around here but all the things I've seen that I've liked were well out of my price range and I don't want a big mortgage that I'd struggle to pay for the next twenty five years; I wanna pay cash, really, but there's no way I could afford five hundred grand!"

"So what are you going to do?"

I closed my eyes and took a deep breath. "I don't really know, to be honest; ask me again in six months; maybe I'll get a promotion and a pay rise, if I do enough brown-nosing."

She giggled. "Well, you were always good enough at that."

"Oh, gimme a break; you know me: I just keep my head down and try never to get caught!" I said, and Ness giggled again. "I've really got to shoot home and get an early night, Ness," I told her. "I haven't had one in months."

"Oh, don't be boring," she said. "Here, let me get you another drink."

"Nah, I've got a bottle here, look," I told her, pointing at the Bacardi on the floor.

"Let me top you up, then; here," she went, taking my glass and doing the honours. "So what are the girls like at the casino; have you made any 'special friends' yet?"

Now it was my turn to laugh. "No I haven't, and don't hold your breath."

"Why?" She was brushing my hair again.

"Well, how can I put it? The nice ones are all married or seeing someone, and the others are all minging; how's that?" I took a swig.

"Yeah, but minging how?"

"In nature, I mean; they're so far up themselves it's untrue – and that's just the average-looking ones! Hardly any of the girls are particularly good dealers but they get away with it because most of the managers are men, know what I mean? We blokes have to push twice as hard just to tread water."

"Yeah; well now you know what it feels like!"

"Oh, have a word; so now you want to blame me for thousands of years of ignorant male chauvinism? Do me a favour, it's your own fault for putting up with it for so long!"

"Oh, yeah?" The brushing of my hair had now stopped, for some reason. "So what are you going to do about it, Einstein?" I looked up at her and smiled. "Ooh, Christopher, don't smile like that; you look evil," Ness said. But then she'd often said that sort of thing to me.

"I've got some plans," I said, taking another swig.

"What plans?" she interrogated, pinching my cheek playfully.

"Oh, they're far too advanced for you to understand," I said imprudently, and she viciously tweaked my poor cheek but I just grinned; I'd long since worked out that displaying the opposite reaction to the one people were expecting was by far the most sensible way to behave.

"*What plans*?" she asked again, more playfully this time.

"Well," I said, drunk, "I thought I might put in an offer for the casino."

"What, for the casino?" Ness yelped, "Is it up for sale, then?"

"Everything's for sale if you've got enough money," I

336

told her with another evil grin. "Our place is always open to offers; in fact I think I heard that a big finance house is putting in a bid at the moment."

"Yeah; so how much are they offering?"

"'Bout nine million, so I heard on the grapevine," I said.

"Nine million *pounds*? *Sterling*? Where are you going to get nine million pounds? *Christopher*, are you being naughty again?"

"No, but I bet you'd like me to be," I said, gently taking her hand and delicately brushing her palm with the tips of my fingers; Ness had gorgeous green eyes, almost as nice as mine, and I stared into them, smiling.

But Ness knew me too well; "You bastard, don't try and change the subject," she said, but she left her hand in mine. I'd always been good with my hands; maybe that's what made me such a good dealer. "Where are you going to get your hands on nine million pounds?"

"I dunno."

"So what are you saying? You're going to put in a bid for nine million, but you're happy to let me keep driving that old Mini? Shilling, you're *so* full of shit!"

"What?" I went.

"You say you can put in a bid nine mil, but you pulled up here tonight in an MX5 worth a couple of grand, max! Who's bullshitting who here?" But at least she was laughing as she said it; girls with no sense of humour absolutely did my head in!

"Oh, so you were looking out of the window for me, were ya?" I said, and she shrugged; "Jeez, you sad loser!" I went, and she giggled. "So how come you can't get a normal guy, considering the number of single blokes who come in your pub?"

"I don't want a normal guy," she said, running her fingertips along my jaw and then undoing a couple of my shirt buttons; none of the off-duty social workers seemed to be paying any attention to us (more fool them) but than that's what wine will do to a man: how pathetic, alcohol had never affected *me* that way! Ness began moving her hands downwards – she'd obviously been on the cider – and then I remembered the bulging package that I had down my pants... and yet something made me want to let her hands stray, to let my good friend discover the money, to let her add two and two together and make five, to let her think that I was making a *lot* more money than I really was... and it was nice to feel the tips of her fingers caressing my chest and now starting to snake downwards....

I jerked my entire body up and swivelled out from under where Ness had somehow sat down on my lap.

"Gotta go to the little boys room," I lied, staggered towards the incredibly steep wooden stairs and clawed my way up; they were, in estate-agent speak, a 'feature' of Lesley's house/cottage, and tried not to make a mess; after I'd washed my hands and splashed water on my face, I carefully manoeuvred myself back down the stairs.

Ness was still there and had now been joined by Fiona, and all my resolutions of the immediate past started melting away especially since I now had Ness on one side and Fiona on the other (both of whom I knew liked me), and I could always make drunken excuses to myself; after all, what was the good in making loads of money in a risky way if one didn't get something worthwhile out of it, right?

"So wot sort of car shall I get meself next week?" I slurred to the girls.

"A Jaguar!" said Ness.

"A Lotus!" said Fiona.

"Both!" I cried drunkenly, "Cheers!" as Vanessa took my empty glass and poured me another drink.

I was so drunk that night that I forgot to force down a couple of pints of water before falling into bed, so consequently woke up mid-morning with a pounding headache and dodgy guts, and the feeling remained with me all day, even when I was digging poxy holes all

339

over the place.

Last night's alcoholic stupidity had elevated my paranoia to epidemic proportions, and as soon as I heard the rest of the family depart for Grandma's I was out of bed and downstairs like a shot, digging fiendishly to retrieve the ten grand I'd buried behind the shed. It took me over an hour of sweaty (and curse-filled) digging to get my little package – at it did look blooming small, sitting there in my palm – and then I was straight in the car and off up the Totternhoe Knolls with nothing more than a large trowel (and thirty large) in my backpack.

There were two other cars in the Knolls picnic site when I rocked up just after one o'clock, so I knew I'd have to keep my eyes peeled, but I wasn't really bothered because if there were too many walkers out that afternoon I could always come back on Tuesday afternoon. I left the crappy and embarrassing MX5 and stalked off up the bridleway, following the dry, rutted track and sweating off my hangover.

Making a mental note of the area, even though I knew it well already – about half-way along the track, just before it dipped down towards a pair of trees on the path – I glanced around to ensure no-one was about and then ducked off the edge of the path and up the bank, pulling myself up through the bushes by grabbing hold of roots and branches; I now found myself on a secluded ledge next to an old barbed-wire fence, with a

340

view over fields and ancient chalk workings.

I knelt down and crawled along the top of the ledge; it was obvious no-one ever came up here, but I stopped to catch my breath anyway and also to have a good listen. But it was as I thought: there was no-one around; I got out my trowel and started gouging away into the side of the bank, underneath the roots of an old bush. There wasn't too much impacted chalk, and soon enough I had a hole of about two feet in depth, into which I shoved ten grand, all double-wrapped in cling-film, inside a small Tupperware box and then taped up in a plastic bag.

Making another note of my immediate surroundings – the bush in relation to the nearest fence posts and the view beyond – I filled in the hole and scattered mud and leaves all around till it looked completely natural, and then made my way back to the path, having a quick scan around before sliding back down on to it: good! There was no-one to witness my sudden re-appearance! And then I was marching off along the track again, wiping the sweat off my brow as I went, cos I was pouring.

When I eventually arrived at the small field, I saw it had plenty of rabbits around the edges of it, a sure sign that no-one had passed by recently. I hurried across it, and then clambered down and then up a small but steep gully, underneath some huge old oak trees; now I was at the edge of the large, square field, which itself sat underneath the old hill of the site of the Norman 'castle mound.'

I skirted round to my right and came to one of the corners of the field, where I slumped down and rested for a few minutes; seeing as it was such a nice mild, sunny day, I was surprised there weren't more walkers about, but there was no sign of anyone at all, and I couldn't hear any dogs, either... so with one final glance around, I dragged myself under the low bushes and squirmed through the undergrowth, till I was covered in mud and fully enclosed by bushes and trees. The ground looked undisturbed, so I chose the largest of the bushes nearby and once more dug a hole of around two feet in depth, into which I pushed another bundle of ten thousand pounds; Jeez Louise, I prayed, please don't let any rabbit dig it up one day and then have some mangy old mongrel drag it off and hand it over to its master; damn!

Squirming back out of there, I lay low and scanned the field: still empty. So I pulled myself out, stood up, dusted myself down and went walking on, eventually burying my last ten grand under the bushes at another corner of the same field. By now, I was both knackered and covered in scratches, mud and grime, so I flopped down and had a rest for about half an hour, committing to memory where I'd buried my cash; no doubt I'd write the details down on a scrap of paper later, and then have to find yet another place to secrete the bit of paper – but that was just me. And I knew I'd probably

342

have nightmares about the money being found by some passing dog, bird-watcher or vagrant, but it was certainly the lesser of two evils compared to all that cash being discovered by the Old Bill should they raid the house, which was becoming an odds-on certainty what with us shovelling out seventy grand a week to bloody Albert.

After all that digging, I was so knackered that I overslept on Monday and didn't rock up for work till just gone one-thirty; I was sweating with nerves as I buzzed the back door for them to let me in, but nothing was said as I scurried in, dumping my jacket in the staff-room and sprinting out onto the gaming floor; I received a couple of looks from the other dealers, but nothing was said to me by Keith – the idiot pit-boss – or, as luck would have it, by Mary, again our manager for the afternoon.

Mary had been quite noticeable by her absence these last few weeks – something to do with the latest take-over bid, so I gathered – but now here she was, bustling around and checking all our pit-control float-sheets, and all of us waiting for her to agree after checking every piddling little thing before we could whack the chips into the plastic, lockable, float 'bubbles'.

I went into the staff-room and slumped into the nearest seat, and a moment later Sincs followed me in.

Before he could say anything – we both glanced around to make sure there was no-one else in there – I said:

"I don't give a fuck, mate; I really don't!" Sincs giggled, sat down next to me and straightened the creases of his dress trousers. "I'm gonna pay that twat out as much as I can today, and I don't give a screw if they fire me or not; fuck 'em!" He laughed again and I snorted, but in actual fact I'd done a lot of cogitating over the last few days and come to an inevitable – and potentially dangerous – conclusion: the scam couldn't go on indefinitely, not with Mary MacCreith forever hanging around it couldn't.

I had also belatedly twigged that Sincs, Wendy and Albert would continue with the scam till the heat became so intense that even the most *bone-stupid* of inspectors would be bound to sniff a rat and suss that there was a fiddle going on, bringing me down in flames when the scam was finally discovered – lovely! So what to do? I'd obsessed about it for days and the difficult decision that I'd arrived at was: I was fucked no matter what I did! So what the hell; in for a penny, in for a pound! (Though I would still keep trying to figure a way out.)

The afternoon was a complete pain: Albert hanging around, Mary hovering like a hawk, Sincs paying him out on every shoe and me doing my damnedest to signal to him that I wasn't interested. It was only at around six-thirty that Mary sloped off to hobnob with some regular high-rollers that I felt safe enough to shell Albert out about seven grand, which only took half an hour till I was replaced; and then I did another shovelling-out session from eight till half-past, till I got removed yet again by a furious Blackwood; I even got another go at midnight (with Wendy inspecting and cooking the books) and decided once more to do the crooked shuffle and ended up passing him out yet another five k before being yanked off the table by our senior pit boss, Percy Collins; before I could scoot off to the staff-room, he took me to one side.

"What do you think he's up to, Shills; is he counting?" It was a question I'd been asked by just about everyone and so I'd been working carefully on some good responses.

I pursed my lips and tried to look intelligent. "Do you know what? I'm not sure, but I don't think he can be counting; not entirely, anyway, cos he seems to place large bets at the start of the shoe and no regular counter does that, though that might be just to try to put us off, you know? Nah, I reckon it's a combination of basic strategy, counting, going with the flow, trying to fluster us, doubling-up when he loses, I mean, you name it! But I'll give him this: he's a good enough player, the bastard! Why, what do you reckon?"

Percy had been nodding throughout my little soliloquy; he wasn't the sharpest knife in the drawer but he was all right; he had been in the casino business for over thirty years (it may well have been his only job), and – for what it was worth – he was an OK pit boss.

He was always immaculately turned out, knew all our punters by name, achieved good results for the club, had enough savvy to be an effective interface between the egotistical managers and our highly-strung dealers, and he was usually all right with me – and that was the main thing.

He dyed his grey hair blond, but apart from that (and having a rather long nose) he looked somewhat like Frank Sinatra. I didn't know a lot about him, only that he had grown-up kids, a disabled wife and was originally from the East End of London, and so it was something of a shame that here he was, now in his late fifties but still driving a clapped-out old red Mini (similar to my Mum's) and living on one of the worst council estates in Watford; but I liked him most because he could put on a show like the best of them. And now he was asking me: "Do you think we can beat him?"

I nodded, carefully. "Yeah, it stands to reason we'll get him in the end; trouble is, he's such a good player that he might have some really lucky nights, cane us to the tune of fifty grand a night and then it'll take us ages to recoup the money – if indeed we ever do; there's definitely a case to be made for cutting our losses, I reckon," I said – for I'd just that second realised that if I could get the slag barred it'd be no bad thing for any of us, particularly me!

"Okay; go and take off Tina on AR2," Percy told me, still nodding, and I headed off to give some old English boys a hammering on roulette.

For the rest of the week Mary and Albert played a game of slag and mouse, and it proved pretty difficult for any of us to pay him out more than a couple of grand here and there, even for Sincs, who was normally completely cool and utterly brazen about it; but the bosses had obviously handed down instructions to change the dealer as soon as money started going out, so it was only on the afternoon shifts that I worked with Wendy that I could get away with shovelling out a few grand here and there.

Maurice Miller was sitting at his office desk and eating his lunch-time sandwich. He was feeling very depressed about the number of bills he'd got to pay and thinking – yet again – about the package he'd seen in his friend Chris' jeans the other night.

Maurice and Chris had been friends for years, and although Mo didn't consider Chris to be his closest friend, it wasn't far off – which was why Maurice was fairly sure that if he asked Chris to lend him a grand he wouldn't be turned down flat (he'd borrowed small sums of cash from Chris over the years, and always paid him back). Judging by the outline of the wad in Chris' pocket the other night, it *had* to be money, and by the size of it, it had to be over five grand; five grand!

It had bugged Mo during the night of the party, but before he'd been able to confront Chris he'd disappeared with Vanessa; Mo was fairly sure that Chris wasn't short of a bob or two (he never had been, come to think of it), but now he was almost certain that his old friend was doing something naughty – again.

For as long as they'd known each-other, Chris was always on the make, always on the look-out for a deal; Chris maintained a flexible ethical stance to making money (which was one of the reasons why Mo would never quite think of Chris as his very best friend), an approach which had helped considerably when Chris had started selling cigarettes, air guns and flick-knives to all the under-age hooligans at school.

It had never seemed to bother Chris that he'd been responsible for starting a hive of local industry, most of it criminal, when most of the naughtier boys at Chris' school had started shoplifting (or worse) so they could afford to buy Chris' overpriced (but otherwise unobtainable) weapons, and he was similarly uncaring when the same thing happened towards the end of October every year (when he'd sold the same tearaways thousands of fireworks) or and when he started flogging duty-free fags (that his Uncle Uncle had smuggled in from Spain), and he was just as undaunted by the fact that he was destroying the health of hundreds of kids (and possibly turning them into lifelong nicotine addicts); Chris was making a healthy profit, and that was all that mattered to him.

Indeed, Chris was genuinely gleeful when he'd come up with the idea of buying an old motorbike and hiring it out – at his usual rates – to all the local school-age (and thus under-age) bikers, and one of the stories Chris loved to tell the most was when he was teaching a local lad how to ride (naturally without tax, MOT, insurance and helmets) and they'd been spotted (and chased) by an unmarked patrol car, and Chris had eluded them by driving through the alleys of a council estate and then rapidly over the fields beyond.

'Victimless Crimes', Chris called his all business deals, was forever telling Mo he was an entrepreneur and that he that was proud he had both the brains and the balls to pull off all his little stunts.

Another favourite was when Chris had signed-up the entire engineering class at school to make him knuckle-dusters (and paying the class £10 for five hours' work; a paper-round only netted a tenner a week!); old Mr Morris, the failed engineer who taught the class, had never understood why his class was suddenly so industrious (by all accounts Chris and his mate Jerry had no problem flogging them off in the dodgy pubs around town for fifty quid a pop).

"But what if you get caught?" Mo asked him.

"Oh, I'm only a kid, and they never bang you up for a first offence... and anyway, the prisons are all full!" Chris would laugh (and then he'd go back to figuring out yet another scam).

There were certain things Chris did that really annoyed Mo: forever speeding around in his parents' cars; always carrying a whopping great wad of cash (so nothing had changed there); arranging shooting contests in the woods; cheating everyone at cards; often carrying a CO_2 pistol (or throwing knife, or knuckle-duster); silly little things.

And then there were other things that Mo had witnessed Chris do over the years, things that weren't quite so harmless, the worst one being the first time that Mo was invited to the Shillings' for lunch.

It was intended to be a nice quiet lunch with just himself, Chris and Chris' parents in attendance; but, on the day, Chris' younger brother Simon had been hanging around, so Chris' mum – Kathy – had invited Simon to join them; and it had still been a very pleasant lunch, with Mo, Chris' dad (Jim) and Kathy treating him exactly like he was a grown-up... until Simon had made a mildly unflattering comment about his older brother and then tried to spear one of Chris' roast potatoes with his fork.

Striking with snake-like speed, Chris had snatched up his heavy pint glass – a solid glass 'jug' with a handle – and viciously smashed it down upon his brother's hand. The glass had smashed, there was blood everywhere, Kathy had been aghast – and there had been all the predictable mayhem – but what had shocked Maurice most was how nonchalant Chris had been by the incident.

"Aw, it was barely a scratch," Chris said (as Simon was driven off to hospital by Jim, with Simon bawling in the back seat, his hand wrapped in a kitchen towel and being comforted by Kathy); "Come on, let's go for a spin!"

Mo had also heard from various school mates of dubious tales involving Chris: how he'd shot his brother on numerous occasions; Chris being attacked by a gang led by his brother, and not only facing them down but giving them all an awful hiding; how accurate he was with his throwing knife; and how he laughed when he made even the smallest of deals.

Although Chris had never been arrested for any of these transgressions over the years, he'd developed a certain reputation, yet to the best of Mo's knowledge Chris had barely been given even the mildest rebuke by any teacher or person in authority.

The only time that Chris ever got into trouble at school was when he was caught by a science master hiding in a science lab, bunking off a cross country run (in the height of winter) with his mates Jerry and Andrew – and they were playing cards to boot – but Chris had even weaselled out of that one, by somehow convincing the master that he was explaining the true mathematical odds of poker and blackjack and convincing the science master that exercising their brains was a more fruitful than doing a cross country run in a blizzard. He was simply let off with a 'don't let me catch you a second time' – and he never was.

And by the time Chris' mate Jerry got expelled from school, Chris was looking forward to college and pulling new scams and didn't need a business partner.

And so now, after over ten years of friendship with him, Mo was finding Chris even harder to read (not that he'd ever been easy to read: he was always up-beat and up for a laugh, and when he wasn't out and about, wheeling and dealing, he had his nose buried in a book, and he never revealed his true feelings about much of anything); and now he was in the casino business, a business that, Mo admitted to himself, suited him perfectly; he was probably working for gangsters and loving every minute of it. Mo was, slowly but surely, becoming very wary of his old friend; he desperately needed to borrow a thousand pounds, but he didn't want the source to be 'blood money'.

Mo finished eating his tasteless chicken sandwich and wondered – yet again – who else he could ask for a (very) long-term loan.

I was becoming increasingly surprised that our little blackjack ruse hadn't been sussed out, and could only conclude that we were but days away from being arrested, so much so that I was mulling over other things, even other jobs that I could do; the one good thing – and the reason that I could rest fairly easy – was that at least I'd saved (and hidden) all the money, and I knew they'd never get it back; they'd have had to sentence me to five years hard labour (not that British prisons did that sort of thing any more) before I'd have given it back (and the prisons were full anyway).

I collected a measly eight grand from Sincs when he passed by my house on the Saturday afternoon; we'd had a brief chat in my bedroom, where I'd been listening to the Cocteau Twins, and he again refused my request to ask Albert if we could give it a rest for a couple of weeks.

"Why be greedy?" I wailed, turning up the stereo.

"Oh, stop being such a pussy," Sincs told me. "And do me a favour: turn this shit off!" I laughed. "Albert wants us to carry on till either he gets barred or we all get jobs at another club; they've got bigger maximums in London."

"Yeah, and cameras up the ass – an' I don't wanna work in London, or abroad!"

"Oh, stop whining," he went as I slumped down on my bed and moaned in desperation. Sincs could tell I wasn't in the mood to go out on the town (though he might have convinced me), but he made his excuses and left, and I spent the next couple of hours alternately dozing and wondering where I was going to dig my next hole to hide my next ten large. Then I struggled up and went to meet Vanessa for a drink.

The Hope and Anchor was a small pub/restaurant in the village of Eaton Bray, which lay about ten miles from where we lived. Ness had worked there for about a year and seemed to enjoy it, and the landlord, staff and regulars all seemed nice enough. Because of my working hours I normally only ever saw the early-evening crowd, when I might pop by for a quick drink and a chat with Ness on the way home from an afternoon's fishing, but even these trips had dwindled lately, what with all the overtime I had been doing. I steered the MX5 into the small pub car park and squeezed in between a blue TVR convertible and a silver Mercedes coupé; I supposed I was lucky to get a space at all on a Saturday night, especially when I saw all the up-market, larger vehicles parked out on the road; it was a tiny little pub, with an equally minuscule restaurant and pathetically small car park.

I walked in through the front door of the pub directly into the bar area, which always reminded me of a sitting room in a country cottage: rose-coloured carpeting, muted wall lighting, armchairs and wooden 'barrel' seats, small tables with candles on them, a short, ten-foot-long bar and no sign (or sound) of any jukeboxes, fruit machines or even a radio; the regulars all seemed to drink G&T, real ale or Guinness. It was busy tonight, but not too crowded for me to want to go elsewhere; I pressed my way politely through to the bar, where I was greeted by name and served my usual glass of large Bacardi with diet coke, ice but no slice.

As it was not quite 9.30pm, Ness hadn't finished her shift yet, so I remained at the bar drinking and making small-talk with one of the regulars, an old-timer called Joe Green; he asked me how things were going, so I regaled him with some stories of the bigger winners and losers we'd had in the casino that week; Joe knew I was croupier, I'd seen him in the Hope just about every time I'd been in there (he seemed like part of the furniture), and seeing as he was well into his seventies and living on a comfortable pension I could relax with him, since I wasn't too worried that he'd be quizzing me for information about how to fiddle the place (or trying to involve me in some ridiculous swindle where he had everything to gain and I had everything to lose).

"We had a bloke in this week," I told him truthfully, "and all he ever does is play the far end of the table; the last dozen, you know?" Joe nodded; he'd been around the block long enough for me not to have to explain every minute detail of the game to him.

"Well, I hammered him and hammered him, this bloke; I was hitting the zero and the three, the seven and the twelve, but never the high numbers, and it was a bit of a shame as this guy's quite a polite bloke – for a punter; anyway – and it was coming to the end of my stint, so just as I was about to go I said to the bloke to place a bet on number seven, just in case like, and blow me if he didn't stick a pony down on number seven, I spun and bang, it went straight into seven, so I had to pay him out over eight hundred quid!

"So he says 'thanks', lays out about another two hundred on the next spin, doubling up on the seven and stone me if I didn't repeat it! I passed him out two and a half grand in two spins, which was just about all the money he'd punted across the table in the previous hour; I couldn't bloody believe it! I mean, he called me a 'wonderful young man' and all that, but Jesus, that was all I needed! And so for working hard for an entire hour, all I got as a reward was a filthy look from both the inspector and the pit boss! Charming, isn't it? I'll tell you, Joe, you can't do anything right up there!"

"But surely the punters have to win sometimes, otherwise they'd never come back?" Joe put in.

"Tell me about it!" I went. "But you try telling that to the managers! They seem to think that we should be nailing fifty percent of the drop each and every night, the morons!" I took a breath, finished my drink and looked up to try and catch the attention of a barmaid or the landlord, who was called Daryl of all things, who was allegedly floating around somewhere.

"Here, I'll get that," Joe said; he was probably grateful to have someone to talk to. Glancing into the restaurant I could see that the place was packed, and I doubted if Vanessa would be finished for some time, so I said thanks to Joe and kept looking out for someone who could serve me a drink.

"And I'll tell you what," I went, "doing all this night work and all this overtime is going to kill me."

"Rubbish!" said Daryl, bustling up to pour half a real ale for Joe and then my usual. "Do you the world of good!" He was a nice bloke, was Daryl; easy-going, tall, slim, blond-haired, blue-eyed and good-looking; all the ladies in the village adored him yet he somehow managed to get on with the men as well (probably because they thought he was gay). Vanessa had told me he was a brilliant boss, but I liked him most because he was outgoing and friendly to *everyone*, even a young bloke like me (who admittedly didn't really spend much over his bar and nothing in his restaurant); it was a pleasant change for me, seeing as most of the adults that I came into contact with gave me a wide berth (if they knew me) or ignored me completely.

"Ha!" I said. "You don't know the stress we get, working in a casino!"

"Stress?" he queried; "You don't know the meaning of the word! Try running a pub and trying to control all the women I've got here, seventeen hours a day! I'll tell you what, Joe: these kids today don't know they've been born!"

"Oh please!" I went, drawing the word out and laughing. "Er, say, Daryl; when is Ness going to be finished, roughly?" I enquired.

"It'll be a while yet, Chris," he replied; "They haven't even finished doing most of the main courses."

"Oh, well; might as well stay for another then," I said with a shrug.

Ness and I got away just after ten and went for a drive in her old Mini (a 'gift' from her Dad; a *gift*, for fucks sake! I was still coughing-up £100 per month for my shitty MX5). It was something we often used to do all the time when we were at college: go for a drive somewhere, chatting all the way. We talked about the party the previous week-end and how our friends were changing – mostly for the worse.

"What about me?" I asked her. "Have I changed?"

She glanced over at me with a wry look on her face. "You haven't changed since the day I met you," she answered, and I grinned.

We proceeded up to a car park overlooking the Dunstable Downs, where Ness parked up, turned off the engine and rested a hand upon my knee. "So how's it been this week?" she asked. "I couldn't get much sense out of you last week."

"Er, yeah; well, I'd had a few, hadn't I?" I squirmed.

"So what's new?" she laughed. "But you were saying something about there was a lot that went on behind the scenes and that you didn't like it, or something? What did you mean?"

"Oh, I dunno," I said. "The punters come in and try it on when they're losing; the managers are always telling us to speed the games up, which basically means they want us to try to take more money; some of the dealers have got little arrangements on the side with some of the punters; the Gaming Board haven't got the foggiest about what goes on; we're supposed to be on our guard to catch cheats, but the biggest cheats of all are the managers, like when they tell you to go and 'kill' a game; oh, I could go on. I tell you what, Ness: it's one big den of iniquity, and I'm stuck in the middle taking it from all sides!" She laughed.

"Ha! So what are you going to do about it, Einstein?"

"Do? What can I do? At the end of the day, I actually like the job; I just don't like most of the people. And who else is going to take me on – and pay me two grand a month plus bonuses – just to spin a poxy ball around a wheel like a trained monkey?" She laughed again. Of course, I had to give Ness an inflated figure of my salary just in case I did go out and buy that Lotus, or something even better!

"So can the dealers actually spin their preferred numbers then, or what?" she asked. I smiled to myself in the darkness; I was continually trying to section spin, all to no avail.

"Well, that's a bit of an urban myth," I told her; "The casinos don't really want you to be able to 'section spin', as they call it, unless of course they're losing a lot of money: then they'd love us to be able to do it in the house's favour! In fact, they deny such a skill is even possible; nevertheless, all dealers still try to miss the big numbers, the big players; I mean, who wants to always be making big payouts, you know? But then you just become more confident and seem to miss the big numbers naturally; of course, it'd be handy to be able to 'spin-to-miss' the big bets – because I've often seen a player place just one bet and it'll come in, funny that – but to actually be able to do it at will seems beyond the grasp of most dealers."

"But I suppose if someone *could* do it, then in theory they could cheat the casino, couldn't they?" she asked.

"Well exactly, and this is exactly why the casino don't really want you to be able to do it – though that don't stop me trying!" I laughed. "I mean, I've occasionally seen dealers spinning away at the wheel, and it's seemed pretty obvious to me that they're trying to avoid a certain section, but when they miss a big bet, who is to say that it was skill and not just luck, do you know what I mean? I mean, how do you prove it? And if they did manage to miss a big punter, and the casino won all the money, the managers are hardly going to

360

complain!"

"No, I suppose not," she said; "Be nice if you could do it, though."

"Tell me about it!" I said. Her hand was moving slowly up and down my thigh, and I wasn't doing anything to prevent it; one couldn't help but be intimate in something as small as a Mini. I reached over and gently brushed her brown hair across her cheek, and then continued stroking her hair as she began softly moaning.

"I always loved it when you did that," she said, and I nodded. "You know, we don't do this nearly enough." I nodded again. "When are you going to get a place of your own? I hate making out in the back of a car."

"So you don't want me to get a Lotus then," I said, and she giggled. Now her hand was resting above my you-know-what, which was throbbing unmercifully; I was brushing the tips of my fingers up and down the nape of her neck, Vanessa was rolling her head from side to side, and up and down, and after a few more minutes of this we suddenly found ourselves naked and on the back seat, enthusiastically doing what Ness had said moments before she hated doing.

But Ness was right: it maybe it was about time that I got my own place. So on the afternoons that I wasn't doing overtime I started browsing on the net at the rental agencies of all the nearby towns and villages, on the look-out for a small country cottage with a large drive and double garage; they weren't very common, such requirements, and soon enough I was looking at two or three bedroom semi-detached houses with astronomical rents; the problem wasn't that I couldn't afford the money, the problem was that anyone looking at my monthly salary statements would have assumed that I couldn't, and there was no way I was going to leave a dreaded paper trail.

At work, we continued the scam but under increasingly difficult conditions; Wendy, Sincs and I were still agreeing to do as much overtime as possible, which was just as well as it was only on these shifts that we had any real chance of doing the crooked shuffle.

On the evening shifts, the pit boss – under direct orders from the managers – would replace a dealer as soon as they started making any sizeable payouts, so one crooked shoe was often all we could manage, and that was only once a night (unless you were lucky).

On the afternoon shifts the manager as well as the pit-boss would be in constant attendance in the blackjack pit if Albert were around, and would stand at a nearby table and stare blatantly at the proceedings, in which case I wouldn't even bother to do the bent shuffle but Albert was obliged to keep on playing because (a) it would have looked too suspicious if he'd walked off

362

every time a certain croupier stopped dealing to him, and (b) he'd lose his prized position at the table, i.e. the end boxes. Slowly, very slowly, the dealers seemed to be chipping away at him – at least until Wendy, Sincs or I would each pay him out three or four grand in one afternoon.

But I was growing more and more apprehensive, and feeling very uneasy about Wendy doctoring the paperwork, what with the managers hanging around all the time and continually checking the figures. And to cap it all, we now had the awful Mary MacCreith, the casino's recently promoted 'gaming manager' skulking around and interrogating us over every minor incident, and then she'd go stalking back to the far-end of the pit and write everything up in the 'Incidents Book.' Another month went by like this, with me only managing to eke out another twelve grand from Albert (via Sincs), and then it all came to a head one day, just as I knew it would, and guess whose fault it was? Yeah, you guessed it: Sir Christopher Muggins Himself!

Right from the word go, on that fateful Wednesday afternoon, Wendy was inspecting me deal to Albert and since there was no-one on the gaming floor that we had to be particularly wary of, I'd managed to hurriedly pay Albert out about five grand before she decided to take me off and instructed me to go and get the day-shift pit boss, Keith Blackwood (again), who was eating his breakfast in the staff-room, which I duly did; but before I went scurrying off Wendy told me that she'd already doctored the figures to make it look as if she'd been doing the dealing: good old Wendy, she didn't care!

As soon as I broke the news to Blackwood, he jumped up (leaving his great mound of bacon, eggs, sausages and chips) and ran off towards the pit, and a few seconds later we got a call summoning all gaming staff into the pit, so out we trooped, muttering and moaning; Blackwood was leaning on the bureau, staring at the pit control sheet and pulling out what little hair he had left; seeing as he was the afternoon's designated pit boss, the 'result' was down to him, at least it was in Mary MacCreith's eyes!

"Right, we're going on to fifteens," he said, "and unless you nail him, I'm going to change the dealer every fifteen minutes, okay?" We all nodded. "Right then: who's feeling lucky?" We all kept nodding and dutifully raised our hands, and he chose me to start the ball rolling, dismissing the others. "Right then, Mr Shilling, I want you to get on there, give it a quick double shuffle and then cut it nice and deep, okay?"

"Got it, boss," I said, with a look of intent eagerness on my face, heading over to take Wendy off.

"Thank-you, you have a new dealer," she announced properly, wiping her hands and showing her palms upwards, and I in turn showed 'clean hands' – though why one had to do this at the beginning of a stint at the tables I'd never understood – and then I speedily dealt out the remainder of Wendy's shoe which I followed with a totally straight double shuffle of my own. Out of the corner of my eye, I could see Keith and Wendy talking in low tones over by the bureau.

"How are you today, sir?" I enquired loudly of Albert, and before he could reply I whispered: "Er, it wouldn't hurt if you could do back a tiny bit."

He looked at me, looked at Blackwood and Wendy, looked back at me and muttered, "Okay." I then dealt blackjack to him for two god-rotting hours as he did back, in dribs and drabs, about two grand. Of course, Blackwood was going to leave me on for as long as I took money, which naturally pissed me off no end but I knew better than to ask him for a break. However, at five o'clock some of the other dealers issued forth from the staff-room, I knew that I was well overdue a break plus I had just come to the end of a shoe, and yet I still wasn't taken off; right then: fuck 'em!

So I caught Albert's eye and winked, did a very fast crooked shuffle, dealt it out slow then fast, did it again and then did it a third time.

"Okay!" he whispered, placing seven bets of £500, sticking on all and – surprise, surprise – I bust, so out went £3,500, just as it did on the second hand, seven grand in just two hands, thank-you very much!

Then I started raced through the rest of the shoe. Quickly doing the crooked shuffle again, I'd just

365

completed it when I received a tap on the shoulder. After allowing Albert to cut the deck, I slapped the cards into the shoe, showed clean palms, announced the change of dealer and walked off to the staff-room, slumping down into an chair, closing my eyes and enjoying my first proper break of the afternoon – and figuring that, even though he'd done back a bit, Albert should at least pay me a goodly portion of what he would now be plundering from the shoe that I'd just shuffled (but hadn't had a chance to deal), i.e. at least £7k, plus what I'd paid him just before (another £7k), minus roughly £2k I'd told him to do back, plus what I'd paid him first thing (£5k); in other words, I was due at least eight grand, whoopee!

But that wasn't my main concern; my main concern was how to get rid of Albert, as I knew he would keep plugging away at our place forever – or until we all got caught. I just sat there rubbing my forehead and trying to figure out a way of getting shot of the bloke without making a scene in front of him (or Sincs), but I simply couldn't come up with anything.

And after my break, Keith directed me straight back on to BJ5, where Albert was still punting away. I tapped Wendy on the shoulder, and clocked the chip tray: it was almost empty of ponies and hundreds; Wendy hadn't been mucking around! So I took over and rushed through the remainder of her shoe, and by the time it came to shuffle the cards, Keith had got Wendy inspecting so I did the bent shuffle, grateful that I could continue from where Wendy left off and that she could cook the books. I paid him out nearly seven grand in the next shoe and quickly shuffled again, even though I'd spotted Mary MacCreith sharking around near the cage and bottom end of the pit, and then hurriedly dished out another seven grand.

During my next shuffle – I decided to do straight one – I waited for Wendy to mooch off and glance at a roulette game and whispered to fuck face: "Now you're gonna have to do back a bit, unless you want them to take me off."

He made a face, but then shrugged and nodded, placing a one one-hundred pound bet on each of the seven boxes, so then I began to deal, very slowly, and it was then that Mary chose to come slinking over.

"How are you doing today, sir; winning?" She had a sort-of smile on her face as she enquired after him but failed to prevent the disgust in her voice, and all but spat the question out. Albert shrugged, and drawled:

"Oh, I've just lost a grand to this guy; "He's terrible!"

"Tell me about it," Mary said.

"I never have much luck against this guy," he went on. "It must be his aftershave!"

"Or his ridiculous haircut," MacCreith chipped in, the bitch, causing Albert to laugh, the wanker.

"And look at his shirt!" Albert went on, while I seethed; "It's obvious he can't afford an iron – and he can't deal to save his life!" he laughed, and The Wicked Witch just stood there, laughing along with him! I needed this like I needed a hole in the head, and when I finished the shuffle – another straight one – I made a point of banging the cards down into the shoe as loudly as I could; I knew that if I said even one word, MacCreith would have a pathetic excuse to haul me over the coals, and I wasn't going to give her a chance, the horrible old witch!

So I proceeded to deal the next shoe, as professionally as I could, clearly announcing the value of the hands, dealing the cards out and sweeping the bets in as smoothly as I was able (it had been a while since I'd really tried to deal a smooth game of blackjack, but I did OK).

After half a shoe of me raking in the money, Mary walked off – and as soon as her back was turned, Albert gave a quick glance around, and then gave me a broad wink. "Yeah, whatever," I muttered under my breath. "But I ain't paying you out any more today, so you might as well go and play roulette for a while."

"One more shoe," he whispered.

"Okay, but then you'll have to wait for Sinclair or Wendy, okay?" He nodded, and so I hurriedly (and messily) completed that shoe, did the crooked shuffle yet again and, once he'd had a couple of shoes to remember it, I paid him out another seven large, and after coughing up so much I wasn't all that surprised to feel a tap on my left shoulder indicating that I was being taken off; I glanced to my side and saw that it was Sincs who was taking me off, so didn't bother doing another crooked shuffle, merely announcing: "New dealer," wiping my palms face upward, and heading over to the pit desk, where Keith Blackwood was leaned over, holding his head in his palms.

"Fucking bloke!" I went, "I was doing all right against him till he started slagging me off; put me right off, he did!" But then I shut-up, as I'd suddenly just had an inkling of an idea.

"Oh, don't worry about it, mate," Keith said; "Go and take a quick break."

"Thanks, boss," I said, and glanced down to the bottom end of the pit where I could make out Mary sitting on AR10, looking through some paperwork. I closed my eyes, took a deep breath, and made my decision… and, taking some more very deep breaths, walked down the pit to talk to her. "Um, excuse me," I said.

"Fucking cunt!" she spat.

I raised my eyebrows in polite enquiry. "Er…"

"We're already about thirty thousand down on the day," she snarled, "And I'm thinking he's been taking

369

the piss out of us for too many weeks now!"

"Er, yeah; that's what I wanted to talk to you about," I said. "I keep getting the mark of the guy but just when I start hammering him he takes the piss, deliberately, and it puts me right off; I've sort of noticed him do it before, but this afternoon took the bloody biscuit: today he was blatantly rude; I mean you heard him!"

"Yes, I did," Mary hissed, eyes narrowing dangerously.

"I mean, I'm always polite and everything, you know that, but there's only so much one can take, you know? Hmph!" I went, somewhat theatrically.

She slapped her perfectly manicured fingertips down on the Incidents Book, and went: "Right! That's it; that's exactly the excuse I've been looking for! Not only is he a bastard to beat, but now he's actually insulting my staff, and I know because I witnessed it!" she smiled up at me, victoriously.

Yeah, after you deliberately provoked him, I thought, smiling and nodding along with her.

"Er…" I went, wanting him gone whilst at the same time wondering if we couldn't keep the scam going for just another month or so, as I suddenly realised I was witnessing about twenty thousand pounds going up in smoke; oh sweet Jesus!

"No, my mind's made up; as of today, he's barred –

and fuck him!"

"Er, hang on," I blurted, almost against my better judgement; "Isn't he up on us, overall?"

"Maybe, but not by all that much." That's what you think, I thought. "I can afford to get rid of him," she replied.

"If you let him play a bit more, we might nail him." I said, helpfully (though inside I was cringing, my mouth writing cheques my brain couldn't cash).

"No, my mind's made up; go on, off you go," she went, glaring nastily and waving me away, and so off I went, off to the pit for a shortened break and trying to weigh the consequences of my actions.

Was she really going to bar him? Probably. So ought I pop round tonight and collect the money I was due from the day's scamming? Probably. Should I tell Sincs what The Wicked Witch had just told me? Probably not. Should I mention to Sincs the fact that I had initiated the conversation between myself and Mary and so was probably instrumental in getting Albert barred? *Definitely not.*

I made it to the staff room and slumped down for ten minutes rest, but it wasn't really a rest as my pea-brain tried to assimilate what had just happened; oh, shit!

Later that evening, I managed to whisper to Sincs (in

the changing room) that I wanted to pop round Wendy's after work, telling him that I wanted all the money due to me, and when he asked why I needed it so urgently I quickly made up some codswallop about going round looking at some cars I was thinking about buying the next day. He shrugged, and said he'd tell her if he got a chance.

I knew he would go ballistic if he realised that I was to blame for getting Albert barred – as would Wendy – but I knew that as soon as Albert received a letter telling him he was barred we wouldn't see the bastard for dust (and any money we were owed would disappear with him).

After an interminable night dealing crummy, small-time games of roulette and boring, depressing games of blackjack, I was finally 'chopped' and allowed to shoot off, so as soon as I got in the MX5 I fired her up and headed off towards Wendy's, with Sincs racing up behind; I'll give him that: his Escort might have looked like a complete pile of shit but it was fast enough. I'd convinced him to come with me to get his cash as well, which I knew was risky as it might tip Albert off that we knew he was going to get barred; it was stupid, but it was a gesture I had to make out of loyalty to my friend. Sincs had tried to talk me out of going round, saying that it was a bit risky, but I'd insisted, so here we were, tooling into Watford at a quarter past four in the morning.

I decided to take my buddy for a race, to give Wendy time to get home as much as anything and seeing as she always changed out of her smart casino evening dress before leaving I knew it might take a while, so we hared off up the road along a dual carriageway, with Sincs trying to overtake me and me just managing to fend him off, and then we turned off up a narrow lane which took us up towards a village, and I got the old MX5 up to ninety, along roads which should have been a thirty zone, with Sincs right on my tail and flashing and hooting, as was his wont. I was finding it hard to concentrate as I was laughing so much, heedless of any prowling Old Bill; anyway, they were more interested in hidden stashes of drugs or naughty drink-drivers, neither of which I had to worry about when leaving work. Eventually, however, I headed back towards where Wendy lived.

There were quite a few parking spaces along Wendy's road but I didn't want to be parking-up outside her house only to have Malcolm bloody Philby pulling up outside and clocking us leaving, and as I knew that getting any money out of Albert was liable to be a bit of a palaver I drove round the corner and parked on a side-street that I hoped – all things being equal – that Philby wouldn't drive past.

"Hi guys," Wendy said, letting us in and looking tired (as usual). Albert was sitting in the lounge smoking a cigarette and had a pile of cash out on the coffee table; Sincs had managed to get word to Wendy, and she must

373

have told Albert we were on our way.

"All right lads, how's it goin'?" he went in his American drawl, getting up and shaking our hands; it was only the second time he'd ever seen me outside of work, so it was quite an occasion (especially considering the amount of 'business' we had done together). However, I didn't want to muck about, so told him:

"Look, sorry to hassle you, but I'm going car-hunting tomorrow and need some cash to hopefully get a better deal, you know? I think you owe me around fifteen grand."

"Yeah, well I figured around twelve," he said, surprising me, and handed me a wad of fifties. "Sinclair, do you want your cut as well?" he asked Sincs, holding out another wad, equally as thick as the one he'd given me. Sincs nodded, and shoved the bundle into his jacket (I'd undone a couple of my shirt buttons and pushed my bundle of bills into my shirt; I figured this was marginally less risky than leaving the stack in a jacket pocket, where it might be found by the police should I get pulled for speeding or, even worse, my old dear, should I forget to remove it from my jacket pocket).

"Say, don't you think we ought to cool it for a while?" I said to everyone. "I mean, Mary MacCreith has been hanging around like a cheap suit, and every time you come in the managers are all over us like a rash! Look,

374

all I'm saying," I said calmly, not wanting Sincs to kick-off, "is that I think you ought to give it a break for a couple of weeks; pretend you're going back to America for a while. Or come in, and do back a bit to me and Sincs and play for longer with some of the other dealers, you know?"

Albert smiled, and looked at me like I was completely barking yet didn't seem too much against the idea; Wendy just glanced between Sincs and Albert; Sincs, however, just stood there shaking his head, and then let out a massive, theatrical sigh.

"Oh, for god's sake!" he said. "You know what? If they haven't caught us by now, they're never going to catch us!" Sincs said. "You're always panicking, always shitting in your pants!" he laughed.

"Oh, all right then, forget I even mentioned it," I went, waving my hand in front of me; "Maybe you're right. But you know what they say: it's the greed that finally gets you. So please, just have a think about cooling it for a while; we can always do it again in a couple of months time, you know? Anyway, I gotta shoot; see y'all tomorrow, yeah? Cheers, Albert." And with that, I zipped up my little black jacket and made for the door, as did Sinclair and everyone said their goodbyes. I went to the front door, cracked it open and peered around outside, paranoid. Then, with a muttered 'laters,' I hurried off up the street and round the corner towards my car, on the look-out for any approaching headlights that might have been that Malcolm Philby.

I didn't go out looking for a new car the following day (I needed a lie-in anyway), though when I did finally surface the first thing I did was get the twelve grand that I'd been paid by Albert last night, along with eighteen more from the previous month's scamming, and hot-tailed it over to Totternhoe with my little gardening trowel in my rucksack. I buried the latest monies (as usual, wrapped in cling-film and in a sealed plastic box) in another three holes (after I'd reconnoitred the area and made sure it was free from walkers or witnesses) relatively close to the other three caches; I did not want to have more than ten grand in any one hole, and I now had sixty grand buried in six separate holes.

Job done, I took the car for a spin (top down), pondering as to whether my next set of wheels should be an Lotus Esprit or a Jaguar (and whether Albert knew he'd been barred yet). Then I stopped for a drink, went for a walk along the Grand Union Canal and tried to relax; I ended up walking for about two miles before I felt relaxed enough to head back to the car.

Cerebrally, I knew that trying to get Albert barred was the smartest thing to do, but there was still a big part of me that was wondering whether, as Sincs clearly thought, we could have gone on undetected for another couple of months and I could have made myself another sixty grand; sweet Jesus!

Albert didn't show up in the casino that night, and since neither Wendy nor Sincs said anything, neither did I; and I was on yet another double-shift on the Friday, with Sincs again but not with Wendy, and, again, Sincs didn't mention anything to me as to Albert's membership status.

Sincs and I were put mostly on roulette that afternoon, so both of us went into 'pay and spin' mode to try and impress the bosses, and overall we both did OK. When Wendy started her shift at ten to nine, she gave no indication that anything untoward had happened, and I started wondering whether Mary MacCreith had changed her mind about barring Albert (needless to say, I could hardly go up to her and ask point-blank). I didn't have a very enjoyable or lucky night, and was finally put out of my misery when Sincs turned up unannounced the following lunchtime whilst I was having a bowl of home-made soup and a cheese roll with my parents.

My parents always made a fuss whenever I brought friends round (because it happened so rarely, I suppose), and I was always terribly embarrassed, but today, although I could see Sincs wanted to be away and talk privately, I let them force him to eat something and then third degree him – in the nicest possible sense – as to how he was enjoying it at work. He played along admirably, saying that he was saving up to buy a flat, that we were two of the best dealers they had, that the management respected us, that we were both due a pay rise and that everyone liked me. Well, my old Mum positively *glowed*, and even Dad looked somewhat proud (albeit surprised).

Because I hardly ever talked about what went on at work – seeing as I didn't want to tell a porky pie and then be caught out at a later date – Mum and Dad were still pretty much in the dark as to the intricacies of casino dealing, so in a way I was grateful to Sincs for rambling on; he was a very smooth, credible liar, and had the knack of being able to make something up on the spot and run with it, and Mum lapped it up. He even asked for some more of Mum's home-made soup, and after that she didn't want him to go. However, go we eventually did, up to my room for a quick chat (behind locked doors and to the sound of Dead Can Dance). Sincs flopped onto my single bed and I looked out of the window.

"You ain't going to believe this," he said.

"What's that?" I asked.

"They've banned Albert! He came in yesterday afternoon and they wouldn't let him in, said they'd sent him a letter telling him was banned!"

"You're joking!" I went, in a shocked sort of way. "Well what're we gonna do now? Fuck!"

"Dunno," Sincs said, shaking his head. "And it was all going so well! Another couple of months and I could've left the fuckin' place – shit!"

Not knowing what to say – and not fully trusting my flapping mouth – I kept schtum and just stood there, trying to keep a thoughtful expression on my face. Sincs seemed distraught, completely different from the bloke he'd been when chatting to my parents five minutes beforehand and I felt for him, I really did, but I knew that getting Albert barred had been the sensible thing to do.

"You've paid off your flat, right?" I asked him, "and got some money put by?" He nodded, looking very unhappy, but I laughed. "Well, that's more than I can say I have. So what are you gonna do now? We could just stay on at work for a while; consider our options; try not to do anything rash."

"Fuck it!" he said, and punched by pillow case. "I just needed another two or three months! Then I could've had another flat paid for, which I could've rented out and then gone and got a cushy job in London; fuck it!" I just stood there, nodding thoughtfully.

"Come on, let's go for a spin," I said – it's amazing what a change of scene can do for someone who's depressed – and Sincs nodded. We went outside, got the MX5 fired up and drove over to Ashridge Forest, where we could walk and talk and discuss delicate things without anyone eavesdropping.

I woke up on Sunday morning feeling more relaxed than I had done in ages; working as a dealer wasn't the easiest occupation in the world but try doing it whilst committing a massive casino scam at the same time; for a good couple months I'd been under a lot of stress from all sides, and in the last few weeks I was sure it was all going to end in disaster, but now it seemed I had made it through safely.

I had gone out for a few drinks with Sincs the previous evening and we'd ended up in Totternhoe down The Hope and Anchor, but it hadn't been a particularly late one because I didn't really want one; I hadn't needed a massive session to help me forget my troubles since I no longer had any!

I was over the moon that I'd got sixty grand safely buried (plus another three grand in change under the bed) and I was happy to simply go home for an early night, and I'd woken up feeling relaxed and for an hour I just lay in bed coming to terms with the fact that the scam was over, I'd come out of it unscathed and hopefully I'd never have to get involved in such foolishness again. The money that I'd saved was a *huge* amount, and would hopefully become the deposit on a house, and for an hour I just lay there smiling, giggling and not even needing a wank to cheer me up.

When I surfaced just before noon, Mum and Dad were getting ready to go round my Grandmother's for lunch, and – since I knew my Bonehead Baby Brother was out misbehaving with his mates – when Mum asked if I wanted to come and I said yes I think she nearly collapsed in surprise. So after I'd showered and changed, we climbed in the Citroen and headed up the road, where we spent a pleasant afternoon eating a roast, playing Canasta, and chatting, and I entertained them with a few stories of the milder goings-on at work.

But it hadn't been solely out of social responsibility that I'd gone to see my Grandma, because I wanted to try to collar my Old Man for a loan, so waited for the right moment and grabbed my chance after the second game of Canasta, when he popped outside to smoke his filthy pipe for a while.

After a few minutes of companionable silence, I said: "I remember you told me once that if I saved enough money for a deposit for a house, you'd double it; does that offer still stand?"

He stood there silently, puffing away and regarding me steadily.

"Perhaps," he said. "How much have you saved?"

"Nearly five grand," I lied, "but I want to wait till I've got ten; could you double it?"

"Perhaps," he said again.

"Good," I told him, "because all things being equal I'll want to buy my own place in a couple of months; Jesus Christ, when are you going to quit?" I asked, nodding at his stinking pipe.

"Sooner rather than later, if it means getting you out from under our hair!" He laughed, but I just stood there, stone-faced. "Of course, you're going to have to pay back all of the money we lent you for the Mazda first, you realise that I trust?"

"Oh, you can't even give your own son a break, can you!" I wheedled, hoping he'd forgotten about the car debt, which of course he hadn't. "Well you can forget it!" I yelled, and stomped back inside and slammed the door on him, fuming.

Chapter 6

To be back at work without worrying that I was going to have my collar felt at any second was a real joy!

 I got stuck into the games of roulette and blackjack like I never had before, and tried to be as amenable as possible to the idiotic demands of the pit bosses and management. I also tried to angle for a result whenever I could. It was like a weight had been removed from my shoulders and I started walking tall, realising that although I might not have as much 'experience' as some of the other dealers, I was, actually, as good as any of them and better than most.

 A few pleasant weeks went by like this, with me concentrating on the finer points of blackjack – obviously I thought I knew everything there was to know about roulette – when Sincs grabbed me after work one night and summoned me to a meeting with Albert.

 I didn't want to go, but there wasn't a lot I could do to refuse, so shrugged and raced his old Escort to the meeting at Wendy's house. As I followed him along the road at ninety, nudging his rear bumper with my front one, I was crapping myself, sweating and panicking and imagining all kinds of horrendously awful scenarios, all of which involved the scam having finally being uncovered and them cutting a deal and me about to get pinched; as before, it was only my respect and trust for Sincs that kept me following him. When we got to Wendy's road I drove past her house, as usual, and parked out of the way around the corner and walked back to her gaff.

By the time she let me in, Sincs was already sitting comfortably in her lounge swigging on a beer and chatting amiably to Albert because here he was, sitting there on the settee with a foxy grin all over his face, the cheating slag.

"All right?" I asked everyone; "So what's up? I'm shagged and wanna go home, so can we make it snappy, yeah?" Since starting at the casino my social skills had come on in leaps and bounds.

"All right Shilling, keep your hair on!" Sincs told me. "Sit down, have a beer and listen to what Albert's got to say."

"Yeah, what's that?" I went. "And I don't want a beer; you got any Bacardi and diet coke?" I asked Wendy.

"Yeah, I think so," she replied; "Sinclair told me to get some in, just in case you came round."

"Oh, cool," I grunted, slumping down onto one of Wendy's old armchairs and resigning myself to the fact that I was going to be here for a while (and still wondering whether we'd been sussed, they'd all cut a deal with the authorities and I was about to be dragged off to the cells; then again, I was coming to accept that I'd always have these doubts and general paranoia).

When Wendy brought in the B n C, I poured myself a strong glass and took some quick slugs, deciding it was a crappy situation and there was nothing for it but to get pissed, and after a few minutes of small talk Albert began telling me what he'd got in mind, and after a few more minutes of listening to him I stopped concentrating on the booze and started concentrating on his scheme.

Firstly, he rambled on for ages about how difficult it was to make (private) contact with any casino dealer, how vigilant the casinos were to try to prevent any collusion and on top of that how uncommon it was to find a casino which had decent action but little or no camera surveillance; in fact, managing to get all these factors in place successfully was so rare that Albert did not want his getting barred to put an end to (his words) our partnership (I had to stifle a guffaw).

So he had decided to make us an offer, whereby we could continue safely scamming even if he did get barred occasionally, to wit: rather than apply for jobs in another provincial casino or in London, which was a bit close to home, we would apply for jobs with an agency and go abroad and do it all over again at a casino in a completely different country, one that Albert had cased, found to be suitable and was – obviously – already a member of. Once said jobs were applied for, offered and accepted, we would start working there and, lo and behold, Albert could begin plundering the blackjack tables all over again.

And every six months or so, we would go through the whole process yet again; and (all things being equal, Albert assured us) if we could skank two casinos a year for the next five years, and thus, as night follows day – his words – we would all make our fortunes and be millionaires in less than five years. Moreover, as a final sweetener – his words again – he was prepared to offer us a better cut: sixty-forty in our favour, and as soon as he came out with that it was all I could do not to jump up and accuse him of basically admitting to ripping us off these last months.

I looked over at Sincs and he was nodding away with a silly grin plastered all over his face; I glanced at Wendy and she was gazing at Albert with a soppy expression; Albert was looking at me expectantly, so I faked a yawn and took a big swig of Bacardi.

"Well," he asked, looking at me; "What do you think, guy? Ain't that a plan?" he went, like an excited kid.

I took another long drink, looked at him and shrugged. "It's not a bad idea, actually," I told him honestly; "But obviously I'll have to think it over," I lied, because I already knew I wanted no part of it; I would keep in touch with Sincs and I could always meet up and do it again at a later date (assuming I ever needed the money that badly), but not for the moment.

Sincs muttered a load of abuse – no doubt he'd spend the next couple of months trying to talk me into it – but Wendy didn't seem too surprised with my answer. I finished my drink, poured myself another stiff one and took another mighty sip. "Obviously you think it's a good idea, then?" I asked looking at Sincs, who nodded and shrugged as if it was as clear as crystal.

"Makes perfect sense to me," he said.

"Yeah, it's not a bad idea, I'll give you that," I told them. "Give me a couple of days to mull it over and I'll let you know." They nodded, clearly unsurprised by my reaction. I got up and took my empty glass into Wendy's kitchen, taking a final swig before rinsing it out. "Well, I'll let myself out," I said, seeing as none of them appeared interested in getting up; Sincs would probably spend another couple of hours there, shooting the breeze. I wandered up the road, fired up the MX5, drove home and went straight to bed, but of course I couldn't sleep and lay there tossing and turning and wondering how I could weasel out of this latest problem, as I knew that there was just no way I could do the offski and leave my dog Cinnamon behind.

Two more weeks went by with me dealing away at work and keeping my head down; I'd managed to put off giving Sincs a decision so far and thought I'd done bloody well to delay it for so long. I'd really been clearing up on the tables at work and had been enjoying it tremendously. But when Sincs came over late one afternoon on the last Saturday of July, I knew he wanted an answer and I gave it to him straight (well, as straight as anything ever could be if I was involved). I locked my bedroom door and turned up the stereo (the Cocteau Twins, as usual).

"Dude, I ain't coming abroad with you," I said, "But if you want to go somewhere, get set up and let me know that it's all going okay then I might come out; I've got too much to do here, what with getting a place of my own and all that shit, you know?"

He nodded, grimacing.

"I thought that's what you were going to say," he said.

"Well, you know me," I muttered, and he laughed and sat down on my bed.

"Yeah," he went. "We've all been thinking, and overall we think it'd be better if we go abroad instead of doing it here; too much moving around in this country and the fuckin' Gaming Board will have all the records, know what I mean?" I nodded. "So I'm applying to the agencies for a contract and we're going to see what they come up with; could be the Caribbean, could be the cruise ships, could be the Far East, we'll just have to wait and see. I'm going to go out first and then Wendy and Albert – and then you – can come over once I've got the place sussed out, all right?"

388

"Yeah, that sounds like an okay idea," I lied; "Now are we going on the piss tonight, or what?"

"Yeah," Sincs nodded. "I got a mate coming over, and we're meeting him in the Nag's at half seven."

"Jeez, the Caribbean, eh? Fuck me, that sounds all right!"

"Yeah, though anywhere really, as long as it's warm and sunny," he said.

"Yeah, too right," I said; "Er, what about your bird?" I asked him delicately; "What does she say about it?"

"Oh, Judy's all right about it," he told me. "Of course, I've told her fuck-all about our little business arrangement, but now that we've got a flat she's happy and since I bought her that car she wanted, that Vauxhall Astra convertible, she lets me do pretty-much whatever I want." He laughed. "I've already told her I might be going abroad for six months, but she's cool with it; I've also told her that I'll be able to save enough to buy another flat by working abroad for six months, so she's fine with it." I nodded, and turned the music up a fraction.

"But what if they've got cameras everywhere, or a more switched-on management team, or better inspectors or whatever?" I asked.

"Well, we'll have to play it by ear, but if we're only

going to be hitting them for three months out of every six and then moving on I don't think it'll be a problem no matter how good they are. The only place Albert don't want to go is Russia; he reckons that if we got sussed in Russia they'd just blow us away cos it's all run by the Russian Mafia out there, but anywhere else he reckons they'd just deport us." He shrugged and grinned; "I can live with getting deported every six months!"

"Yeah, but then the agencies would get to hear about it and might not give you another job," I said.

"Oh, they're only interested in their percentage," he breezed; "And anyway, we're never going to get sussed; in five years time I'm gonna be a millionaire an' you're still going to be sweating your cobs off working in Watford!"

"Bollocks!" I yelled.

"Then you better get your arse in gear and come with us!" he expostulated. "Where are your glasses?" I got a couple of good glasses out of a box underneath my bed and we helped ourselves to the vodka and Bacardi that I now had on an optic on a shelf above my chest of drawers, topping them up with some warm diet coke from a bottle also stashed under the bed.

We talked about what we thought would happen over the next six months and after we'd finished what little there was left in the bottles we headed into town, to that shit-hole The Nag's Head, where Sincs introduced me to his school-friend Alastair and they told tall stories, acted flash, bought girls drinks, landed the (£200) jackpot on the fruit machine and spent money like it was going out of fashion; I watched the proceedings, became gradually deafened by the music and ended up getting horrendously pissed.

The day Sincs left for his foreign contract I thought all my worries were over... and I couldn't believe it when just two days later another dealer dropped me in it all over again by telling me about another scam that was taking place at work: *I couldn't believe it!*

It's funny how things happen: you plod along for months and months doing the same old boring things and then suddenly some momentous events take place in just a few days.

I slogged away at work throughout the August until my birthday, right at the end of the month; for my 19th, my friends and I had a massive bonfire party in Ashridge Forest near The Monument, with fireworks, plenty of booze and insane amounts of crazy, off-road drunken driving; it was a great night – but I couldn't wait to get back to work.

No longer under the pressure of the blackjack scam, I could feel my dealing becoming smoother and I was growing more confident with every week that passed and then, in the final week of September, it all happened: Sincs disappeared off abroad, Wendy resigned (and went to work in a London club), I moved in to a small rented cottage in a village close to Berko and a dealer at work dropped me right in the shit by telling me all about another scam that was going on at work: I couldn't believe it! Just when I thought I'd escaped by the skin of my teeth from being banged-up over a dodgy scam, here I was right back in the shit again: I couldn't believe it!

The village of Wilstone sat about ten miles north of Berkhamsted near the Grand Union Canal; it had a quaint little pub (which I was familiar with), one post office (including a sorry excuse for a shop), one church and a pretty little stream running through its meadows.

Because it was surrounded on all sides by lovely countryside, one could easily forget that it was only twenty-five miles from the festering shit hole that was Watford (and over twenty of those miles were dual carriageway, so the commute was never going to take more than half an hour); in many ways it was perfect for me (I could think of sixty thousand of them straight off), and most importantly I could afford, on paper, the rent (£700 a month, plus bills). I'd seen it up for rent whilst driving through the village en route to going fishing on the Grand Union canal.

I'd finally paid off the remaining MX5 debt to my parents, and when I announced that I would shortly be moving out the old parents seemed not unduly surprised and somewhat proud, with Mum apparently somewhat upset that I might be moving out, though I couldn't fathom why.

"My lovely boy," she'd say, with a tear in her eye, stroking my hair (like I was some kind of pet) before I left for to work; "All grown up!" In all fairness though she'd seen very little of me lately, and it was only when I was off to work or moving out altogether that she showed any maternal concern.

I'd decided it would be better for the time being if Cinnamon remained at home with mum and dad, along with my old motorbike and VW Beetle, because it wouldn't be fair to her being left on her own in my new place most of the time, and I could pop in and see her two or three times a week when I took a present of my clothes over for mum to launder and get some free food.

Wendy resigned the same week that Sincs did the offski abroad (to Sun City in South Africa, as it turned out), and he took two other dealers with him, Doug Gill and Peter Connaught, both of whom had come up at the same time as he did from The Palace Casino down the road. We never talked much, but before she left Wendy told me she'd secured a job in one of the best London casinos (for twice the money we were on); I wasn't sure how this was going to affect the arrangement between herself, Albert, Sincs and the ongoing scam (if any) but we had no plans to keep in touch – I hadn't even got her phone number – and I wondered if I'd ever see her again.

So there I was, sitting in the staff-room late one night, minding my own business as usual, when in saunters Philip Heron, one of our better dealers. He lit up a fag, got a coffee and sat himself down next to me. We were the only ones present; losing three good dealers and an inspector had, once again, left us short-staffed.

"How's it going, Shills?" he asked. I shrugged and nodded.

"All right, I guess," I said, shrugging again. "Same old bollocks, you know."

He nodded and dragged on his cigarette. He was tall, slim, had a chiselled face with full lips and kept his naturally curly hair cut extremely short; he was a very capable dealer, popular at work (since he continually slagged-off the punters and managers), went to all the parties (of which there was normally at least two every week, usually round someone's flat, where they stayed up late talking about work and smoking pot), and on his days off usually went to nightclubs in London (and doing ecstasy, speed and cocaine).

Although he had a clique at work (they all did the same sort of things), he generally got along with everyone and he had always been OK with me, particularly in these last few months; no doubt he'd seen me dealing bigger and bigger games and managing them well. Like many dealers at our club, he had originally come up from The Palace Casino, our 'competition' in Watford, and he was quite experienced in both roulette and blackjack. I had heard that he lived with his parents in Watford, but seeing as I tried to avoid the town at all costs (apart from going to work) I didn't know for sure.

"Didn't I see you arrive in a different car tonight?" Philip asked, eyebrows raised (he had a very expressive face).

"Yeah, could've been," I shrugged. "I borrowed me old man's Citroen," I told him. "My MX5's having a bit of welding done and I can't afford a new car on the money these cunts pay, know what I mean?"

"Tell me about it! You like your cars, don't you?" Philip said with a knowing look.

"Yeah, I guess so," I replied. "At least with an MX5 I get the shake, rattle and leak," I quipped, and he smiled. "It's don't go very fast, but it sits so low that even at seventy it feels like it's doing a ton!"

"Nice," Philip nodded, dragging deeply on his fag. Then there was a long pause, which I had no intention of breaking and just stared at the second-hand of the large black-and-white clock above the door as it ticked slowly round; eventually Philip said: "So what did that set you back?"

"About three grand," I told him.

"But seriously, you're doing okay, money-wise?" he asked; "You seem to do enough doubles."

I shrugged and nodded. "Yeah, I guess so," I replied.

"You live with your parents, don't you?" he asked.

"Well, yeah, I was until recently," I lied smoothly. "But I've just moved into a little cottage in in Wilstone; you know it?" He shook his head, frowning. Amazing – he didn't know where Wilstone was, what a mong! "It's a village just the other side of Berkhamsted," I explained. "I've been doing all the overtime I can and saving like buggery these last six months; plus I do a few things on the side, if you know what I mean." To this, he gave me a strange look, but I breezed on: "The cottage is in a bit of a bit of a state, but the old man's going to do it up and when it's all done I'll invite everyone round for a massive piss-up," I lied. He nodded, pursing his lips, apparently impressed.

"You know, you should come out with us a bit more Shills; come to some of the do's after work," Philip said.

"Yeah?" I went. "I don't know, I don't get on with most of them that work here; I think most of them are cunts, to be honest." He laughed.

"Yeah, you're right there," he said, frowning and

nodding authoritatively; "But we have some bloody good parties, now that a few more people have come up from The Palace; a lot of the dealers who were trained here are a bit up themselves," he whispered, even though we were on our own in there.

"Tell me about it!" I replied.

"And the new training school they're doing is superb," he said. "I've been helping out, it's almost all girls and they're an absolute scream; we had a party the end of last week – last Friday – and it was a riot, everyone smoking dope, doing Ecstasy and stuff, dancing in the street, you name it," he said.

"Really?" I went.

"Yeah, it was amazing; we nearly destroyed Matt's house!" he laughed, referring to one of our dealers who also lived in Watford (with his parents) called Matt Jenkins. "We were still going for it when his parents came home, I thought they were going to shit themselves!" He laughed again.

"Nice!" I said; "Well, you gotta take advantage whenever you can!"

"Too right," Philip went, nodding enthusiastically. He glanced around the room – we were still alone; the 'staff mum' had long since gone home – and then he turned to stare at me.

"What?" I went.

"Listen, Shills; top secret, okay?" he whispered, staring hard.

"Yeah; course," I replied, nodding and staring back.

"Me and some of the boys are doing a bit of fiddling."

"Yeah?" I went, my heart sinking like the *fucking Titanic*.

"Yeah," he nodded; "We're doing a bit of top-hatting for a couple of Paki geezers."

"Oh; right," I went, shaking my head and unable to concentrate; I couldn't *fucking* believe it! Talk about out of the frying pan, in to the fire! I could have strangled the bastard!

He nodded again, finishing his coffee and fag. "Tell you more about it later, okay? See if you want to come in on it for a bit, yeah?" He stood up to go, but I grasped his forearm.

"Yeah, that's fine but listen Philip; don't tell anyone you've told me, yeah? No-one at all, okay?" I looked at him seriously.

"Yeah, no, definitely," he said as we left the staff room and returned to the pit, me walking behind him shaking my head, not quite believing that I'd just been dropped back in it: *fuck*!

And for the rest of the night I was all over the place, unable to concentrate properly on the tables, and what's more I was unlucky, so had to be taken off my stints early and moved around; I was so bad that Percy Collins even asked what the hell I was playing at, and I had to make up some codswallop that I was coming down with a flu bug or something.

At the end of the night I was fidgeting to get away, but what I really wanted to do was get some quality time with Philip Heron and either silence the bastard for good or try to impress upon him how crucial it was to keep the fact that he'd told me about the scam from anyone else; I had severe doubts that he was as anything like as circumspect as Sincs had been (he was forever out of his face on drugs, for one thing), and I would've invited myself out with him later if I hadn't been driving the Citroen DS.

The professional welding on the MX5 was going to cost me some three hundred quid (on top of the fifty quid my old man had charged me for doing some work on it before he found that he couldn't quite complete the job; unbelievable!). Also, the hood was leaking and a new hood would cost five hundred quid – and we were coming into the autumn – so I knew I had to seriously consider getting a new car, so began religiously browsing the net and small ads in the local papers and shortly thereafter ended up – because the seller was local (Whipsnade, near the zoo) and a Lotus dealer/enthusiast, more than anything else – part-exchanging the MX5 (and coughing up five grand) for a 1982 Lotus Esprit: whoopee!

It came in a black shell with a cream half-leather interior, but at least it had no rust (being fibreglass) and sounded mechanically OK; Dad assured me he was capable of doing any minor work needed (yeah, *right*!) and the seller promised he could do just about any work on it at a much better rate than any proper dealer could, and what with the internet, parts were much more readily available and not too costly.

It only had a 2.2 litre engine but being so light it certainly went fast enough; furthermore, it was a coupé (after my experiences with leaking roofs, I'd gone right off the idea of convertibles), had a face-off stacking CD and an alarm (both of which one needed if one parked in Watford regularly) but by far the most important thing was that I thought it looked *fucking amazing*, and had always wanted one ever since watching 'The Spy Who Loved Me' as a kid: my first real dream had been achieved and I was over the moon, and it definitely wouldn't look out of place in the staff car park alongside the senior casino employees' second-hand Porsches, BMW's and Alfa Romeo's.

I was, in fact, more than delighted with my purchase; it had put me in a genuinely good mood for once and I spent all my free time driving around in it, mostly visiting friends and various pubs and generally showing off.

Now that I was no longer scamming the casino, I didn't think that my Lotus would raise any issues at work and even if it did, it didn't matter anyway; but even so, I had concocted a story that I was setting myself up as a 'classic' car dealer, and for quite a few weeks would alternatively turn up for work in the orange VW Beetle, my Dad's Citroen DS and now the Lotus Esprit.

It didn't create any issues at work whatsoever; a couple of people (after seeing me pull up in it) enquired after it, but most of them seemed to prefer the Citroen, and rightly so; quite of few of them asked about the cars in a friendly way, rather than a 'where would someone like you get the money from' sense; and when I attended a casino party the following week, it turned out to be much better than I'd been expecting, and – typically – I wished I'd been a little bit more forgiving with my casino colleagues.

At work, I had been chatting quite a bit with Philip Heron and his clique of mates, Stewart Davies, Ian Alderton and Johnny Slocombe, all of whom had come up from the other casino in town (we poached so many of their staff I wondered if they had to hold nigh-on continuous training schools), and they'd all insisted I came to the next party, so here I was, along with all the girls from the latest training school (and some of them were gorgeous!), plus a few dealers and some inspectors from work; the 'do' was being held in a house in Watford that three of our older dealers were renting; apparently there was a get-together round there just about every night of the week, but this do was the one big do of the week (and on this particular night there must have been a good twenty people in attendance).

With unusual foresight, I had brought along a half-bottle of Bacardi and some diet coke, and was now stood in the kitchen chatting to Philip and another dealer, Mike Connors, who was, skilfully and quickly, industriously churning out numerous 'spliffs' (whilst puffing away on a gigantic one of his own); occasionally, a stoned dealer would wander into the kitchen, mutter something, pick up a handful of spliffs and disappear. Music was coming from two different rooms: loud dance music from the lounge and quieter, chilled-out stuff from the dining-room; it was a smallish, terraced house and I wondered what the neighbours made of it all, though it was entirely possible that they left early for work just as our party was warming up.

Philip, Mike, various other dealers and I discussed work and (in particular) the various assholes that we had to put up with at work, and I made wisecracks, threw insults about that made them laugh, hinted that my parents were well off and that they'd bought my Lotus and the Citroen to set myself up in the car business since I'd completed a full year at the casino but they wanted me to have something else on the side; hopefully, they would repeat what I'd told them and word would gradually filter round that I came from a well-to-do background and this was where the money came from for sales of cars, rather than, say, me stealing over sixty grand from right under their noses.

So we drank, smoked and talked, and when Mike finally headed off into the lounge (to hand out his joints) I seized the moment and quizzed Philip about the fiddle he was doing and I was flabbergasted not only as to how mickey-mouse it was, but also how incredible it was that they hadn't already been caught.

Apparently two blokes – they were called Moy and Lahara – had been playing roulette in our club for quite a while (when I got Philip to describe them, I knew them straight off: Moy looked like a short, greasy snake and Lahara looked like a big, shaggy-haired Columbian drug dealer, though Philip said they were both Pakistanis); they hardly ever punted at my table, and now I was beginning to understand why. Philip told me that one day Jimmy Slocombe had bumped into one of them in a betting shop in Watford, and they'd got chatting, gone for a smoke, chatted some more... and one thing had led to another.

Philip was asking me:

"Shills, what would you say was the least popular part of the roulette wheel?"

"What, for the players to punt on?" He nodded, and I shrugged and said: "The numbers from twenty-five round to thirty-six, no question." He nodded again.

"Exactly; you get punters going for the voisons du zero or the tier, but hardly ever for numbers like 25, 34, 6, 27, 13, right?"

"Right," I agreed. "They'll bet on 17, and even 'seventeen-neighbours', but hardly ever place chips on the outer column numbers."

"Exactly! So if we've got a game, we try to aim for that section of the wheel, and that's where Moy and Lahara place their chips; they only ever play fives and ponies, and if we miss... well," he shrugged, "if no-one's looking, we'll top-hat it anyway!" He laughed. "We've been paying them out thousands and thousands for the last couple of months or so; trouble is, they tend to take what we've paid them and punt it back on other tables." He paused and took a deep inhalation from his spliff.

"So how's it going? Are they paying you half?" I politely enquired. He pursed his lips and thought for a second.

"Yeah, we're not doing too badly," he said. "But no, we're not getting half, no-where near; I dunno, maybe a couple of hundred quid a week apiece," he said.

"What?" I went. "Nah, that can't be right!" I told him. "Surely if you're going to do it you wanna to go halves on the profits, no? After all, you're the ones taking the risk." He shook his head.

"No Shills, you don't understand; listen: for it to look right, they can't go playing pound chips on one table and suddenly start playing ponies when one of us starts dealing, you know? So half the time they have to keep on punting with other dealers just so it don't look suspicious," he told me.

"But that's madness!" I told him. "You might end up paying them five grand only for them to tell you that they did it all back!" But Philip didn't seem bothered; he just shrugged, and said:

"Well, that's what happens, mate!" He took another long drag and shrugged again. "Me? To tell you the truth, I fuckin' hate work, Shills; I only like coming in when I'm stoned, and yeah, this fiddling thing has made it a bit more more interesting, and shit, if I can pick up another three hundred quid in cash every week — in other words, doubling my wages — then I'm well happy." We just stood there for a while, him smoking and me drinking, but me mainly thinking.

"So can you actually section-spin, then?" I asked him. "That's amazing, cos I've tried it loads of times and I can't manage it! Jeez, if I could I reckon I'd be the richest bastard in Hertfordshire!"

"In Britain!" he cackled. "Yes mate, I can do it sometimes, but it's tricky even if you're always aiming to hit the same section, but you know, even if I miss I can usually palm a pony; it depends on a lot of things, like how busy we are, which inspector I've got, how much money the table is winning, how many other tables the inspector is watching, what other players I've got at the table, whether the managers are hanging around, and oh, so many other little things. It's certainly not easy, but like I said, we've been doing it for a couple of months and got away with it no problem, so I don't think anyone's cottoned-on. They punt all night anyway, which takes the pressure off." He stopped explaining and took another hit.

"So how many people are in on it?" I asked.

"Not many," he said, "only me, Stew, Ian and Johnny Slo... and the two punters, of course. I don't want it getting too big," he said, though I didn't really believe him. I didn't know whether I trusted him or not, but my instincts were not to; if he could tell me all about it – and I tried to come across as was one of the straightest blokes you'd ever meet – then he could tell anyone... especially if you mixed plenty of drugs into the equation. Oh, shit! Now I had plenty more to worry and stress about; if only I hadn't come out with the line: 'I do a few things on the side'; I was only going to tell him about selling air guns and flick knives to the other kids at school, that's all; shit!

Shaking my head in despair, I had the deep desire to do the only sensible thing available to me at that moment (to wit: get completely pissed), but I had too much to think (and worry) about, so grunted something to Philip again about not telling anyone he'd told me about the scam and took my drink for a walk through the house, nodding to everyone and chatting to a few. I got introduced to the trainees from the latest school, and they all seemed all right (i.e. without massive attitudes or chips on their shoulders). Most of them lived in Watford, though two lived in Hemel Hempstead and another in Leighton Buzzard, so I chatted to them, discovering that the girl from Leighton, Rebecca Westoning, travelled in on the bus every day.

"Well how the hell are you going to get home at four in the morning?" I went to her, half-pissed.

"I dunno!" she yelled back, over the racket of the stereo. She had an empty glass in her hand and looked pretty hammered herself (though was very good-looking: petite, with nice brown eyes and dark brown hair). "Try to get a lift off someone or wait for the bus!"

"What time's the first bus?" I hollered.

"Dunno, about half-five I guess!" she screamed in my ear-hole.

"Fuck that," I muttered.

"What?" she shrieked.

"Fair enough, I said!" I bawled. "I'm going for a drink!" I shouted, waving my empty glass at her; "Want one?" and she nodded, following me out to the kitchen. Philip had disappeared, so I got her another beer from the fridge, topped up my rum and coke and told her that I'd just rented a cottage just past Berko and en route to Leighton Buzzard. "So I can always drop you back if we finish about the same time." She nodded, and asked how long I'd worked there, so I told her a year, and then she started asking other things and we ended up getting completely pissed together, after which I drove her home.

Adam Charte was a multi-millionaire, but like everyone else he had his problems. He was certainly a millionaire on paper, though cash-flow had become a bit scarce over the last year: another divorce, another marriage, a sizeable VAT bill, a wilfully beautiful twenty-three year old daughter, an unwise investment and a health scare had all taken their toll.

Bloody doctors: he'd been told to lose five stone in weight, which was simply ridiculous; his family were big-boned, and his high blood pressure had nothing whatsoever to do with his weight: it was all down to his brother's three criminal sons hassling him for a fifty grand loan so they could import a load of cocaine, that was where it all started (not that he could tell the doctor that).

And the latest wife's constant nagging that he was never home didn't help (even if all she wanted to do was stay in and watch the soaps); and he was convinced that one of his daughter's boyfriends was only seeing her because she had a wealthy father.

At least most of his businesses were still churning the money out: a 4x4 garage; two riding schools; seventeen rented houses, thirty eight lock-up garages, various fields and a large gypsy site that he owned but rented out to the local council (though this last was causing him a headache since some of the councillors were threatening to stop paying the rent unless he did something about the 'travellers' bothering the local villagers, as if he could do anything! And even if he could, he could hardly tell a few unruly members of his own family how to behave!).

Maybe this was why he had enjoyed going to the casino so much: to escape from all the things he couldn't control. When he was in the casino he found he could relax because he could put everything out of his mind and focus solely on the moment. He lived just outside Milton Keynes and so had three casinos within a half-hour drive: two in Watford and one in Northampton, and out of the three he preferred The Metropolitan in Watford, if only for to its easy access from the motorway and ample parking; Adam hated bringing his big Toyota Amazon or Range Rover into town, but the Met had good, secure parking and even a valet service – and outside of London that was unheard of!

He liked going to the casino, the money-rinsing aspects of it being merely a pleasant bonus; he'd long-ago worked out that by far the best odds in the building were the even-chance bets on roulette and he'd stuck to them ever since. He played randomly, on either red or black; for one thing, you could play them without actually having to sit at the table; for another, you could often play two tables at once; also, seeing as you were only placing one bet per spin, the dealer couldn't try to rush you (as he'd seen dealers do to table-chip players); furthermore, it was relatively easy to achieve good wins whilst minimising losses; and moreover – and most important of all – the dealer couldn't single you out for special attention because it was impossible for dealers to deliberately miss a particular number (a section, maybe, but not an individual number).

Adam always waited for the dealer to spin before placing his bet (as he'd seen the Chinese punters do), and would choose his red or black bet by following pure gut instinct; it had served him well in business over the years, and it rarely let him down in the casino. Of course, it was simple common sense to never take more cash than he could afford to lose, just as it was to avoid playing against dealers that had recently beaten him (as they might be experiencing a lucky streak), and he always tried to remember faces (and the naughty little stunts they'd sometimes pull when trying to beat a player – such as speeding the game up or altering the speed of the wheel every time – pathetic!).

He often brought his daughter along with him — nowadays often accompanied by her latest paramour — so he could keep an eye on her as much as for the company; at least she never told him to stop playing, which was a relief (and made a nice change from his previous wife). She was called Penelope, was his only child and the apple of his eye; she was a product of his first marriage (to a real head-turner, which Pen had now become herself) and somewhere along the line — at university, probably — she had developed a taste for men. She had a heart-breaking, angelic, innocent face on top of a tall centrefold's body; black shimmering hair, deep blue eyes, glowing skin, pouting lips and a certain way about her — and men fell at her feet. She'd already been through six or seven (that he knew of) in the last year and he couldn't help but worry about her; these days he simply hoped that a man would either sweep her off her feet or break her heart, but unfortunately that hadn't happened. Because he adored her, he never begrudged her the house he'd given her, or the car, or the 'wardrobe allowance' of two thousand a month; and he knew she loved him, much more than any of his ex-wives did (she had him round for dinner at least twice a week, which was a sight more than his three ex-wives ever did).

He'd been doing very well against The Metropolitan lately; he meticulously recorded all his results in the back of his pocket diary and so far for this month (September) he was up (after six sessions) £7,600, which meant he was winning £32,200 on the year. Of course, he'd usually have a couple of losing sessions each month (which was merely par for the course), but in these cases he would aim to walk out losing less than a grand; however, on the flip-side was that if his luck was in, he'd regularly leave the casino winning over two or three grand and — seeing as he'd been playing this way for quite a few years now — he saw no reason for this to change.

I'd enjoyed the casino party but had spent all day Saturday in bed nursing a hangover; I'd finally surfaced at seven in the evening, after which I'd taken the Lotus for a spin, visiting my friend David and several hostelries; I loved my new car!

Life carried on like this for a another month, with me explaining to Phil Heron that I didn't want to get involved in doing any fiddling just yet, what with my little cottage being done-up with the help of my parents (I'd ordered Dad to get his arse in gear and finish the place off so I could move in properly).

One Sunday in November I went out to lunch with my parents at a country pub/ restaurant that Dad liked called The Five Bells in the village of Stanbridge, over near Leighton Buzzard; it was a bit up-market, but Dad and I had been popping in there for donkey's years for a drink on the way home from one of our fishing trips;

also it was Mum's birthday, so I suppose that was why Dad had chosen it; it was a bit pricey, but they did a superb lunch and seeing as Dad was driving I was allowed to have a drink, and I ended up getting half-pissed and then shocked both of them (and myself) by paying the £100 bill with two crisp fifty pound notes (I must have been half-pissed!).

On the way out Mum decided she fancied an Irish coffee in their relaxing saloon bar, which gave Dad an ideal opportunity to say hello to a couple of the local blokes and trade bits of insider information on the best local fishing spots at the moment. Mum was all weepy due to my coughing-up for the bill, so I excused myself, grabbed another surreptitious large Bacardi and diet coke and eavesdropped on Dad and the local lads and in fact I thought I recognised one of them as an occasional punter, but couldn't be sure and certainly gave no indication of it, but I did remember his face.

Back at work, I witnessed Moy and Lahara loitering on the roulette tables whenever Philip, Stew, Ian or Johnny Slo-mo were dealing and they were picking up shed-loads; over the week-end, I'd done a lot of thinking and I'd decided that my best course of action was just to do what I'd always done: keep my head down and not get involved with Phil & Co's little fiddle, which I was sure was going to be sussed at any moment; surely not even our managers could be that thick!

I focused on my games and always angled to try to get a result for the house, at least on roulette; there wasn't much a dealer could do if a player got a lucky shoe on blackjack, and now that Albert and Sincs had gone I hated dealing the game; I really missed Sincs!.

On the Thursday of that week we were quieter than usual (Thursday always being our quietest night in any case), for the first time in ages no-one had called in sick, only half our gaming tables had been opened and we even had some of the new trainees from the latest school starting 'on the floor', so, if anything, we were actually over-staffed; I couldn't ever remember it happening before!

When I came out of the staff-room from a break at midnight (we'd been doing forty on, twenty off all night), I was instructed by Percy to 'take off' Stanley Marsh, so trooped off down the pit looking out for him and, for a second, couldn't see the twat; now I knew Percy wouldn't have made a mistake since that never happened, so I thought: oh no, please don't tell me he's up in the blackjack pit and I missed him, and I was just about to walk back to the bj pit when I clocked Stanley bending over (and emptying) the chipping machine on AR6 and he was chipping, I couldn't believe it! I hadn't had a 'chip' in six months (not since I'd become a competent dealer, in fact); anyone with any sense loved to have the occasional chip since it was the only completely stress-free job in the building, though it was usually reserved for only the freshest or most useless

414

dealers; because we'd been so short staffed lately, no-one had been chipping, so much so that I'd even seen the managers having the odd go; I walked up behind Marsh and slapped him on the shoulder.

"Off you go fuck-face!" I whispered; "Go and have a quick wank in the gents!" He cackled, showed clean palms and whispered a quiet 'fuck you' as he sloped off. As the machine on AR6 was nigh-on empty, I looked around and saw Mike Connors across on AR5 dealing to a small crowd of elderly Jewish women and young Chinese blokes so stepped over and whispered: "All right Connors, ya twat?"

"All right Shilling, you old tart!" he replied *sotto voce*. Out of everyone working at the casino I liked Connors the best (since Sincs had gone); he was older than most of the dealers but had only been in the game a couple of years. I think he was twenty-eight or twenty-nine, which was a good eight to ten years older than most people starting in the industry, but he was a tall, handsome, young-looking bloke; he'd worked abroad as a barman on various cruise ships in the Caribbean and had travelled around the States doing a variety of jobs (and drugs). He was into meditation, yoga, smoking pot and – for some unaccountable reason – drove a grey 1980's Renault 5 Turbo.

"You still driving that piece of French crap?" I asked.

"Yeah; you still driving that lump of fibreglass tat? I'd

piss all over ya!"

"Bollocks, you snail loving flid!" I went, causing him to laugh when he should have been announcing 'no more bets'. So as not to get bollocked, I turned around to help Kara Allsop – who'd just taken Sharon Jacobs off AR4 – and witnessed what was to be both a revelation and the major turning point of my career.

It was rare to see an inspector as senior as Kara dealing, especially as she was dealing at an almost empty table, which was probably why I paused to see what was going on and then I spotted a well-dressed man standing half-way between AR3 and AR4 with a stack of ponies in his hand; I recognised him immediately, though couldn't remember the last time he'd played against me.

I remembered him because he had always struck me as an intelligent (and therefore dangerous) player; for one thing, he was one of only a few punters – correction, the *only* punter – who only ever played big money on the outside-chance bets, never on the layout (which was something I could never understand, as it was without doubt the best way to play, and, indeed, the way I would play). For another thing, he was one of the very few roulette players who hardly ever played at my table, tending – I suspected – to seek out the less competent dealers (which was probably why he'd been playing against the useless Sharon Jacobs).

What also made me wary of him was that I'd seen him increase his even-money bets when on a winning streak and stick to the minimums when up against a strong dealer, whereas most players tended to chase their losses (doubling-up and trying to recoup, which was a sure-fire recipe for disaster); plus, I'd seem him hit a lucky streak, press it and then immediately cash-in his chips and leave the building, and I was *seriously* hard-pushed to think of another punter that I'd witnessed do this.

So he was definitely no fool, but most of all, I think I was impressed by his quiet way of playing, and due to the way he played he could never be hurried or pressured by a dealer, and he was one of these middle-aged men (I put him around fifty) that you see every now and then who are completely at home in their own skin. He dressed well but there was nothing flash about him; I suppose it was just the way he spoke and carried himself (in other words, he was about as unlike me as it was possible to get).

I vaguely recalled that the last time I'd seen him he'd been accompanied by an absolutely stunning dark-haired young woman, and when I'd dared to ask an inspector about him I'd been given a look and moodily told his name was Charte and that he was a regular but that was all, and I'd made a point of watching out for him ever since.

As Kara spun, I saw him clock the wheel (both ball and

wheel were spinning rapidly round) and place a stack of ponies (£500) on red. The ball bounced once and fell into number thirty-two, so Kara paid him out £500 – which was the table 'maximum' on the even chances – and no sooner had she done so than she was spinning the ball and wheel again, Charte was scooping up his winning chips and leaving a stack on red again, and again the ball and inner wheel were whizzing round. With a bounce and a couple of clicks, the ball settled into number twelve, red again, forcing Kara to pay out another stack of ponies. Her hand was spinning the ball almost as soon as she'd retrieved the dolly, and I noticed that she did the same spin: fast wheel and fast ball.

I didn't really have any reason to be loitering at her table, so turned and hurriedly took some stacks of chips out of Connors' machine, but I turned back in time to witness the ball fall into number nineteen, and this time Kara pulled in a losing bet of £500, because Mr Charte had switched on black. The ball was spinning again before I had time to place the losing bet back in the float. I then nipped over to AR6 and AR7, but the dealers on those games were coping on their own, so I shot back to AR4 and saw the ball fall away from the inner rim and bounce into number thirty-five, but Charte had bet on black and so won that time. Another spin, with Kara keeping to the same strategy: fast wheel, fast ball and fast spins. The next number was twelve, next to thirty-five on the wheel, and she raked

418

in Mr Charte's losing £500 bet on black.

I was so mesmerised by the game that I hung around AR4 for the entire forty minutes of my stint, and when someone tapped me on the shoulder I wiped my palms and strode off to the staff-room but I couldn't sit still as my mind was in overdrive because for almost her entire forty-minute stint on AR4 Kara had done nothing but spin the 'voisins' (i.e. neighbours) of the zero section of the wheel! After a minute of sitting in the staff-room I had to get up and go for a walk along the corridor to the gents changing room otherwise I thought I'd freak out! She had kept the ball doing the same spin, the inner wheel going the same speed, and almost every time the ball had fallen into the voisins du zero! Stone me, if that wasn't section-spinning I don't know what was!

And if my eyes had needed any more proof (which they didn't any more) it was when I'd seen the ball fall into the zero-section but hit one of the tiny metal struts separating each number's pocket, making the ball bounce wildly and go spinning round for another half of the wheel ending up in number ten – opposite zero. So what did Kara do? Well, on her next spin she did the same spin of the ball as always but slowed the inner wheel down a fraction – I spotted it, even if Mr Charte didn't – and bang! Lo and behold, the ball fell straight back into the zero section again!

Of course, we dealers are all told to spin the ball from the last number it fell in (thereby making each spin a

419

'new event'); also, we are told to keep the wheel revolving relatively quickly (furthermore randomising each spin); plus we are told to do fairly long spins (thereby making prediction harder); furthermore, we are told to concentrate on getting the payouts right (thereby making it harder to remember the previous spin); moreover, we are told to 'pay and spin' and deal a fast game (thereby also making it harder to remember the previous spin) – and if that wasn't bad enough, we also had to reverse the direction of the ball and wheel on every spin! So it would only be on the quietest of games that a good dealer would ever be likely to put section-spinning to the test, but even then – assuming he thought he could do it – as soon as he got stuck into dealing a busy game he'd soon forget about section-spinning.

And on top of all *that*, every ball and wheel in the casino were slightly different, so it was pointless for a dealer to consider purchasing a wheel of his own to practise on – and don't think I hadn't – since it might well turn out to be a wheel (and/or ball) completely unlike the ones used in his club.

The fact was that most dealers, due to the house percentage and inherent greed and bad play by the punters, would win money whether they could section-spin or not; and due to the intrinsic difficulties involved in section spinning, most dealers would soon give it up as a waste of time and effort (since they were probably going to win money anyway).

And due to how casinos were operated, if a dealer could do it, and somehow managed to pay out big money to a cheating confederate, he'd soon be removed from the table by an alert inspector, pit boss or manager; in fact, unless they trusted him implicitly he might very well be fired merely on suspicion that he could section spin.

What I'd seen Kara do was a masterful display of skill, and it was all the more impressive as I hadn't seen her deal a game in months – months! Obviously Percy Collins had primed her before sending her to the table but even so, I'd been there for her entire stint and it was like nothing I'd ever seen before: brilliant! And obviously the reason Kara had been aiming for the zero section was because Mr Charte had been playing decent money on the even-chance bets and thus the only advantage for the house was to hit zero (in which case it took half the bet). Well, I knew I'd seen her hit zero a couple of times, but no more than that; she'd simply been 'unlucky'.

But she had hit the numbers 3, 15, 26 and 32 more times than I could remember, and they were right next to zero; she had simply been very unlucky. When I felt my replacement tap me on the shoulder I had checked the float and the table only seemed to be ahead by one extra stack of ponies (i.e. five hundred quid), which didn't seem a helluva lot but then again neither was it a bad rate of profit; if every table won just £500 per hour, the casino would be netting something in the region of a hundred grand a day!

I was reminded of what I'd seen Carl Hunter do whilst I was on the training school – spin zero with just one attempt – but then, that had been on a spin with a very slow wheel and a ball that only made a few revolutions of the wheel; what I'd seen Kara do was much more impressive, so much so that for the first time I think I truly believed that section spinning was not only possible, every now and then, but realistically possible at any time.

For the rest of the night I could hardly sit still and when I dealt roulette I didn't give a damn about getting my payouts correct or being polite or anything else: I just tried to spin the section of nine numbers from 21 through to 36, and from that moment on all I wanted to do was learn the art of section spinning.

END OF BOOK ONE; PLEASE DO NOT INVEST IN BOOK TWO UNTIL YOU HAVE STOPPED LOSING AND STARTED WINNING FROM THE INSIDER INFORMATION GAINED FROM BOOK ONE!